KU-287-433

Animals
Famous and
Curious Stories

Animals
Famous and
Curious Stories

Octopus Books Limited

First published 1982 by

Octopus Books Limited
59 Grosvenor Street
London W1

Illustrated by Rowan Clifford

Copyright © 1982 selection, arrangement and illustrations
Octopus Books Limited

ISBN 0 7064 1797 6

Printed in Czechoslovakia

50 438

Contents

Bel Ria   Sheila Burnford   9

Life With Mij   Gavin Maxwell   23
(from 'Ring of Bright Water')

Gilded Cage   Alan Coren   43

The Race   Leo Tolstoy   47
(from 'Anna Karenina')   (trans. Constance Garnett)

The Rat Who Wasn't Having   William Garnett   70
    Any

The Grey Cub   Jack London   77
(from 'White Fang')

Animals at Alconleigh   Nancy Mitford   92
(from 'The Pursuit of Love')

The Triumph of Moby Dick   Herman Melville   99

Trinket's Colt   E. Œ. Somerville &
    Martin Ross   120

A Sea of Headwaiters   Gerald Durrell   131
(from 'The Whispering Land')

Stumberleap   Henry Williamson   152

The Dog That Bit People   James Thurber   167

The Bull That Thought   Rudyard Kipling   172

The Pacing Mustang   Ernest Thompson Seton   184

Tobermory   Saki   199

Pig-Hoo-o-o-o-ey!   P. G. Wodehouse   206

The Hound of the Baskervilles	Sir Arthur Conan Doyle	223
It Shouldn't Happen to a Vet	James Herriot	246
The Country of the Houyhnhnms (from 'Gulliver's Travels')	Jonathan Swift	258
Lady Into Fox	David Garnett	271
A Cat in the Window	Derek Tangye	285
Flush	Virginia Woolf	298
African Game (from 'Maiwa's Revenge')	Sir H. Rider Haggard	309
And Who, With Eden . . .	John Collier	330
A Buffalo Hunt	Washington Irving	342
Troubles in the Fold (from 'Far From the Madding Crowd')	Thomas Hardy	348
We Think the World of You	J. R. Ackerley	354
The Stolen White Elephant	Mark Twain	363
Acknowledgments		379

Bel Ria

SHEILA BURNFORD

The wartime life of a tough little terrier among a travelling circus troupe in the Basque country, takes him through the rigours of life aboard a British naval vessel on active service, and leaves him, finally, in Plymouth at the height of an air raid . . .

ALICE TREMORNE HAD been trapped for two nights and days when the dog found her. She had been alone in the house as Miss Carpenter, her companion help, was away on a week's holiday, and the daily help had left soon after putting the evening meal in the oven. After listening to the nine o'clock news, restless and so bored with her own company that she had even cleared away the supper dishes for the first time in her life, Mrs. Tremorne suddenly thought of sloe gin. At the beginning of the war she had put up several bottles. They should be pleasantly aged by now, maturing in the inspection pit of the garage, a place which she had found, after much trial and error, maintained an excellent temperature for her home-made wines. She would tell Janet Carpenter to fetch a sample bottle when she returned . . .

But the more she thought about the sloe gin, the more she wanted to try it now; how very inconsiderate of the woman not to have foreseen this wish. Why should she have to wait five days before it was realised? She could not. She would not. *She would fetch some herself* – she would show Carpenter she was not indispensable. It would be interesting to see how the Elderflower '37 was faring too. Wincing, but still majestic, Mrs. Tremorne rose stiffly to her feet.

Taking a small torch, a fur wrap, and her stick from the hall cupboard, she shuffled slowly down the path to the garage, grimly enjoying the outing, savouring each detail of the hazards of steps and path to relate to Carpenter in due course. She hoped she would be able to manipulate the bottles, for her hands as well as her legs were stiff and swollen with arthritis. Anticipating difficulty, she had put two small bottles and a funnel in the string bag over her arm so that at least she could transfer some of the contents in the garage itself.

Where the cobbles had been taken up from the stable yard, the surface had been paved; very easy to negotiate, even for an elderly woman who normally never set foot outside without her companion's arm being available. But when she opened the garage door and shone the light around, she realised that she had forgotten the fitted boards covering the pit. She would have to remove the ones over the steps. Her knees twinged at the thought. But Mrs. Tremorne was not one to turn back from her determined course; somehow she managed to lever up enough boards. Puffing and panting, giddy with the effort, cursing Carpenter, she now realised that it would be sheer foolhardiness to attempt the cement steps of the pit without a handrail. She decided to investigate instead the deep cupboard in which the matured bottles of Elderberry, Ginger and Blackcurrant wines were kept, under the stairs leading to the loft.

Outside the sirens wailed, such a normal event almost every evening since the war had begun that she took no notice. She unlocked the door, closing it carefully behind her before switching on the light. The neat rows of labelled bottles filled her orderly soul with pleasure, dating back to – let me see when – she adjusted her pince-nez and bent closer. It was at this precise moment that she realised the sirens had heralded business this time; the anti-aircraft defences ringing the town burst out into an excited crackling, and now the great thudding of the naval guns from the dockyard joined in. Above all this was another seldom heard but unmistakable noise, a very unpleasant noise indeed, with the spaced finality of its dreadful thuds rattling her bottles and sending the suspended light-bulb into a crazy flickering dance: *those unspeakable Germans were actually having the effrontery to bomb Plymouth.*

Mrs. Tremorne switched off the light, and re-opened the cupboard door. The open garage door now framed a bright orange sky across which searchlight fingers moved, and a garden illuminated as clearly as a stage setting. A flare floated down towards the paddock beyond, and as she watched her fascination changed to irritation as the bright unearthly glow revealed unseemly mounds of fresh mole-hills on her lawn. There was a sudden clanging as fragments of metal rained down on the path, an unpleasant pattering on the roof above. She found herself longing for the comfortable haven of her armchair in the shelter of the cellar stairs of the house, three comforting floors and the concrete stairs overhead.

Then her world was filled with a rushing screaming noise like an express train coming straight at her. Arthritis and all, Mrs. Tremorne dropped to the floor and lay flat, her head buried in her arms. The stone floor rocked, she felt as though all air were being sucked out of her body, her head exploding, then her body became strangely weightless. Without in any way feeling conscious of her passage across the garage, she had been neatly picked up and as neatly deposited on the straw on top of her own bottles at the bottom of the pit. At the same time, almost as though she had activated some lever, the roof collapsed, the first beams to fall straddling the pit, and so supporting the remainder that fell in crazy order on top. Terribly shaken, her head spinning, her eardrums thudding, Mrs. Tremorne lay on her straw mattress and wondered if this was the end. Before she could find out, she dropped off into unconsciousness.

When she came to some hours later, lying there with her arms by her sides, in thick black silence, she thought that she was in her coffin, additional proof being that when she spoke up indignantly to say that there had been some mistake, she heard no words. She resigned herself, with black fury, to eternal rest.

After a while, she became conscious of sharp things boring through the straw, like fakirs' nails into her back, and memory returned: the tops of her wine bottles. She lifted her arms then each leg cautiously in turn; everything worked. She felt herself carefully, but could not find even a scratch; her shoes had been blown off, but she still clutched the torch in one hand, the string bag was still over her arm, the medicine bottles were intact inside. After much painful effort, she managed to get to her feet, resting her elbows on a cleared space at floor level. She saw now that there were occasional chinks of red light in the otherwise impenetrable mass over her. She swept the beam of the light around the roof of her prison and saw that even if she had had the strength to remove some of the obstruction, the balance was so delicately conserved that she might well loosen a key support and bring the whole jumble crashing down. She would have to resign herself to waiting. Conserving her light, her strength. Thank goodness, even although the night was not cold, she had put on her cape. It irritated her very much that she had no one except herself to blame for her predicament, this unnerving silence – only those dreadful Germans, and she concentrated all her hate on them.

She did not know when the All Clear sounded at last in the early morning; she did not even know if it was day or night, only that she was now very cold and ached in every bone. She shouted and shouted not knowing that her voice had become a whisper, and tears of fury and weakness furrowed down her dusty cheeks. Falling silent at last from sheer exhaustion, she realised that the A.R.P. post at the corner of the street where the listed occupants of all the houses around were kept, would probably check the house only. Knowing that Miss Carpenter was away – one of the wardens was her cousin – and finding no evidence of Mrs. Tremorne (if only she had not been so altruistic with that supper tray . . .) they would assume that she had gone out for the evening. They would never think of looking in the garage, for everyone knew that she was unable to get around without assistance. But the daily would come at 9 o'clock, Mrs. Tremorne reassured herself, she would know, she would come searching. . . .

But no one came. She had no idea of the passage of time for her watch had stopped. She moved some bottles to form a straw nest. Sometimes she fell into an exhausted sleep, sometimes she forced herself to move her arms and legs and stand leaning on the edge of the pit, shouting. Sometimes, lightheaded, she sang, her fingers pressed over her vocal chords to assure herself that sound was indeed coming forth. Thirsty, she remembered the sloe gin; transferring some to a small bottle in total darkness occupied her for a long time. She spilled a lot before she learned the art, but the result – taken strictly medicinally – was very comforting. And the more sips she took, the more it seemed that her hearing was returning; she could even hear occasional sounds of traffic from the road beyond the garden. But they only increased her feeling of a terrible loneliness and desertion – the rest of the world going about its business, uncaring of Alice Tremorne.

It was in one of these more lonely moments, during the second night if she had known it, that as she learned against the pit edge, and clenched and unclenched her fingers against their growing stiffness, she suddenly heard an unfamiliar creaking in the immediate timbers. She shone the weak beam of the light in this direction, calling for help in a husky whisper, then suddenly, out of nowhere came the warm wet touch of a tongue on her finger. Instinctively repelled she jerked her arm back; then as though to reassure her, she heard a soft whining, and knew that this was not the repulsive questing of a hopeful rat. Her fingers moved again to touch a muzzle, ears, to be covered again by an eager tongue – it was a dog that had come out of the blackness to her, the only living thing that knew or cared, apparently, that she still existed.

Unfamiliar tears of gratitude welled up in Mrs. Tremorne's eyes. When the pile shifted, and high agonised yelps followed she forgot her own splitting head and aching bones; she longed only to comfort this warm miraculous link with life, to show it by the soft stroking of her fingers how much she cared. From that moment, Mrs. Tremorne determined that if she had to spend another month here, living on gin in total darkness, she would somehow come out of it and see the reality of this small creature that had risked its life to come to her need out of the terrible night.

It was undoubtedly the same sloe gin that put her there in the first place that brought her out alive again, for it was to be another two days before she was found by the conscientious Janet Carpenter who had cut short her holiday to come back when she could receive no satisfaction on the telephone, the lines being down. She had arrived only that morning, after travelling for two nightmarishly slow days. She had been unable to find the daily help who had promised so faithfully to look after Mrs.

Tremorne. She had vanished without a trace, padlocking her cottage behind her, and for a while Miss Carpenter thought Mrs. Tremorne might have vanished with her, to some safer hideout in the country. She knew that her mistress would not have gone out with friends that evening, as the warden suggested, for the simple reason that she had no friends. No one even liked her sufficiently to ask her out and put up with her overbearing bitterness for an evening. But it never occurred to her to think beyond the house at first; Mrs. Tremorne elsewhere, solo, was unthinkable.

It was not until after her fruitless investigations that she came out into the garden to survey the wreckage and heard a faint muffled barking. Puzzled, she traced it to the garage. Plainly there was a dog trapped somewhere in that pile; but how to set about getting it out was another matter, for the whole structure above it looked perilous in the extreme. She sniffed the air; it smelled as though some Bacchanalian orgy had recently taken place. The cupboard under the stairs hung drunkenly, one hinge on the shelves buckled and a pile of broken bottles covered in white dust lying below. On top was a curiously familiar shape under its coating of dust. Picking her way carefully over she picked it up: she held Alice Tremorne's ivory-headed cane, as much a part of her normally as though it were an extension of her left arm. Janet Carpenter turned and ran for the A.R.P. post.

They uncovered, piece by precarious piece, first the dog, a small white shadow of a dog who gazed blindly up at them from thickly encrusted eyes behind a matted fringe of hair, dusty white save for the contrasting red of a clean licked, mangled fore-paw, so light that as it was lifted out it seemed there could be nothing but dry bones within the enveloping whiteness. The man who held it was conscious of the sweet sickly smell of infection, the dry hot skin below the coat. Nevertheless, it acknowledged man's presence by a brief quivering of the end of its tail. He laid it on the floor and they set to again for the urgent, yet frustratingly slow uncovering of Mrs. Tremorne's body.

It was unveiled at last. Stretched out neatly on a bed of straw, her head pillowed on a flat square of empty bottles, hands folded tidily on her chest under the sable cape, her stockinged feet together, Mrs. Tremorne lay. The string of pearls on the massive shelf of her bosom moved up and down with peaceful regularity. Even as they gazed upon her, the slack lower jaw dropped another fraction, she hiccoughed gently, and then a loud imperious snore fell upon their astonished ears.

She was taken to hospital, where – almost incredibly for a seventy-six-year-old semi-invalid – no damge other than a bruising which discoloured almost her entire body had been found, and now it was a matter of time and rest only.

The overworked nursing staff hoped fervently that the time with them would be brief, for she was a despotic bell-ringer of a patient. The first thing she had asked for when she recovered from her monumental but merciful hangover was the dog, her rescuer, in whom, as she declared, had lain her salvation. Miss Carpenter, hovering dutifully by the bed, was bidden to find out about this canine hero forthwith. What did it look like? It was just a dog, a small dog, Miss Carpenter said, remembering with aversion the limp, dirty, blood-stained bundle, but adding only that it appeared to have a shortish tail and longish ears. Mrs. Tremorne regarded her with scorn.

'It was a miracle,' she said, her words still somewhat slurred, 'I held ish paw and strength flowed out, poshitively *flowed* out . . .' Her glazed eyes glared from the pillow, challenging anyone to dispute the source of the miracle working flow, and Miss Carpenter left to track it down.

She was able to report next day that one of the rescue team had taken the dog home with him, and his wife was looking after it; its eyes were open, the wound on the paw was clean, but possibly there were internal injuries or severe shock for the animal seemed to have lost the will to live – it simply lay in a box without stirring, and was kept going only by the efforts of the woman with spoonfuls of warm milk laced with precious whisky.

She must be suitably rewarded, and a vet must be called immediately, commanded Mrs. Tremorne – two, three vets if necessary. A taxi must be summoned so that dog could be installed at The Cedars straightaway. Carpenter must go forth and – here was her alligator bag – set the machinery in motion; a dog basket, the best, to be bought; leads, brushes, bones and tempting dog delicacies – dogs liked liver, she knew: fetch then, quantities of liver . . .

Liver was very hard to get nowadays, offered Miss Carpenter apologetically. 'Tell Hobbs the Butcher I wish liver,' said Mrs. Tremorne, weakly but majestically. The butcher's had received a direct hit, Carpenter had heard. 'What has that to do with Hobbs obtaining liver?' enquired Mrs. Tremorne in genuine surprise.

It was useless explaining; no one tried. The war to Alice Tremorne was simply an interlude of personal inconvenience. Miss Carpenter departed dispiritedly into the ruins of the shopping centre.

'Good dog, good little doggie,' mumbled Alice Tremorne, drifting off again. 'Did it hurt then? Poor little doggie . . . never mind . . . Alice is here . . .'

If miraculous strength had flowed out of the dog's paw to Alice Tremorne, now the procedure was reversed and strength flowed back through every means that the hand dipping into its alligator bag could provide. The little dog entered a new stage of his life that held everything a solicitous parent might give its child, a life of extreme contrast to all he had ever known, in its quiet stability and ordained pattern of day following upon day. By the time Mrs. Tremorne was allowed home to her well-aired bed, still stiff and sore, he was installed in a basket (the best) in her bedroom, his coat brushed to gleaming point, his hair tied back from his eyes with a red ribbon, and combed to a silken length that would have sent MacLean rushing in shame for scissors. The hair around his delicate hocks had been shaved to match the area around the injured paw over which a baby's blue bootee was drawn to hold the dressing in place. He hopped on three legs, and several times a day Miss Carpenter, mouth buttoned into a thin line, clipped a leash on to the lightest and finest of red collars and took her charge for an airing in the garden. After the first day of Mrs. Tremorne's homecoming she no longer returned him to the basket, but lifted him – her lips by now almost invisible – into the fastness of Mrs. Tremorne's bed, who then drew her pink silk eiderdown tenderly over.

At first he had hardly stirred, lying with dull apathetic eyes that were wide open yet seemed to focus on nothing. When they closed and he slept briefly, his body twitched convulsively, and then Mrs. Tremorne would reach out to pat and talk the reassuring baby talk that she had never used in her life but which seemed to come naturally to her now, until he lay quiet again. As the days passed, his tail gradually stirred more and more, his eyes cleared and focused, his ears rose fractionally – until one day she woke from a light sleep to find him lightly brushing her arm with one paw, his eyes beaming with interest. Yet another indomitable little dog had risen from the ashes.

Now to find a name for him. It seemed to Alice Tremorne that if she tried enough words she might run into a chance combination of vowels that would sound near enough to the dog's ears. Propped up against her pillows, her anonymous audience's eyes fixed upon her with unwavering attention, she started off by running through all the fictional or traditional canine names that she could remember: Rover, Fido, Blackie, Spot, Kim . . . She sent Carpenter down to the library: Garm, Argus, Owd Bob, Beautiful Joe, Luath, Beowulf, Greyfriars Bobby . . . She ran through name after name but none met with any recognition. Matthew, Mark, Luke, John . . . she persevered: Tinker, Tailor, Soldier, Sailor . . . She was about to dip into the telephone book when she remembered John Peel and his hounds.

'*Yes, I ken John Peel, and Ruby too!/ And Ranter and Rover/ . . .*' She trailed off; no, it wasn't Rover, it was . . . *Raver? Ringworm?* She started off at the beginning again, hoping to get carried along unconsciously: '*Do ye ken John Peel,/Wi' his coat so gay,*' she sang determinedly, only to get stuck again at Ranter. It was very irritating to one who prided herself on her memory.

She was still at it when Miss Carpenter arrived to take the dog out, and when commanded to make a duet she outran Mrs. Tremorne convincingly: '*Ranter and Ringwood,/Bellman and True!*' She continued in a surprisingly sweet soprano.

It was irritating to be bested; but as Mrs. Tremorne repeated the new names, suddenly the ears before her rose and flickered and the round eyes lit up in seeming recognition. She repeated the names, and this time the dog jumped off the bed and sat quivering expectantly, his eyes never leaving her face. It was Bellman that excited him, but she soon found that the first half of the word had the same effect: 'Bell!' she said, *'Bell* - good Bell!' and each time she spoke, the dog's tail wagged more furiously.

'You see,' she said triumphantly, 'that's his name - Bell! Time for walkies then, my darling Bell—' She gazed down dotingly.

In glum silence, Carpenter clipped on the lead. Then, almost unheard of, she produced an opinion of her own. 'I think Bell's a silly name for a dog,' she said. 'It sounds like a girl one way or a chime the other.' she sniffed.

Mrs. Tremorne was not used to mutiny, but she quelled it now with cunning ease: 'Neither the feminine nor the ding dong,' she said with lofty dismissal, 'but *Bel*, who - as I am sure you will remember - was the god of heaven and earth in Babylonian mythology.'

Many years addiction to *The Times* crossword had paid off. Bel he became, despite Carpenter sniffs, the sound of the name near enough to the one to which he must have responded for so many years before he became Ria.

Measure for measure, he returned the love and care lavished on him, and all his uninhibited affection and natural gaiety, so long denied, returned. He filled out to an attractive alert healthiness, becoming in the process the closest thing to a poodle to which the united efforts of his mistress and a kennel maid skilled in the art could clip and comb him, the dark curls of the outer coat stripping down to a pale, almost lavender, grey. The multilation of his toes left him with a permanent slight limp but did not seem to inconvenience him at all.

The gardener, the milkman, the postman, every tradesman who came to the door - in fact, any human who entered the house or garden - was greeted with enthusiastic interest, and if it were not immediately returned he would stand on his hindlegs to draw attention to the oversight.

Soon, even the reluctant Miss Carpenter, who had lived only for retirement one day with an undemanding canary, fell under his spell. She no longer looked so haunted, for now that Mrs. Tremorne had an all-engrossing interest, the spotlight of attention had shifted, and an atmosphere of almost cosy warmth gradually permeated the normally gloomy house with their mutual absorption. Suddenly one day she became Janet. Bel loved her, and more and more she enjoyed his company and the interest he brought to her formerly solitary walks. But undoubtedly the one who received his full devotion was the one whom he had found himself, his own human bounty, Mrs. Tremorne.

He seemed to be completely content in his role of the perfect companion to her; a dog who had quickly learned to interpret yet another vocabulary, who roused no antagonism in other dogs, whose presence did not raise the hair or flatten the ears of cats, friendly with all worlds; a perfect dog, obedient, fastidiously clean, with faultless manners, even towards food, for at first he would eat nothing, however tempting, unless she were eating too. To all appearances a dog for old ladies to pamper, who could fit right into a gentle purposeless life as though he had known no other; a chameleon little dog. Yet there were times when Mrs. Tremorne felt that it was like living with some kind of ghostly X, the unknown quantity – who and whatever had formed his life before he came to her. There was a certain excitement in finding new clues towards the solving, but mostly they only tantalised further with fragmentary glimpses of an unshared world.

There were times when he lay for hours on top of the garden wall, watching the world that passed below as though he was waiting to recognise some familiar form. Watching him herself. Mrs. Tremorne gradually discovered the pattern of his interests: the clip-clop of a horse-drawn milk van or coal cart always brought the most eager attention; servicemen, and sailors in particular, always aroused attention; children were accorded only a flicker of interest, passing dogs no more than a polite ritual acknowledgement. But this knowledge only added up to the questionable composite of an equestrian batchelor sailor for a former owner, and was not much help. He made many friends among the regular passers-by. They would stop and have a word with him, and he would receive their attentions with dignified polite interest, but he would never jump down off the security of his garden wall. He also made an excellent early warning system, for minutes before the sirens wailed to the approaching throb of German raiders he had abandoned the wall to make for the furthermost corner of the shelter under the kitchen stairs. A bonfire one day in the garden terrified him into this refuge as well.

There were the occasional times too when he lay listless and unresponsive, his eyes infinitely sad and faraway. One afternoon, eerily, he had sat up suddenly, thrown his head back and howled, a high haunting sound that had rung in Mrs. Tremorne's ears for days afterwards, unable to gauge at the depths from which such sorrow must find outlet. Sometimes she found herself almost willing him to speak, to tell her what he was so obviously imploring her to do on those occasions when he would sit before her, or crouch at the top of the stairs, tense, searching her eyes, straining every nerve to get his message across as to the part she must play in some ritual ... 'Darling Bel, what *is* it?' she would implore. 'What are you trying to tell me?'

'Sit up!' and 'salute' and 'catch' had been translated into immediate action, and she had discovered that he would toss and catch biscuits balanced on his nose, but whatever other time-honoured canine trick command she gave – speak, say please, roll over, jump – a puzzled shadow only would flit over his eyes, and it seemed as though she would never find the key words that would unlock any further response. But as the bond between them grew, his quivering need to communicate became stronger.

One day, he rose to his hindlegs in a bid to keep her attention longer. She took his forepaws. The wireless was playing Irish jigs, and she laughed down at him, moving his paws in time to the music. 'Come on, my darling,' she said, 'dance with me—' She moved three stiff close steps to the right, and then to the left, and he followed her. 'One, two, three,' sang Mrs. Tremorne to her eager little partner, 'and a one, two, *three*—' Breathless, she let his paws go, but to her astonishment he circled on, nodding his head and pawing the air in a quaint little dance.

Her reaction, of course, was one of unmitigated admiration and enchantment as she clapped her hands – and relief too, for it was as though some barrier had been broken down. Her pleasure was so patent that thereafter he volunteered this performance from time to time; but only, she noticed, when the need to communicate or demonstrate affection to her became so overwhelming that he had no other recourse, a unique bestowal of himself. A barrier had indeed been broken down but she could never know how strong and deeply entrenched it had been.

Because she wanted more than anything else to participate in the life that now ran with hers, she forced herself to walk more and more so that she could go further afield to the garden and watch her darling's enjoyment there. Unheeding of the almost impossible goal she had set for her arthritic legs, her ambition was to take Bel for a proper country walk one day. Sometimes she ached in every other part of her body as well, but whitefaced with effort, she persevered, and was rewarded in more ways than one, for not only did she begin to feel better physically, but through Bel she made daily contact with the outside world. She had actually been seen at the far end of the orchard talking over the fence – about Bel naturally – to her neighbour. But she was so slow that she decided he must have more from her than this sedate accompaniment; he must have more outdoor pursuits and more interests to keep his mind off himself and overcome these lonely listless periods.

She planned to buy a ball for a start; he would chase it, retrieve it, she would throw it up in the air and over gates and he would jump and leap and have all the exercise she could not give him.

Fortunately she was spared the bending and stretching of these activities. That afternoon, she and Bel had reached the far end of the garden at their customary tortoise pace when suddenly he stopped, his ears pricked, tense and quivering. Then he gathered himself and shot like an arrow down through the hedge, across the small orchard beyond, and leaped at the barred gate to the paddock. He paused there, poised on the top bar, his tail moving in the strange nervous vibration that was his version of the more usual wagging of other dogs. Clinging on with his front paws, his tail moving more rapidly than ever, he looked so like a fluffy hovering dragonfly that Mrs. Tremorne laughed out loud.

Now she saw the object of his excitement, her neighbour's donkey, the long-retired Fred who grazed her paddock from time to time – he must have been turned out there again only today. She watched Bel streak across the grass, then slow down to a halt a few feet away, his excitement apparently diminished. However, he sniffed around, examining from every angle, returning with his nose the compliments of the donkey as it gently nudged his head. He crouched, sprang, and dropped lightly on the shaggy back. Fortunately it was not the first time that Fred had felt an unexpected weight there; fifteen years of children had accustomed him to almost anything. Mrs. Tremorne leaned on her cane and revelled in the light-hearted spectacle of Bel, his mouth open, pink tongue lolling as though in laughter, his forepaws so rigid before him that they looked as though they pushed back his head and trunk. Fred moved off slowly, cropping the grass, the small motionless rider still on his back.

When Mrs. Tremorne called at last Bel came running immediately, his eyes still alight with excitement. She filed away another clue towards the unknown X. After this there was no problem about outdoor interest: if not bound for a session on the wall he would trot off briskly in search of Fred, sometimes pottering around the paddock in his company, sometimes lying close by as the donkey whiled away the long summer afternoons in the shade of the trees, sometimes bounding in a beautifully co-ordinated arc on to the broad patient back, there to dream with head thrown back, erect and totally still. Yet if Mrs Tremorne tried to persuade him to repeat this leap to order, he would simply sit before her, looking more and more puzzled the more she exhorted.

The withdrawn hours became fewer and fewer as the timeless weeks stretched into months within the garden walls, the war intruding only in domestic inconvenience, sporadic sorties to the air raid shelter, or through the impersonal voices of the BBC bringing news of the disastrous world that lay beyond:

'Today's official reports from Singapore indicate a grave situation . . . our troops have again had to fall back . . .' 'Dreadful, dreadful,' said Mrs. Tremorne.
'A great sea and air battle is going on in the English Channel . . . Scharnhorst, Geneisenau . . . Prinz Eugen . . . The cost to us: six Swordfish aircraft are missing . . . twenty bombers . . . sixteen fighters . . .'
That *unspeakable* little Hilter—' said Mrs. Tremorne.

The convoys battled on against the ever multiplying U-boat packs, such a terrible toll exacted that rationing became even more stringent. A strange tinned fish called snoek – popularly supposed to have originated in very old Rhodesian rain barrels – made its appearance on ration points. Whalemeat was expensive but required no points. Succulent slabs of horsemeat destined for British dogs were dyed blue to discourage human consumption. However, 'The introduction of soap rationing will reduce the consumption of soap by one-fifth,' declared the 9 o'clock news voice. Lord Woolton created his Wartime Pie.

Terrible, *terrible!*, said Mrs. Tremorne when he revealed its ingredients.

But it was only when she was faced with the prospect of one egg per fortnight and an ounce of butter to spread over seven slices of morning toast that the full impact of the war was brought home. She was unable to dismiss the inconvenience any longer; it was clearly here to stay, and for some time. Unable to do anything about the butter, she turned her attention to a long range solving of the egg problem: they would keep hens. Fortunately Janet showed unexpected enthusiasm for this project. Even more happily, yet another interest was provided for Bel. Six day-old chicks were bought; for the first few days they were reared in the kitchen under a lamp in a box, and under the unwavering gaze of Bel who appeared to be almost mesmerised by them. When they huddled together under the lamp for a brief sleep he relaxed; when they awoke, their cheepings brought him scurrying back. When they were let out they followed him around as though he were a mother hen; and if he lay down they climbed all over him. His retinue persisted even when they were grown birds and had the run of the orchard and, for a while, the garden. They would converge on him from all quarters with hysterical clucking excitement when he appeared, and were greatly frustrated when their wings were clipped and they were no longer able to fly up and perch beside him on the donkey's back. Mrs. Tremorne was greatly amused by his feathery following until they took to searching him out in the house, perching on windowsills, peering through, gaining access through any open door or window. After she and Bel had woken up one morning to the sound of their triumphant voices outside the bedroom door, they were exiled from the garden.

Now Bel's days were full indeed, and by the time a year had passed and the months of the second were marching on, he was indirectly contributing to the war effort as well, for in a combination of patriotism – stirred into activity by the fall of Singapore where she had once lived – and the effort to arrest the stiffness of her fingers in order to groom him, Mrs. Tremorne had learned to knit. Slowly and painfully she knitted for the Naval Comforts Fund, working her way up through the endless tedium of scarves to balaclavas and mitts, and then the ultimate triumph of socks. When the articles were collected the names and addresses of the knitters were pinned on, and sometimes they were despatched this way. Months later Mrs. Tremorne received acknowledgment of her labours from two of the recipients, a Wren stationed in

Scapa Flow, into whose hands.a pair of mitts had found their way, and a Leading Seaman who might well have been on the Arctic convoy routes from his description of the cold.

Mrs. Tremorne was strangely touched by their letters; for the first time she was in personal contact with the war. So touched, that from now on she and Janet saved from their rations of sugar, margarine and dried fruits, and one day two cakes were despatched.

She wrote regularly to her protégés, long inconsequential letters totally unrelated to the war; about what was coming up in the garden, the hens, a book she had read – but always the longest paragraphs were about Bel, and Bel's day to day activities. Perhaps her age and infirmity were apparent in her writing, perhaps the youngsters to whom she wrote appreciated this other-worldliness in the midst of service life, or perhaps she was just exceptionally fortunate, but she received many long letters in return, and even from time to time small presents. The one which she particularly treasured was a diagonally-sliced silver of tusk, minutely engraved with an endless procession of infinitesimal dogs. She had it set into a brooch and never wore any other.

If her life had been completely altered by Bel's coming, so was Janet Carpenter's, who looked ten years younger – almost within five years of her actual thirty-four. Having looked after her elderly ailing parents until they died, she had been untrained for any job. Unable, because of a slight congenital heart defect, to escape into the more colourful life of the women's services, she had resigned herself to the grey future of a light-duties companion. Now that Mrs. Tremorne was so occupied, and content to be left in the company of Bel, she had nerved herself to ask if she might join one of the voluntary services, and now slaved most happily two afternoons and two evenings a week in a railway canteen.

She proved to be an unexpectedly amusing raconteuse, and brought back a breath of outside life each time as she regaled Mrs. Tremorne with her various encounters over the coffee urns. Mrs. Tremorne, eager to expand her Bel audience, encouraged her to invite lonely or stranded young service men and women back to The Cedars.

At Christmas, by now well-launched into under-counter or behind-haystack deals, she procured a magnificent turkey, wine, and even crackers, and eight young people sat down to an unforgettable dinner. Afterwards, one of them produced a pennywhistle, another a concertina, and they sang carols. Then, as though to put the final seal of pleasure on this happiest of days, Bel judged his moment, and rose to perform his solemn little dance to the music.

It had been some time since he had expressed himself this way to Mrs. Tremore, and as she watched him circle now with nodding head and outstretched paws, she saw that his eyes sought hers with the same strange intensity of those first weeks. At that moment, with a sudden jealous stab of helplessness, as though she had somehow failed him, she

21

knew without doubt that this was only a part of a presentation: it should go on, but it could not for something was missing, and she could not provide it. Everything else in his life she could provide, but not this release that belonged to someone else.

She did not speak of this to Janet; if she had become such an absurd old woman that she was jealous of a ghost then it was better to keep it to herself. She comforted herself in bed that night by thinking of all his ways that belonged only to her, that had no part of any other life but The Cedars; how he brought her stick, carried up the morning newspaper, retrieved a fallen ball of wool, searched out the sites of cunningly concealed eggs – and a dozen examples that had sprung from her alone. She felt his reassuring warmth at the end of the bed. He was hers. She was just about to fall asleep when she realised that she herself had taught him none of these tricks: all had evolved from Bel himself.

Life with Mij
GAVIN MAXWELL

*After the death of his beloved dog, Jonnie, Gavin Maxwell left
his home in Camusfeàrna in the Western Highlands of Scotland
to travel in Iraq. On his return he brought with him to London
a new companion, an otter called Mijbil, who was to transform
his life . . .*

IT WAS NOW EARLY MAY, and I had been in London for more than three
weeks, three weeks of impatience and nostalgia for Camusfeàrna, and I
felt I could wait no longer to see Mij playing, as I visualized him, under
the waterfall, or free about the burn and the island beaches. I went by
way of my family home in the south of Scotland, where Mij could taste
a partial but guarded liberty before emancipation to total freedom in the
north.

Travelling with otters is a very expensive business. There was now no
question of again confining Mij to a box, and there is, unfortunately, no
other legitimate means of carrying an otter by train. For the illegitimate
means which I followed then and after, I paid, as do all who have
recourse to black markets, highly. He travelled with me in a first-class
sleeper, a form of transport which for some reason he enjoyed hugely;
indeed from the first he showed a perverse predilection for railway
stations, and a total disregard for their deafening din and alarming crowd
scenes.

At the barrier the railway official punched for me a dog ticket (on
which I had noticed the words 'Give full Description') and had already
turned to the next in the queue before his eyes widened in a perfect
double take; then Mij was tugging up the crowded platform at the end

of his lead, heedless of the shouts and the bustle, the screaming train hooters and rumbling luggage trolleys.

I had planned this operation with some care, visualizing each hazard and circumventing it as far as possible in advance; my hush money was already paid; the basket I carried contained everything conceivably necessary to Mij for the journey; over my left arm was an army blanket ready to protect the sheets from Mij's platform-grimed paws as soon as he entered the sleeper. When the initial penetration of the citadel, as it were, passed off without the slightest hitch, I felt that I had reaped no more than the just rewards of my forethought.

Mij had an instant eye for anything connected with water, and the most cursory inspection of the sleeping compartment convinced him that in the wash basin, however dry at the moment, lay the greatest pleasure-potential; he curled up in it, his form fitting the contours as an apple fits a dumpling, and his paws began increasingly feverish experiments with the chromium tap. It was, however, of a type entirely new to him, operating by downward pressure, and not a drop could he draw from it for a full five minutes; at last, trying to lever himself into an upright position, he put his full weight on the tap handle and found himself, literally, in his element.

There was only one incident that evening, an incident however, that for a moment bade fair to bring the whole train to a stop and to expose to the outraged eyes of officialdom my irregular travelling companion. My attention had wandered from Mij; the train was roaring up through the Midlands in summer dusk, and I was watching out of the window the green corn and the blackthorn hedges and the tall trees heavy with leaf, and thinking how effectively the glass and the movement of the train insulated one from any intimacy with these desirable things while seeming to offer no protection against the impact of drab industrial landscapes. Thus occupied, it had not occurred to me that Mij could, in that very confined space, get into any serious mischief; it had not crossed my mind, for example that by standing on the piled luggage he could reach the communication cord. This, however, was precisely what he had done, and when my eye lit on him he already had it firmly between his teeth while exploring with his paws the tunnel into which its ends disappeared. It was probably nothing but this insatiable curiosity as to detail that had so far saved the situation; now as I started towards him he removed his fingers from the recess and braced them against the wall for the tug. It takes a surprisingly strong pull to ring the communication bell (I have once done so, when the only other passenger in my compartment died while lighting his pipe), but Mij had the necessary strength, and it seemed, the determination. I caught him round the shoulders, but he retained his grip, and as I pulled him I saw the chain bulge ominously outward; I changed my tactics and pushed him towards it, but he merely braced his arms afresh. It seemed a deadlock, and one that might end in ignominy, until suddenly inspiration came to me. Mij was extremely ticklish, particularly over the region of the ribs. I began to tickle him feverishly, and at once his jaws relaxed into the foolish grin that he reserved for such occasions and he began to squirm. Later that evening he tried several times to reach the cord again, but by then I had redisposed the suitcases, and it was beyond the furthest stretch of his elastic body.

It was in unfamiliar surroundings such as these that Mij appeared most often to copy my actions; that night, though by now he had become accustomed to sleep inside the bed with his head to my feet, he arranged himself as he had on the first night at my flat, on his back with his head on the pillow and his arms outside the bedclothes. He was still so disposed when the attendant bought my tea in the morning. He stared at Mij, and said, 'Was it tea for one, or two, sir?'

During his stay at Monreith, the home of my family, Mij's character began to emerge and to establish itself. At first on farm mill dams, then in the big loch over which the house looks out, and finally in the sea – which, though he had never known salt water, he entered without apparent surprise – he demonstrated not only his astonishing swimming powers but his willingness to reject the call of freedom in favour of human company. At first, guessing the urgency of the summons that his instincts would experience, I allowed him to swim only on the end of a long fishing line. I had bought a spring reel, which automatically took up the slack, and attached this to the butt end of a salmon rod, but the danger of underwater snags on which the line might loop itself soon seemed too great, and after the first week he ran free and swam free. He wore a harness to which a lead could be attached in emergency, but its function was as much to proclaim his domesticity to would-be human aggressors as one of restraint. The design of this harness, one that would neither impede movement nor catch upon submerged branches and drown him, was a subject that occupied my imagination for many months, and was not perfected for nearly a year.

This time of getting to know a wild animal on terms, as it were, of mutual esteem, was wholly fascinating to me, and our long daily walks by stream and hedgerow, moorland and loch, were a source of perpetual delight. Though it remained difficult to lure him from some enticing piece of open water, he was otherwise no more difficult than a dog, and infinitely more interesting to watch. His hunting powers were still underdeveloped, but he would sometimes corner an eel in the mill dams, and in the streams he would catch frogs, which he skinned with a dexterity seemingly born of long practice. I had rightly guessed that his early life in a Marsh Arab household would have produced an enlightened and progressive attitude towards poultry – for no Ma'dan would tolerate a predator among the sparse and scrawny scarecrows that pass in the marshes for chickens – and in fact I found that Mij would follow me through a crowded and cackling farmyard without a glance to right or to left. To most domestic livestock he was indifferent, but black cattle he clearly identified with the water buffaloes of his home, and if they gathered at the edge of water in which he was swimming he became wild with excitement, plunging and porpoising and chittering with pleasure.

Even in the open countryside he retained his passion for playthings, and would carry with him for miles some object that had caught his fancy, a fallen rhododendron blossom, an empty twelve-bore cartridge case, a fir-cone, or, on one occasion, a woman's comb with an artificial brilliant set in the bar; this he discovered at the side of the drive as we set off one morning, and carried it for three hours, laying it down on the bank when he took to water and returning for it as soon as he emerged.

In the traces left by wild otters he took not the slightest interest. Following daily the routines for which Mij expressed preference, I found myself almost imperceptibly led by his instinct into the world in which the otters of my own countryside lived, a watery world of deep-cut streams between high, rooty banks where the leaves of the undergrowth met overhead; of unguessed alleys and tunnels in reedbeds by a loch's edge; of mossy culverts and marsh-marigolds; of islands tangled with fallen trees among whose roots were earthy excavations and a whisper of the wind in the willows. As one may hear or read a strange, unusual name, and therafter be haunted by its constant coincidental recurrence, so, now that I had through Mijbil become conscious of otters, I saw all around me the signs of their presence where I had been oblivious to them before; a smoothed bank of steep mud which they had used for tobogganing; a hollowed-out rotten tree-stump whose interior had been formed into a dry sleeping place; the print of a broad, capable, webbed foot; a small tarry dropping, composed mainly of eel-bones, deposited upon a stone in midstream. In these last I had expected Mij to show at least an equal interest to that which he had displayed in their canine counterparts, but whether because otters do not use their excreta in an anecdotal or informative way, or because he did not recognise in these the product of his own kind, he treated them as if they did not exist.

During all the time that I had him he killed, so far as I know, only one warm-blooded animal, and then he did not eat it, for he seemed to have a horror of blood and of the flesh of warm-blooded animals. On this occasion he was swimming in a reedy loch when he caught a moorhen chick of a few days old, a little black gollywog of a creature half the size of a day-old chick. He had a habit of tucking his treasures under one arm when he was swimming – for an otter swimming under-water uses its fore-limbs very little – and here he placed the chick while he went on in a leisurely way with his underwater exploration. It must have drowned during the first minute or so, and when at length he brought it ashore for a more thorough investigation he appeared disapointed and irritated by this unwarrantable fragility; he nuzzled it and pushed it about with his paws and chittered at it in a pettish sort of way, and then, convinced of its now permanent inertia, he left it where it lay and went in search of something more co-operative.

In the library at Monreith I explored what natural historians of earlier generations had to say about otters. There were no recent works, for the relevant section of the library had received no addition for many years past. That garrulous eighteenth-century clown the Comte de Buffon, whose nineteen volumes had acquired a petulant flavour by his contemporary translator's insistence on the use of the English word 'pretend' for the French *prétendre*, did not, on the whole, approve of otters. He was a whimsical man, much concerned with the curious, and credulous as to the existence of most patently improbable creatures, which he himself tried assiduously to produce by arranging monstrous matings (after much experiment he was disappointedly forced to the conclusion that a bull and a mare 'could copulate neither with pleasure nor profit'); furthermore he appeared to attach some mystic significance to whether an animal could or could not be persuaded to eat honey. Otters, he found, could not.

'Young animals are generally beautiful; but the young otter is not so handsome as the old. A head ill shaped, ears placed low, eyes small and covered, a lurid aspect, awkward motions, an ignoble and deformed figure, and a kind of mechanical cry, which he repeats every moment, seem to indicate a stupid animal. The otter, however, acquires industry with age, sufficient, at least, to carry on a successful war against the fishes, who, both with regard to sentiment and instinct, are much inferior to other animals. But I can hardly allow him to have the talents of the beaver. . . . All I know is, that the otters dig no habitations for themselves, . . . that they often change their places of abode; that they banish their young at the end of six weeks or two months; that those I attempted to tame endeavoured to bite; that some days after they became more gentle, perhaps because they were weak or sick; that, so far from being easily accustomed to a domestic life, all of them that I attempted to bring up, died young; that the otter is naturally of a cruel and savage disposition. . . . His retreats exhale a noxious odour, from the remains of putrid fishes; and his own body has a bad smell. The flesh is extremely fishy and disagreeable. The Romish Church permits the use of it on maigre days. In the kitchen of the Carthusian convent, near Dijon, Mr. Pennant saw one preparing for the dinner of the rigid order, who, by their rules, are prohibited, during their whole lives, the eating of flesh.'

This description might perhaps have proved somewhat discouraging had I not such abundant first-hand evidence to refute it, but if Buffon had been the otter's principal detractor, the great American naturalist Ernest Thompson Seton was certainly champion in chief. Writing soon after the turn of this century he said, 'Of all the beasts whose lives I have tried to tell, there is one that stands forth, the Chevalier Bayard of the wilds – without fear and without reproach. That is the otter, the joyful, keen, and fearless otter; mild and loving to his own kind, and gentle with his neighbour of the stream; full of play and gladness in his life, full of courage in his stress; ideal in his home, steadfast in death; the noblest little soul that ever went four-footed through the woods.' In his writings I recognized the animal that I knew, 'the most beautiful and engaging of all elegant pets. There seems no end to its fun, its energy, its drollery, its good nature, and its postures of new and surprising grace. I never owned a pet otter, but I never yet saw one without shamelessly infringing article number ten of the Decalogue,'[1] While noting that in its structural affinities 'the otter is nothing but a big water weasel' he adds, writing of the tobogganing habit: 'It is a delightful proof of growth and uplift when we find an adult animal setting aside a portion of its time and effort for amusement, and especially for social amusement. A large number of the noblest animals thus relax from sordid life and pursue amusement with time and appliances after a fashion that finds its highest development in man.'

Yet another early writer, whose name I find elusive, remarked, with a certain quaint charm in choice of words, that 'the Otter is of course a giant amphibious stoat whose nature has been softened by the gentling and ennobling influence of the fisher life'.

We arrived at Camusfeàrna in early June, soon after the beginning of a long spell of Mediterranean weather. My diary tells me that summer begins on 22nd June, and under the heading for 24th June there is a somewhat furtive aside to the effect that it is Midsummer's day, as though to ward off the logical deduction that summer lasts only for four days in every year. But that summer at Camusfeàrna seemed to go on and on through timeless hours of sunshine and stillness and the dapple of changing cloud shadow upon the shoulders of the hills.

When I think of early summer at Camusfeàrna a single enduring image comes forward through the multitude that jostle in kaleidoscopic patterns before my mind's eye – that of wild roses against a clear blue sea, so that when I remember that summer alone with my curious namesake who had travelled so far, those roses have become for me the symbol of a whole complex of peace. They are not the pale, anaemic flowers of the south, but a deep, intense pink that is almost a red; it is the only flower of that colour, and it is the only flower that one sees habitually against the direct background of the ocean, free from the green stain of summer. The yellow flag irises flowering in dense ranks about the burn and the foreshore, the wild orchids bright among the heather and mountain grasses, all these lack the essential contrast, for the eye may move from them to the sea beyond them only through the intermediary, as it were, of the varying greens among which they grow. It is in June and October that the colours at Camusfeàrna run riot, but in

[1] *Life Histories of Northern Animals* (Constable, 1910).

June one must face seaward to escape the effect of wearing green-tinted spectacles. There at low tide the rich ochres, madders and oranges of the orderly strata of seaweed species are set against glaring, vibrant whites of barnacle-covered rock and shell sand, with always beyond them the elusive, changing blues and purples of the moving water, and somewhere in the foreground the wild roses of the north.

Into this bright, watery landscape Mij moved and took possesion with a delight that communicated itself as clearly as any articulate speech could have done; his alien but essentially appropriate entity occupied and dominated every corner of it, so that he became for me the central figure among the host of wild creatures with which I was surrounded. The waterfall, the burn, the white beaches and the islands; his form became the familiar foreground to them all – or perhaps foreground is not the right word, for at Camusfeàrna he seemed so absolute a part of his surroundings that I wondered how they could ever have seemed to me complete before his arrival.

At the beginning, while I was still imbued with the caution and forethought that had so far gone to his tending, Mij's daily life followed something of a routine; this became, as the week went on, relaxed into a total freedom at the centre point of which Camusfeàrna house remained Mij's holt, the den to which he returned at night, and in the daytime when he was tired. But this emancipation, like most natural changes, took place so gradually and unobtrusively that it was difficult for me to say at what point the routine had stopped.

Mij slept in my bed (by now, as I have said, he had abandoned the teddy-bear attitude and lay on his back under the bedclothes with his whiskers tickling my ankles and his body at the crook of my knees) and would wake with bizarre punctuality at exactly twenty past eight in the morning. I have sought any possible explanation for this, and some 'feed-back' situation in which it was actually I who made the first unconcious movement, giving him his cue, cannot be altogether discounted; but whatever the reason, his waking time, then and until the end of his life, summer or winter, remained precisely twenty past eight. Having woken, he would come up to the pillow and nuzzle my face and neck with small attenuated squeaks of pleasure and affection. If I did not rouse myself very soon he would set about getting me out of bed. This he did with the business-like, slightly impatient efficiency of a nurse dealing with a difficult child. He played the game by certain defined and self-imposed rules; he would not, for example, use his teeth even to pinch, and inside these limitations it was hard to imagine how a human brain could, in the same body, have exceeded his ingenuity. He began by going under the bedclothes and moving rapidly up and down the bed with a high-hunching, caterpillar-like motion that gradually untucked the bed-clothes from beneath the sides of the mattress; this achieved he would redouble his efforts at the foot of the bed, where the sheets and blankets had a firmer hold. When everything had been loosened up to his satisfaction he would flow off the bed onto the floor – except when running on dry land the only appropriate word for an otter's movement is flowing; they pour themselves, as it were, in the direction of their objective – take the bedclothes between his teeth, and, with a series of violent tugs, begin to yank them down beside him. Eventually, for I do not wear pyjamas, I would be left quite naked on the undersheet, clutching the pillows rebelliously. But they, too, had to go; and it was here that he demonstrated the extraordinary strength concealed in his small body. He would work his way under them and execute a series of mighty hunches of his arched back, each of them lifting my head and whole shoulders clear of the bed, and at some point in the procedure he invariably contrived to dislodge the pillows while I was still in mid-air, much as a certain type of practical joker will remove a chair upon which someone is in the act of sitting down. Left thus comfortless and bereft both of covering and of dignity, there was little option but to dress, while Mij looked on with all-that-shouldn't-really-have-been-necessary-you-know sort of expression. Otters usually get their own way in the end; they are not dogs, and they co-exist with humans rather than being owned by them.

His next objective was the eel-box in the burn, followed, having breakfasted, by a tour of the water perimeter, the three-quarter circle formed by the burn and the sea; shooting like an under-water arrow after trout where the burn runs deep and slow between the trees; turning over stones for hidden eels where it spreads broad and shallow over sun-reflecting scales of mica; tobogganing down the long, loose sand slope by the sand-martin colony; diving through the waves on the sand beach and catching dabs; then, lured in with difficulty and subterfuge from starting on a second lap, home to the kitchen and ecstatic squirming among his towels.

This preamble to the day, when Mij had a full stomach and I had not, became, as he established favoured pools and fishing grounds which had every morning to be combed as for a lost possesion, even longer and longer, and after the first fortnight I took, not without misgiving, to going back indoors myself as soon as he had been fed. At first he would return after an hour or so, and when he had dried himself he would creep up under the loose cover of the sofa and form a round breathing hump at the centre of the seat. But as time went on he stayed longer about the burn, and I would not begin to worry until he had been gone for half the day.

There were great quantities of cattle at Camusfeàrna that year, for the owner of the estate was of an experimental turn of mind, and had decided to farm cattle on the lines of the Great Glen Cattle Ranch. The majority of these beasts were black, and, as at Monreith in the spring, Mij seemed to detect in them an affinity to his familiar water buffaloes of the Tigris marshes, for he would dance round them with excited chitterings until they stampeded. Thus massed they presented too formidable an appearance for him, and after a week or two he devised for himself a means of cattle-baiting at which he became a past master. With extreme stealth he would advance *ventre à terre* towards the rear end of some massive stirk whose black-tufted tail hung invitingly within his reach; then, as one who makes a vigorous and impatient tug at a bell-rope, he would grab the tuft between his teeth and give one tremendous jerk upon it with all his strength, leaping backward exactly in time to dodge the lashing hooves. At first I viewed this sport with the gravest alarm, for, owing to the structure of the skull, a comparatively light blow on the nose can kill an otter, but Mij was able to gauge the distance to an inch, and never a hoof so much as grazed him. As a useful by-product of his impish sense of humour, the cattle tended to keep farther from the house, thus incidentally reducing the number of scatological hazards to be skirted at the door.

I had a book to write during those summer months at Camusfeàrna, and often I would lie for hours in the sun by the waterfall; from time to time Mij would appear from nowhere, bounding up the bank from the water, to greet me as though we had been separated for weeks.

There is a patron saint of otters, St. Cuthbert – the eider duck, too, shares his patronage; clearly he was a man who bestowed his favours with the most enlightened discrimination – and there exists an eye-witness account of his converse with them.

'It was his way for the most part to wander in those places and to preach in those remote hamlets, perched on steep rugged mountain sides, where other men would have a dread of going, and whose poverty and rude ignorance gave no welcome to any scholar.... Often for a whole week, sometimes for two or three, and even for a full month, he would not return home, but would abide in the mountains, and call these simple folk to heavenly things by his words and ways....

'(*He was, moreover, easily entreated, and came to stay at the abbey of Coldingham on a cliff above the sea.*)

'As was his habit, at night while other men took their rest, he would go out to pray: and after long vigils kept far into the night, he would come home when the hour of common prayer drew near. One night, a brother of this same monastery saw him go silently out, and stealthily followed on his track, to see where he was going or what he would do. And so he went out from the monastery and, his spy following him, went down to the sea, above which the monastery was built: and wading into the depths till the waves swelled up to his neck and arms, kept his vigil through the dark with chanting voiced like the sea. As the twilight of dawn drew near, he waded back up the beach, and kneeling there, again began to pray: and as he prayed, straight from the depths of the sea came two four-footed beasts which are called by the common people otters.

These, prostrate before him on the sand, began to busy themselves warming his feet with pantings, and trying to dry them with their fur; and when this good office was rendered, and they had his benediction they slipped back again beneath their native waters. He himself returned home, and sang the hymns of the office with the brethren at the appointed hour. But the brother who had stood watching him from the cliffs was seized with such panic that he could hardly make his way home, tottering on his feet: and early in the morning came to him and fell at his feet, begging forgiveness with his tears for his foolish attempt, never doubting but that his behaviour of the night was known and discovered.

'To whom Cuthbert: "What ails you, my brother? What have you done? Have you been out and about to try to come at the truth of this night wandering of mine? I forgive you, on this one condition: that you promise to tell no man what you saw, until my death." And the promise given, he blesed the brother and absolved him alike of the fault and the annoyance his foolish boldness had given: and the brother kept silence on the piece of valour that he had seen, until after the saint's death, when he took pains to tell it to many."[2]

Now it is apparent to me that whatever other saintly virtues St. Cuthbert possessed he well merited canonization by reason of his forebearance alone. I know all about being dried by otters. I have been dried by them more times than I care to remember. Like everything else about otters, it takes place the wrong way round, so to speak. When one plays ball with a puppy, one throws the ball and the puppy fetches it back and then one throws it again; it is all comparatively restful and orderly. But when one plays ball with an otter the situation gets out of hand from the start; it is the otter who throws the ball – to a remarkable distance – and the human who fetches it. With the human who at the beginning is not trained to this the otter is fairly patient, but persistent and obstinate refusal meets with reprisals. The same upside-down situation obtains when being dried by otters. The otter emerges tempestuously from the sea or the river or the bath, as the case may be, carrying about half a gallon of water in its fur, and sets about drying you with a positively terrifying zeal and enthusiasm. Every inch of you requires, in the view of a conscientious otter, careful attention. The otter uses its back as the principal towel, and lies upon it while executing a series of vigorous, eel-like wriggles. In a surprisingly short space of time the otter is quite dry except for the last four inches of its tail, and the human being is soaking wet except for nothing. It is no use going to change one's clothes; in a few minutes the otter will come rampaging out of the water again intent upon its mission of drying people.

I have but little doubt what the good brother of Coldingham monastery really saw. St. Cuthbert had been praying at the water's edge, not, as the

[2] Helen Waddell, *Beasts and Saints* (Constable, 1934).

brother thought (it was, one must bear in mind, night, and the light was poor), up to his neck in the waves; and it was entirely the condition of the saint's clothing after he had been dried by the otters that led the observer to deduce some kind of sub-marine devotion. Clearly, too, it was an absolution rather than a simple benediction that the now shivering and bedraggled saint bestowed upon his tormentors. In the light of my interpretation St. Cuthbert's injunction to silence falls neatly into place, for he could not know of the brother's misapprehension, and not even a saint enjoys being laughed at in this kind of misfortune.

While otters undoubtedly have a special vocation for drying human beings they will also dry other objects, most particularly beds, between the sheets, all the way from the pillows to the bed-foot. A bed dried by this process is unusable for a week, and an otter-dried sofa is only tolerable in the heat of summer. I perceive why St. Cuthbert required the ministrations of the eider ducks and the warm down of their breasts; the unfortunate man must have been constantly threatened with an occupational pneumonia.

This aspect of life with an otter had never really struck me before I brought Mij to Camusfeàrna; in London one could run the water out of the bath, and by using a monster towel could render him comparatively harmless before he reached the sitting-room, while at Monreith the loch was far enough from the house for him to be dry before reaching home. But at Camusfeàrna, with the sea a stone's throw on one side and the burn on the other, I have found no satisfactory solution beyond keeping the bedroom door closed, and turning, as it were, a blind posterior to wet sofas and chairs.

The manuscript that I was writing that summer became blurred and stained as though by tears; I would lie, as I have said, sunbathing and writing in the grass by the burn, and every now and again Mij's busy quartering of the stream's bed from the falls to the sea and back again would bring him to the point above which I lay. With delighted squeaks and gurgles he would rush through the shallows and come bounding up the bank to deposit his skin-load of water indiscriminately upon myself and my manuscript, sometimes adding insult to injury by confiscating my pen as he departed.

In the sea, Mij discovered his true, breath-taking aquabatic powers; until he came to Scotland he had never swum in deep waters, for the lakes and lagoons of his native marshes are rarely more than a fathom or two deep. He would swim beside me as I rowed in the little dinghy, and in the glass-clear waters of Camusfeàrna bay, where the white shell sand alternates with sea tangle and outcrops of rock, I could watch him as he dived down, down, down through fathom after fathom to explore the gaudy sea forests at the bottom with their flowered shell glades and mysterious, shadowed caverns. He was able, as are all otters and seals, to walk on the bottom without buoyancy, for an otter swims habitually underwater and does not dive with full lungs, depending for oxygen – we must presume in the absence of knowledge – upon a special adaptation of the venous system. The longest that I ever timed Mij below the surface was almost six minutes, but I had the impression that he was in no way taxing his powers, and could greatly have exceeded that time in emergency. Normally, however, if he was not engrossed, he would return to the surface every minute or so, breaking it for only a second, with a forward diving roll like that of a porpoise. Swimming at the surface, as he did if he wanted to keep some floating object in view, he was neither very fast nor graceful, a labouring dog-paddle in amazing contrast to his smooth darting grace below water. For hours he would keep pace with the boat, appearing now on this side and now on that, sometimes mischievously seizing an oar with both arms and dragging on it, and from time to time bouncing inboard with a flurry of water, momentarily recalled to his mission of drying people.

Only when I was fishing did I have to leave Mij shut up in the house, for he was a creature who must test everything with his mouth, and my worst nightmare was the vision of a mackerel hook in his jaw. At first I fished little, having no great liking for the lythe and coal fish that are all one may depend upon in early summer round the Camusfeàrna skerries. Though by mid-June there are all the signs of summer; the teeming, clangorous bird life of the islands established for many weeks and the samphire and goose-grass alive with downy chicks, it is not until July that with the coming of the mackerel the sea appears to burst into life; for following them come all the greater creatures that prey upon them, and the mackerel in their turn force up to the surface the lesser fishes upon which they feed, the small, glittering, multitudinous fry of many species, including their own. When far out on the blank face of the summer sea there are screaming patches of gulls that dip and swoop, half running, half flying, alighting with wings still open to grab and to swallow, one may guess that somewhere beneath them lies a great shoal of mackerel, who are pushing up to the surface and the waiting gulls the little fish fleeing in panic from, perhaps, their own parents. Sometimes there are curiously local patches of fry at the surface, and at sunset when the surface is really as smooth as glass – a much misused simile, for it rarely is – I have seen, miles from shore, little dancing foot-wide fountains of blue and silver mackerel no longer than a man's thumb, and have found no predator below them.

After the mackerel had arrived I fished for a few minutes in the cool of every evening; for them Mij, though he never caught one himself, so far as I knew, had an insatiable passion, as had Jonnie before him; and I too welcomed them, perhaps because of childhood associations. When I was a child in Galloway we used to fish for mackerel by trolling from a sailing-boat a single hook baited with bright metal, or with a sliver of flesh and skin sliced from a mackerel's flank (how well I recall the horror of seeing for the first time this operation performed upon the living fish; the tears, the reassurance, all among the blue waves and the spindrift and the flapping brown sail). We caught our fish singly and rebaited the hook each time, and if we caught twenty or thirty fish in an afternoon we chattered about it for weeks. It was not, I think, until shortly before the last war that the murderous darrow came into general use in the West Highlands, and at Camusfeàrna, where there is no means of disposing of surplus fish but dumping them, it has the disadvantge of limiting fishing time to a few minutes. A darrow consists of a twelve-foot cast carrying up to twenty-two flies of crudely-dyed hen's feathers, weighted at the bottom with a two-pound sinker. The boat is stationary in anything from six to twenty fathoms of water, and the darrow and line are allowed to run out until the sinker bumps the bottom. By that time, as often as not in Camusfeàrna bay, there are half a dozen or so mackerel on the hooks. If there are not, it is simply a question of hauling in two fathoms of line and letting it run out again, and repeating this process until either the boat drifts over a shoal or a moving shoal happens to pass beneath the boat. Sometimes the mackerel are in shallower water, clear water where one can see fathoms down to pale sand and dark sea-tangle and rushing shoals of aquamarine fish as they dart at the bright feathers. Quite often every single fly is taken at once; then at one moment the line is lead-heavy, tugging and jerking, and at the next light as floating string as the mackerel swim upward carrying the sinker with them. There is a great art in dealing with a full darrow, for twenty-two large fish-hooks flipping wildly about the hold of a small boat catch more than fish. In the days of the Soay Shark Fishery I saw many barbs sunk deep in hands and legs of mackerel fishers; there was only one way of extraction, and a very painful one it was – to push the hook clean through, as opposed to pulling on it, then to snip off the barb with wire cutters and work the hook all the way back again.

It is not always mackerel that take the darrow flies; there are saith and lythe and the strangely heraldic gurnards, so fantastically armoured with spikes and thorns as to make their capture by anything but man seem nothing short of impossible, yet I have watched, with the same sensations as a man might view a big snake swallowing an ox whole, a shag swallow a large gurnard tail first – against the grain, as it were. This extraordinary and surely gratuitously painful feat took the shag just over half an hour of grotesque convulsion, and when the stunt was at last completed the bird had entirely changed its shape. From being a slim, graceful, snake-like creature with a neck like an ebony cane, it had become an amorphous and neck-less lump – its crop so gigantically distended as to force the head far back down the spine and flush with it – unable to rise or even to swim without danger of ridicule.

Mij himself caught a number of fish on his daily outings; and week by week, as his skill and speed grew, their size and variety increased. In the burn he learned to feel under stones for eels, reaching in with one paw and averted head; and I in turn learned to turn over the larger stones for him, so that after a time he would stand in front of some boulder too heavy for him to move, and chitter at me to come and lift it for him. Often, as I did this, an eel would streak out from it into deeper water and he would fire himself after it like a brown torpedo beneath the surface. Near the edge of the tide he would search out the perfectly camouflaged flounders until they shot of with a wake of rising sand-grains like smoke from an express train – and farther out in the bay he would kill an occasional sea trout; these he never brought ashore, but ate them treading water as he did so, while I thought a little wistfully of the Chinese who are said to employ trained otters to fish for them. Mij, I thought, with all his delightful camaraderies, would never offer me a fish; I was wrong, but when at last he did so it was not a sea trout but a flounder. One day he emerged from the sea on to the rock ledge where I was standing and slapped down in front of me a flounder a foot across. I took it that he had brought this for congratulation, for he would often bring his choicer catches for inspection before consuming them, so I said something encouraging and began to walk on. He hurried after me and slammed it down again with a wet smack at my feet. Even then I did not understand, assuming only that he wished to eat in company, but he just sat there looking up and chittering at me. I was in no hurry to take the gesture at its face value, for, as I have said, one of the most aggressive actions one can perform to a wild animal is to deprive it of its prey, but after perhaps half a minute of doubt, while Mij redoubled his invitation, I reached down slowly and cautiously for the fish, knowing that Mij would give me vocal warning if I misinterpreted him. He watched me with the plainest approval while I picked it up and began a mime of eating it; then he plunged off the rock into the sea and sped away a fathom down in the clear water.

Watching Mij in a rough sea – and the equinoctial gales at Camusfeàrna produce very rough seas indeed – I was at first sick with apprehension, then awed and fascinated, for his powers seemed little less than miraculous. During the first of the gales, I remember, I tried to keep him to the rock pools and the more sheltered corners, but one day his pursuit of some unseen prey had taken him to the seaward side of a high dry reef at the very tide's edge. As the long undertow sucked outward he was in no more than an inch or two of marbled water with the rock at his back, crunching the small fish he had caught; then, some forty yards to seaward of him I saw a great snarling comber piling up higher and higher, surging in fifteen feet tall and as yet unbreaking. I yelled to Mij as the wave towered darkly towards him, but he went on eating and paid no heed to me. It curled over and broke just before it reached him; all those tons of water just smashed down and obliterated him, enveloping the whole rock behind in a booming tumult of sea, Somewhere under it I visualized

Mij's smashed body swirling round the foot of the black rock. But as the sea drew back in a long hissing undertow I saw, incredulously, that nothing had changed; there was Mij still lying in the shallow marbled water, still eating his fish.

He rejoiced in the waves; he would hurl himself straight as an arrow right into the great roaring grey wall of an oncoming breaker and go clean through it as if it had neither weight nor momentum; he would swim far out to sea through wave after wave until the black dot of his head was lost among the distant white manes, and more than once I thought that some wild urge to seek new lands had seized him and that he would go on swimming west into the Sea of Hebrides and that I should not see him again.

As the weeks went by his absences did grow longer, and I spent many anxious hours searching for him, though as yet he had never stayed away for a night. When I had drawn blank at the falls and at all his favourite pools in the burn or among the rock ledges by the sea, I would begin to worry and to roam more widely, calling his name all the while. His answering note of recognition was so like the call of some small dowdy bird that inhabits the trees by the waterside that my heart would leap a hundred times before I knew with certainty that I had heard his voice, and then my relief was so unbounded that I would allow him to dry me without protest.

The first time that I found him in distress was in the dark ravine above the waterfall. The waterfall divides, in some sense, the desert from the sown; the habitable world from the strange, beautiful, but inhospitable world of the dark gorge through which the burn flows above it. In summer, when the water is low, one may pick one's way precariously along the rock at the stream's edge, the almost sheer but wooded sides rising a hundred feet at either hand. Here it is always twilight, for the sun never reaches the bed of the stream, and in summer the sky's light comes down thin and diffused by a stipple of oak and birch leaves whose branches lean out far overhead. Here and there a fallen tree-trunk spans the narrow gorge, its surface worn smooth by the passage of the wildcats' feet. The air is cool, moist, and pungent with the smell of wild garlic and watery things such as ferns and mosses that grow in the damp and the dark. Sometimes the bed of the stream widens to deep pools whose rock flanks afford no foothold, and where it looks as though the black water must be bottomless.

Once Morag asked me, in an offhand way behind which I sensed a tentative probing, whether I felt at ease in that place. It was a question that held a tacit confession, and I replied frankly. I have never been at ease in it; it evokes in me an unpleasant sensation that I associate only with the unfurnished top floor of a certain house, a sensation which makes me want to glance constantly over my shoulder, as though, despite the physical impossibility, I were being followed. I catch myself trying

37

to step silently from stone to stone, as though it were important to my safety that my presence should remain undetected. I should have been abashed to tell Morag of this had she not given me the lead, but she told me then that she had had a horror of the place ever since she was a child, and could offer no explanation.

To conform to the spirit of my confession the gorge ought, of course, to be shunned by bird and animal alike, but it has, in fact, more of both than one might expect. There are foxes' and badgers' and wildcats' dens in the treacherous, near-vertical walls of the ravine; the buzzards and hooded crows nest every year in the branches that lean out over the dark water; below them there are the dippers and grey wagtails (a crass ornithological misnomer for this canary-yellow creature), and, for some reason, an unusual number of wrens that skulk and twitter among the fern. Whatever makes the gorge an unpleasant place to some people does not extend its influence beyond human beings.

The deep pools spill in unbroken falls a few feet high, and after two hundred yards or so there is the second real waterfall, dropping fifty feet interrupted by a ledge pool half-way down. That is the upper limit of the 'haunting', though the physical details of the gorge above the second falls differ little from those of the stretch below it; then, a further hundred yards up the burn's course, the way is blocked by the tall cataract, eighty feet of foaming white water falling sheer.

Mij, certainly, found nothing distasteful in the reach where my ghosts walked, and he had early used his strength and resource to scale the Camusfeàrna waterfall and find out what lay beyond. Thereafter this inaccessible region had become his especial haunt, and one from which his extraction presented, even when he was not in difficulties, almost insuperable problems. The clamour of the falling water effectively drowned the calling human voice, and even if he did hear it there was little chance of the caller perceiving his faint, bird-like response. On this occasion there was more water in the burn than is usual in summer, and there had been, too, a recent landslide, temporarily destroying the only practicable access from above. I lowered myself into the ravine on a rope belayed to the trunk of a tree, and I was wet to the waist after the first few yards of the burn's bed. I called and called, but my voice was diminished and lost in the sound of rushing water, and the little mocking birds answered me with Mij's own note of greeting. At length one of these birds, it seemed, called so repeatedly and insistently as to germinate in me a seed of doubt, but the sound came from far above me, and I was looking for Mij in the floor of the burn. Then I saw him; high up on the cliff, occupying so small a ledge that he could not even turn to make his way back, and with a fifty-foot sheer drop below him; he was looking at me, and, according to his lights, yelling his head off. I had to make a long detour to get above him with the rope and all the while I was terrified that the sight of me would have spurred him to some effort that would bring tragedy; terrified, too, that I myself might dislodge him as I tried to lift him from his eyrie. Then I found that the trees at the cliff-top were all rotten, and I had to make the rope fast to a stump on the hill above, a stump that grew in soft peat and that gave out from its roots an ominous squelching sound when I tugged hard on it. I went down that rock with the rope knotted round my waist and the feeling that Mij would probably survive somehow, but that I should most certainly die. He tried to stand on his hind legs when he saw me coming down above him, and more than once I thought he had gone. I had put the loop of his lead through the rope at my waist, and I clipped the other end to his harness as soon as my arm could reach him, but the harnesses, with their constant immersion, never lasted long, and I trusted this one about as much as I trusted the stump to which my rope was tied. I went up the rope with Mij dangling and bumping at my side like a cow being loaded on to a ship by crane, and in my mind's eye were two jostling, urgent images – the slow, sucking emergence of the tree roots above me, and the gradual parting of the rivets that held Mij's harness together. All in all it was one of the nastiest five minutes of my life; and when I reached the top the roots of the stump were indeed showing – it took just one tug with all my strength to pull them clean out.

But the harness held, though, mercifully, it broke the next time it was put to strain. Mij had been missing, that day in the ravine, for nine hours, and had perhaps passed most of them on that ledge, for he was ravenously hungry, and ate until I thought he must choke.

There were other absences, other hours of anxiety and search, but one in particular stands out in my mind, for it was the first time that he had been away for a whole night, the first time that I despaired of him. I had left him in the early morning at the burn side eating his eels, and began to be uneasy when he had not returned by mid-afternoon. I had been working hard at my book; it was one of those rare days of authorship when everything seemed to go right; the words flowed unbidden from my pen, and the time had passed unheeded, so that it was a shock to realize that I had been writing for some six hours. I went out and called for Mij down the burn and along the beach, and when I did not find him I went again to the ravine above the falls. But there was no trace of him anywhere, though I explored the whole dark length of it right to the high falls, which I knew that even Mij could not pass. Just how short a distance my voice carried I realized when, above the second falls, I came upon two wildcat kittens at play on the steep bank; they saw me and were gone in a flash, but they had never heard my voice above the sound of the water. I left the burn then and went to the nearer islands; it was low tide, and there were exposed stretches and bars of soft white sand. Here I found otter footprints leading towards the lighthouse island, but I could not be certain that they were Mij's. Later that summer his claws became worn so that his pad-marks no longer showed the nails, but at that stage I was still unsure of distinguishing his tracks from those of a wild otter, unless the imprints were very precise. All that evening I searched and called, and when dusk came and he still did not return I began to despair, for his domestic life had led him to strictly diurnal habits, and by sundown he was always asleep in front of the fire.

It was a cloudy night with a freshening wind and a big moon that swam muzzily through black rags of vapour. By eleven o'clock it was blowing strong to gale from the south, and on the windward side of the islands there was a heavy sea beginning to pile up; enough, I thought, for him to loose his bearings if he were trying to make his way home through it. I put a light in each window of the house, left the doors open, and dozed fitfully in front of the kitchen fire. By three o'clock in the morning there was the first faint paling of dawn, and I went out to get the boat, for by now I had somehow convinced myself that Mij was on the lighthouse island. That little cockleshell was in difficulties from the moment I launched her; I had open water and a beam sea to cross before I could reach the lee of the islands, and she was taking a slosh of water over her gunwale all the way. If I shipped oars to bale I made so much leeway that I was nearly ashore again before I had done, and after half an hour I was both wet and scared. The bigger islands gave some shelter from the south wind, but in the passages between them the north-running sea was about as much as the little boat would stand, and over the many rocks and skerries the water was foaming white and wicked-looking in the half light. A moment to bale and I would have been swept on to these black cusps and molars; the boat would have been crunched on them like a squashed matchbox, and I, who canno' swim a stroke, would have been feeding the lobsters. To complete my discomfort, I met a Killer whale. In order to keep clear of the reefs I had rowed well north of the small islands that lie to landward of the lighthouse; the water was calmer here, and I did not have to fight to keep the nose of the boat into the waves. The Killer broke the surface no more than twenty yards to the north of me, a big bull whose sabre fin seemed to tower a man's height out of the water; and, probably by chance, he turned straight for me. My nerves were strung and tensed, and I was in no frame of mind to assess the true likelihood of danger; I swung and rowed for the nearest island as though man were a Killer's only prey. I grounded on a reef a hundred yards from the tern island, and I was not going to wait for the tide to lift me. Slithering and floundering in thigh-deep water over a rock ledge I struggled until I had lifted the flat keel clear of the tooth on which it had grated; the Killer, possibly intent upon his own business and with no thought, of me, cruised round a stone's throw away. I reached the tern island, and the birds rose screaming around me in a dancing canopy of ghostly wings, and I sat down on the rock in the dim windy dawn and felt as desolate as an abandoned child.

The lighthouse island was smothered in its jungle-growth of summer briars that grip the clothing with octopus arms and leave trails of blood-drops across hands and face; on it I felt like a dream walker who never moves, and my calling voice was swept away northwards on gusts of cold, wet wind. I got back to the house at nine in the morning, with a dead-weight boat more than half full of water and a sick emptiness in my mind and body. By now part of me was sure that Mij too had met the Killer, and that he was at this moment half digested in the whale's belly.

All that day until four o'clock in the afternoon I wandered and called, and with every hour grew the realization of how much that strange animal companion had come to signify to me. I resented it, resented my dependence upon this subhuman presence and companionship, resented the void that his absence was going to leave at Camusfeàrna. It was in this mood, one of reassertion of human independence, that about five in the evening I began to remove the remaining evidence of his past existence. I had taken from beneath the kitchen table his drinking bowl, had returned for the half-full bowl of rice and egg, had carried this to the scullery, what the Scots call the back kitchen, and was about to empty it into the slop pail, when I thought I heard Mij's voice from the kitchen behind me. I was, however, very tired, and distrustful of my own reactions; what I thought I had heard was the harshly whispered 'Hah?' with which he was accustomed to interrogate a seemingly empty room. The impression was strong enough for me to set down the bowl and hurry back into the kitchen. There was nothing there. I walked to the door and called his name, but all was as it had been before. I was on my way back to the scullery when I stopped dead. There on the kitchen floor, where I had been about to step, was a large, wet footprint. I looked at it, and I thought; I am very tired and very overwrought; and I went down on my hands and knees to inspect it. It was certainly wet, and it smelled of otter. I was still in a quadrupedal attitude when from the doorway behind me I heard the sound again, this time past mistaking – 'Hah?' Then Mij was all over me, drenched and wildly demonstrative, squeaking, bouncing round me like an excitable puppy, clambering on my shoulders, squirming on his back, leaping, dancing. I had been reassuring myself and him for some minutes before I realized that his harness was burst apart, and that for many hours, perhaps a day or more, he must have been caught like Absalom, struggling, desperate, waiting for a rescue that never came.

I am aware that this scene of reunion, and the hours that for me had preceded it, must appear to many a reader little short of nauseous. I might write of it and subsequent events with a wry dishonesty, a negation of my feeling for that creature, which might disarm criticism, might forestall the accusation of sentimentality and slushiness to which I now lay myself open. There is, however, a certain obligation of honesty upon a writer, without which his words are worthless, and beyond that my feeling for animals that I adopt would, despite any dissimulation that I might essay, reveal itself as intense, even crucial. I knew by that time that Mij meant more to me than most human beings of my aquaintance, that I should miss his physical presence more than theirs, and I was not ashamed of it. In the penultimate analysis, perhaps, I knew that Mij trusted me more utterly than did any of my own kind, and so supplied a need that we are slow to admit.

Gilded Cage
ALAN COREN

THE WATERY DAWN came up, to little interest. A cassowary honked, half-heartedly; Moskisson's potto squeaked, once; an elderly scorpion broke wind.

They had seen dawns before. There was no point kicking up an atavistic fuss. For one thing, you didn't have to scare breakfast into submission. It came on tin plates.

The lion yawned. Bound to be horse again. Nothing wrong with horse, mind, nice piece of shoulder, can't complain. Slides down a treat, horse.

The only thing was, you couldn't chase a chop. That was the whole trouble with convenience foods. You couldn't bring them down, play with them, scare the life out of them. Be nice, thought the lion wistfully, to hear your breakfast scream a bit, now and again.

He strolled to the bars, looked out.

'Hallo,' he said. 'Here's a do.'

His lioness turned over slowly on her hygienic concrete shelf. Her tail flopped down. She let it swing, idly. Cleaner up here than a tree, she thought, more modern, chamfered for easy maintenance, no moss, insects. And yet.

'What is it?' she said.

'They've duffed up another chimpanzee,' said her mate.

The lioness opened one eye. In the cage across the way, a chimpanzee lay on its back, hands, feet, teeth all clenched in an unmistakable rigor.

'Oh, that,' she murmured. She shut the eye again. 'New frail old chimp horror, anthropoid granny another victim of senseless violence, where will it end, see fabulous free knickers offer page nine.'

'You know who I blame?' said the lion. 'I blame the parents.'

The lioness snored.

At eight o'clock, two keepers came with a black polythene sack and removed the battered corpse.

The lion watched.

The tiger next door came to the front of its cage.

'Keepers won't even bother finding out who did it,' said the tiger. 'Right?'

'What's the point?' said the lion.

'What's the point?'

'Only let 'em off with a bloody caution,' said the lion.

'If that,' said the tiger.

'They'll blame it all on the environment,' said the lion gloomily. 'Am I right?'

'No question,' said the tiger.

'Impersonal high-rise steel cages, parents out picking one another's fleas off all day, lack of properly supervised play areas, catch my drift?'

'Absolutely,' said the tiger. 'Not to mention a cry for help.'

'I'd give 'em bleeding cry for help!' snapped the lion. 'When I was a cub, they'd have got the chop.'

He drew a burnished claw across his throat, as only lions can.

'Bloody good job, too,' said the tiger.

'No messing about,' said the lion, 'eye for an eye, know what I mean?'

'Those were the days,' said the tiger.

At 11.30 am, the lioness jumped down from her shelf.

A keeper let her four cubs in.

She played with them for half an hour.

Then the keeper came and took them out again.

She jumped back up on her shelf, and began to groom.

'I don't call that motherhood,' said the lion.

The lioness shrugged. She rolled on her back, and looked at the ceiling of the cage.

'I ought to get a job,' she said. 'There's more to life than bringing up cubs.'

'You what?' cried the lion. 'A *lioness*? Getting a *job*?'

'While we're at it,' said his mate, 'I think I'll drop the ess. It is discriminatory; it is degrading. Lion, is what I am.'

The lion's claws sprang from their soft sheaths, instinctively.

'What kind of job?' he growled.

'Oh, I dunno,' she said. 'I could roar. I could terrorise visitors. I could attack the keeper.'

'*I* DO THAT!' thundered the lion, with such force that, on the other side of the Zoo, a small herd of antelope woke up, trembled violently, and ran into the wall. 'Any roaring, any terrorising, is down to *me*!'

'I could be just as good,' said the lioness.

'Oh yes! Ha, ha! Oh yes!' muttered the lion. He paced up and down furiously. 'Ha, ha! Oh yes! Very droll. Ha, ha!'

He hurled himself at the bars, and bit them.

'She'll be growing a mane next,' said the tiger next door.

'I blame the Zoo,' said the lion. 'The Zoo does everything for 'em, these days. Food, housing, education, all laid on, know what I mean, whatever happened to self-sufficiency, independence, responsibility?'

'You've been talking to Rhodes Bison,' said the tiger.

'Why not?' said the lion.

'Look at them dingoes,' said the lion, an hour or two later. 'They're at it like knives!'

'When I was young,' said the tiger, 'there was such a thing as courtship.'

'The magic's gone,' muttered the lion. 'I blame the Zoo. No restrictions any more. They used to move in and stop all that. They used to keep 'em apart, except for breeding seasons.'

'Permissiveness,' grunted the tiger.

'Comes back to what I was saying ' said the lion firmly. 'Too much time on their hands, too much done for 'em. In the old days, before the Zoo stepped in and took over everything, they never had no time for all that. Out foraging for food, fighting off enemies, building your own home, competing to survive – it bred a different class, built character, follow me?'

'You're talking about the jungle, now,' said the tiger, wistfully.

'Right!' cried the lion. 'Definitely!'

The dingoes shrieked to an umpteenth climax.

'They're like bloody animals,' muttered the lion.

The sparrow zipped through the bars, and landed on the edge of the lion's trough.

'I've just been up the Bird House,' it chirped. 'You wouldn't bloody credit it!'

'What?' said the lion.

'They just took delivery of two gross chrome bells, anodised ladders, mirrors, prefabricated nesting-boxes, you name it.'

'Oh, very nice!' said the lion sarcastically. 'I wonder how much that little lot set the Zoo back?'

'Birds,' twittered the sparrow, 'used to make their own entertainment. There's no end of things you can do with a good pebble, couple of bottle tops, fag-packets, all that. Now they just sit around waiting for the Zoo to provide everything, have you noticed?'

'Have *I* noticed?' cried the lion.

'Has *he* noticed?' said the tiger.

'They'll have Zoo-subsidised tellies next,' said the lion.

'He's not joking,' said the tiger.

The white Range Rover of the Zoo Vet Service rolled past. They watched it turn the bend.

'Elephant,' explained the sparrow. 'Got a bit of colic. I was just round there.'

'*Bit of colic?*' exclaimed the lion. 'Bloody stroll on! What would he do up India?'

'Wouldn't bother about it,' said the tiger, 'would he? More important things to think about. Knocking down trees, leading herds, working out how to get to the graveyard.'

'Stepping on tigers,' said the sparrow.

'Why not?' retorted the tiger. 'Part of life's rich texture. *And* if he did, would I go running to the doctor's? Would I buggery, I'd have a bit of a lick, pull myself together, get on with things, right?'

'You'd probably nip down the village and knock a couple of tribesmen back.' said the lion dreamily. He ran his purple tongue over his muzzle. 'Set you up a treat, that.'

'Better than free bloody medical treatment, anyway,' said the tiger.

'You know what bothers me more than anything?' said the lion, after a moment or two.

'What's that?' enquired the sparrow.

'It's like this,' said the lion. 'All our offspring are growing up in this mollycoddling bloody environment, right? Everything done for 'em, nothing demanded of 'em, all they got to do if they want anything is ask the Zoo, they get a handout, okay?'

'Get on with it,' muttered the tiger.

'What I'm saying is,' said the lion, 'what I'm saying *is*, what happens if the Zoo runs out of money? Overspends on services or whatever, and the whole operation starts falling to bits, health service breaks down, cages crumble, keepers pack it in, food gets short, amenities fold up. So there's all the bars fallen off, and there's all these animals wandering about with no-one to look after 'em or tell 'em what to do next, and because they've all grown up in the Zoo, would they have any idea of how to fend for themselves?'

'He's a bit of a thinker, this one,' said the sparrow.

'It'd all come back to them, wouldn't it?' said the tiger. 'I mean, it's in the blood. It's *natural*, right?'

The lion shrugged. He looked at his paw, wondering what it would be like to feel grass under it.

'It's only a thought,' he said.

The Race
LEO TOLSTOY

*At a critical point in his affair with Anna Karenina, Count
Vronsky's only distraction from the passion that is absorbing
and torturing them both is the preparation for the Krasnoe
Selo steeplechase . . .*

ON THE DAY OF THE races at Krasnoe Selo, Vronsky had come earlier
than usual to eat beefsteak in the common mess-room of the regiment.
He had no need to be strict with himself, as he had very quickly been
brought down to the required light weight; but still he had to avoid
gaining flesh, and so he eschewed farinaceous and sweet dishes. He sat
with his coat unbuttoned over a white waistcoat, resting both elbows on
the table, and while waiting for the steak he had ordered he looked at
a French novel that lay open on his plate. He was only looking at the
book to avoid conversation with the officers coming in and out; he was
thinking.

He was thinking of Anna's promise to see him that day after the races.
But he had not seen her for three days, and as her husband had just
returned from abroad, he did not know whether she would be able to
meet him today or not, and he did not know how to find out. He had had
his last interview with her at his cousin Betsy's summer villa. He visited
the Karenins' summer villa as rarely as possible. Now he wanted to go
there, and he pondered the question how to do it.

'Of course I shall say Betsy has sent me to ask whether she's coming
to the races. Of course, I'll go,' he decided, lifting his head from the book.
And as he vividly pictured the happiness of seeing her, his face lighted
up.

'Send to my house, and tell them to have out the carriage and three horses as quick as they can,' he said to the servant, who handed him the steak on a hot silver dish, and moving the dish up he began eating.

From the billiard-room next door came the sound of balls knocking, of talk and laughter. Two officers appeared at the entrance-door: one, a young fellow, with a feeble, delicate face, who had lately joined the regiment from the Corps of Pages; the other, a plump, elderly officer, with a bracelet on his wrist, and little eyes, lost in fat.

Vronsky glanced at them, frowned, and looking down at his book as though he had not noticed them, he proceeded to eat and read at the same time.

'What? Fortifying yourself for your work?' said the plump officer, sitting down beside him.

'As you see,' responded Vronsky, knitting his brows, wiping his mouth, and not looking at the officer.

'So you're not afraid of getting fat?' said the latter, turning a chair round for the young officer.

'What?' said Vronsky angrily, making a wry face of disgust, and showing his even teeth.

'You're not afraid of getting fat?'

'Waiter, sherry!' said Vronsky, without replying, and moving the book to the other side of him, he went on reading.

The plump officer took up the list of wines and turned to the young officer.

'You choose what we're to drink,' he said, handing him the card, and looking at him.

'Rhine wine, please,' said the young officer, stealing a timid glance at Vronsky, and trying to pull his scarcely visible moustache. Seeing that Vronsky did not turn round, the young officer got up.

'Let's go into the billiard-room,' he said.

The plump officer rose submissively, and they moved towards the door.

At that moment there walked into the room the tall and well-built Captain Yashvin. Nodding with an air of lofty contempt to the two officers, he went up to Vronsky.

'Ah! here he is!' he cried, bringing his big hand down heavily on his epaulet. Vronsky looked round angrily, but his face lighted up immediately with his characteristic expression of genial and manly serenity.

'That's it, Alexey,' said the captain, in his loud baritone. 'You must just eat a mouthful, now, and drink only one tiny glass.'

'Oh, I'm not hungry.'

'There go the inseparables,' Yashvin dropped, glancing sarcastically at the two officers who were at that instant leaving the room. And he bent his long legs, swathed in tight riding-breeches, and sat down in the chair, too low for him, so that his knees were cramped up in a sharp angle.

'Why didn't you turn up at the Red Theatre yesterday? Numerova wasn't at all bad. Where were you?'

'I was late at the Tverskoys',' said Vronsky.

'Ah!' responded Yashvin.

Yashvin, a gambler and a rake, a man not merely without moral principles, but of immoral principles, Yashvin was Vronsky's greatest friend in the regiment. Vronsky liked him both for his exceptional physical strength, which he showed for the most part by being able to drink like a fish, and do without sleep without being in the slightest degree affected by it; and for his great strength of character, which he showed in his relations with his comrades and superior officers, commanding both fear and respect, and also at cards, when he would play for tens of thousands, and however much he might have drunk, always with such skill and decision, that he was reckoned the best player in the English Club. Vronsky respected and liked Yashvin particularly because he felt Yashvin liked him, not for his name and his money, but for himself. And of all men he was the only one with whom Vronsky would have liked to speak of his love. He felt that Yashvin, in spite of his apparent contempt for every sort of feeling, was the only man who could, so he fancied, comprehend the intense passion which now filled his whole life. Moreover, he felt certain that Yashvin, as it was, took no delight in gossip and scandal, and interpreted his feeling rightly, that is to say, knew and believed that this passion was not a jest, not a pastime, but something more serious and important.

Vronsky had never spoken to him of his passion, but he was aware that he knew all about it, and that he put the right interpretation on it, and he was glad to see that in his eyes.

'Ah! yes,' he said, to the announcement that Vronsky had been at the Tverskoys'; and his black eyes shining, he plucked at his left moustache, and began twisting it into his mouth, a bad habit he had.

'Well, and what did you do yesterday? Win anything?' asked Vronsky.

'Eight thousand. But three don't count; he won't pay up.'

'Oh, then you can afford to lose over me,' said Vronsky, laughing. (Yashvin had betted heavily on Vronsky in the races.)

'No chance of my losing. Mahotin's the only one that's risky.'

And the conversation passed to forecasts of the coming race, the only thing Vronsky could think of just now.

'Come along, I've finished,' said Vronsky, and getting up he went to the door. Yashvin got up too, stretching his long legs and his long back.

'It's too early for me to dine, but I must have a drink. I'll come along directly. Hi, wine!' he shouted, in his rich voice, that always rang out so loudly at drill, and set the windows shaking now.

'No, all right,' he shouted again immediately after. 'You're going home, so I'll go with you.'

And he walked out with Vronsky.

Vronsky was staying in a roomy, clean, Finnish hut, divided into two by a partition. Petritsky lived with him in camp too. Petritsky was asleep when Vronsky and Yashvin came into the hut.

'Get up, don't go on sleeping,' said Yashvin, going behind the partition and giving Petritsky, who was lying with ruffled hair and with his nose in the pillow, a prod on the shoulder.

Petritsky jumped up suddenly on to his knees and looked round.

'Your brother's been here,' he said to Vronsky. 'He waked me up, damn him, and said he'd look in again.' And pulling up the rug he flung himself back on the pillow. 'Oh, do shut up, Yashvin!' he said, getting furious with Yashvin, who was pulling the rug off him. 'Shut up!' He turned over and opened his eyes. 'You'd better tell me what to drink; such a nasty taste in my mouth, that . . .'

'Brandy's better than anything,' boomed Yashvin. 'Tereshtchenko! brandy for your master and cucumbers,' he shouted, obviously taking pleasure in the sound of his own voice.

'Brandy do you think? Eh?' queried Petritsky, blinking and rubbing his eyes. 'And you'll drink something? All right then, we'll have a drink together! Vronsky, have a drink?' said Petritsky, getting up and wrapping the tiger-skin rug round him. He went to the door of the partition wall, raised his hands, and hummed in French, 'There was a king in Thule.' 'Vronsky, will you have a drink?'

'Go along,' said Vronsky, putting on the coat his valet handed him.

'Where are you off to?' asked Yashvin. 'Oh, here are your three horses,' he added, seeing the carriage drive up.

'To the stables, and I've got to see Bryansky, too, about the horses,' said Vronsky.

Vronsky had as a fact, promised to call at Bryansky's, some eight miles from Peterhof, and to bring him some money owing for some horses; and he hoped to have time to get that in too. But his comrades were at once aware that he was not only going there.

Petritsky, still humming, winked and made a pout with his lips, as though he would say: 'Oh yes, we know your Bryansky.'

'Mind you're not late!' was Yashvin's only comment; and to change the conversation: 'How's my roan? is he doing all right?' he inquired, looking out of window at the middle one of the three horses, which he had sold Vronsky.

'Stop!' cried Petritsky to Vronsky as he was just going out. 'Your brother left a letter and a note for you. Wait a bit; where are they?'

Vronsky stopped.

'Well, where are they?'

'Where are they? That's just the question!' said Petritsky solemnly, moving his forefinger upwards from his nose.

'Come, tell me; this is silly!' said Vronsky smiling.

'I have not lighted the fire. Here somewhere about.'

'Come, enough fooling! Where is the letter?'

'No, I've forgotten really. Or was it a dream? Wait a bit, wait a bit! But what's the use of getting in a rage. If you'd drunk four bottles yesterday as I did you'd forget where you were lying. Wait a bit, I'll remember!'

Petritsky went behind the partition and lay down on his bed.

'Wait a bit! This was how I was lying, and this was how he was standing. Yes – yes – yes . . . Here it is!' – Petritsky pulled a letter out from under the mattress, where he had hidden it.

Vronsky took the letter and his brother's note. It was the letter he was expecting – from his mother, reproaching him for not having been to see her – and the note was from his brother to say that he must have a little talk with him. Vronsky knew that it was all about the same thing. 'What business is it of theirs!' thought Vronsky, and crumpling up the letters he thrust them between the buttons of his coat so as to read them carefully on the road. In the porch of the hut he was met by two officers; one of his regiment and one of another.

Vronsky's quarters were always a meeting-place for all the officers.

'Where are you off to?'

'I must go to Peterhof.'

'Has the mare come from Tsarskoe?'

'Yes, but I've not seen her yet.'

'They say Mahotin's Gladiator's lame.'

'Nonsense! But however are you going to race in this mud?' said the other.

'Here are my saviours!' cried Petritsky, seeing them come in. Before him stood the orderly with a tray of brandy and salted cucumbers. 'Here's Yashvin ordering me to drink a pick-me-up.'

'Well, you did give it to us yesterday,' said one of those who had come in; 'you didn't let us get a wink of sleep all night.'

'Oh, didn't we make a pretty finish!' said Petritsky. 'Volkov climbed on to the roof and began telling us how sad he was. I said: "Let's have music, the funeral march!" He fairly dropped asleep on the roof over the funeral march.'

'Drink it up; you positively must drink the brandy, and then seltzer water and a lot of lemon,' said Yashvin, standing over Petritsky like a mother making a child take medicine, 'and then a little champagne – just a small bottle.'

'Come, there's some sense in that. Stop a bit, Vronsky, we'll all have a drink.'

'No; good-bye all of you. I'm not going to drink today.'

'Why, are you gaining weight? All right, then we must have it alone. Give us the seltzer water and lemon.'

'Vronsky!' shouted someone when he was already outside.

'Well?'

'You'd better get your hair cut, it'll weigh you down, especially at the top.'

Vronsky was in fact beginning, prematurely, to get a little bald. He laughed gaily, showing his even teeth, and pulling his cap over the thin place, went out and got into his carriage.

'To the stables!' he said, and was just pulling out the letters to read them through, but he thought better of it, and put off reading them so as not to distract his attention before looking at the mare. 'Later!'

The temporary stable, a wooden shed, had been put up close to the racecourse, and there his mare was to have been taken the previous day. He had not yet seen her there.

During the last few days he had not ridden her out for exercise himself, but had put her in the charge of the trainer, and so now he positively did not know in what condition his mare had arrived yesterday and was today. He had scarcely got out of his carriage when his groom, the so-called 'stable-boy', recognising the carriage some way off, called the trainer. A dry-looking Englishman, in high boots and a short jacket, clean shaven, except for a tuft below his chin, came to meet him, walking with the uncouth gait of a jockey, turning his elbows out and swaying from side to side.

'Well, how's Frou-Frou?' Vronsky asked in English.

'All right, sir,' the Englishman's voice responded somewhere in the inside of his throat. 'Better not go in,' he added, touching his hat. 'I've put a muzzle on her, and the mare's fidgety. Better not go in, it'll excite the mare.'

'No, I'm going in. I want to look at her.'

'Come along, then,' said the Englishman, frowning, and speaking with his mouth shut, and, with swinging elbows, he went on in front with his disjointed gait.

They went into the little yard in front of the shed. A stable-boy, spruce and smart in his holiday attire, met them with a broom in his hand, and followed them. In the shed there were five horses in their separate stalls, and Vronsky knew that his chief rival, Gladiator, a very tall chestnut horse, had been brought there, and must be standing among them. Even more than his mare, Vronsky longed to see Gladiator, whom he had never seen. But he knew that by the etiquette of the racecourse it was not merely impossible for him to see the horse, but improper even to ask questions about him. Just as he was passing along the passage, the boy opened the door into the second horse-box on the left, and Vronsky caught a glimpse of a big chestnut horse with white legs. He knew that this was Gladiator, but, with the feeling of a man turning away from the sight of another man's open letter, he turned round and went into Frou-Frou's stall.

'The horse is here belonging to Mak . . . Mak . . . I never can say the name,' said the Englishman, over his shoulder, pointing his big finger and dirty nail towards Gladiator's stall.

'Mahotin? Yes, he's my most serious rival,' said Vronsky.

'If you were riding him,' said the Englishman, 'I'd bet on you.'

'Frou-Frou's more nervous; he's stronger,' said Vronsky, smiling at the compliment to his riding.

'In a steeplechase it all depends on riding and on pluck,' said the Englishman.

Of pluck – that is, energy and courage – Vronsky did not merely feel that he had enough; what was of far more importance, he was firmly convinced that no one in the world could have more of this 'pluck' than he had.

'Don't you think I want more thinning down?'

'Oh no,' answered the Englishman. 'Please, don't speak loud. The mare's fidgety,' he added, nodding towards the horse-box, before which they were standing, and from which came the sound of restless stamping in the straw.

He opened the door, and Vronsky went into the horse-box, dimly lighted by one little window. In the horse-box stood a dark bay mare, with a muzzle on, picking at the fresh straw with her hoofs. Looking round him in the twilight of the horse-box, Vronsky unconsciously took in once more in a comprehensive glance all the points of his favourite mare. Frou-Frou was a beast of medium size, not altogether free from reproach, from a breeder's point of view. She was small-boned all over; though her chest was extremely prominent in front, it was narrow. Her hind-quarters were a little drooping, and in her fore-legs, and still more in her hind-legs, there was a noticeable curvature. The muscles of both hind and fore legs were not very thick; but across her shoulders the mare was exceptionally broad, a peculiarity specially striking now that she was lean from training. The bones of her leg below the knees looked no thicker than a finger from in front, but were extraordinarily thick seen from the side. She looked altogether, except across the shoulders, as it were pinched in at the sides and pressed out in depth. But she had in the highest degree the quality that makes all defects forgotten: that quality was *blood*, the blood *that tells*, as the English expression has it. The muscles stood up sharply under the network of sinews, covered with the delicate, mobile skin, as soft as satin, and they were hard as bone. Her clean-cut head, with prominent, bright, spirited eyes, broadened out at the open nostrils, that showed the red blood in the cartilage within. About all her figure, and especially her head, there was a certain expression of energy, and, at the same time, of softness. She was one of those creatures, which seem only not to speak because the mechanism of their mouth does not allow them to.

To Vronsky, at any rate, it seemed that she understood all he felt at that moment, looking at her.

Directly Vronsky went towards her, she drew in a deep breath, and, turning back her prominent eye till the white looked bloodshot, she stared at the approaching figures from the opposite side, shaking her muzzle, and shifting lightly from one leg to the other.

'There, you see how fidgety she is,' said the Englishman.

'There, darling! There!' said Vronsky, going up to the mare and speaking soothingly to her.

But the nearer he came, the more excited she grew. Only when he stood by her head, she was suddenly quieter, while the muscles quivered under her soft, delicate coat. Vronsky patted her strong neck, straightened over her sharp withers a stray lock of her mane that had fallen on the other side, and moved his face near her dilated nostrils, transparent as a bat's wing. She drew a loud breath and snorted out through her tense nostrils, started, pricked up her sharp ear, and put out her strong, black lip towards Vronsky, as though she would nip hold of his sleeve. But remembering the muzzle, she shook it and again began restlessly stamping one after the other her shapely legs.

'Quiet, darling, quiet!' he said, patting her again over her hindquarters; and with a glad sense that his mare was in the best possible condition, he went out of the horse-box.

The mare's excitement had infected Vronsky. He felt that his heart was throbbing, and that he too, like the mare, longed to move, to bite; it was both dreadful and delicious.

'Well, I rely on you, then,' he said to the Englishman; 'half-past six on the ground.'

'All right,' said the Englishman. 'Oh, where are you going, my lord?' he asked suddenly, using the title 'my lord', which he had scarcely ever used before.

Vronsky in amazement raised his head, and stared, as he knew how to stare, not into the Englishman's eyes, but at his forehead, astounded at the impertinence of his question. But realising that in asking this the Englishman had been looking at him not as an employer, but as a jockey, he answered—

'I've got to go to Bryansky's; I shall be home within an hour.'

'How often I'm asked that question today!' he said to himself, and he blushed, a thing which rarely happened to him. The Englishman looked gravely at him; and, as though he, too, knew where Vronsky was going, he added—

'The great thing's to keep quiet before a race,' said he; 'don't get out of temper or upset about anything.'

'All right,' answered Vronsky, smiling; and jumping into his carriage, he told the man to drive to Peterhof.

Before he had driven many paces away, the dark clouds that had been threatening rain all day broke, and there was a heavy downpour of rain.

'What a pity!' thought Vronsky, putting up the roof of the carriage.

'It was muddy before, now it will be a perfect swamp.' As he sat in solitude in the closed carriage, he took out his mother's letter and his brother's note, and read them through.

Yes, it was the same thing over and over again. Everyone, his mother, his brother, everyone thought fit to interfere in the affairs of his heart. This interference aroused in him a feeling of angry hatred – a feeling he had rarely known before. 'What business is it of theirs? Why does everybody feel called upon to concern himself about me? And why do they worry me so? Just because they see that this is something they can't understand. If it were a common, vulgar, wordly intrigue, they would have left me alone. They feel that this is something different, that this is not a mere pastime, that this woman is dearer to me than life. And this is incomprehensible, and that's why it annoys them. Whatever our destiny is or may be, we have made it ourselves, and we do not complain of it,' he said, in the word *we* linking himself with Anna. 'No, they must needs teach us how to live. They haven't an idea of what happiness is; they don't know that without our love, for us there is neither happiness nor unhappiness – no life at all,' he thought.

He was angry with all of them for their interference just because he felt in his soul that they, all these people, were right. He felt that the love that bound him to Anna was not a momentary impulse, which would pass, as wordly intrigues do pass, leaving no other traces in the life of either but pleasant or unpleasant memories. He felt all the torture of his own and her position, all the difficulty there was for them, conspicuous as they were in the eye of all the world, in concealing their love, in lying and deceiving; and in lying, deceiving, feigning, and continually thinking of others, when the passion that united them was so intense that they were both oblivious of everything else but their love.

He vividly recalled all the constantly recurring instances of inevitable necessity for lying and deceit, which were so against his natural bent. He recalled particularly vividly the shame he had more than once detected in her at this necessity for lying and deceit. And he experienced the strange feeling that had sometimes come upon him since his secret love for Anna. This was a feeling of loathing for something – whether for Alexey Alexandrovitch, or for himself, or for the whole world, he could not have said. But he always drove away this strange feeling. Now, too, he shook it off and continued the thread of his thoughts.

'Yes, she was unhappy before, but proud and at peace; and now she cannot be at peace and feel secure in her dignity, though she does not show it. Yes, we must put an end to it,' he decided.

And for the first time the idea clearly presented itself that it was essential to put an end to this false position, and the sooner the better. 'Throw up everything, she and I, and hide ourselves somewhere alone with our love,' he said to himself.

The rain did not last long, and by the time Vronsky arrived, his shaft-horse trotting at full speed, and dragging the trace-horses galloping through the mud, with their reins hanging loose, the sun had peeped out again, the roofs of the summer villas and the old lime-trees in the gardens on both sides of the principal streets sparkled with wet brilliance, and from the twigs came a pleasant drip and from the roofs rushing streams of water. He thought no more of the shower spoiling the racecourse, but was rejoicing now that – thanks to the rain – he would be sure to find her at home and alone, as he knew that Alexey Alexandrovitch, who had lately returned from a foreign watering-place, had not moved from Petersburg.

Hoping to find her alone, Vronsky alighted, as he always did, to avoid attracting attention, before crossing the bridge, and walked to the house. He did not go up the steps to the street door, but went into the court.

'Has your master come?' he asked a gardener.

'No, sir. The mistress is at home. But will you please go to the front door; there are servants there,' the gardener answered. 'They'll open the door.'

'No, I'll go in from the garden.'

And feeling satisfied that she was alone, and wanting to take her by surprise, since he had not promised to be there today, and she would certainly not expect him to come before the races, he walked, holding his sword and stepping cautiously over the sandy path, bordered with flowers, to the terrace that looked out upon the garden. Vronsky forgot now all that he had thought on the way of the hardships and difficulties of their position. He thought of nothing but that he would see her directly, not in imagination, but living, all of her, as she was in reality. He was just going in, stepping on his whole foot so as not to creak, up the worn steps of the terrace, when he suddenly remembered what he always forgot, and what caused the most torturing side of his relations with her, her son with his questioning – hostile, as he fancied – eyes.

This boy was more often than anyone else a check upon their freedom. When he was present, both Vronsky and Anna did not merely avoid speaking of anything that they could not have repeated before everyone; they did not even allow themselves to refer by hints to anything the boy did not understand. They had made no agreement about this, it had settled itself. They would have felt it wounding themselves to deceive the child. In his presence they talked like acquaintances. But in spite of this caution, Vronsky often saw the child's intent, bewildered glance fixed upon him, and a strange shyness, uncertainty, at one time friendliness, at another, coldness and reserve, in the boy's manner to him; as though the child felt that between this man and his mother there existed some important bond, the significance of which he could not understand.

As a fact the boy did feel that he could not understand this relation, and he tried painfully, and was not able to make clear to himself what feeling he ought to have for this man. With a child's keen instinct for every manifestation of feeling, he saw distinctly that his father, his governess, his nurse, – all did not merely dislike Vronsky, but looked on him with horror and aversion, though they never said anything about him, while his mother looked on him as her greatest friend.

'What does it mean? Who is he? How ought I to love him? If I don't know, it's my fault; either I'm stupid or a naughty boy,' thought the child. And this was what caused his dubious, inquiring, sometimes hostile, expression, and the shyness and uncertainty which Vronsky found so irksome. This child's presence always and infallibly called up in Vronsky that strange feeling of inexplicable loathing which he had experienced of late. This child's presence called up both in Vronsky and in Anna a feeling akin to the feeling of a sailor who sees by the compass that the direction in which he is swiftly moving is far from the right one, but that to arrest his motion is not in his power, that every instant is carrying him further and further away, and that to admit to himself his deviation from the right direction is the same as admitting his certain ruin.

This child, with his innocent outlook upon life, was the compass that showed them the point to which they had departed from what they knew, but did not want to know.

This time Seryozha was not at home, and she was completely alone. She was sitting on the terrace waiting for the return of her son, who had gone out for his walk and been caught in the rain. She had sent a manservant and a maid out to look for him. Dressed in a white gown, deeply embroidered, she was sitting in a corner of the terrace behind some flowers, and did not hear him. Bending her curly black head, she pressed her forehead against a cool watering-pot that stood on the parapet, and both her lovely hands, with the rings he knew so well, clasped the pot. The beauty of her whole figure, her head, her neck, her hands, struck Vronsky every time as something new and unexpected. He stood still, gazing at her in ecstasy. But, directly he would have made a step to come nearer to her, she was aware of his presence, pushed away the watering-pot, and turned her flushed face towards him.

'What's the matter? You are ill?' he said to her in French, going up to her. He would have run to her, but remembering that there might be spectators, he looked round towards the balcony door, and reddened a little, as he always reddened, feeling that he had to be afraid and be on his guard.

'No; I'm quite well,' she said, getting up and pressing his outstretched hand tightly. 'I did not expect . . . thee.'

'Mercy! what cold hands!' he said.

'You startled me,' she said. 'I'm alone, and expecting Seryozha; he's out for a walk; they'll come in from this side.'

But, in spite of her efforts to be calm, her lips were quivering.

'Forgive me for coming, but I couldn't pass the day without seeing you,' he went on, speaking French, as he always did to avoid using the stiff Russian plural form, so impossibly frigid between them, and the dangerously intimate singular.

'Forgive you? I'm so glad!'

'But you're ill or worried,' he went on, not letting go her hands and bending over her. 'What were you thinking of?'

'Always of the same thing,' she said, with a smile.

She spoke the truth. If ever at any moment she had been asked what she was thinking of, she could have answered truly: of the same thing, of her happiness and her unhappiness. She was thinking, just when he came upon her, of this: why was it, she wondered, that to others, to Betsy (she knew of her secret connection with Tushkevitch) it was all easy, while to her it was such torture? Today this thought gained special poignancy from certain other considerations. She asked him about the races. He answered her questions, and, seeing that she was agitated, trying to calm her, he began telling her in the simplest tone the details of his preparations for the races.

'Tell him or not tell him?' she thought, looking into his quiet, affectionate eyes. 'He is so happy, so absorbed in his races that he won't understand as he ought, he won't understand all the gravity of this fact to us.'

'But you haven't told me what you were thinking of when I came in,' he said, interrupting his narrative; 'please, tell me!'

She did not answer, and, bending her head a little, she looked inquiringly at him from under her brows, her eyes shining under their long lashes. Her hand shook as it played with a leaf she had picked. He saw it, and his face expressed that utter subjection, that slavish devotion, which had done so much to win her.

'I see something has happened. Do you suppose I can be at peace, knowing you have a trouble I am not sharing? Tell me, for God's sake,' he repeated imploringly.

'Yes; I shan't be able to forgive him if he does not realise all the gravity of it. Better not tell; why put him to the proof?' she thought, still staring at him in the same way, and feeling the hand that held the leaf was trembling more and more.

'For God's sake!' he repeated, taking her hand.

'Shall I tell you?'

'Yes, yes, yes . . .'

'I'm with child,' she said, softly and deliberately. The leaf in her hand shook more violently, but she did not take her eyes off him, watching how he would take it. He turned white, would have said something, but stopped; he dropped her hand, and his head sank on his breast. 'Yes, he realises all the gravity of it,' she thought, and gratefully she pressed his hand.

But she was mistaken in thinking he realised the gravity of the fact as she, a woman, realised it. On hearing it, he felt come upon him with tenfold intensity that strange feeling of loathing of someone. But at the same time, he felt that the turning-point he had been longing for had come now; that it was impossible to go on concealing things from her husband, and it was inevitable in one way or another that they should soon put an end to their unnatural position. But, besides that, her emotion physically affected him in the same way. He looked at her with a look of submissive tenderness, kissed her hand, got up, and, in silence, paced up and down the terrace.

'Yes,' he said, going up to her resolutely. 'Neither you nor I have looked on our relations as a passing amusement, and now our fate is sealed. It is absolutely necessary to put an end' – he looked round as he spoke – 'to the deception in which we are living.'

'Put an end? How put an end, Alexey?' she said softly.

She was calmer now, and her face lighted up with a tender smile.

'Leave your husband and make our life one.'

'It is one as it is,' she answered, scarcely audibly.

'Yes, but altogether; altogether.'

'But how, Alexey, tell me how?' she said in melancholy mockery at the hopelessness of her own position. 'Is there any way out of such a position? Am I not the wife of my husband?'

'There is a way out of every position. We must take our line,' he said. 'Anything's better than the position in which you're living. Of course, I see how you torture yourself over everything – the world and your son and your husband.'

'Oh, not over my husband,' she said, with a quiet smile. 'I don't know him, I don't think of him. He doesn't exist.'

'You're not speaking sincerely. I know you. You worry about him too.'

'Oh, he doesn't even know,' she said, and suddenly a hot flush came over her face; her cheeks, her brow, her neck crimsoned, and tears of shame came into her eyes. 'But we won't talk of him.'

Vronsky had several times already, though not so resolutely as now, tried to bring her to consider their position, and every time he had been confronted by the same superficiality and triviality with which she met his appeal now. It was as though there were something in this which she could not or would not face, as though directly she began to speak of this, she, the real Anna, retreated somehow into herself, and another strange and unaccountable woman came out, whom he did not love, and whom he feared, and who was in opposition to him. But today he was resolved to have it out.

'Whether he knows or not,' said Vronsky, in his usual quiet and resolute tone, 'that's nothing to do with us. We cannot . . . you cannot stay like this, especially now.'

'What's to be done, according to you?' she asked with the same frivolous irony. She who had so feared he would take her condition too lightly was now vexed with him for deducing from it the necessity of taking some step.

'Tell him everything, and leave him.'

'Very well, let us suppose I do that,' she said. 'Do you know what the result of that would be? I can tell you it all beforehand,' and a wicked light gleamed in her eyes, that had been so soft a minute before. '"Eh, you love another man, and have entered into criminal intrigues with him?"' (Mimicking her husband, she threw an emphasis on the word 'criminal', as Alexey Alexandrovitch did.) '"I warned you of the results in the religious, the civil, and the domestic relation. You have not listened to me. Now I cannot let you disgrace my name,—"' and my son, she had meant to say, but about her son she could not jest, – '"disgrace my name, and"' – and more in the same style,' she added. 'In general terms, he'll say in his official manner, and with all distinctness and precision, that he cannot let me go, but will take all measures in his power to prevent scandal. And he will calmly and punctually act in accordance with his words. That's what will happen. He's not a man, but a machine, and a spiteful machine when he's angry,' she added, recalling Alexey Alexandrovitch as she spoke, with all the peculiarities of his figure and manner of speaking, and reckoning against him every defect she could find in him, softening nothing for the great wrong she herself was doing him.

'But, Anna,' said Vronsky, in a soft and persuasive voice, trying to soothe her, 'we absolutely must, anyway, tell him, and then be guided by the line he takes.'

'What, run away?'

'And why not run away? I don't see how we can keep on like this. And not for my sake – I see that you suffer.'

'Yes, run away, and become your mistress,' she said angrily.

'Anna,' he said, with reproachful tenderness.

'Yes,' she went on, 'become your mistress, and complete the ruin of . . .'

Again she would have said 'my son', but she could not utter that word.

Vronsky could not understand how she, with her strong and truthful nature, could endure this state of deceit, and not long to get out of it. But he did not suspect that the chief cause of it was the word – *son*, which she could not bring herself to pronounce. When she thought of her son, and his future attitude to his mother, who had abandoned his father, she felt such terror at what she had done, that she could not face it; but, like a woman, could only try to comfort herself with lying assurances that everything would remain as it always had been, and that it was possible to forget the fearful question of how it would be with her son.

'I beg you, I entreat you,' she said suddenly, taking his hand, and speaking in quite a different tone, sincere and tender, 'never speak to me of that!'

'But, Anna . . .'

'Never. Leave it to me. I know all the baseness, all the horror of my position; but it's not so easy to arrange as you think. And leave it to me, and do what I say. Never speak to me of it. Do you promise me? . . . No, no, promise! . . .'

'I promise everything, but I can't be at peace, especially after what you have told me. I can't be at peace, when you can't be at peace . . .'

'I?' she repeated. 'Yes, I am worried sometimes; but that will pass, if you will never talk about this. When you talk about it – it's only then it worries me.'

'I don't understand,' he said.

'I know,' she interrupted him, 'how hard it is for your truthful nature to lie, and I grieve for you. I often think that you have ruined your whole life for me.'

'I was just thinking the very same thing,' he said; 'how could you sacrifice everything for my sake? I can't forgive myself that you're unhappy.'

'I unhappy?' she said, coming closer to him, and looking at him with an ecstatic smile of love. 'I am like a hungry man who has been given food. He may be cold, and dressed in rags, and ashamed, but he is not unhappy. I unhappy? No, this is my happiness . . .'

She could hear the sound of her son's voice coming towards them, and, glancing swiftly round the terrace, she got up impulsively. Her eyes glowed with the fire he knew so well; with a rapid movement she raised her lovely hands, covered with rings, took his head, looked a long look into his face, and, putting up her face with smiling, parted lips, swiftly kissed his mouth and both eyes, and pushed him away. She would have gone, but he held her back.

'When?' he murmured in a whisper, gazing in ecstasy at her.

'Today, at one o'clock,' she whispered, and, with a heavy sigh, she walked with her light, swift step to meet her son.

Seryozha had been caught by the rain in the big garden, and he and his nurse had taken shelter in an arbour.

'Well, *au revoir*,' she said to Vronsky. 'I must soon be getting ready for the races. Betsy promised to fetch me.'

Vronsky, looking at his watch, went away hurriedly.

When Vronsky looked at his watch on the Karenins' balcony, he was so greatly agitated and lost in his thoughts that he saw the figures on the watch's face, but could not take in what time it was. He came out on to the high road and walked, picking his way carefully through the mud, to his carriage. He was so completely absorbed in his feeling for Anna, that he did not even think what o'clock it was, and whether he had time to go to Bryansky's. He had left him, as often happens, only the external faculty of memory, that points out each step one has to take, one after the other. He went up to his coachman, who was dozing on the box in the shadow, already lengthening, of a thick lime-tree; he admired the shifting clouds of midges circling over the hot horses, and, waking the coachman, he jumped into the carriage, and told him to drive to Bryansky's. It was only after driving nearly five miles that he had sufficiently recovered himself to look at his watch, and realise that it was half-past five, and he was late.

There were several races fixed for that day: the Mounted Guards' race, then the officers' mile-and-a-half race, then the three-mile race, and then the race for which he was entered. He could still be in time for his race, but if he went to Bryansky's he could only just be in time, and he would arrive when the whole of the court would be in their places. That would be a pity. But he had promised Bryansky to come, and so he decided to drive on, telling the coachman not to spare the horses.

He reached Bryansky's, spent five minutes there, and galloped back. The rapid drive calmed him. All that was painful in his relations with Anna, all the feeling of indefiniteness left by their conversation, had slipped out of his mind. He was thinking now with pleasure and excitement of the race, of his being, anyhow, in time, and now and then the thought of the blissful interview awaiting him that night flashed across his imagination like a flaming light.

The excitement of the approaching race gained upon him as he drove further and further into the atmosphere of the races, overtaking carriages driving up from the summer villas or out of Petersburg.

At his quarters no one was left at home; all were at the races, and his valet was looking out for him at the gate. While he was changing his clothes, his valet told him that the second race had begun already, that a lot of gentlemen had been to ask for him, and a boy had twice run up from the stables. Dressing without hurry (he never hurried himself, and never lost his self-possession), Vronsky drove to the sheds. From the sheds he could see a perfect sea of carriages, and people on foot, soldiers surrounding the racecourse, and pavilions swarming with people. The second race was apparently going on, for just as he went into the sheds he heard a bell ringing. Going towards the stable, he met the white-legged chestnut, Mahotin's Gladiator, being led to the racecourse in a blue forage horsecloth, with what looked like huge ears edged with blue.

'Where's Cord?' he asked the stable-boy.

'In the stable, putting on the saddle.'

In the open horse-box stood Frou-Frou, saddled ready. They were just going to lead her out.

'I'm not too late?'

'All right! All right!' said the Englishman; 'don't upset yourself!'

Vronsky once more took in in one glance the exquisite lines of his favourite mare, who was quivering all over, and with an effort he tore himself from the sight of her, and went out of the stable. He went towards the pavilions at the most favourable moment for escaping attention. The mile-and-a-half race was just finishing, and all eyes were fixed on the horse-guard in front and the light hussar behind, urging their horses on with a last effort close to the winning-post. From the centre and outside of the ring all were crowding to the winning-post, and a group of soldiers and officers of the horse-guards were shouting loudly their delight at the expected triumph of their officer and comrade. Vronsky moved into the middle of the crowd, unnoticed, almost at the very moment when the bell rang at the finish of the race, and the tall, mud-spattered horse-guard who came in first, bending over the saddle, let go the reins of his panting grey horse that looked dark with sweat.

The horse, stiffening out its legs, with an effort stopped its rapid course, and the officer of the horse-guards looked round him like a man waking up from a heavy sleep, and just managed to smile. A crowd of friends and outsiders pressed round him.

Vronsky intentionally avoided that select crowd of the upper world, which was moving and talking with discreet freedom before the pavilions. He knew that Madame Karenin was there, and Betsy, and his brother's wife, and he purposely did not go near them for fear of something distracting his attention. But he was continually met and stopped by acquaintances, who told him about the previous races, and kept asking him why he was so late.

At the time when the racers had to go to the pavilion to receive the prizes, and all attention was directed to that point, Vronsky's elder brother, Alexander, a colonel with heavy fringed epaulets, came up to him. He was not tall, though as broadly built as Alexey, and handsomer and rosier than he; he had a red nose, and an open drunken-looking face.

'Did you get my note?' he said. 'There's never any finding you.'

Alexander Vronsky, in spite of the dissolute life, and in especial the drunken habits, for which he was notorious, was quite one of the court circle.

Now, as he talked to his brother of a matter bound to be exceedingly disagreeable to him, knowing that the eyes of many people might be fixed upon him, he kept a smiling countenance, as though he were jesting with his brother about something of little moment.

'I got it, and I really can't make out what *you* are worrying yourself about,' said Alexey.

'I'm worrying myself because the remark has just been made to me that you weren't here, and that you were seen in Peterhof on Monday.'

'There are matters which only concern those directly interested in them, and the matter you are so worried about is . . .'

'Yes, but if so, you may as well cut the service . . .'

'I beg you not to meddle, and that's all I have to say.'

Alexey Vronsky's frowning face turned white, and his prominent lower jaw quivered, which happened rarely with him. Being a man of very warm heart, he was seldom angry; but when he was angry, and when his chin quivered, then, as Alexander Vronsky knew, he was dangerous. Alexander Vronsky smiled gaily.

'I only wanted to give you mother's letter. Answer it, and don't worry about anything just before the race. *Bonne chance,*' he added, smiling, and he moved away from him. But after him another friendly greeting brought Vronsky to a standstill.

'So you won't recognise your friends! How are you, *mon cher?*' said Stepan Arkadyevitch, as conspicuously brilliant in the midst of all the Petersburg brilliance as he was in Moscow, his face rosy, and his whiskers sleek and glossy. 'I came up yesterday, and I'm delighted that I shall see your triumph. When shall we meet?'

'Come tomorrow to the mess-room,' said Vronsky, and squeezing him by the sleeve of his coat, with apologies, he moved away to the centre of the racecourse, where the horses were being led for the great steeplechase.

The horses who had run in the last race were being led home, steaming and exhausted, by the stable-boys, and one after another the fresh horses for the coming race made their appearance, for the most part English racers, wearing horse-cloths, and looking with their drawn-up bellies like strange, huge birds. On the right was led in Frou-Frou, lean and beautiful, lifting up her elastic, rather long pasterns, as though moved by springs. Not far from her they were taking the rug off the lop-eared Gladiator. The strong, exquisite, perfectly correct lines of the stallion, with his superb hind-quarters and excessively short pasterns almost over his hoofs, attracted Vronsky's attention in spite of himself. He would have gone up to his mare, but he was again detained by an acquaintance.

'Oh, there's Karenin!' said the acquaintance with whom he was chatting. 'He's looking for his wife, and she's in the middle of the pavilion. Didn't you see her?'

'No,' answered Vronsky, and without even glancing round towards the pavilion where his friend was pointing out Madame Karenin, he went up to his mare.

Vronsky had not had time to look at the saddle, about which he had to give some direction, when the competitors were summoned to the pavilion to receive their numbers and places in the row at starting. Seventeen officers, looking serious and severe, many with pale faces, met together in the pavilion and drew the numbers. Vronsky drew the number seven. The cry was heard: 'Mount!'

Feeling that with the others riding in the race, he was the centre upon which all eyes were fastened, Vronsky walked up to his mare in that state of nervous tension in which he usually became deliberate and composed in his movements. Cord, in honour of the races, had put on his best clothes, a black coat buttoned up, a stiffly starched collar, which propped up his cheeks, a round black hat, and top-boots. He was calm and dignified as ever, and was with his own hands holding Frou-Frou by both reins, standing straight in front of her. Frou-Frou was still trembling as though in a fever. Her eye, full of fire, glanced sideways at Vronsky. Vronsky slipped his finger under the saddle-girth. The mare glanced aslant at him, drew up her lip, and twitched her ear. The Englishman puckered up his lips, intending to indicate a smile that anyone should verify his saddling.

'Get up; you won't feel so excited.'

Vronsky looked round for the last time at his rivals. He knew that he would not see them during the race. Two were already riding forward to the point from which they were to start. Galtsin, a friend of Vronsky's and one of his more formidable rivals, was moving round a bay horse that would not let him mount. A little light hussar in tight riding-breeches rode off at a gallop, crouched up like a cat on the saddle, in imitation of English jockeys. Prince Kuzovlev sat with a white face on his thoroughbred mare from the Gabrovsky stud, while an English groom led her by the bridle. Vronsky and all his comrades knew Kuzovlev and his peculiarity of 'weak nerves' and terrible vanity. They knew that he was afraid of everything, afraid of riding a spirited horse. But now, just because it was terrible, because people broke their necks, and there was a doctor standing at each obstacle, and an ambulance with a cross on it, and a sister of mercy, he had made up his mind to take part in the race. Their eyes met, and Vronsky gave him a friendly and encouraging nod. Only one he did not see, his chief rival, Mahotin on Gladiator.

'Don't be in a hurry,' said Cord to Vronsky, 'and remember one thing: don't hold her in at the fences, and don't urge her on; let her go as she likes.'

'All right, all right,' said Vronsky, taking the reins.

'If you can, lead the race; but don't lose heart till the last minute, even if you're behind.'

Before the mare had time to move, Vronsky stepped with an agile, vigorous movement into the steel-toothed stirrup, and lightly and firmly seated himself on the creaking leather of the saddle. Getting his right foot in the stirrup, he smoothed the double reins, as he always did, between his fingers, and Cord let go.

As though she did not know which foot to put first, Frou-Frou started, dragging at the reins with her long neck, and as though she were on springs, shaking her rider from side to side. Cord quickened his step, following him. The excited mare, trying to shake off her rider first on one side and then the other, pulled at the reins, and Vronsky tried in vain with voice and hand to soothe her.

They were just reaching the dammed-up stream on their way to the starting-point. Several of the riders were in front and several behind, when suddenly Vronsky heard the sound of a horse galloping in the mud behind him, and he was overtaken by Mahotin on his white-legged, lop-eared Gladiator. Mahotin smiled, showing his long teeth, but Vronsky looked angrily at him. He did not like him, and regarded him now as his most formidable rival. He was angry with him for galloping past and exciting his mare. Frou-Frou started into a gallop, her left foot forward, made two bounds, and fretting at the tightened reins, passed into a jolting trot, bumping her rider up and down. Cord too scowled, and followed Vronsky almost at a trot.

There were seventeen officers in all riding in this race. The racecourse was a large three-mile ring of the form of an ellipse in front of the pavilion. On this course nine obstacles had been arranged: the stream, a big and solid barrier five feet high, just before the pavilion, a dry ditch, a ditch full of water, a precipitous slope, an Irish barricade (one of the most difficult obstacles, consisting of a mound fenced with brushwood, beyond which was a ditch out of sight for the horses, so that the horse had to clear both obstacles or might be killed); then two more ditches filled with water, and one dry one; and the end of the race was just facing the pavilion. But the race began not in the ring, but two hundred yards away from it, and in that part of the course was the first obstacle, a dammed-up stream, seven feet in breadth, which the racers could leap or wade through as they preferred.

Three times they were ranged ready to start, but each time some horse thrust itself out of line, and they had to begin again. The umpire who was starting them, Colonel Sestrin, was beginning to lose his temper, when at last for the fourth time he shouted 'Away!' and the racers started.

Every eye, every opera-glass, was turned on the brightly coloured group of riders at the moment they were in line to start.

'They're off! They're starting!' was heard on all sides after the hush of expectation.

And little groups and solitary figures among the public began running from place to place to get a better view. In the very first minute the close group of horsemen drew out, and it could be seen they were approaching the stream in twos and threes and one behind another. To the spectators it seemed as though they had all started simultaneously, but to the racers there were seconds of difference that had great value to them.

Frou-Frou, excited and over-nervous, had lost the first moment, and several horses had started before her, but before reaching the stream, Vronsky, who was holding the mare with all his force as she tugged at the bridle, easily overtook three, and there were left in front of him Mahotin's chestnut Gladiator, whose hind-quarters were moving lightly and rhythmically up and down exactly in front of Vronsky, and in front of all, the dainty mare Diana, bearing Kuzovlev more dead than alive.

For the first instant Vronsky was not master either of himself or his mare. Up to the first obstacle, the stream, he could not guide the motions of his mare.

Gladiator and Diana came up to it together and almost at the same instant; simultaneously they rose above the stream and flew across to the other side; Frou-Frou darted after them, as if flying; but at the very moment when Vronsky felt himself in the air, he suddenly saw almost under his mare's hoofs Kuzovlev, who was floundering with Diana on the further side of the stream. (Kuzovlev had let go the reins as he took the leap, and the mare had sent him flying over her head). Those details Vronsky learned later; at the moment all he saw was that just under him, where Frou-Frou must alight, Diana's legs or head might be in the way. But Frou-Frou drew up her legs and back in the very act of leaping, like a falling cat, and, clearing the other mare, alighted beyond her.

'O the darling!' thought Vronsky.

After crossing the stream Vronsky had complete control of his mare, and began holding her in, intending to cross the great barrier behind Mahotin, and to try to overtake him in the clear ground of about five hundred yards that followed it.

The great barrier stood just in front of the imperial pavilion. The Tsar and the whole court and crowds of people were all gazing at them – at him, and Mahotin a length ahead of him, as they drew near the 'devil', as the solid barrier was called. Vronsky was aware of those eyes fastened upon him from all sides, but he saw nothing except the ears and neck of his own mare, the ground racing to meet him, and the back and white legs of Gladiator beating time swiftly before him, and keeping always the same distance ahead. Gladiator rose, with no sound of knocking against anything. With a wave of his short tail he disappeared from Vronsky's sight.

'Bravo!' cried a voice.

At the same instant, under Vronsky's eyes, right before him flashed the palings of the barrier. Without the slightest change in her action his mare flew over it; the palings vanished, and he heard only a crash behind him. The mare, excited by Gladiator's keeping ahead, had risen too soon before the barrier, and grazed it with her hind hoofs. But her pace never changed, and Vronsky, feeling a spatter of mud in his face, realised that he was once more the same distance from Gladiator. Once more he perceived in front of him the same back and short tail, and again the same swiftly moving white legs that got no further away.

At the very moment when Vronsky thought that now was the time to overtake Mahotin, Frou-Frou herself, understanding his thoughts, without any incitement on his part, gained ground considerably, and began getting alongside of Mahotin on the most favourable side, close to the inner cord. Mahotin would not let her pass that side. Vronsky had hardly formed the thought that he could perhaps pass on the outer side, when Frou-Frou shifted her pace and began overtaking him on the other side. Frou-Frou's shoulder, beginning by now to be dark with sweat, was even with Gladiator's back. For a few lengths they moved evenly. But before the obstacle they were approaching, Vronsky began working at the reins, anxious to avoid having to take the outer circle, and swiftly passed

Mahotin just upon the declivity. He caught a glimpse of his mud-stained face as he flashed by. He even fancied that he smiled. Vronsky passed Mahotin, but he was immediately aware of him close upon him, and he never ceased hearing the even-thudding hoofs and the rapid and still quite fresh breathing of Gladiator.

The next two obstacles, the watercourse, and the barrier, were easily crossed, but Vronsky began to hear the snorting and thud of Gladiator closer upon him. He urged on his mare, and to his delight felt that she easily quickened her pace, and the thud of Gladiator's hoofs was again heard at the same distance away.

Vronsky was at the head of the race, just as he had wanted to be and as Cord had advised, and now he felt sure of being the winner. His excitement, his delight, and his tenderness for Frou-Frou grew keener and keener. He longed to look round again, but he did not dare do this, and tried to be cool and not to urge on his mare, so to keep the same reserve of force in her as he felt that Gladiator still kept. There remained only one obstacle, the most difficult; if he could cross it ahead of the others, he would come in first. He was flying towards the Irish barricade, Frou-Frou and he both together saw the barricade in the distance, and both the man and the mare had a moment's hesitation. He saw the uncertainty in the mare's ears and lifted the whip, but at the same time felt that his fears were groundless; the mare knew what was wanted. She quickened her pace and rose smoothly, just as he had fancied she would, and as she left the ground gave herself up to the force of her rush, which carried her far beyond the ditch; and with the same leg forward, Frou-Frou fell back into her pace again.

'Bravo, Vronsky!' he heard shouts from a knot of men – he knew they were his friends in the regiment – who were standing at the obstacle. He could not fail to recognise Yashvin's voice though he did not see him.

'O my sweet!' he said inwardly to Frou-Frou, as he listened for what was happening behind. 'He's cleared it!' he thought, catching the thud of Gladiator's hoofs behind him. There remained only the last ditch, filled with water and five feet wide. Vronsky did not even look at it, but anxious to get in a long way first began sawing away at the reins, lifting the mare's head and letting it go in time with her paces. He felt that the mare was at her very last reserve of strength; not her neck and shoulders merely were wet, but the sweat was standing in drops on her mane, her head, her sharp ears, and her breath came in short, sharp gasps. But he knew that she had strength left more than enough for the remaining five hundred yards. It was only from feeling himself nearer the ground and from the peculiar smoothness of his motion that Vronsky knew how greatly the mare had quickened her pace. She flew over the ditch as though not noticing it. She flew over it like a bird; but at the same instant Vronsky, to his horror, felt that he had failed to keep up with the mare's pace, that he had, he did not know how, made a fearful, unpardonable mistake, in recovering his seat in the saddle. All at once his position had shifted and he knew that something awful had happened. He could not yet make out what had happened when the white legs of a chestnut horse flashed by close to him, and Mahotin passed at a swift gallop. Vronsky was touching the ground with one foot, and his mare was sinking on that foot. He just had time to free his leg when she fell on one side, gasping painfully, and, making vain efforts to rise with her delicate, soaking neck, she fluttered on the ground at his feet like a shot bird. The clumsy movement made by Vronsky had broken her back. But that he only knew much later. At that moment he knew only that Mahotin had flown swiftly by, while he stood staggering alone on the muddy, motionless ground, and Frou-Frou lay gasping before him, bending her head back and gazing at him with her exquisite eye. Still unable to realise what had happened, Vronsky tugged at his mare's reins. Again she struggled all over like a fish, and her shoulders setting the saddle heaving, she rose on her front legs, but unable to lift her back, she quivered all over and again fell on her side. With a face hideous with passion, his lower jaw trembling, and his cheeks white, Vronsky kicked her with his heel in the stomach and again fell to tugging at the rein. She did not stir, but thrusting her nose into the ground, she simply gazed at her master with her speaking eyes.

'A – a – a!' groaned Vronsky, clutching at his head. 'Ah! what have I done!' he cried. 'The race lost! And my fault! shameful, unpardonable! And the poor darling, ruined mare! Ah! what have I done!'

A crowd of men, a doctor and his assistant, the officers of his regiment, ran up to him. To his misery he felt that he was whole and unhurt. The mare had broken her back, and it was decided to shoot her. Vronsky could not answer questions, could not speak to anyone. He turned, and without picking up his cap that had fallen off walked away from the racecourse, not knowing where he was going. He felt utterly wretched. For the first time in his life he knew the bitterest sort of misfortune, misfortune beyond remedy, and caused by his own fault.

Yashvin overtook him with his cap, and led him home, and half an hour later Vronsky had regained his self-possession. But the memory of that race remained for long in his heart, the cruellest and bitterest memory of his life.

The Rat Who Wasn't Having Any

WILLIAM GARNETT

THERE WAS ONCE A RAT, among many rats, and he lived in a wood-pile. At a short distance from the wood-pile stood an old ramshackle shed full of broken flower-pots and bits of wheelbarrows. This shed had a window in it that faced the wood-pile, so that it was an easy matter for the rat to run up the side of the shed and squeeze in through one of the broken panes. Next door to the shed stood the cow-house, which was built of brick and had a concrete floor; and in a corner of the shed under a pile of beeswax and half-rotten seed potatoes was the entrance to the passage which led under the cow-house floor, and joined all the other secret passages, and was linked to the main alleyway which came up, very conveniently, under a heap of mouldy sacks that lay in a corner of the food-store under an old wooden grain bin with a hole in the bottom. For it was in this food-store, just beyond the cow-house, that the rat was in the habit of feeding, and the mouldy sacks had lain in that same corner as far back as he could remember.

In the food-store there was almost always a reasonably good supply of oil-cake and oats and tail-wheat and sometimes a few bags of beet pulp or brewers' grains; so that the smell in there was simply delicious even though most of the food might be shut up in bins. Now there were times of the day when, as the rat knew, these bins were apt to be left open and there was nobody much about; but despite this fact he usually took the precaution of only coming out of the wood-pile for his meals at night time.

So one day, as darkness was falling, he poked his nose out of the wood-pile to see if the coast was clear, and was somewhat surprised to smell a fox. So he hailed the fox and said:

'I see you, you stinking son of a ditch-crawling corpse-snatcher, lurking in the shadows just out there. What hare-brained plot has bitten you in the brush this time? I suppose you thought I would be loopy enough to try a sprint for the window with you trailing your fly-blown carcase around. Likely, isn't it, when I know another way that's just as quick and a damned sight safer! Ta-ta for now.'

The fox breathed a sigh of relief.

'That's just what I've come to warn you about,' he said. 'My! it's a good thing for you that you showed up when you did. You know that old owl who hangs about here most nights? Well, he's ever so wise . . .'

'I'll bet he is if you say so, Dogsbody. Why, what does he know?'

'He knows about Fate,' said the fox. 'Reads all about it in the stars, so he says. And if I'm not much mistaken he knows a thing or two about your fate.'

'The Hell he does!' said the rat with some alarm.

'He says that everything that has ever happened was ordained by Fate at the beginning of Time,' explained the fox; 'and that was long long ago before you or I or the owl were born. And at the beginning of Time the fate of each one of us was ordained; and Fate ordained that Robert Rat would be eaten by an owl. And he says that what has been ordained by Fate at the beginning of Time can never be unordained. I just thought you'd like to know.'

'Oh, can't it just!' retorted the rat. 'Are you trying to string me along that if I jumped out in front of your flea-bitten nose I'd stand an earthly? Go and tell that to my grandmother.'

'Oh, it's not my affair how you meet your fate,' said the fox; 'but I'm always glad to be of service in any way I can. If you don't believe what I say, you can go and talk it over with the owl himself: he's sitting on the cow-house roof watching the end of the drain. That's your other way round I believe.'

'How the Devil did you find that out, you great gutful of maggot puddings?'

'The owl told me,' replied the fox.

So the rat scurried through the wood-pile, slipped out the other side into a patch of nettles, ran along a row of cloches ending in a jungle of weeds and broken glass, picked his way over this, flattened himself through a fence, made his way under the shelter of this, and disappeared into a secret entrance to the cesspit. Here he carefully edged round to a place from which he could jump into the protecting end of the drain, jumped, and scampered nimbly up it until he arrived at the end by the cow-house.

When he came by this route he usually made a bee-line for the cat's hole in the cow-house door, and once through this two or three quick strides took him to the manger, and a short distance along the manger was the water pipe which led slanting up the wall, and when he had clambered up this he had only to run along the tie-beam, pop out of the hole under the tiles behind it, trot a few paces down the gutter and pop back into the hole in the roof on the other side of the wall, and after that it was all plain sailing.

But on this occasion he paused at the end of the drain and looked about him warily. There, sure enough, was the owl, sitting on the edge of the gutter just at the very spot where he would have jumped into it if he had not been on the alert, and had managed to get that far.

'Hullo, old Feather-Brain,' said the rat genially. 'What's all this rot the fox tells me about Fate?'

'Whose fate?' asked the owl.

'Mine of course, you moth-eaten mouse's nest in an undertaker's wig. As if you didn't know!'

'Yours, eh?' said the owl looking down at him with his head on one side. 'I shall eat you myself, as it happens.'

'Who said?'

'Fate,' said the owl. 'At the beginning of Time there was nothing in the whole world except an egg: a great big egg with a silver shell inscribed all over with mysterious cyphers written in gold that shone like the moon. And when the egg hatched out the shell burst into a thousand fragments, and all the animals came out, and each one went his way and thought himself free; but in reality, as anyone knows who has studied the mysterious cyphers in the sky, every single thing that has happened to an animal since the beginning of Time was ordained by Fate when she first laid the egg.'

'I know that for a lousy festering addle-pated lie!' said the rat, 'because if I'd been there I'd have sucked that egg as clean as a whistle.'

'Foolish fellow,' said the owl, 'your fate was sealed in that egg long before you were born, and nobody – not even I – can unseal it. You are to be eaten by an owl.'

'Meaning you?'

'O-ho,' said the owl; 'we shall see. It will all happen just as Fate has ordained it.'

'So the fox said, but I'll chew my own tail if I'm sold on a cock-and-bull yarn like that. I reckon I can do just as I bloody well please; and you and the fox can do your damnedest.'

'It was stupid of him to mention it, and it is quite absurd of you to think you can dodge your fate. As it's bound to happen in any case, what's the use of setting your face against it? You'd much better give yourself up with a good grace while I'm still here, and get it all over and done with. I shall be flying away to the rick-yard in five minutes, so you haven't got all night.'

All this was spoken in so solemn a tone that the rat nearly fell over

backwards with laughing at the owl; but he recovered himself sufficiently
to hear the owl conclude his little speech with the remark:

'And you'd better be quick about it as there's a weasel just nipping
into the other end of the drain.'

'That's O.K., old bird: Robertus Rat was earmarked for an owl,' he
replied with what seemed to him a brilliant stroke of repartee. All the
same he didn't like the sound of the owl's last remark, and if there was
a weasel anywhere about he wasn't going to hang about in order to
exchange platitudes about Fate. In the nick of time he remembered a
turning that some of the younger rats had been excavating where there
was a broken tile in the drain. If his suspicions were right this turning
should lead underneath the muck-heap where it would join up with
another passage which linked up with the network under the cow-house
floor. The turning proved to be very narrow and uncomfortable, but the
thought that the weasel, if there was a weasel, might catch him in his
present defenceless position spurred him on, and by dint of pausing for
breath after each effort he made, and telling himself it was only a few
more inches to safety, he shinned his way painfully along it and poked
his nose out through the muck-heap just in time to hear the weasel, who
was now at the end of the drain where he himself had been only a minute
before, saying to the owl:

'Hi, you up there! Did that rat come out of here just now?'

'You won't catch him,' said the owl.

'I'll catch him quick enough if you tell me which way he went.'

'The other way.'

'There is no other way. He couldn't get through the run to the
muck-heap; he's too fat. Must've heard me coming and squashed himself
in backwards till he heard me go by.'

'Good,' said the owl. 'I like them fat.'

'Do you indeed? You don't think I'm going to let you have him when
I've got him?'

'You won't get him.'

'Who says I won't get him?'

'Well,' said the owl; 'you know how clever that old fox is?'

'No, I don't,' said the weasel.

'Well, he must be clever,' said the owl, 'because he can read the cyphers
in the stars, and they tell him what's lying in store for us.'

'And what's that?'

'Fate,' said the owl.

'Phooey,' said the weasel. 'I don't believe in Fate.'

'Nor did the rat when I told him he was going to be eaten by an owl.
But the fox says – and he ought to know – that long ago at the beginning
of Time, before he or I or you or the rat were born, there was nothing
in the whole world but an egg and the dove who had laid it. And she
brooded it for ages and millenniums and aeons and then one day it

hatched out into all the animals, and the pieces of shell flew in all directions, and the dove flew away and left us to our fate, which had been ordained on the day that she laid the egg – and before that, for aught I know – and was inscribed on the egg before it hatched. But as the shell is now split up in so many pieces and scattered in all corners of the sky, only somebody as clever as the fox can make head or tail of the cyphers and read what was ordained by Fate at the beginning of Time.'

'Well, it's my opinion,' said the weasel, 'that he's having you on with all this trumped-up tale of a pie-faced pigeon sitting on an egg covered with stars and bung-full of animals. And if you're dolt enough to swallow anything the fox tells you, you'll very quickly find yourself out of business. Why, if I or any other weasel had been sucking that egg the pigeon would never have got away alive! As for the rat, I've an idea. What will you bet me I can't catch him?'

'Don't be silly,' said the owl. 'I tell you the fate of that rat is as certain as if I had him all trussed up ready.'

'I'll lay you a couple of fieldmice: two to one.'

'Nothing doing. I don't give a hoot for your odds; you'll only be wasting your money.'

'Make it an even three then. Four, if you like. You see, you daren't.'

The owl shook his head. 'It's not that the mice mean anything to me,' he said. 'I'm not a betting owl.'

'Well,' said the weasel, 'I'm betting you five fieldmice, straight and level, that I'll catch that rat. That's my final offer: take it or leave it.'

'I take it,' said the owl; 'but you're a fool to do it.'

'Make it a round half-dozen then?'

'Done.'

The rat heard the weasel turn and run back down the drain. He looked across at the cat's hole in the cow-house door. He could be away and through that hole and up on the tie-beam before that fossilised old bird could stir a feather; and he could always slip through the hole on the far side of the roof. Should he make a dash for it? Then he looked up at the owl, who sat up there as still as death; and then he looked at the stars, which glinted down at him like the eyes of an army of stoats; and he glanced at the moon, which hung over his head like a huge Cheshire cheese that had been nibbled on one side. And then he thought about Fate and the egg: and he shivered. And he drew a little closer into the sheltering warmth of the muck-heap. But just then he heard the weasel's little piping voice addressing somebody at the other end of the drain. What's this? he thought; not more haggling over my living body? But it wasn't every rat, he told himself with an inward smile of self-satisfaction, that carried a price of six fieldmice on his head.

'Hi, you out there! Has that rat been through here just now?' he heard the weasel say. Then he heard the fox reply:

'He went back the way you've come.'

'The owl said he went this way, and there is no other way, unless he's got himself stuck fast in the run to the muck-heap.'

'The owl was pulling your leg,' said the fox. 'He caught him before you arrived. I knew he'd get him in the end.'

'You don't mean to say that downy old fly-by-night was pulling a fast one? He egged me on till I bet him six fieldmice that I'd catch him before he took me on. Why, to think that all the time he was shooting his head off about a pigeon that brooded a lot of rats and mice and a fox that could read the stars he was only pulling the wool over my eyes! He did seem mighty sure of his ground, now that I think of it. And I thought I was on to a good thing: a bit of kickshaws to pave the way for the savoury.'

'I heard everything he told you,' said the fox. 'He's a wily bird. You should learn to take what he says with a grain of salt.'

'He led me up the garden path good and proper,' said the weasel; 'but, trust me, I'll even the score before he's much older. You wait till I see him.'

The rat waited a moment or two longer, uncertain whether to stay and hear what the owl and the weasel would have to say to each other, or whether to push on before the weasel got on to the right track. But the owl at that moment deciding that it was time he flew round to the rick-yard, he was left with no option but to follow the latter course.

So Robert Rat groped cautiously under the muck-heap, not making a sound, and presently he found the passage that led in from the other side. This was a bit wider than the other, and it was not long before he crawled out into one of the well-trodden alleyways of the cow-house floor, turned right, bore left, and then it was left again: yes, he knew this road like the back of his hand. Let those clot-headed creatures out there fret themselves silly about Fate and fieldmice! He fairly laughed aloud as he rounded the last bend. Now came the familiar feel of those mouldy sacks. Only a matter of seconds now and he would be ripping his teeth into a nice fat sack of crushed oats . . .

To look at her by the faint moonlight that seeped in through the cobwebby windows of the food-store, you would think that Tabitha was asleep. Her master had put her in there soon after the cows were milked; and many watchful hours had passed since then. He had run short of corn to give his chickens, and had been scraping the last grains from the bin when he noticed the hole in the bottom. So he had moved the bin to see if there was any corn on the floor, and it was then that he had come upon the heap of mouldy sacks.

Tabitha had been sitting in practically the same position ever since, and her only movements, made upwards of two and three-quarter hours ago, had been to shift her haunches slightly and settle herself in a rather more relaxed attitude than before. One ear drooped a little more than the other and her nose was more or less tucked away behind one of her paws. A layer of mealy dust had settled on the tips of her fur wherever her coat was most exposed: several particles clung to her whiskers. But though nine-tenths of her was fast asleep, there was one whisker that seemed a little less recumbent than the others, and the tip of one ear was still perceptibly turned in the direction of the mouldy sacks. And when Robert Rat began to pick his way among their well-remembered folds, the ear twitched, and the whisker straightened, and then the other ear moved in sympathy with the first, and the end of the tail lifted itself off the floor, and Tabitha's green eyes, which had never really been closed, opened a little wider.

Robert gave a little squeal and a squeak that might just have been heard outside the window if there was anybody there to hear. Then the claws tightened and the teeth bit through all the life that was left in him.

Then began a dance of triumph in which Tabitha tossed Robert up and caught him, and juggled with him behind her back, and sent him spinning across the floor. Then she pretended to lose him, and then she pretended to lose interest in the whole rigmarole, and started to lick herself. Then she stalked him, and then she killed him three or four times over, and then she sat down on top of him pretending to wash her face. Then she bit his head off and ate him, morsel by morsel, all except the gall-bladder.

After that she stretched herself and yawned very wide, until her whiskers nearly touched in front of her nose and her eyes were completely shut. Then she walked back and deliberately settled herself down in front of the mouldy sacks in almost exactly the same position as she had occupied before she was interrupted in her vigil.

Moral

FATE CAN WAIT

The Grey Cub
JACK LONDON

In the savage, frozen-hearted Northland Wild, a pair of wolves survive the rigours of cold, hunger and exhaustion. Among their litter is White Fang, the grey cub whose life begins here, in a rugged cave beside the Mackenzie river . . .

HE WAS DIFFERENT FROM his brothers and sisters. Their hair already betrayed the reddish hue inherited from their mother, the she-wolf; while he alone, in this particular, took after his father. He was the one little grey cub of the litter. He had bred true to the straight wolf-stock – in fact, he had bred true to old One Eye himself, physically, with but a single exception, and that was – he had two eyes to his father's one.

The grey cub's eyes had not been open long, yet already he could see with steady clearness. And while his eyes were still closed, he had felt, tasted, and smelled. He knew his two brothers and his two sisters very well. He had begun to romp with them in a feeble, awkward way, and even to squabble, his little throat vibrating with a queer rasping noise (the forerunner of the growl), as he worked himself into a passion. And long before his eyes had opened, he had learned by touch, taste, and smell to know his mother – a fount of warmth and liquid food and tenderness. She possessed a gentle, caressing tongue that soothed him when it passed over his soft little body, and that impelled him to snuggle against her and to doze off to sleep.

Most of the first month of his life had been passed thus in sleeping; but now he could see quite well, and he stayed awake for longer periods of time, and he was coming to learn his world quite well. His world was gloomy; but he did not know that, for he knew no other world. It was dim-lighted; but his eyes had never had to adjust themselves to any other light. His world was very small. Its limits were the walls of the lair; but as he had no knowledge of the wide world outside, he was never oppressed by the narrow confines of his existence.

But he had early discovered that one wall of his world was different from the rest. This was the mouth of the cave and the source of light. He had discovered that it was different from the other walls long before he had any thoughts of his own, any conscious volitions. It had been an irresistible attraction before ever his eyes opened and looked upon it. The light from it had beat upon his sealed lids, and the eyes and the optic nerves had pulsated to little, sparklike flashes, warm-coloured and strangely pleasing. The life of his body and of every fibre of his body, the life that was the very substance of his body and that was apart from his own personal life, had yearned toward this light, and urged his body toward it in the same way that the cunning chemistry of a plant urges it toward the sun.

Always, in the beginning, before his conscious life dawned, he had crawled toward the mouth of the cave. And in this his brothers and sisters were one with him. Never, in that period, did any of them crawl toward the dark corners of the back wall. The light drew them as if they were plants; the chemistry of the life that composed them demanded the light as a necessity of being; and their little puppet-bodies crawled blindly and chemically, like the tendrils of a vine. Later on, when each developed individuality and became personally conscious of impulsions and desires, the attraction of the light increased. They were always crawling and sprawling toward it, and being driven back from it by their mother.

It was in this way that the grey cub learned other attributes of his mother than the soft, soothing, tongue. In his insistent crawling toward the light, he discovered in her a nose that with a sharp nudge administered rebuke, and later, a paw, that crushed him down and rolled him over and over with a swift, calculating stroke. Thus he learned hurt; and on top of it he learned to avoid hurt – first, by not incurring the risk of it; and second, when he had incurred the risk, by dodging and by retreating. These were conscious actions, and were the results of his first generalizations upon the world. Before that he had recoiled automatically from hurt, as he had crawled automatically toward the light. After that he had recoiled from hurt because he *knew* that it was hurt.

He was a fierce little cub. So were his brothers and sisters. It was to be expected. He was a carnivorous animal. He came of a breed of meat-killers and meat-eaters. His father and mother lived wholly upon meat. The milk he had sucked with his first flickering life was milk transformed directly from meat; and now, at a month old, when his eyes had been open for about a week, he was beginning himself to eat meat – meat half digested by the she-wolf and disgorged for the five growing cubs that already made too great demand upon her breast.

But he was, further, the fiercest of the litter. He could make a louder rasping growl than any of them. His tiny rages were much more terrible than theirs. It was he that first learned the trick of rolling a fellow-cub over with a cunning paw-stroke. And it was he that first gripped another cub by the ear and pulled and tugged and growled through jaws tight-clenched. And certainly it was he that caused the mother the most trouble in keeping her litter from the mouth of the cave.

The fascination of the light for the grey cub increased from day to day. He was perpetually departing on yard-long adventures toward the cave's entrance, and as perpetually being driven back. Only he did not know it for an entrance. He did not know anything about entrances – passages whereby one goes from one place to another place. He did not know any other place, much less of a way to get there. So to him the entrance of the cave was a wall – a wall of light. As the sun was to the outside dweller, this wall was to him the sun of his world. It attracted him as a candle attracts a moth. He was always striving to attain it. The life that was so swiftly expanding within him urged him continually toward the wall of light. The life that was within him knew that it was the one way out, the way he was predestined to tread. But he himself did not know anything about it. He did not know there was any outside at all.

There was one strange thing about this wall of light. His father (he had already come to recognize his father as the one other dweller in the world, a creature like his mother, who slept near the light and was a bringer of meat) – his father had a way of walking right into the white far wall and disappearing. The grey cub could not understand this. Though never permitted by his mother to approach that wall, he had approached the other walls, and encountered hard obstruction on the end of his tender nose. This hurt. And after several such adventures, he left the walls alone. Without thinking about it, he accepted this disappearing into the wall as a peculiarity of his father, as milk and half-digested meat were peculiarities of his mother.

In fact, the grey cub was not given to thinking – at least, to the kind of thinking customary of men. His brain worked in dim ways. Yet his conclusions were as sharp and distinct as those achieved by men. He had a method of accepting things without questioning the way and wherefore. In reality, this was the act of classification. He was never disturbed over *why* a thing happened. *How* it happened was sufficient for him. Thus, when he had bumped his nose on the back wall a few times, he accepted that he would not disappear into walls. In the same way he accepted that his father could disappear into walls. But he was not in the least disturbed by desire to find out the reason for the difference between his father and himself. Logic and physics were no part of his mental make-up.

Like most creatures of the Wild, he early experienced famine. There came a time when not only did the meat-supply cease, but the milk no longer came from his mother's breast. At first, the cubs whimpered and cried, but for the most part they slept. It was not long before they were reduced to a coma of hunger. There were no more spats and squabbles, no more tiny rages nor attempts at growling; while the adventures toward the far white wall ceased altogether. The cubs slept, while the life that was in them flickered and died down.

One Eye was desperate. He ranged far and wide, and slept but little in the lair that had now become cheerless and miserable. The she-wolf, too, left her litter and went out in search of meat. In the first days after the birth of the cubs, One Eye had journeyed several times back to the Indian camp and robbed the rabbit snares; but, with the melting of the snow and the opening of the streams, the Indian camp had moved away, and that source of supply was closed to him.

When the grey cub came back to life and again took interest in the far white wall, he found that the population of his world had been reduced. Only one sister remained to him. The rest were gone. As he grew stronger, he found himself compelled to play alone, for the sister no longer lifted her head nor moved about. His little body rounded out with the meat he now ate; but the food had come too late for her. She slept continuously, a tiny skeleton flung round with skin in which the flame flickered lower and lower and at last went out.

Then there came a time when the grey cub no longer saw his father appearing and disappearing in the wall, nor lying down asleep in the entrance. This had happened at the end of a second and less severe famine. The she-wolf knew why One Eye never came back, but there was no way by which she could tell what she had seen to the grey cub. Hunting herself for meat, up the left fork of the stream where lived the lynx, she had followed a day-old trail of One Eye. And she had found him, or what remained of him, at the end of the trail. There were many signs of the battle that had been fought, and of the lynx's withdrawal to her lair after having won the victory. Before she went away, the she-wolf had found this lair, but the signs told her that the lynx was inside, and she had not dared to venture in.

After that, the she-wolf in her hunting avoided the left fork. For she knew that in the lynx's lair was a litter of kittens, and she knew the lynx for a fierce, bad-tempered creature and a terrible fighter. It was all very well for half a dozen wolves to drive a lynx, spitting and bristling, up a tree; but it was quite a different matter for a lone wolf to encounter a lynx – especially when the lynx was known to have a litter of hungry kittens at her back.

But the Wild is the Wild, and motherhood is motherhood, at all times fiercely protective whether in the wild or out of it; and the time was to come when the she-wolf, for her grey cub's sake would venture the left fork, and the lair in the rocks, and the lynx's wrath.

By the time his mother began leaving the cave on hunting expeditions, the cub had learned well the law that forbade his approaching the entrance. Not only had this law been forcibly and many times impressed on him by his mother's nose and paw, but in him the instinct of fear was developing. Never, in his brief cave-life, had he encountered anything of which to be afraid. Yet fear was in him. It had come down to him from a remote ancestry through a thousand thousand lives. It was a heritage he had received directly from One Eye and the she-wolf; but to them, in turn, it had been passed down through all the generations of wolves that had gone before. Fear! – that legacy of the Wild which no animal may escape nor exchange for pottage.

So the grey cub knew fear, though he knew not the stuff of which fear was made. Possibly he accepted it as one of the restrictions of life. For he had already learned that there were such restrictions. Hunger he had known; and when he could not appease his hunger he had felt restriction. The hard obstruction of the cave-wall, the sharp nudge of his mother's nose, the smashing stroke of her paw, the hunger unappeased of several famines, had borne in upon him that all was not freedom in the world – that to life there were limitations and restraints. These limitations and restraints were laws. To be obedient to them was to escape hurt and make for happiness.

He did not reason the question out in this man fashion. He merely classified the things that hurt and the things that did not hurt. And after such classification he avoided the things that hurt – the restrictions and restraints – in order to enjoy the satisfactions and the remunerations of life.

Thus it was that in obedience to the law laid down by his mother, and in obedience to the law of that unknown and nameless thing, fear, he kept away from the mouth of the cave. It remained to him a white wall of light. When his mother was absent, he slept most of the time, while during the intervals that he was awake he kept very quiet, suppressing the whimpering cries that tickled in his throat and strove for noise.

Once, lying awake, he heard a strange sound in the white wall. He did not know that it was a wolverine, standing outside, all a-trembling with its own daring, and cautiously scenting out the contents of the cave. The cub knew only that the sniff was strange, a something unclassified, therefore unknown and terrible – for the unknown was one of the chief elements that went into the making of fear.

The hair bristled up on the grey cub's back, but it bristled silently. How was he to know that this thing that sniffed was a thing at which to bristle? It was not born of any knowledge of his, yet it was the visible expression of the fear that was in him, and for which, in his own life, there was no accounting. But fear was accompanied by another instinct – that of concealment. The cub was in a frenzy of terror, yet he lay without movement or sound, frozen, petrified into immobility, to all appearances dead. His mother, coming home, growled as she smelt the wolverine's track, and bounded into the cave and licked and nozzled him with undue vehemence of affection. And the cub felt that somehow he had escaped a great hurt.

But there were other forces at work in the cub, the greatest of which was growth. Instinct and law demanded of him obedience. But growth demanded disobedience. His mother and fear impelled him to keep away from the white wall. Growth is life, and life is for ever destined to make for light. So there was no damming up the tide of life that was rising within him – rising with every mouthful of meat he swallowed, with every breath he drew. In the end, one day, fear and obedience were swept away by the rush of life, and the cub straddled and sprawled toward the entrance.

Unlike any other wall with which he had had experience, this wall seemed to recede from him as he approached. No hard surface collided with the tender little nose he thrust out tentatively before him. The substance of the wall seemed as permeable and yielding as light. And as condition, in his eyes, had the seeming form, so he entered into what had been wall to him, and bathed in the substance that composed it.

It was bewildering. He was sprawling through solidity. And ever the light grew brighter. Fear urged him to go back, but growth drove him on. Suddenly he found himself at the mouth of the cave. The wall, inside which he had thought himself, as suddenly leaped back before him to an immeasurable distance. The light had become painfully bright. He was dazzled by it. Likewise he was made dizzy by this abrupt and tremendous extension of space. Automatically, his eyes were adjusting themselves to the brightness, focusing themselves to meet the increased distance of objects. At first, the wall had leaped beyond his vision. He now saw it again; but it had taken upon itself a remarkable remoteness. Also, its appearance had changed. It was now a variegated wall, composed of the trees that fringed the stream, the opposing mountain that towered above the trees, and the sky that out-towered the mountain.

A great fear came upon him. This was more of the terrible unknown. He crouched down on the lip of the cave and gazed out on the world. He was very much afraid. Because it was unknown, it was hostile to him. Therefore the hair stood up on end along his back, and his lips wrinkled weakly in an attempt at a ferocious and intimidating snarl. Out of his puniness and fright he challenged and menaced the whole wide world.

Nothing happened. He continued to gaze, and in his interest he forgot to snarl. Also, he forgot to be afraid. For the time, fear had been routed by growth, while growth had assumed the guise of curiosity. He began to notice near objects – an open portion of the stream that flashed in the sun, the blasted pine-tree that stood at the base of the slope, and the slope itself, that ran right up to him and ceased two feet beneath the lip of the cave on which he crouched.

Now the grey cub had lived all his days on a level floor. He had never experienced the hurt of a fall. He did not know what a fall was. So he stepped boldly out upon the air. His hind-legs still rested on the cave-lip, so he fell forward head downward. The earth struck him a harsh blow on the nose that made him yelp. Then he began rolling down the slope, over and over. He was in a panic of terror. The unknown had caught him at last. It had gripped savagely hold of him and was about to wreak upon him some terrific hurt. Growth was now routed by fear, and he ki-yi'd like any frightened puppy.

The unknown bore him on he knew not to what frightful hurt, and he yelped and ki-yi'd unceasingly. This was a different proposition from crouching in frozen fear while the unknown lurked just alongside. Now the unknown had caught tight hold of him. Silence would do no good. Besides, it was not fear, but terror, that convulsed him.

But the slope grew more gradual, and its base was grass-covered. Here the cub lost momentum. When at last he came to a stop, he gave one last agonized yelp and then a long, whimpering wail. Also, and quite as a matter of course, as though in his life he had already made a thousand toilets, he proceeded to lick away the dry clay that soiled him.

After that he sat up and gazed about him, as might the first man of the earth who landed upon Mars. The cub had broken through the wall of the world, the unknown had let go its hold of him, and here he was without hurt. But the first man on Mars would have experienced less unfamiliarity than did he. Without any antecedent knowledge, without any warning whatever that such existed, he found himself an explorer in a totally new world.

Now that the terrible unknown had let go of him, he forgot that the unknown had any terrors. He was aware only of curiosity in all the things about him. He inspected the grass beneath him, the moss-berry plant just beyond, and the dead trunk of the blasted pine that stood on the edge of an open space among the trees. A squirrel, running around the base of the trunk, came full upon him, and gave him a great fright. He cowered down and snarled. But the squirrel was as badly scared. It ran up the tree, and from a point of safety chattered back savagely.

This helped the cub's courage, and though the wood-pecker he next encountered gave him a start, he proceeded confidently on his way. Such was his confidence, that when a moose-bird impudently hopped up to him, he reached out at it with a playful paw. The result was a sharp peck on the end of his nose that made him cower down and ki-yi. The noise he made was too much for the moose-bird, who sought safety in flight.

But the cub was learning. His misty little mind had already made an unconscious classification. There were live things and things not alive. Also, he must watch out for the live things. The things not alive remained always in one place; but the live things moved about, and there was no telling what they might do. The thing to expect of them was the unexpected, and for this he must be prepared.

He travelled very clumsily. He ran into sticks and things. A twig that he thought a long way off would the next instant hit him on the nose or rake along his ribs. There were inequalities of surface. Sometimes he overstepped and stubbed his nose. Quite as often he understepped and stubbed his feet. Then there were the pebbles and stones that turned under him when he trod upon them; and from them he came to know that the things not alive were not all in the same state of stable equilibrium as was his cave; also, that small things not alive were more liable than large things to fall down or turn over. But with every mishap he was learning. The longer he walked, the better he walked. He was adjusting himself. He was learning to calculate his own muscular movements, to know his physical limitations, to measure distances between objects, and between objects and himself.

His was the luck of the beginner. Born to be a hunter of meat (though he did not know it), he blundered upon meat just outside his own cave-door on his first foray into the world. It was by sheer blundering that he chanced upon the shrewdly hidden ptarmigan nest. He fell into it. He had essayed to walk along the trunk of a fallen pine. The rotten bark gave way under his feet, and with a despairing yelp he pitched down the rounded descent, smashed through the leafage and stalks of a small bush, and in the heart of the bush, on the ground, fetched up in the midst of seven ptarmigan chicks.

They made noises, and at first he was frightened at them. Then he perceived that they were very little, and he became bolder. They moved. He placed his paw on one, and its movements were accelerated. This was a source of enjoyment to him. He smelled it. He picked it up in his mouth. It struggled and tickled his tongue. At the same time he was made aware of a sensation of hunger. His jaws closed together. There was a crunching of fragile bones, and warm blood ran in his mouth. The taste of it was good. This was meat, the same as his mother gave him, only it was alive between his teeth and therefore better. So he ate the ptarmigan. Nor did he stop till he had devoured the whole brood. Then he licked his chops in quite the same way his mother did, and began to crawl out of the bush.

He encountered a feathered whirlwind. He was confused and blinded by the rush of it and the beat of angry wings. He hid his head between his paws and yelped. The blows increased. The mother-ptarmigan was in a fury. Then he became angry. He rose up, snarling, striking out with his paws. He sank his tiny teeth into one of the wings and pulled and tugged sturdily. The ptarmigan struggled against him, showering blows upon him with her free wing. It was his first battle. He was elated. He forgot all about the unknown. He was fighting, tearing at a live thing that was striking at him. Also, this live thing was meat. The lust to kill was on him. He had just destroyed little live things. He would now destroy a big live thing. He was too busy and happy to know that he was happy. He was thrilling and exulting in ways new to him and greater to him than any he had known before.

He held on to the wing and growled between his tight-clenched teeth. The ptarmigan dragged him out of the bush. When she turned and tried to drag him back into the bush's shelter, he pulled her away from it and on into the open. And all the time she was making outcry and striking with her free wing, while feathers were flying like a snowfall. The pitch to which he was aroused was tremendous. All the fighting blood of his breed was up in him and surging through him. This was living, though he did not know it. He was realising his own meaning in the world; he was doing that for which he was made – killing meat and battling to kill it. He was justifying his existence, than which life can do no greater; for life achieves its summit when it does to the uttermost that which it was equipped to do.

After a time the ptarmigan ceased her struggling. He still held her by the wing, and they lay on the ground and looked at each other. He tried to growl threateningly, ferociously. She pecked on his nose, which by now, what of previous adventures, was sore. He winced but held on. She pecked him again and again. From wincing he went to whimpering. He tried to back away from her, oblivious to the fact that by his hold on her he dragged her after him. A rain of pecks fell on his ill-used nose. The flood of fight ebbed down in him, and, releasing his prey, he turned tail and scampered off across the open in inglorious retreat.

He lay down to rest on the other side of the open, near the edge of the bushes, his tongue lolling out, his chest heaving and panting, his nose still hurting him and causing him to continue to whimper. But as he lay there, suddenly there came to him a feeling as of something terrible impending. The unknown with all its terrors rushed upon him, and he shrank back instinctively into the shelter of the bush. As he did so, a draught of air fanned him, and a large, winged body swept ominously and silently past. A hawk, driving down out of the blue, had barely missed him.

While he lay in the bush, recovering from this fright and peering fearfully out, the mother-ptarmigan on the other side of the open space fluttered out of the ravaged nest. It was because of her loss that she paid no attention to the winged bolt of the sky. But the cub saw, and it was a warning and a lesson to him – the swift downward swoop of the hawk, the short skin of its body, just above the ground, the strike of its talons in the body of the ptarmigan, the ptarmigan's squawk of agony and fright, and the hawk's rush upward into the blue, carrying the ptarmigan away with it.

It was a long time before the cub left his shelter. He had learned much. Live things were meat. They were good to eat. Also, live things, when they were large enough, could give hurt. It was better to eat small live things like ptarmigan chicks, and to let alone large live things like ptarmigan hens. Nevertheless he felt a little prick of ambition, a sneaking desire to have another battle with that ptarmigan hen – only the hawk had carried her away. Maybe there were other ptarmigan hens. He would go and see.

He came down a shelving bank to the stream. He had never seen water before. The footing looked good. There were not inequalities of surface. He stepped boldly out on it, and went down, crying with fear, into the embrace of the unknown. It was cold, and he gasped, breathing quickly. The water rushed into his lungs instead of the air that had always accompanied his act of breathing. The suffocation he experienced was like the pang of death. To him it signified death. He had no conscious knowledge of death, but like every animal of the Wild, he possessed the instinct of death. To him it stood as the greatest of hurts. It was the very essence of the unknown, it was the sum of the terrors of the unknown – the one culminating and unthinkable catastrophe that could happen to him, about which he knew nothing and about which he feared everything.

He came to the surface, and the sweet air rushed into his open mouth. He did not go down again. Quite as though it had been a long-established custom of his, he struck out with all his legs and began to swim. The near bank was a yard away; but he had come up with his back to it, and the first thing his eyes rested upon was the opposite bank, toward which he immediately began to swim. The stream was a small one, but in the pool it widened out to a score of feet.

Midway in the passage, the current picked up the cub and swept him down-stream. He was caught in the miniature rapid at the bottom of the pool. Here was little chance for swimming. The quiet water had become suddenly angry. Sometimes he was under, sometimes on top. At all times he was in violent motion, now being turned over or around, and again, being smashed against a rock. And with every rock he struck he yelped. His progress was a series of yelps, from which might have been adduced the number of rocks he encountered.

Below the rapid was a second pool, and here, captured by the eddy, he was gently borne to the bank and as gently deposited on a bed of gravel. He crawled frantically clear of the water and lay down. He had learned some more about the world. Water was not alive. Yet it moved. Also, it looked as solid as the earth, but was without any solidity at all. His conclusion was that things were not always what they appeared to be. The cub's fear of the unknown was an inherited distrust, and it had now been strengthened by experience. Thenceforth, in the nature of things, he would possess an abiding distrust of appearances. He would have to learn the reality of a thing before he could put his faith into it.

One other adventure was destined for him that day. He had recollected that there was such a thing in the world as his mother. And then there came to him a feeling that he wanted her more than all the rest of the things in the world. Not only was his body tired with the adventures it had undergone, but his little brain was equally tired. In all the days he had lived it had not worked so hard as on this one day. Furthermore, he was sleepy. So he started out to look for the cave and his mother, feeling at the same time an overwhelming rush of loneliness and helplessness.

He was sprawling along between some bushes, when he heard a sharp, intimidating cry. There was a flash of yellow before his eyes. He saw a weasel leaping swiftly away from him. It was a small live thing, and he had no fear. Then, before him, at his feet, he saw an extremely small live thing, only several inches long – a young weasel, that, like himself, had disobediently gone out adventuring. It tried to retreat before him. He turned it over with his paw. It made a queer, grating noise. The next moment the flash of yellow reappeared before his eyes. He heard again the intimidating cry, and at the same instant received a severe blow on the side of the neck, and felt the sharp teeth of the mother-weasel cut into his flesh.

While he yelped and ki-yi'd and scrambled backward, he saw the mother-weasel leap upon her young one and disappear with it into the neighbouring thicket. The cut of her teeth in his neck still hurt, but his feelings were hurt more grievously, and he sat down and weakly whimpered. The mother-weasel was so small and so savage! He was yet to learn that for size and weight the weasel was the most ferocious, vindictive, and terrible of all the killers of the Wild. But a portion of this knowledge was quickly to be his.

He was still whimpering when the mother-weasel reappeared. She did not rush him, now that her young one was safe. She approached more cautiously, and the cub had full opportunity to observe her lean, snake-like body, and her head, erect, eager, and snakelike itself. Her sharp, menacing cry sent the hair bristling along his back, and he snarled warningly at her. She came closer and closer. There was a leap, swifter than his unpractised sight, and the lean, yellow body disappeared for a moment out of the field of his vision. The next moment she was at his throat, her teeth buried in his hair and flesh.

At first he snarled and tried to fight; but he was very young, and this was only his first day in the world, and this snarl became a whimper, his fight a struggle to escape. The weasel never relaxed her hold. She hung on, striving to press down with her teeth to the great vein where his life-blood bubbled. The weasel was a drinker of blood, and it was ever her preference to drink from the throat of life itself.

The grey cub would have died, and there would have been no story to write about him, had not the she-wolf come bounding through the bushes. The weasel let go the cub and flashed at the she-wolf's throat, missing, but getting a hold on the jaw instead. The she-wolf flirted her head like the snap of a whip, breaking the weasel's hold and flinging it high in the air. And, still in the air, the she-wolf's jaws closed on the lean, yellow body, and the weasel knew death between the crunching teeth.

The cub experienced another access of affection on the part of his mother. Her joy at finding him seemed greater even than his joy at being found. She nozzled him, and caressed him, and licked the cuts made in him by the weasel's teeth. Then, between them, mother and cub, they ate the blood-drinker, and after that went back to the cave and slept.

The cub's development was rapid. He rested for two days, and then ventured forth from the cave again. It was on this adventure that he found the young weasel whose mother he had helped eat, and he saw to it that the young weasel went the way of its mother. But on this trip he did not get lost. When he grew tired, he found his way back to the cave and slept. And every day thereafter found him out and ranging a wider area.

He began to get accurate measurement of his strength and his weakness, and to know when to be bold and when to be cautious. He found it expedient to be cautious all the time, except for the rare moments when, assured of his own intrepidity, he abandoned himself to petty rages and lusts.

He was always a little demon of fury when he chanced upon a stray ptarmigan. Never did he fail to respond savagely to the chatter of the squirrel he had first met on the blasted pine. While the sight of a moose-bird almost invariably put him into the wildest rages, for he never forgot the peck on the nose he had received from the first of that ilk he encountered.

But there were times when even a moose-bird failed to affect him, and those were times when he felt himself to be in danger from some other prowling meat-hunter. He never forgot the hawk, and its moving shadow always sent him crouching into the nearest thicket. He no longer sprawled and straddled, and already he was developing the gait of his mother, slinking and furtive, apparently without exertion, yet sliding along with a swiftness that was as deceptive as it was imperceptible.

In the matter of meat, his luck had been all in the beginning. The seven ptarmigan chicks and the baby weasel represented the sum of his killings. His desire to kill strengthened with the days, and he cherished hungry ambitions for the squirrel that chattered so volubly and always informed all wild creatures that the wolf-cub was approaching. But as birds flew in the air, squirrels could climb trees, and the cub could only try to crawl unobserved upon the squirrel when it was on the ground.

The cub entertained a great respect for his mother. She could get meat, and she never failed to bring him his share. Further, she was unafraid of things. It did not occur to him that this fearlessness was founded upon experience and knowledge. Its effect on him was that of an impression of power. His mother represented power; and as he grew older he felt this power in the sharper admonishment of her paw; while the reproving nudge of her nose gave place to the slash of her fangs. For this, likewise, he respected his mother. She compelled obedience from him, and the older he grew the shorter grew her temper.

Famine came again, and the cub with clearer consciousness knew once more the bite of hunger. The she-wolf ran herself thin in the quest for meat. She rarely slept any more in the cave, spending most of her time on the meat-trail, and spending it vainly. This famine was not a long one, but it was severe while it lasted. The cub found no more milk in his mother's breast, nor did he get one mouthful of meat for himself.

Before, he had hunted in play, for the sheer joyousness of it; now he hunted in deadly earnestness, and found nothing. Yet the failure of it accelerated his development. He studied the habits of the squirrel with great carefulness, and strove with greater craft to steal upon it and surprise it. He studied the wood-mice, and tried to dig them out of their burrows; and he learned much about the ways of moose-birds and woodpeckers. And there came a day when the hawk's shadow did not drive him crouching into the bushes. He had grown stronger, and wiser, and more confident. Also, he was desperate. So he sat on his haunches, conspicuously in an open space, and challenged the hawk down out of the sky. For he knew that there, floating in the blue above him, was meat – the meat his stomach yearned after so insistently. But the hawk refused to come down and give battle, and the cub crawled away into a thicket and whimpered his disappointment and hunger.

The famine broke. The she-wolf brought home meat. It was strange meat, different from any she had ever brought before. It was a lynx kitten, partly grown, like the cub, but not so large. And it was all for him. His mother had satisfied her hunger elsewhere, though he did not know that it was the rest of the lynx that had gone to satisfy her. Nor did he know the desperateness of her deed. He knew only that the velvet-furred kitten was meat, and he ate and waxed happier with every mouthful.

A full stomach conduces to inaction, and the cub lay in the cave, sleeping against his mother's side. He was aroused by her snarling. Never had he heard her snarl so terribly. Possibly in her whole life it was the most terrible snarl she ever gave. There was reason for it, and none knew it better than she. A lynx's lair is not despoiled with impunity. In the full glare of the afternoon light, crouching in the entrance of the cave, the cub saw the lynx-mother. The hair rippled up along his back at the sight. Here was fear, and it did not not require his instinct to tell him of it. And if sight alone were not sufficient, the cry of rage the intruder gave, beginning with a snarl and rushing abruptly upward in a hoarse screech, was convincing enough in itself.

The cub felt the prod of the life that was in him, and stood up and snarled valiantly by his mother's side. But she thrust him ignominiously away and behind her. Because of the low-roofed entrance the lynx could not leap in, and when she made a crawling rush of it the she-wolf sprang upon her and pinned her down. The cub saw little of the battle. There was a tremendous snarling and spitting and screeching. The two animals threshed about, the lynx ripping and tearing with her claws and using her teeth as well, while the she-wolf used her teeth alone.

Once the cub sprang in and sank his teeth into the hind leg of the lynx. He clung on, growling savagely. Though he did not know it, by the weight of his body he clogged the action of the leg and thereby saved his mother much damage. A change in the battle crushed him under both their bodies and wrenched loose his hold. The next moment the two mothers separated, and before they rushed together again the lynx lashed out at the cub with a huge forepaw that ripped his shoulder open to the bone and sent him hurtling sidewise against the wall. Then was added to the uproar the cub's shrill yelp of pain and fright. But the fight lasted so long that he had time to cry himself out and to experience a second burst of courage; and the end of the battle found him again clinging to a hind-leg and furiously growling between his teeth.

The lynx was dead. But the she-wolf was very weak and sick. At first she caressed the cub and licked his wounded shoulder; but the blood she had lost had taken with it her strength, and for all of a day and a night she lay by her dead foe's side, without movement, scarcely breathing. For a week she never left the cave, except for water, and then her movements were slow and painful. At the end of that time the lynx was devoured, while the she-wolf's wounds had healed sufficiently to permit her to take the meat-trail again.

The cub's shoulder was stiff and sore, and for some time he limped from the terrible slash he had received. But the world now seemed changed. He went about in it with greater confidence, with a feeling of prowess that had not been his in the days before the battle with the lynx. He had looked upon life in a more ferocious aspect; he had fought; he had buried his teeth in the flesh of a foe, and he had survived. And because of all this, he carried himself more boldly, with a touch of defiance that was new in him. He was no longer afraid of minor things and much of his timidity had vanished, though the unknown never ceased to press upon him with its mysteries and terrors, intangible and ever-menacing.

He began to accompany his mother on the meat-trail, and he saw much of the killing of meat, and began to play his part in it. And in his own dim way he learned the law of meat. There were two kinds of life – his own kind and the other kind. His own kind included his mother and himself. The other kind included all live things that moved. But the other kind was divided. One portion was what his own kind killed and ate. This portion was composed of non-killers and the small killers. The other portion killed and ate his own kind, or was killed and eaten by his own kind. And out of this classification arose the law. The aim of life was meat. Life itself was meat. Life lived on life. There were the eaters and the eaten. The law was: EAT, OR BE EATEN. He did not formulate the law in clear, set terms and moralise about it. He did not even think the law; he merely lived the law without thinking about it at all.

He saw the law operating around him on every side. He had eaten the ptarmigan chicks. The hawk had eaten the ptarmigan mother. The hawk would also have eaten him. Later, when he had grown more formidable, he wanted to eat the hawk. He had eaten the lynx kitten. The lynx-mother would have eaten him had she not herself been killed and eaten. And so it went. The law was being lived about him by all live things, and he himself was part of and parcel of the law. He was a killer. His only food was meat, live meat, that ran away swiftly before him, or flew into the air, or climbed trees, or hid in the ground, or faced him and fought with him, or turned the tables and ran after him.

Had the cub thought in man-fashion, he might have epitomized life as a voracious appetite ·and the world as a place wherein ranged a multitude of appetites, pursuing and being pursued, hunting and being hunted, eating and being eaten, all in blindness and confusion, with violence and disorder, a chaos of gluttony and slaughter, ruled over by chance, merciless, planless, endless.

But the cub did not think in man-fashion. He did not look at things with wide vision. He was single-purposed, and entertained but one thought or desire at a time. Besides the law of meat, there were a myriad other and lesser laws for him to learn and obey. The world was filled with surprise. The stir of the life that was in him, the play of his muscles, was an unending happiness. To run down meat was to experience thrills and elations. His rages and battles were pleasures. Terror itself, and the mystery of the unknown led to his living.

And there were easements and satisfactions. To have a full stomach, to doze lazily in the sunshine – such things were remuneration in full for his ardours and toils, while his ardours and toils were in themselves self-remunerative. They were expressions of life, and life is always happy when it is expressing itself. So the cub had no quarrel with his hostile environment. He was very much alive, very happy, and very proud of himself.

Animals at Alconleigh
NANCY MITFORD

THERE IS A PHOTOGRAPH in existence of Aunt Sadie and her six children sitting round the tea-table at Alconleigh. The table is situated, as it was, is now, and ever shall be, in the hall, in front of a huge open fire of logs. Over the chimney-piece plainly visible in the photograph, hangs an entrenching tool, with which, in 1915, Uncle Matthew had whacked to death eight Germans one by one as they crawled out of a dug-out. It is still covered with blood and hairs, an object of fascination to us as children. In the photograph Aunt Sadie's face, always beautiful, appears strangely round, her hair strangely fluffy, and her clothes strangely dowdy, but it is unmistakably she who sits there with Robin, in oceans of lace, lolling on her knee. She seems uncertain what to do with his head, and the presence of Nanny waiting to take him away is felt though not seen. The other children, between Louisa's eleven and Matt's two years, sit round the table in party dresses or frilly bibs, holding cups or mugs according to age, all of them gazing at the camera with large eyes opened wide by the flash, and all looking as if butter would not melt in their round pursed-up mouths. There they are, held like flies in the amber of that moment – click goes the camera and on goes life; the minutes, the days, the years, the decades, taking them further and further from that happiness and promise of youth, from the hopes Aunt Sadie must have had for them, and from the dreams they dreamed for themselves. I often think there is nothing quite so poignantly sad as old family groups.

When a child I spent my Christmas holidays at Alconleigh, it was a regular feature of my life, and, while some of them slipped by with nothing much to remember, others were distinguished by violent occurrences and had a definite character of their own. There was the time, for example, when the servants' wing caught fire, the time when my pony lay on me in the brook and nearly drowned me (not very nearly, he was soon dragged off, but meanwhile bubbles were said to have been observed). There was drama when Linda, aged ten, attempted suicide in order to rejoin an old smelly Border Terrier which Uncle Matthew had had put down. She collected and ate a basketful of yew-berries, was discovered by Nanny and given mustard and water to make her sick. She was then 'spoken to' by Aunt Sadie, clipped over the ear by Uncle Matthew, put to bed for two days and given a Labrador puppy, which soon took the place of the old Border in her affections. There was much worse drama when Linda, aged twelve, told the daughters of neighbours, who had come to tea, what she supposed to be the facts of life. Linda's presentation of the 'facts' had been so gruesome that the children left Alconleigh howling dismally, their nerves permanently impaired, their future chances of a sane and happy sex life much reduced. This resulted in a series of dreadful punishments, from a real beating, administered by Uncle Matthew, to luncheon upstairs for a week. There was the unforgettable holiday when Uncle Matthew and Aunt Sadie went to Canada. The Radlett children would rush for the newspapers every day hoping to see that their parents' ship had gone down with all aboard; they yearned to be total orphans – especially Linda, who saw herself as Katy in *What Katy Did*, the reins of the household gathered into small but capable hands. The ship met with no iceberg and weathered the Atlantic storms, but meanwhile we had a wonderful holiday, free from rules.

But the Christmas I remember most clearly of all was when I was fourteen and Aunt Emily became engaged. Aunt Emily was Aunt Sadie's sister, and she had brought me up from babyhood, my own mother, their youngest sister, having felt herself too beautiful and too gay to be burdened with a child at the age of nineteen. She left my father when I was a month old, and subsequently ran away so often, and with so many different people, that she became known to her family and friends as the Bolter; while my father's second, and presently his third, fourth and fifth wives, very naturally had no great wish to look after me. Occasionally one of these impetuous parents would appear like a rocket, casting an unnatural glow upon my horizon. They had great glamour, and I longed to be caught up in their fiery trails and be carried away, though in my heart I knew how lucky I was to have Aunt Emily. By degrees, as I grew up, they lost all charm for me; the cold grey rocket cases mouldered where they had happened to fall, my mother with a major in the South of France, my father, his estates sold up to pay his debts, with an old Rumanian countess in the Bahamas. Even before I was grown up much of the glamour with which they had been surrounded had faded, and finally there was nothing left, no foundation of childish memories to make them seem any different from other middle-aged people. Aunt Emily was never glamorous but she was always my mother, and I loved her.

At the time of which I write, however, I was at an age when the least imaginative child supposes itself to be a changeling, a Princess of Indian blood, Joan of Arc, or the future Empress of Russia. I hankered after my parents, put on an idiotic face which was intended to convey mingled suffering and pride when their names were mentioned, and thought of them as engulfed in deep, romantic, deadly sin.

Linda and I were very much preoccupied with sin, and our great hero was Oscar Wilde.

'But what did he *do?*'

'I asked Fa once and he roared at me – goodness, it was terrifying. He said: "If you mention that sewer's name again in this house I'll thrash you, do you hear, damn you?" So I asked Sadie and she looked awfully vague and said: "Oh, duck, I never really quite knew, but whatever it was was worse than murder, fearfully bad. And, darling, don't talk about him at meals, will you?" '

'We must find out.'

'Bob says he will, when he goes to Eton.'

'Oh, good! Do you think he was worse than Mummy and Daddy?'

'Surely he couldn't be. Oh, you are so lucky, to have wicked parents.'

This Christmas-time, aged fourteen, I stumbled into the hall at Alconleigh blinded by the light after a six-mile drive from Merlinford station. It was always the same every year. I always came down by the same train, arriving at tea-time, and always found Aunt Sadie and the children round the table underneath the entrenching tool, just as they were in the photograph. It was always the same table and the same tea-things; the china with large roses on it, the tea-kettle and the silver dish for scones simmering over little flames – the human beings of course were getting imperceptibly older, the babies were becoming children, the children were growing up, and there had been an addition in the shape of Victoria now aged two. She was waddling about with a chocolate biscuit clenched in her fist, her face was smothered in chocolate and was a horrible sight, but through the sticky mask shone unmistakably the blue of two steady Radlett eyes.

There was a tremendous scraping of chairs as I came in, and a pack of Radletts hurled themselves upon me with the intensity and almost the ferocity of a pack of hounds hurling itself upon a fox. All except Linda. She was the most pleased to see me, but determined not to show it. When the din had quieted down and I was seated before a scone and a cup of tea, she said:

'Where's Brenda?' Brenda was my white mouse.

'She got a sore back and died,' I said. Aunt Sadie looked anxiously at Linda.

'Had you been riding her?' said Louisa, facetiously. Matt, who had recently come under the care of a French nursery governess, said in a high-pitched imitation of her voice: '*C'était, comme d'habitude, les voies urinaires.*'

'Oh, dear,' said Aunt Sadie, under her breath.

Enormous tears were pouring into Linda's plate. Nobody cried so much or so often as she; anything, but especially anything sad about animals, would set her off, and, once begun, it was a job to stop her. She was delicate, as well as a highly nervous child, and even Aunt Sadie, who lived in a dream as far as the health of her children was concerned, was aware that too much crying kept her awake at night, put her off her food, and did her harm. The other children, and especially Louisa and Bob, who loved to tease, went as far as they dared with her, and were periodically punished for making her cry. *Black Beauty, Owd Bob, The Story of a Red Deer*, and all the Seton Thompson books were on the nursery index because of Linda, who, at one time or another, had been prostrated by them. They had to be hidden away, as, if they were left lying about, she could not be trusted not to indulge in an orgy of self-torture.

Wicked Louisa had invented a poem which never failed to induce rivers of tears:

> *A little, houseless match, it has no roof, no thatch,*
> *It lies alone, it makes no moan, that little, houseless match.*

When Aunt Sadie was not around the children would chant this in a gloomy chorus. In certain moods one had only to glance at a match-box to dissolve poor Linda; when, however, she was feeling stronger, more fit to cope with life, this sort of teasing would force out of her very stomach an unwilling guffaw. Linda was not only my favourite cousin, but, then and for many years, my favourite human being. I adored all my cousins, and Linda distilled, mentally and physically, the very essence of the Radlett family. Her straight features, straight brown hair and large blue eyes were a theme upon which the faces of the others were a variation; all pretty, but none so absolutely distinctive as hers. There was something furious about her, even when she laughed, which she did a great deal, and always as if forced to against her will. Something reminiscent of pictures of Napoleon in youth, a sort of scowling intensity.

I could see that she was really minding much more about Brenda than I did. The truth was that my honeymoon days with the mouse were long since over; we had settled down to an uninspiring relationship, a form, as it were, of married blight, and, when she had developed a disgusting sore patch on her back, it had been all I could do to behave decently and treat her with common humanity. Apart from the shock it always is to find somebody stiff and cold in their cage in the morning, it had been a very great relief to me when Brenda's sufferings finally came to an end.

'Where is she buried?' Linda muttered furiously, looking at her plate.

'Beside the robin. She's got a dear little cross and her coffin was lined with pink satin.'

'Now, Linda darling,' said Aunt Sadie, 'if Fanny has finished her tea why don't you show her your toad?'

'He's upstairs asleep,' said Linda. But she stopped crying.

'Have some nice hot toast, then.'

'Can I have Gentleman's Relish on it?' she said, quick to make capital out of Aunt Sadie's mood, for Gentleman's Relish was kept strictly for Uncle Matthew, and supposed not to be good for children. The others made a great show of exchanging significant looks. These were intercepted, as they were meant to be, by Linda, who gave a tremendous bellowing boo-boo and rushed upstairs.

'I wish you children wouldn't tease Linda,' said Aunt Sadie, irritated out of her usual gentleness, and followed her.

The staircase led out of the hall. When Aunt Sadie was beyond earshot, Louisa said: 'If wishes were horses beggars would ride. Child hunt tomorrow, Fanny.'

'Yes, Josh told me. He was in the car – been to see the vet.'

My Uncle Matthew had four magnificent bloodhounds, with which he used to hunt his children. Two of us would go off with a good start to lay the trail, and Uncle Matthew and the rest would follow the hounds on horseback. It was great fun. Once he came to my home and hunted Linda and me over Shenley Common. This caused the most tremendous stir locally, the Kentish week-enders on their way to church were appalled by the sight of four great hounds in full cry after two little girls. My uncle seemed to them like a wicked lord of fiction, and I became more than ever surrounded with an aura of madness, badness, and dangerousness for their children to know.

The child hunt on the first day of this Christmas visit was a great success. Louisa and I were chosen as hares. We ran across country, the beautiful bleak Cotswold uplands, starting soon after breakfast when the sun was still a red globe, hardly over the horizon, and the trees were etched in dark blue against a pale blue, mauve and pinkish sky. The sun rose as we stumbled on, longing for our second wind; it shone, and there dawned a beautiful day, more like late autumn in its feeling than Christmas-time.

We managed to check the bloodhounds once by running through a flock of sheep, but Uncle Matthew soon got them on the scent again, and, after about two hours of hard running on our part, when were were only half a mile from home, the baying slavering creatures caught up with us, to be rewarded with lumps of meat and many caresses. Uncle Matthew was in a radiantly good temper; he got off his horse and walked home with us, chatting agreeably. What was most unusual, he was even quite affable to me.

'I hear Brenda has died,' he said; 'no great loss I should say. That mouse stank like merry hell. I expect you kept her cage too near the radiator, I always told you it was unhealthy, or did she die of old age?'

'She was only two,' I said, timidly.

Uncle Matthew's charm, when he chose to turn it on, was considerable, but at that time I was always mortally afraid of him, and made the mistake of letting him see that I was.

'You ought to have a dormouse, Fanny, or a rat. They are much more interesting than white mice – though I must frankly say, of all the mice I ever knew, Brenda was the most utterly dismal.'

'She was dull,' I said, sycophantically.

'When I go to London after Christmas, I'll get you a dormouse. Saw one the other day at the *Army & Navy*.'

'Oh Fa, it *is* unfair,' said Linda, who was walking her pony along beside us. 'You know how I've always longed for a dormouse.'

'It is unfair' was a perpetual cry of the Radlets when young. The great advantage of living in a large family is that early lesson of life's essential unfairness. With them I must say it nearly always operated in favour of Linda, who was the adored of Uncle Matthew.

To-day, however, my uncle was angry with her, and I saw in a flash that this affability to me, this genial chat about mice, was simply designed as a tease for her.

'You've got enough animals, miss,' he said sharply. 'You can't control the ones you have got. And don't forget what I told you – that dog of yours goes straight to the kennel when we get back, and stays there.'

Linda's face crumpled, tears poured, she kicked her pony into a canter and made for home. It seemed that her dog Labby had been sick in Uncle Matthew's business-room after breakfast. Uncle Matthew was unable to bear dirtiness in dogs, he flew into a rage, and, in his rage, had made a rule that never again was Labby to set foot in the house. This was always happening, for one reason or another, to one animal or another, and, Uncle Matthew's bark being invariably much worse that his bite, the ban seldom lasted more than a day or two, after which would begin what he called the Thin End of the Wedge.

'Can I bring him in just while I fetch my gloves?'

'I'm so tired – I can't go to the stables – do let him stay just till after tea.'

'Oh, I see – the thin end of the wedge. All right, this time he can stay, but if he makes another mess – or I catch him on your bed – or he chews up the good furniture (according to whichever crime it was that had resulted in banishment), I'll have him destroyed, and don't say I didn't warn you.'

All the same, every time sentence of banishment was pronounced, the owner of the condemned would envisage her beloved moping his life away in the solitary confinement of a cold and gloomy kennel.

'Even if I take him out for three hours every day, and go and chat to him for another hour, that leaves twenty hours for him all alone with nothing to do. Oh, why can't dogs read?'

The Radlett children, it will be observed, took a highly anthropomorphic view of their pets.

To-day, however, Uncle Matthew was in a wonderfully good temper, and, as we left the stables, he said to Linda, who was sitting crying with Labby in his kennel:

'Are you going to leave that poor brute of yours in there all day?'

Her tears forgotten as if they had never been, Linda rushed into the house with Labby at her heels. The Radletts were always either on a peak of happiness or drowning in black waters of despair; their emotions were on no ordinary plane, they loved or they loathed, they laughed or they cried, they lived in a world of superlatives. Their life with Uncle Matthew was a sort of perpetual Tom Tiddler's ground. They went as far as they dared, sometimes very far indeed, while sometimes, for no apparent reason, he would pounce almost before they had crossed the boundary. Had they been poor children they would probably have been removed from their roaring, raging, whacking papa and sent to an approved home, or, indeed, he himself would have been removed from them and sent to prison for refusing to educate them. Nature, however, provides her own remedies, and no doubt the Radletts had enough of Uncle Matthew in them to enable them to weather storms in which ordinary children like me would have lost their nerve completely.

The Triumph of Moby Dick
HERMAN MELVILLE

*Captain Ahab's insane pursuit of the great white whale cul-
minates in a dramatic three-day chase. The reluctant crew of
the Pequod, urged on by the offer of a gold doubloon for the
first man to sight Moby Dick's snowy hump, prepares for the
final struggle . . .*

LIKE NOISELESS NAUTILUS shells, their light prows sped through the sea;
but only slowly they neared the foe. As they neared him, the ocean grew
still more smooth; seemed drawing a carpet over its waves; seemed a
noon-meadow, so serenely it spread. At length the breathless hunter came
so nigh his seemingly unsuspecting prey, that his entire dazzling hump
was distinctly visible, sliding along the sea as if an isolated thing, and
continually set in a revolving ring of finest, fleecy, greenish foam. He saw
the vast, involved wrinkles of the slightly projecting head beyond. Before
it, far out on the soft Turkish-rugged waters, went the glistening white
shadow from his broad, milky forehead, a musical rippling playfully
accompanying the shade; and behind, the blue waters interchangeably
flowed over into the moving valley of his steady wake; and on either hand
bright bubbles arose and danced by his side. But these were broken again
by the light toes of hundreds of gay fowl softly feathering the sea,
alternate with their fitful flight; and like to some flagstaff rising from the
painted hull of an argosy, the tall but shattered pole of a recent lance
projected from the white whale's back; and at intervals one of the cloud
of soft-toed fowls hovering, and to and fro skimming like a canopy over
the fish, silently perched and rocked on this pole, the long tail feathers
streaming like pennons.

A gentle joyousness – a mighty mildness of repose in swiftness, invested the gliding whale. Not the white bull Jupiter swimming away with ravished Europa clinging to his graceful horns; his lovely, leering eyes sideways intent upon the maid; with smooth bewitching fleetness, rippling straight for the nuptial bower in Crete; not Jove, not that great majesty Supreme! did surpass the glorified White Whale as he so divinely swam.

On each soft side – coincident with the parted swell, that but once laving him, then flowed so wide away – on each bright side, the whale shed off enticings. No wonder there had been some among the hunters who namelessly transported and allured by all this serenity, had ventured to assail it; but had fatally found that quietude but the vesture of tornadoes. Yet calm, enticing calm, oh whale! thou glidest on, to all who for the first time eye thee, no matter how many in that same way thou may'st have bejuggled and destroyed before.

And thus, through the serene tranquilities of the tropical sea, among waves whose hand-clappings were suspended by exceeding rapture, Moby Dick moved on, still withholding from sight the full terrors of his submerged trunk, entirely hiding the wrenched hideousness of his jaw. But soon the fore part of him slowly rose from the water; for an instant his whole marbleized body formed a high arch, like Virginia's Natural Bridge, and warningly waving his bannered flukes in the air, the grand god revealed himself, sounded, and went out of sight. Hoveringly halting, and dipping on the wing, the white sea-fowls longingly lingered over the agitated pool that he left.

With oars apeak, and paddles down, the sheets of their sails adrift, the three boats now stilly floated, awaiting Moby Dick's reappearance.

'An hour,' said Ahab, standing rooted in his boat's stern; and he gazed beyond the whale's place, towards the dim blue spaces and wide wooing vacancies to leeward. It was only an instant; for again his eyes seemed whirling round in his head as he swept the watery circle. The breeze now freshened; the sea began to swell.

'The birds! – the birds!' cried Tashtego.

In long Indian file, as when herons take wing, the white birds were now all flying towards Ahab's boat; and when within a few yards began fluttering over the water there, wheeling round and round, with joyous, expectant cries. Their vision was keener than man's; Ahab could discover no sign in the sea. But suddenly as he peered down and down into its depths, he profoundly saw a white living spot no bigger than a white weasel, with wonderful celerity uprising, and magnifying as it rose, till it turned, and then there were plainly revealed two long crooked rows of white, glistening teeth, floating up from the undiscoverable bottom. It was Moby Dick's open mouth and scrolled jaw; his vast, shadowed bulk still half blending with the blue of the sea. The glittering mouth yawned beneath the boat like an open-doored marble tomb; and giving one sidelong sweep with his steering oar, Ahab whirled the craft aside from this tremendous apparition. Then, calling upon Fedallah to change places with him, went forward to the bows, and seizing Perth's harpoon, commanded his crew to grasp their oars and stand by to stern.

Now, by reason of this timely spinning round the boat upon its axis, its bow, by anticipation, was made to face the whale's head while yet under water. But as if perceiving this stratagem, Moby Dick, with that malicious intelligence ascribed to him, sidelingly transplanted himself, as it were, in an instant, shooting his pleated head lengthwise beneath the boat.

Through and through; through every plank and each rib, it thrilled for an instant, the whale obliquely lying on his back, in the manner of a biting shark, slowly and feelingly taking its bows full within his mouth, so that the long, narrow, scrolled lower jaw curled high up into the open air, and one of the teeth caught in a row-lock. The bluish pearl-white of the inside of the jaw was within six inches of Ahab's head, and reached higher than that. In this attitude the White Whale now shook the slight cedar as a mildly cruel cat her mouse. With unastonished eyes Fedallah gazed, and crossed his arms; but the tiger-yellow crew were tumbling over each other's heads to gain the uttermost stern.

And now, while both elastic gunwales were springing in and out, as the whale dallied with the doomed craft in this devilish way; and from his body being submerged beneath the boat, he could not be darted at from the bows, for the bows were almost inside of him, as it were; and while the other boats involuntarily paused, as before a quick crisis impossible to withstand, then it was that monomaniac Ahab, furious with this tantalizing vicinity of his foe, which placed him all alive and helpless in the very jaws he hated; frenzied with all this, he seized the long bone with his naked hands, and wildly strove to wrench it from its gripe. As now he thus vainly strove, the jaw slipped from him; the frail gunwales bent in, collapsed, and snapped, as both jaws, like an enormous shears, sliding further aft, bit the craft completely in twain, and locked themselves fast again in the sea, midway between the two floating wrecks. These floated aside, the broken ends drooping, the crew at the stern-wreck clinging to the gunwales, and striving to hold fast to the oars to lash them across.

At that preluding moment, ere the boat was yet snapped, Ahab, the first to perceive the whale's intent, by the crafty upraising of his head, a movement that loosed his hold for the time; at that moment his hand had made one final effort to push the boat out of the bite. But only slipping further into the whale's mouth, and tilting over sideways as it slipped, the boat had shaken off his hold on the jaw; spilled him out of it, as he leaned to the push; and so he fell flat-faced upon the sea.

Ripplingly withdrawing from his prey, Moby Dick now lay at a little distance, vertically thrusting his oblong white head up and down in the billows; and at the same time slowly revolving his whole spindled body; so that when his vast wrinkled forehead rose – some twenty or more feet out of the water – the now rising swells, with all their confluent waves, dazzlingly broke against it; vindictively tossing their shivered spray still higher into the air.* So, in a gale, the but half baffled Channel billows only recoil from the base of the Eddystone, triumphantly to overleap its summit with their scud.

But soon resuming his horizontal attitude, Moby Dick swam swiftly round and round the wrecked crew; sideways churning the water in his vengeful wake, as if lashing himself up to still another and more deadly assault. The sight of the splintered boat seemed to madden him, as the blood of grapes and mulberries cast before Antiochus's elephants in the book of Maccabees. Meanwhile Ahab half smothered in the foam of the whale's insolent tail, and too much of a cripple to swim, – though he could still keep afloat, even in the heart of such a whirlpool as that; helpless Ahab's head was seen, like a tossed bubble which the least chance shock might burst. From the boat's fragmentary stern, Fedallah incuriously and mildly eyed him; the clinging crew, at the other drifting end, could not succour him; more than enough was it for them to look to themselves. For so revolvingly appalling was the White Whale's aspect, and so planetarily swift the ever-contracting circles he made, that he seemed horizontally swooping upon them. And though the other boats, unharmed, still hovered hard by; still they dared not pull into the eddy to strike, lest that should be the signal for the instant destruction of the jeopardized castaways, Ahab and all; nor in that case could they themselves hope to escape. With straining eyes, then, they remained on the outer edge of the direful zone, whose centre had now become the old man's head.

Meantime, from the beginning all this had been descried from the ship's mast heads; and squaring her yards, she had borne down upon the scene; and was now so nigh, that Ahab in the water hailed her; – 'Sail on the' – but that moment a breaking sea dashed on him from Moby Dick, and whelmed him for the time. But struggling out of it again, and chancing to rise on a towering crest, he shouted, – 'Sail on the whale! – Drive him off!'

The Pequod's prow was pointed; and breaking up the charmed circle, she effectually parted the white whale from his victim, As he sullenly swam off, the boats flew to the rescue.

Dragged into Stubb's boat with blood-shot, blinded eyes, the white brine caking in his wrinkles; the long tension of Ahab's bodily strength did crack, and helplessly he yielded to his body's doom: for a time, lying all crushed in the bottom of Stubb's boat, like one trodden under foot of

*This motion is peculiar to the sperm whale. It receives its designation (pitch-poling) from its being likened to that preliminary up-and-down poise of the whale-lance, in the exercise called pitchpoling, previously described. By this motion the whale must best and most comprehensively view whatever objects may be encircling him.

herds of elephants. Far inland, nameless wails came from him, as desolate sounds from out ravines.

But this intensity of his physical prostration did but so much the more abbreviate it. In an instant's compass, great hearts sometimes condense to one deep pang, the sum total of those shallow pains kindly diffused through feebler men's whole lives. And so, such hearts, though summary in each one suffering; still, if the gods decree it, in their life-time aggregate a whole age of woe, wholly made up of instantaneous intensities; for even in their pointless centres, those noble natures contain the entire circumferences of inferior souls.

'The harpoon,' said Ahab, half way rising, and draggingly leaning on one bended arm – 'is it safe?'

'Aye, sir, for it was not darted; this is it,' said Stubb, showing it.

'Lay it before me; – any missing men?'

'One, two, three, four, five; – there were five oars, sir, and here are five men.'

'That's good. – Help me, man; I wish to stand. So, so, I see him! there! there! going to leeward still; what a leaping spout! – Hands off from me! The eternal sap runs up in Ahab's bones again! Set the sail; out oars; the helm!'

It is often the case that when a boat is stove, its crew, being picked up by another boat, help to work that second boat; and the chase is thus continued with what is called double-banked oars. It was thus now. But the added power of the boat did not equal the added power of the whale, for he seemed to have treble-banked his every fin; swimming with a velocity which plainly showed, that if now, under these circumstances, pushed on, the chase would prove an indefinitely prolonged, if not a hopeless one; nor could any crew endure for so long a period, such an unintermitted, intense straining at the oar; a thing barely tolerable only in some one brief vicissitude. The ship itself, then, as it sometimes happens, offered the most promising intermediate means of overtaking the chase. Accordingly, the boats now made for her, and were soon swayed up to their cranes – the two parts of the wrecked boat having been previously secured by her – and then hoisting everything to her side, and stacking her canvas high up, and sideways outstretching it with stun-sails, like the double-jointed wings of an albatross; the Pequod bore down in the leeward wake of Moby Dick. At the well known, methodic intervals, the whale's glittering spout was regularly announced from the manned mast-heads; and when he would be reported as just gone down, Ahab would take the time, and then pacing the deck, binnacle-watch in hand, so soon as the last second of the allotted hour expired, his voice was heard. – 'Whose is the doubloon now? D'ye see him?' and if the reply was, No, sir! straightway he commanded them to lift him to his perch. In this way the day wore on; Ahab, now aloft and motionless; anon, unrestingly pacing the planks.

As he was thus walking, uttering no sound, except to hail the men aloft, or to bid them hoist a sail still higher, or to spread one to a still greater breadth – thus to and fro pacing, beneath his slouched hat, at every turn he passed his own wrecked boat, which had been dropped upon the quarterdeck, and lay there reversed; broken bow to shattered stern. At last he paused before it; and as in an already over-clouded sky fresh troops of clouds will sometimes sail across, so over the old man's face there now stole some such added gloom as this.

Stubb saw him pause; and perhaps intending, not vainly, though, to evince his own unabated fortitude, and thus keep up a valiant place in his Captain's mind, he advanced, and eyeing the wreck exclaimed – 'The thistle the ass refused; it pricked his mouth too keenly, sir; ha! ha!'

'What soulless thing is this that laughs before a wreck? Man, man! did I not know thee brave as fearless fire (and as mechanical) I could swear thou wert a poltroon. Groan nor laugh should be heard before a wreck.'

'Aye, sir,' said Starbuck drawing near, ''tis a solemn sight; an omen, and an ill one.'

'Omen? omen? – the dictionary! If the gods think to speak outright to man, they will honorably speak outright; not shake their heads, and give an old wives' darkling hint. – Begone! Ye two are the opposite poles of one thing; Starbuck is Stubb reversed, and Stubb is Starbuck; and ye two are all mankind; and Ahab stands alone among the millions of the peopled earth, nor gods nor men his neighbours! Cold, cold – I shiver! – How now? Aloft there? D'ye see him? Sing out for every spout, though he spout ten times a second!'

The day was nearly done; only the hem of his golden robe was rustling. Soon, it was almost dark, but the look-out men still remained unset.

'Can't see the spout now, sir; – too dark' – cried a voice from the air.

'How heading when last seen?'

'As before, sir – straight to leeward.'

'Good! he will travel slower now 'tis night. Down royals and top-gallant stun-sails, Mr. Starbuck. We must not run over him before morning; he's making a passage now, and may heave-to a while. Helm there! keep her full before the wind! – Aloft! come down! – Mr. Stubb, send a fresh hand to the fore-mast head, and see it manned till morning.' – Then advancing towards the doubloon in the main-mast – 'Men, this gold is mine, for I earned it; but I shall let it abide here till the White Whale is dead; and then, whosoever of ye first raises him, upon the day he shall be killed, this gold is that man's; and if on that day I shall again raise him, then ten times its sum shall be divided among all of ye! Away now! – the deck is thine, sir.'

And so saying, he placed himself half way within the scuttle, and slouching his hat, stood there still dawn, except when at intervals rousing himself to see how the night wore on.

At day-break, the three mast-heads were punctually manned afresh.

'D'ye see him?' cried Ahab, after allowing a little space for the light to spread.

'See nothing, sir.'

'Turn up all hands and make sail! he travels faster than I thought for; – the top-gallant sails! – aye, they should have been kept on her all night. But no matter – 'tis but resting for the rush.'

Here be it said, that this pertinacious pursuit of one particular whale, continued through day into night, and through night into day, is a thing by no means unprecedented in the South sea fishery. For such is the wonderful skill, prescience of experience, and invincible confidence acquired by some great natural geniuses among the Nantucket commanders; that from the simple observation of a whale when last descried, they will, under certain given circumstances, pretty accurately foretell both the direction in which he will continue to swim for a time, while out of sight, as well as his probable rate of progression during that period. And, in these cases, somewhat as a pilot, when about losing sight of a coast, whose general trending he well knows, and which he desires shortly to return to again, but at some further point; like as this pilot stands by his compass, and takes the precise bearing of the cape at present visible, in order the more certainly to hit aright the remote, unseen headland, eventually to be visited: so does the fisherman, at his compass, with the whale; for after being chased, and diligently marked, through several hours of daylight, then, when night obscures the fish, the creature's future wake through the darkness is almost as established to the sagacious mind of the hunter, as the pilot's coast is to him. So that to this hunter's wondrous skill, the proverbial evanescence of a thing writ in water, a wake, is to all desired purposes well nigh as reliable as the steadfast land. And as the mighty iron Leviathan of the modern railway is so familiarly known in its every pace, that, with watches in their hands, men time his rate as doctors that of a baby's pulse; and lightly say of it, the up train or the down train will reach such or such a spot, at such or such an hour; even so, almost, there are occasions when these Nantucketers time that other Leviathan of the deep, according to the observed humor of his speed; and say to themselves, so many hours hence this whale will have gone two hundred miles, will have about reached this or that degree of latitude or longitude. But to render this acuteness at all successful in the end, the wind and the sea must be the whaleman's allies; for of what present avail to the becalmed or windbound mariner is the skill that assures him he is exactly ninety-three leagues and a quarter from his port? Inferable from these statements, are many collateral subtile matters touching the chase of whales.

The ship tore on; leaving such a furrow in the sea as when a cannon-ball, missent, becomes a plough-share and turns up the level field.

'By salt and hemp!' cried Stubb, 'but this swift motion of the deck creeps up one's legs and tingles at the heart. This ship and I are two brave fellows! - Ha! ha! Some one take me up, and launch me, spinewise, on the sea, - for by live-oaks! my spine's a keel. Ha, ha! we go the gait that leaves no dust behind!'

'There she blows - she blows! - she blows! - right ahead!' was now the mast-head cry.

'Aye, aye!' cried Stubb, 'I knew it - ye can't escape - blow on and split your spout, O whale! the mad fiend himself is after ye! blow your trump - blister your lungs! - Ahab will dam off your blood, as a miller shuts his water-gate upon the stream!'

And Stubb did but speak out for well nigh all that crew. The frenzies of the chase had by this time worked them bubblingly up, like old wine worked anew. Whatever pale fears and forebodings some of them might have felt before; these were not only now kept out of sight through the growing awe of Ahab, but they were broken up, and on all sides routed, as timid prairie hares that scatter before the bounding bison. The hand of Fate had snatched all their souls; and by the stirring perils of the previous day; the rack of the past night's suspense; the fixed, unfearing, blind, reckless way in which their wild craft went plunging towards its flying mark; by all these things, their hearts were bowled along. The wind that made great bellies of their sails, and rushed the vessel on by arms invisible as irresistible; this seemed the symbol of that unseen agency which so enslaved them to the race.

They were one man, not thirty. For as the one ship that held them all; though it was put together of all contrasting things - oak, and maple, and pine wood; iron, and pitch, and hemp - yet all these ran into each other in the one concrete hull, which shot on its way, both balanced and directed by the long central keel; even so, all the individualities of the crew, this man's valor, that man's fear; guilt and guiltiness, all varieties were welded into oneness, and were all directed to that fatal goal which Ahab their one lord and keel did point to.

The rigging lived. The mast-heads, like the tops of tall palms, were outspreadingly tufted with arms and legs. Clinging to a spar with one hand, some reached forth the other with impatient wavings; others, shading their eyes from the vivid sunlight, sat far out on the rocking yards; all the spars in full bearing of mortals, ready and ripe for their fate. Ah! how they still strove through that infinite blueness to seek out the thing that might destroy them!

'Why sing ye not out for him, if ye see him?' cried Ahab, when, after the lapse of some minutes since the first cry, no more had been heard. 'Sway me up, men; ye have been deceived; not Moby Dick casts one odd jet that way, and then disappears.'

It was even so; in their headlong eagerness, the men had mistaken some other thing for the whale-spout, as the event itself soon proved; for hardly had Ahab reached his perch; hardly was the rope belayed to its pin on deck, when he struck the key-note to an orchestra, that made the air vibrate as with the combined discharges of rifles. The triumphant halloo of thirty buckskin lungs was heard, as – much nearer to the ship than the place of the imaginary jet, less than a mile ahead – Moby Dick bodily burst into view! For not by any calm and indolent spoutings; not by the peaceable gush of that mystic fountain in his head, did the White Whale now reveal his vicinity; but by the far more wondrous phenomenon of breaching. Rising with his utmost velocity from the furthest depths, the Sperm Whale thus booms his entire bulk into the pure element of air, and piling up a mountain of dazzling foam, shows his place to the distance of seven miles and more. In those moments, the torn, enraged waves he shakes off, seem his mane; in some cases, this breaching is his act of defiance.

'There she breaches! there she breaches!' was the cry, as in his immeasurable bravadoes the White Whale tossed himself salmon-like to Heaven. So suddenly seen in the blue plain of the sea, and relieved against the still bluer margin of the sky, the spray that he raised, for the moment, intolerably glittered and glared like a glacier; and stood there gradually fading and fading away from its first sparkling intensity, to the dim mistiness of an advancing shower in a vale.

'Aye, breach your last to the sun, Moby Dick!' cried Ahab, 'thy hour and thy harpoon are at hand! – Down! down all of ye, but one man at the fore. The boats! – stand by!'

Unmindful of the tedious rope-ladders of the shrouds, the men, like shooting stars, slid to the deck, by the isolated backstays and halyards; while Ahab, less dartingly, but still rapidly was dropped from his perch.

'Lower away,' he cried, so soon as he had reached his boat – a spare one, rigged the afternoon previous. 'Mr. Starbuck, the ship is thine – keep away from the boats, but keep near them. Lower, all!'

As if to strike a quick terror into them, by this time being the first assailant himself, Moby Dick had turned, and was now coming for the three crews. Ahab's boat was central; and cheering his men, he told them he would take the whale head-and-head, – that is, pull straight up to his forehead, – a not uncommon thing; for when within a certain limit, such a course excludes the coming onset from the whale's sidelong vision. But ere that close limit was gained, and while yet all three boats were plain as the ship's three masts to his eye; the White Whale churning himself into furious speed, almost in an instant as it were, rushing among the boats with open jaws, and a lashing tail, offered appalling battle on every side; and heedless of the irons darted at him from every boat, seemed only intent on annihilating each separate plank of which those boats were made. But skilfully manoeuvred, incessantly wheeling like trained chargers in the field; the boats for a while eluded him; though, at times, but by a plank's breadth; while all the time, Ahab's unearthly slogan tore every other cry but his to shreds.

But at last in his untraceable evolutions, the White Whale so crossed and recrossed, and in a thousand ways entangled the slack of the three lines now fast to him, that they fore-shortened, and, of themselves, warped the devoted boats towards the planted irons in him; though now for a moment the whale drew aside a little, as if to rally for a more tremendous charge. Seizing that opportunity, Ahab first paid out more line: and then was rapidly hauling and jerking in upon it again – hoping that way to disencumber it of some snarls – when lo! – a sight more savage than the embattled teeth of sharks!

Caught and twisted – corkscrewed in the mazes of the line, loose harpoons and lances, with all their bristling barbs and points, came flashing and dripping up the chocks in the bows of Ahab's boat. Only one thing could be done. Seizing the boat-knife, he critically reached within – through – and then, without – the rays of steel; dragged in the line beyond, passed it, inboard, to the bowsman, and then, twice sundering the rope near the chocks – dropped the intercepted fagot of steel into the sea; and was all fast again. That instant, the White Whale made a sudden rush among the remaining tangles of the other lines; by so doing, irresistibly dragged the more involved boats of the Stubb and Flask towards his flukes; dashed them together like two rolling husks on a surf-beaten beach, and then, diving down into the sea, disappeared in a boiling maelstrom, in which, for a space, the odorous cedar chips of the wrecks danced round and round, like the grated nutmeg in a swiftly stirred bowl of punch.

While the two crews were yet circling in the waters, reaching out after the revolving line-tubs, oars, and other floating furniture, while aslope little Flask bobbed up and down like an empty vial, twitching his legs upwards to escape the dreaded jaws of sharks; and Stubb was lustily singing out for some one to ladle him up; and while the old man's line – now parting – admitted of his pulling into the creamy pool to rescue whom he could; – in that wild simultaneousness of a thousand concreted perils, – Ahab's yet unstricken boat seemed drawn up towards Heaven by invisible wires, – as, arrow-like, shooting perpendicularly from the sea, the White Whale dashed his broad forehead against its bottom, and sent it, turning over and over, into the air; till it fell again – gunwale downwards – and Ahab and his men struggled out from under it, like seals from a sea-side cave.

The first uprising momentum of the whale – modifying its direction as he struck the surface – involuntarily launched him along it, to a little distance from the centre of the destruction he had made; and with his back to it, he now lay for a moment slowly feeling with his flukes from side to side; and whenever a stray oar, bit of plank, the least chip or crumb of the boats touched his skin, his tail swiftly drew back, and came sideways smiting the sea. But soon, as if satisfied that his work for that time was done, he pushed his pleated forehead through the ocean, and trailing after him the intertangled lines, continued his leeward way at a traveller's methodic pace.

As before, the attentive ship having descried the whole fight, again came bearing down to the rescue, and dropping a boat, picked up the floating mariners, tubs, oars, and whatever else could be caught at, and safely landed them on her decks. Some sprained shoulders, wrists, and ankles; livid contusions; wrenched harpoons and lances; inextricable intricacies of rope; shattered oars and planks; all these were there; but no fatal or even serious ill seemed to have befallen any one. As with Fedallah the day before, so Ahab was now found grimly clinging to his boat's broken half, which afforded a comparatively easy float; nor did it so exhaust him as the previous day's mishap.

But when he was helped to the deck, all eyes were fastened upon him; as instead of standing by himself he still half-hung upon the shoulder of Starbuck, who had thus far been the foremost to assist him. His ivory leg had been snapped off, leaving but one short sharp splinter.

'Aye aye, Starbuck, 'tis sweet to lean sometimes, be the leaner who he will; and would old Ahab had leaned oftener than he has.'

'The ferrule has not stood, sir,' said the carpenter, now coming up; 'I put good work into that leg.'

'But no bones broken, sir, I hope,' said Stubb with true concern.

'Aye! and all splintered to pieces, Stubb! – d'ye see it. – But even with a broken bone, old Ahab is untouched; and I account no living bone of mine one jot more me, than this dead one that's lost. Nor white whale, nor man, nor fiend, can so much as graze old Ahab in his own proper and inaccessible being. Can any lead touch yonder floor, any mast scrape yonder roof? – Aloft there! which way?'

'Dead to leeward, sir.'

'Up helm, then; pile on the sail again, ship keepers! down the rest of the spare boats and rig them – Mr. Starbuck away, and muster the boats' crews.'

'Let me first help thee towards the bulwarks, sir.'

'Oh, oh, oh! how this splinter gores me now! Accursed fate! that the unconquerable captain in the soul should have such a craven mate!'

'Sir?'

'My body, man, not thee. Give me something for a cane – there, that shivered lance will do. Muster the men. Surely I have not seen him yet. By heaven it cannot be! – missing? – quick! call them all.'

The old man's hinted thought was true. Upon mustering the company, the Parsee was not there.

'The Parsee!' cried Stubb – 'He must have been caught in—'

'The black vomit wrench thee! – run all of ye above, alow, cabin, forecastle – find him – not gone – not gone!'

But quickly they returned to him with the tidings that the Parsee was nowhere to be found.

'Aye, sir,' said Stubb – 'caught among the tangles of your line – I thought I saw him dragging under.'

'*My* line! *my* line? Gone? – gone? What means that little word? – What death-knell rings in it, that old Ahab shakes as if he were the belfry. The harpoon, too! – toss over the litter there, – d'ye see it? – the forged iron, men, the white whale's – no, no, no, – blistered fool! this hand did dart it! – 'tis in the fish! – Aloft there! Keep him nailed – Quick! – all hands to the rigging of the boats – collect the oars – harpooneers! the irons, the irons! – hoist the royals higher – a pull on all the sheets! – helm there! steady, steady for your life! I'll ten times girdle the unmeasured globe; yea and dive straight through it, but I'll slay him yet!'

'Great God! but for one single instant show thyself,' cried Starbuck; 'never, never wilt thou capture him, old man – In Jesus' name no more of this, that's worse than devil's madness. Two days chased; twice stove to splinters; thy very leg once more snatched from under thee; thy evil shadow gone – all good angels mobbing thee with warnings: – what more wouldst thou have? – Shall we keep chasing this murderous fish till he swamps the last man? Shall we be dragged by him to the bottom of the sea? Shall we be towed by him to the infernal world? Oh, oh, – Impiety and blasphemy to hunt him more!'

'Starbuck, of late I've felt strangely moved to thee; ever since that hour we both saw – thou know'st what, in one another's eyes. But in this matter of the whale, be the front of thy face to me as the palm of this hand – a lipless, unfeatured blank. Ahab is for ever Ahab, man. This whole act's immutably decreed. 'Twas rehearsed by thee and me a billion years before this ocean rolled. Fool! I am the Fates' lieutenant; I act under orders. Look thou, underling! that thou obeyest mine. – Stand round me, men. Ye see an old man cut down to the stump; leaning on a shivered lance; propped up on a lonely foot. 'Tis Ahab – his body's part; but Ahab's soul's a centipede, that moves upon a hundred legs. I feel strained, half stranded, as ropes that tow dismasted frigates in a gale; and I may look so. But ere I break, ye'll hear me crack; and till ye hear *that*, know that Ahab's hawser tows his purpose yet. Believe ye, men, in the things called omens? Then laugh aloud, and cry encore! For ere they drown, drowning things will twice rise to the surface; then rise again, to sink for evermore. So with Moby Dick – two days he's floated – tomorrow will be the third. Aye, men, he'll rise once more, – but only to spout his last! D'ye feel brave, men, brave?'

'As fearless fire,' cried Stubb.

'And as mechanical,' muttered Ahab. Then as the men went forward, he muttered on: – 'The things called omens! And yesterday I talked the same to Starbuck there, concerning my broken boat. Oh! how valiantly

I seek to drive out of others' hearts what's clinched so fast in mine! – The Parsee – the Parsee! – gone, gone? and he was to go before: – but still was to be seen again ere I could perish – How's that? – There's a riddle now might baffle all the lawyers backed by the ghosts of the whole line of judges: – like a hawk's beak it pecks my brain. *I'll, I'll* solve it, though!'

When dusk descended, the whale was still in sight to leeward.

So once more the sail was shortened, and everything passed nearly as on the previous night; only, the sound of hammers, and the hum of the grindstone was heard till nearly daylight, as the men toiled by lanterns in the complete and careful rigging of the spare boats and sharpening their fresh weapons for the morrow. Meantime, of the broken keel of Ahab's wrecked craft the carpenter made him another leg; while still as on the night before, slouched Ahab stood fixed within his scuttle; his hid, heliotrope glance anticipatingly gone backward on its dial; set due eastward for the earliest sun.

The morning of the third day dawned fair and fresh, and once more the solitary night-man at the fore-mast-head was relieved by crowds of the daylight look-outs, who dotted every mast and almost every spar.

'D'ye see him?' cried Ahab; but the whale was not yet in sight.

'In his infallible wake, though; but follow that wake, that's all. Helm there; steady, as thou goest, and hast been going. What a lovely day again! were it a new-made world, and made for a summer-house to the angels, and this morning the first of its throwing open to them, a fairer day could not dawn upon that world. Here's food for thought, had Ahab time to think; but Ahab never thinks; he only feels, feels, feels; *that's* tingling enough for mortal man! to think's audacity. God only has that right and privilege. Thinking is, or ought to be, a coolness and a calmness; and our poor hearts throb, and our poor brains beat too much for that. And yet, I've sometimes thought my brain was very calm – frozen calm, this old skull cracks so, like a glass in which the contents turn to ice, and shiver it. And still this hair is growing now; this moment growing, and heat must breed it; but no, it's like that sort of common grass that will grow anywhere, between the earthy clefts of Greenland ice or in Vesuvius' lava. How the wild winds blow it; they whip it about me as the torn shreds of split sails lash the tossed ship they cling to. A vile wind that has no doubt blown ere this through prison corridors and cells, and wards of hospitals, and ventilated them, and now comes blowing hither as innocent as fleeces. Out upon it! – it's tainted. Were I the wind, I'd blow no more on such a wicked, miserable world. I'd crawl somewhere to a cave, and slink there. And yet, 'tis a noble and heroic thing, the wind! who ever conquered it? In every fight it has the last and bitterest blow. Run tilting at it, and you but run through it. Ha! a coward wind that strikes stark naked men, but will not stand to receive a single blow. Even Ahab is a braver thing – a nobler thing than *that*. Would now the wind but had a body; but all the things that most exasperate and outrage mortal man, all these things are bodiless, but only bodiless as objects, not as agents. There's a most special, a most cunning, oh, a most malicious difference! And yet, I say again, and swear it now, that there's something all glorious and gracious in the wind. These warm Trade Winds, at least, that in the clear heavens blow straight on, in strong and steadfast, vigorous mildness; and veer not from their mark, however the baser currents of the sea may turn and tack, and mightiest Mississippies of the land shift and swerve about, uncertain where to go at last. And by the eternal Poles! these same Trades that so directly blow my good ship on; these Trades, or something like them – something so unchangeable, and full as strong, blow my keeled soul along! To it! Aloft there! What d'ye see?'

'Nothing, sir.'

'Nothing! and noon at hand! The doubloon goes a-begging! See the sun! Aye, aye, it must be so. I've oversailed him. How, got the start? Aye, he's chasing *me* now; not I, *him* – that's bad; I might have known it, too. Fool! the lines – the harpoons he's towing. Aye, aye, I have run him by last night. About! about! Come down, all of ye, but the regular look outs! Man the braces!'

Steering as she had done, the wind had been somewhat on the Pequod's quarter, so that now being pointed in the reverse direction, the braced ship sailed hard upon the breeze as she rechurned the cream in her own white wake.

'Against the wind he now steers for the open jaw,' murmured Starbuck to himself, as he coiled the new-hauled main-brace upon the rail. 'God keep us, but already my bones feel damp within me, and from the inside wet my flesh. I misdoubt me that I disobey my God in obeying him!'

'Stand by to sway me up!' cried Ahab, advancing to the hempen basket. 'We should meet him soon.'

'Aye, aye, sir,' and straightway Starbuck did Ahab's bidding, and once more Ahab swung on high.

A whole hour now passed; gold-beaten out to ages. Time itself now held long breaths with keen suspense. But at last, some three points off the weather bow, Ahab described the spout again, and instantly from the three mast-heads three shrieks went up as if the tongues of fire had voiced it.

'Forehead to forehead I meet thee, this third time, Moby Dick! On deck there! – brace sharper up; crowd her into the wind's eye. He's too far off to lower yet, Mr. Starbuck. The sails shake! Stand over that helmsman with a topmaul! So, so; he travels fast, and I must down. But let me have one more good round look aloft here at the sea; there's time for that. An old, old sight, and yet somehow so young; aye, and not changed a wink since I first saw it, a boy, from the sand-hills of Nantucket! The same! – the same! – the same to Noah as to me. There's a soft shower to leeward. Such lovely leewardings! They must lead somewhere – to something else than common land, more palmy than the palms. Leeward! the white whale goes that way; to look to windward, then; the better if the bitterer quarter. But good bye, good bye, old mast-head! What's this? – green? aye, tiny mosses in these warped cracks. No such green weather stains on Ahab's head! There's the difference now between man's old age and matter's. But aye, old mast, we both grow old together; sound in our hulls, though, are we not, my ship? Aye, minus a leg, that's all. By heaven this dead wood has the better of my live flesh every way. I can't compare with it; and I've known some ships made of dead trees outlast the lives of men made of the most vital stuff of vital fathers. What's that he said? he should still go before me, my pilot; and yet to be seen again? But where? Will I have eyes at the bottom of the sea, supposing I descend those endless stairs? and all night I've been sailing from him, wherever he did sink to. Aye, aye, like many more thou told'st direful truth as touching thyself, O Parsee; but, Ahab, there thy shot fell short. Good by, masthead – keep a good eye upon the whale, the while I'm gone. We'll talk to-morrow, nay, to-night, when the white whale lies down there, tied by head and tail.'

He gave the word; and still gazing round him, was steadily lowered through the cloven blue air to the deck.

In due time the boats were lowered; but as standing in his shallop's stern, Ahab just hovered upon the point of the descent, he waved to the mate, – who held one of the tackle-ropes on deck – and bade him pause.

'Starbuck!'

'Sir?'

'For the third time my soul's ship starts upon this voyage, Starbuck.'

'Aye, sir, thou wilt have it so.'

'Some ships sail from their ports, and ever afterwards are missing, Starbuck!'

'Truth, sir: saddest truth.'

'Some men die at ebb tide; some at low water; some at the full of the flood; – and I feel now like a billow that's all one crested comb, Starbuck. I am old; – shake hands with me, man.'

Their hands met; their eyes fastened; Starbuck's tears the glue.

'Oh, my captain, my captain! – noble heart – go not – go not! – see, it's a brave man that weeps; how great the agony of the persuasion then!'

'Lower away!' – cried Ahab, tossing the mate's arm from him. 'Stand by the crew!'

In an instant the boat was pulling round close under the stern.

'The sharks! the sharks!' cried a voice from the low cabin-window there; 'O master, my master, come back!'

But Ahab heard nothing; for his own voice was high-lifted then; and the boat leaped on.

Yet the voice spake true; for scarce had he pushed from the ship, when numbers of sharks, seemingly rising from out the dark waters beneath the hull, maliciously snapped at the blades of the oars, every time they dipped in the water; and in this way accompanied the boat with their bites. It is a thing not uncommonly happening to the whale-boats in those swarming seas; the sharks at times apparently following them in the same prescient way that vultures hover over the banners of marching regiments in the east. But these were the first sharks that had been observed by the Pequod since the White Whale had been first descried; and whether it was that Ahab's crew were all such tiger-yellow barbarians, and therefore their flesh more musky to the senses of the sharks – a matter sometimes well known to affect them, – however it was, they seemed to follow that one boat without molesting the others.

'Heart of wrought steel!' murmured Starbuck gazing over the side, and following with his eyes the receding boat – 'canst thou yet ring boldly to that sight? – lowering thy keel among ravening sharks, and followed by them, open-mouthed to the chase; and this the critical third day? – For when three days flow together in one continuous intense pursuit; be sure the first is the morning, the second the noon, and the third the evening and the end of that thing – be that end what it may. Oh! my God! what is this that shoots through me, and leaves me so deadly calm, yet expectant, – fixed at the top of a shudder! Future things swim before me, as in empty outlines and skeletons; all the past is somehow grown dim. Mary, girl! thou fadest in pale glories behind me; boy! I seem to see but thy eyes grown wondrous blue. Strangest problems of life seem clearing; but clouds sweep between – Is my journey's end coming? My legs feel faint, like his who has footed it all day. Feel thy heart, – beats it yet? – Stir thyself, Starbuck! – stave it off – move, move! speak aloud! – Mast-head there! See ye my boy's hand on the hill? – Crazed; – aloft there! – keep thy keenest eye upon the boats: – mark well the whale! – Ho! again! – drive off that hawk! see! he pecks – he tears the vane' – pointing to the red flag flying at the main-truck – 'Ha! he soars away with it? – Where's the old man now? see'st thou that sight, oh Ahab! – shudder, shudder!'

The boats had not gone very far, when by a signal from the mast-heads – a downward pointed arm, Ahab knew that the whale had sounded; but intending to be near him at the next rising, he held on his way a little sideways from the vessel; the becharmed crew maintaining the profoundest silence, as the head-beat waves hammered and hammered against the opposing bow.

'Drive, drive in your nails, oh ye waves! to their uttermost heads drive them in! ye but strike a thing without a lid; and no coffin and no hearse can be mine: – and hemp only can kill me! Ha! ha!'

Suddenly the waters around them slowly swelled in broad circles; then quickly upheaved, as if sideways sliding from a submerged berg of ice, swiftly rising to the surface. A low rumbling sound was heard; a subterraneous hum; and then all held their breaths; as bedraggled with trailing ropes, and harpoons, and lances, a vast form shot lengthwise, but obliquely from the sea. Shrouded in a thin drooping veil of mist, it hovered for a moment in the rainbowed air; and then fell swamping back into the deep. Crushed thirty feet upwards, the waters flashed for an instant like heaps of fountains, then brokenly sank in a shower of flakes, leaving the circling surface creamed like new milk round the marble trunk of the whale.

'Give way!' cried Ahab to the oarsmen, and the boats darted forward to the attack; but maddened by yesterday's fresh irons that corroded in him, Moby Dick seemed combinedly possessed by all the angels that fell from heaven. The wide tiers of welded tendons overspreading his broad white forehead, beneath the transparent skin, looked knitted together; as head on, he came churning his tail among the boats; and once more flailed them apart; spilling out the irons and lances from the two mates' boats, and dashing in one side of the upper part of their bows, but leaving Ahab's almost without a scar.

While Daggoo and Queequeg were stopping the strained planks; and as the whale swimming out from them, turned, and showed one entire flank as he shot by them again; at that moment a quick cry went up. Lashed round and round to the fish's back; pinioned in the turns upon turns in which, during the past night, the whale had reeled the involutions of the lines around him, the half torn body of the Parsee was seen; his sable raiment frayed to shreds; his distended eyes turned full upon old Ahab.

The harpoon dropped from his hand.

'Befooled, befooled!' – drawing in a long lean breath – 'Aye, Parsee! I see thee again. – Aye, and thou goest before; and this, *this* then is the hearse that thou didst promise. But I hold thee to the last letter of thy word. Where is the second hearse? Away, mates, to the ship! those boats are useless now; repair them if ye can in time, and return to me; if not, Ahab is enough to die – Down, men! the first thing that but offers to jump from this boat I stand in, that thing I harpoon. Ye are not other men, but my arms and my legs; and so obey me. – Where's the whale? gone down again?'

But he looked too nigh the boat; for as if bent upon escaping with the corpse he bore, and as if the particular place of the last encounter had been but a stage in his leeward voyage, Moby Dick was now again steadily swimming forward; and had almost passed the ship, – which thus far had been sailing in the contrary direction to him, though for the present her headway had been stopped. He seemed swimming with his utmost velocity, and now only intent upon pursuing his own straight path in the sea.

'Oh! Ahab,' cried Starbuck, 'not too late is it, even now, the third day, to desist. See! Moby Dick seeks thee not. It is thou, thou, that madly seekest him!'

Setting sail to the rising wind, the lonely boat was swiftly impelled to leeward, by both oars and canvas. And at last when Ahab was sliding by the vessel, so near as plainly to distinguish Starbuck's face as he leaned over the rail, he hailed him to turn the vessel about, and follow him, not too swiftly, at a judicious interval. Glancing upwards, he saw Tashtego, Queequeg, and Daggoo, eagerly mounting to the three mast-heads; while the oarsmen were rocking in the two staved boats which had but just been hoisted to the side, and were busily at work in repairing them. One after the other, through the port-holes, as he sped, he also caught flying glimpses of Stubb and Flask, busying themselves on deck among bundles of new irons and lances. As he saw all this; as he heard the hammers in the broken boats; far other hammers seemed driving a nail into his heart. But he rallied. And now marking that the vane or flag was gone from the main-mast-head, he shouted to Tashtego, who had just gained that perch, to descend again for another flag, and a hammer and nails, and so nail it to the mast.

Whether fagged by the three days' running chase, and the resistance to his swimming in the knotted hamper he bore; or whether it was some latent deceitfulness and malice in him: whichever was true, the White Whale's way now began to abate, as it seemed, from the boat so rapidly nearing him once more; though indeed the whale's last start had not been so long as before. And still as Ahab glided over the waves the unpitying sharks accompanied him; and so pertinaciously stuck to the boat; and so continually bit at the plying oars, that the blades became jagged and crunched, and left small splinters in the sea, at almost every dip.

'Heed them not! those teeth but give new rowlocks to your oars. Pull on! 'tis the better rest, the shark's jaw than the yielding water.'

'But at every bite, sir, the thin blades grow smaller and smaller!'

'They will last long enough! pull on! – But who can tell' – he muttered – 'whether these sharks swim to feast on the whale or on Ahab? – But pull on! Aye, all alive, now – we near him. The helm! take the helm; let me pass,' – and so saying, two of the oarsmen helped him forward to the bows of the still flying boat.

At length as the craft was cast to one side, and ran ranging along with the White Whale's flank, he seemed strangely oblivious of its advance – as the whale sometimes will – and Ahab was fairly within the smoky mountain mist, which, thrown off from the whale's spout, curled round his great, Monadnock hump; he was even thus close to him; when, with body arched back, and both arms lengthwise highlifted to the poise, he darted his fierce iron, and his far fiercer curse into the hated whale. As both steel and curse sank to the socket, as if sucked into a morass, Moby Dick sideways writhed; spasmodically rolled his nigh flank against the bow, and, without staving a hole in it, so suddenly canted the boat over, that had it not been for the elevated part of the gunwale to which he then clung, Ahab would once more have been tossed into the sea. As it was, three of the oarsmen – who foreknew not the precise instant of the dart, and were therefore unprepared for its effects – these were flung out; but so fell, that, in an instant two of them clutched the gunwale again, and rising to its level on a combing wave, hurled themselves bodily inboard again; the third man helplessly dropping astern, but still afloat and swimming.

Almost simultaneously, with a mighty volition of ungraduated, instantaneous swiftness, the White Whale darted through the weltering sea. But when Ahab cried out to the steersman to take new turns with the line, and hold it so; and commanded the crew to turn round on their seats, and tow the boat up to the mark; the moment the treacherous line felt that double strain and tug, it snapped in the empty air!

'What breaks in me? Some sinew cracks! – 'tis whole again; oars! oars! Burst in upon him!'

Hearing the tremendous rush of the sea-crashing boat, the whale wheeled round to present his blank forehead at bay; but in that evolution, catching sight of the nearing black hull of the ship; seemingly seeing in it the source of all his persecutions; bethinking it – it may be – a larger and nobler foe; of a sudden, he bore down upon its advancing prow, smiting his jaws amid fiery showers of foam.

Ahab staggered; his hand smote his forehead. 'I grow blind; hands! stretch out before me that I may yet grope my way. Is't night?'

'The whale! The ship!' cried the cringing oarsmen.

'Oars! oars! Slope downwards to thy depths, O sea, that ere it be for ever too late, Ahab may slide this last, last time upon his mark! I see: the ship! the ship! Dash on, my men! Will ye not save my ship?'

But as the oarsmen violently forced their boat through the sledge-hammering seas, the before whale-smitten bowends of two planks burst through, and in an instant almost, the temporarily disabled boat lay nearly level with the waves; its half-wading, splashing crew, trying hard to stop the gap and bale out the pouring water.

Meantime, for that one beholding instant, Tashtego's mast-head hammer remained suspended in his hand; and the red flag, half-wrapping him as with a plaid, then streamed itself straight out from him, as his own forward-flowing heart; while Starbuck and Stubb, standing upon the bowsprit beneath, caught sight of the down-coming monster just as soon as he.

'The whale, the whale! Up helm, up helm! Oh, all ye sweet powers of air, now hug me close! Let not Starbuck die, if die he must, in a woman's fainting fit. Up helm, I say – ye fools, the jaw! the jaw! Is this the end of all my bursting prayers? all my life-long fidelities? Oh, Ahab, Ahab, lo, thy work. Steady! helmsman, steady. Nay, nay! Up helm again! He turns to meet us! Oh, his unappeasable brow drives on towards one, whose duty tells him he cannot depart. My God, stand by me now!'

'Stand not by me, but stand under me, whoever you are that will now help Stubb; for Stubb, too, sticks here. I grin at thee, thou grinning whale! Who ever helped Stubb, or kept Stubb awake, but Stubb's own unwinking eye? And now poor Stubb goes to bed upon a mattrass that is all too soft; would it were stuffed with brushwood! I grin at thee, thou grinning whale! Look ye, sun, moon, and stars! I call ye assassins of as good a fellow as ever spouted up his ghost. For all that, I would yet ring glasses with ye, would ye but hand the cup! Oh, oh! oh, oh! thou grinning whale, but there'll be plenty of gulping soon! Why fly ye not, O Ahab! For me, off shoes and jacket to it; let Stubb die in his drawers! A most mouldy and over salted death, though; – cherries! cherries! cherries! Oh, Flask, for one red cherry ere we die!'

'Cherries? I only wish that we were where they grow. Oh, Stubb, I hope my poor mother's drawn my part-pay ere this; if not, few coppers will now come to her, for the voyage is up.'

From the ship's bows, nearly all the seamen now hung inactive; hammers, bits of plank, lances, and harpoons, mechanically retained in their hands, just as they had darted from their various employments; all their enchanted eyes intent upon the whale, which from side to side strangely vibrating his predestinating head, sent a broad band of overspreading semicircular foam before him as he rushed. Retribution, swift vengeance, eternal malice were in his whole aspect, and spite of all that mortal man could do, the solid white buttress of his forehead smote the ship's starboard bow, till men and timbers reeled. Some fell flat upon their faces. Like dislodged trucks, the heads of the harpooneers aloft shook on their bull-like necks. Through the breach, they heard the waters pour, as mountain torrents down a flume.

'The ship! The hearse! – the second hearse!' cried Ahab from the boat; 'its wood could only be American!'

Diving beneath the settling ship, the whale ran quivering along its keel; but turning under water, swiftly shot to the surface again, far off the other bow, but within a few yards of Ahab's boat, where, for a time, he lay quiescent.

'I turn my body from the sun. What ho, Tashtego! let me hear thy hammer. Oh! ye three unsurrendered spires of mine; thou uncracked keel; and only god-bullied hull; thou firm deck, and haughty helm, and Pole-pointed prow, – death-glorious ship! must ye then perish, and without me? Am I cut off from the last fond pride of meanest shipwrecked captains? Oh, lonely death on lonely life! Oh, now I feel my topmost greatness lies in my topmost grief. Ho, ho! from all your furthest bounds, pour ye now in, ye bold billows of my whole foregone life, and top this one piled comber of my death! Towards thee I roll, thou alldestroying but unconquering whale; to the last I grapple with thee; from hell's heart I stab at thee; for hate's sake I spit my last breath at thee. Sink all coffins and all hearses to one common pool! and since neither can be mine, let me then tow to pieces, while still chasing thee, though tied to thee, thou damned whale! *Thus*, I give up the spear!'

The harpoon was darted; the stricken whale flew forward; with igniting velocity the line ran through the groove; – ran foul. Ahab stooped to clear it; he did clear it; but the flying turn caught him round the neck, and voicelessly as Turkish mutes bowstring their victim, he was shot out of the boat, ere the crew knew he was gone. Next instant, the heavy eye-splice in the rope's final end flew out of the stark-empty tub, knocked down an oarsman, and smiting the sea, disappeared in its depths.

For an instant, the tranced boat's crew stood still; then turned. 'The ship? Great God, where is the ship?' Soon they through dim, bewildering mediums saw her sidelong fading phantom, as in the gaseous Fata Morgana; only the uppermost masts out of the water; while fixed by infatuation, or fidelity, or fate, to their once lofty perches, the pagan harpooneers still maintained their sinking lookouts on the sea. And now, concentric circles seized the lone boat itself, and all its crew, and each floating oar, and every lance-pole, and spinning, animate and inanimate, all round and round in one vortex, carried the smallest chip of the Pequod out of sight.

But as the last whelmings intermixingly poured themselves over the sunken head of the Indian at the mainmast, leaving a few inches of the erect spar yet visible, together with long streaming yards of the flag, which calmly undulated, with ironical coincidings, over the destroying billows they almost touched; – at that instant a red arm and a hammer hovered backwardly uplifted in the open air, in the act of nailing the flag faster and yet faster to the subsiding spar. A sky-hawk that tauntingly had followed the main-truck downwards from its natural home among the stars, pecking at the flag, and incommoding Tashtego there; this bird now chanced to intercept its broad fluttering wing between the hammer and the wood; and simultaneously feeling that etherial thrill, the submerged savage beneath, in his death-gasp, kept his hammer frozen there; and so the bird of heaven, with archangelic shrieks, and his imperial beak thrust upwards, and his whole captive form folding in the flag of Ahab, went down with his ship, which, like Satan, would not sink to hell till she had dragged a living part of heaven along with her, and helmeted herself with it.

Now small fowls flew screaming over the yet yawning gulf; a sullen white surf beat against its steep sides; then all collapsed, and the great shroud of the sea rolled on as it rolled five thousand years ago.

Trinket's Colt

E. Œ. SOMERVILLE AND MARTIN ROSS

IT WAS PETTY SESSIONS day in Skebawn, a cold, grey day of February. A case of trespass had dragged its burden of cross summonses and cross swearing far into the afternoon, and when I left the bench my head was singing from the bellowings of the attorneys, and the smell of their clients was heavy upon my palate.

The streets still testified to the fact that it was market day, and I evaded with difficulty the sinuous course of carts full of soddenly screwed people, and steered an equally devious one for myself among the groups anchored round the doors of the public-houses. Skebawn possesses, among its legion of public-houses, one establishment which timorously, and almost imperceptibly, proffers tea to the thirsty. I turned in there, as was my custom on court days, and found the little dingy den, known as the Ladies' Coffee-room, in the occupancy of my friend Mr. Florence McCarthy Knox, who was drinking strong tea and eating buns with serious simplicity. It was a first and quite unexpected glimpse of that domesticity that has now become a marked feature in his character.

'You're the very man I wanted to see,' I said as I sat down beside him at the oilcloth-covered table; 'a man I know in England who is not much of a judge of character has asked me to buy him a four-year-old down here, and as I should rather be stuck by a friend than a dealer, I wish you'd take over the job.'

Flurry poured himself out another cup of tea, and dropped three lumps of sugar into it in silence.

Finally he said, 'There isn't a four-year-old in this country that I'd be seen dead with at a pig fair.'

This was discouraging, from the premier authority on horseflesh in the district.

'But it isn't six weeks since you told me you had the finest filly in your stables that was ever foaled in the County Cork,' I protested; 'what's wrong with her?'

'Oh, is it that filly?' said Mr. Knox with a lenient smile; 'she's gone these three weeks from me. I swapped her and six pounds for a three-year-old Ironmonger colt, and after that I swapped the colt and nineteen pounds for that Bandon horse I rode last week at your place, and after that again I sold the Bandon horse for seventy-five pounds to old Welply, and I had to give him back a couple of sovereigns luck-money. You see I did pretty well with the filly after all.'

'Yes, yes – oh, rather,' I asserted, as one dizzily accepts the propositions of a bimetallist; 'and you don't know of anything else—?'

The room in which we were seated was closely screened from the shop by a door with a muslin-covered window in it; several of the panes were broken, and at this juncture two voices that had for some time carried on a discussion forced themselves upon our attention.

'Begging your pardon for contradicting you, ma'am,' said the voice of Mrs. McDonald, proprietress of the teashop, and a leading light in Skebawn Dissenting circles, shrilly tremulous with indignation, 'if the servants I recommend you won't stop with you, it's no fault of mine. If respectable young girls are set picking grass out of your gravel, in place of their proper work, certainly they will give warning!'

The voice that replied struck me as being a notable one, well-bred and imperious.

'When I take a barefooted slut out of a cabin, I don't expect her to dictate to me what her duties are!'

Flurry jerked up his chin in a noiseless laugh. 'It's my grandmother!' he whispered. 'I bet you Mrs. McDonald don't get much change out of her!'

'If I set her to clean the pigsty I expect her to obey me,' continued the voice in accents that would have made me clean forty pigsties had she desired me to do so.

'Very well, ma'am,' retorted Mrs. McDonald, 'if that's the way you treat your servants, you needn't come here again looking for them. I consider your conduct is neither that of a lady nor a Christian!'

'Don't you, indeed?' replied Flurry's grandmother. 'Well, your opinion doesn't greatly distress me, for, to tell you the truth, I don't think you're much of a judge.'

'Didn't I tell you she'd score?' murmured Flurry, who was by this time applying his eye to a hole in the muslin curtain. 'She's off,' he went on, returning to his tea. 'She's a great character! She's eighty-three if she's a day, and she's as sound on her legs as a three-year-old! Did you see that old shandrydan of hers in the street a while ago, and a fellow on the box with a red beard on him like Robinson Crusoe? That old

121

mare that was on the near side – Trinket her name is – is mighty near clean bred. I can tell you her foals are worth a bit of money.'

I had heard of old Mrs. Knox of Aussolas; indeed, I had seldom dined out in the neighbourhood without hearing some new story of her and her remarkable *ménage*, but it had not yet been my privilege to meet her.

'Well, now,' went on Flurry in his slow voice, 'I'll tell you a thing that's just come into my head. My grandmother promised me a foal of Trinket's the day I was one-and-twenty, and that's five years ago, and deuce a one I've got from her yet. You never were at Aussolas? No, you were not. Well, I tell you the place there is like a circus with horses. She has a couple of score of them running wild in the woods, like deer.'

'Oh, come,' I said, 'I'm a bit of a liar myself—'

'Well, she has a dozen of them anyhow, rattling good colts too, some of them, but they might as well be donkeys, for all the good they are to me or any one. It's not once in three years she sells one, and there she has them walking after her for bits of sugar, like a lot of dirty lapdogs,' ended Flurry with disgust.

'Well, what's your plan? Do you want to make her a bid for one of the lapdogs?'

'I was thinking,' replied Flurry, with great deliberation, 'that my birthday's this week, and maybe I could work a four-year-old colt of Trinket's she has out of her in honour of the occasion.'

'And sell your grandmother's birthday present to me?'

'Just that, I suppose,' answered Flurry with a slow wink.

A few days afterwards a letter from Mr. Knox informed me that he had 'squared the old lady, and it would be all right about the colt'. He further told me that Mrs. Knox had been good enough to offer me, with him, a day's snipe shooting on the celebrated Aussolas bogs, and he proposed to drive me there the following Monday, if convenient. Most people found it convenient to shoot the Aussolas snipe bog when they got the chance. Eight o'clock on the following Monday morning saw Flurry, myself, and a groom packed into a dogcart, with portmanteaus, gun-cases, and two rampant red setters.

It was a long drive, twelve miles at least, and a very cold one. We passed through long tracts of pasture country, fraught, for Flurry, with memories of runs, which were recorded for me, fence by fence, in every one of which the biggest dog-fox in the country had gone to ground, with not two feet – measured accurately on the handle of the whip – between him and the leading hound; through bogs that imperceptibly melted into lakes, and finally down and down into a valley, where the fir-trees of Aussolas clustered darkly round a glittering lake, and all but hid the grey roofs and pointed gables of Aussolas Castle.

'There's a nice stretch of a demesne for you,' remarked Flurry, pointing downwards with the whip, 'and one little old woman holding it all in the heel of her fist. Well able to hold it she is, too, and always was, and she'll live twenty years yet, if it's only to spite the whole lot of us, and when all's said and done goodness knows how she'll leave it!'

'It strikes me you were lucky to keep her up to her promise about the colt,' I said.

Flurry administered a composing kick to the ceaseless striving of the red setters under the seat.

'I used to be rather a pet with her,' he said, after a pause; 'but mind you, I haven't got him yet, and if she gets any notion I want to sell him I'll never get him, so say nothing about the business to her.'

The tall gates of Aussolas shrieked on their hinges as they admitted us, and shut with a clang behind us, in the faces of an old mare and a couple of young horses, who, foiled in their break for the excitements of the outer world, turned and galloped defiantly on either side of us. Flurry's admirable cob hammered on, regardless of all things save his duty.

'He's the only one I have that I'd trust myself here with,' said his master, flicking him approvingly with the whip; 'there are plenty of people afraid to come here at all, and when my grandmother goes out driving she has a boy on the box with a basket full of stones to peg at them. Talk of the dickens, here she is herself!'

A short, upright old woman was approaching, preceded by a white woolly dog with sore eyes and a bark like a tin trumpet; we both got out of the trap and advanced to meet the lady of the manor.

I may summarise her attire by saying that she looked as if she had robbed a scarecrow; her face was small and incongruously refined, the skinny hand that she extended to me had the grubby tan that bespoke the professional gardener, and was decorated with a magnificent diamond ring. On her head was a massive purple velvet bonnet.

'I am very glad to meet you, Major Yeates,' she said with an old-fashioned precision of utterance; 'your grandfather was a dancing partner of mine in old days at the Castle, when he was a handsome young aide-de-camp there, and I was – You may judge for yourself what I was.'

She ended with a startling little hoot of laughter, and I was aware that she quite realised the world's opinion of her, and was indifferent to it.

Our way to the bogs took us across Mrs. Knox's home farm, and through a large field in which several young horses were grazing.

'There now, that's my fellow,' said Flurry, pointing to a fine-looking colt, 'the chestnut with the white diamond on his forehead. He'll run into three figures before he's done, but we'll not tell that to the old lady!'

The famous Aussolas bogs were as full of snipe as usual, and a good deal fuller of water than any bogs I had ever shot before. I was on my day, and Flurry was not, and as he is ordinarily an infinitely better snipe shot than I, I felt at peace with the world and all men as we walked back, wet through, at five o'clock.

The sunset had waned, and a big white moon was making the eastern

tower of Aussolas look like a thing in a fairy tale or a play when we
arrived at the hall door. An individual, whom I recognised as the Robinson
Crusoe coachman, admitted us to a hall, the like of which one does not
often see. The walls were panelled with dark oak up to the gallery that
ran round three sides of it, and balusters of the wide staircase were
heavily carved, and blackened portraits of Flurry's ancestors on the
spindle side stared sourly down on their descendant as he tramped
upstairs with the bog mould on his hobnailed boots.

We had just changed into dry clothes when Robinson Crusoe shoved
his red beard round the corner of the door, with the information that the
mistress said we were to stay for dinner. My heart sank. It was then
barely half-past five. I said something about having no evening clothes
and having to get home early.

'Sure the dinner'll be in another half hour,' said Robinson Crusoe,
joining hospitably in the conversation; 'and as for evening clothes – God
bless ye!'

The door closed behind him.

'Never mind,' said Flurry, 'I dare say you'll be glad enough to eat
another dinner by the time you get home.' He laughed. 'Poor Slipper!'
he added inconsequently, and only laughed again when I asked for an
explanation.

Old Mrs. Knox received us in the library, where she was seated by a
roaring turf fire, which lit the room a good deal more effectively than the
pair of candles that stood beside her in tall silver candlesticks. Ceaseless
and implacable growls from under her chair indicated the presence of the
woolly dog. She talked with confounding culture of the books that rose
all round her to the ceiling; her evening dress was accomplished by means
of an additional white shawl, rather dirtier than its congeners; as I took
her in to dinner she quoted Virgil to me, and in the same breath screeched
an objurgation at a being whose matted head rose suddenly into view
from behind an ancient Chinese screen, as I have seen the head of a Zulu
woman peer over a bush.

Dinner was as incongruous as everything else. Detestable soup in a
splendid old silver tureen that was nearly as dark in hue as Robinson
Crusoe's thumb; a perfect salmon, perfectly cooked, on a chipped kitchen
dish; such cut glass as is not easy to find nowadays; sherry that, as Flurry
subsequently remarked, would burn the shell off an egg; and a bottle of
port, draped in immemorial cobwebs, wan with age, and probably
priceless. Throughout the vicissitudes of the meal Mrs. Knox's conversation flowed on undismayed, directed sometimes at me – she had installed
me in the position of friend of her youth and talked to me as if I were
my own grandfather – sometimes at Crusoe, with whom she had several
heated arguments, and sometimes she would make a statement of remarkable frankness on the subject of her horse-farming affairs to Flurry, who,
very much on his best behaviour, agreed with all she said, and risked no

original remark. As I listened to them both, I remembered with infinite amusement how he had told me once that 'a pet name she had for him was "Tony Lumpkin", and no one but herself knew what she meant by it.' It seemed strange that she made no allusion to Trinket's colt or to Flurry's birthday, but, mindful of my instructions, I held my peace.

As, at about half-past eight, we drove away in the moonlight, Flurry congratulated me solemnly on my success with his grandmother. He was good enough to tell me that she would marry me to-morrow if I asked her, and he wished I would, even if it was only to see what a nice grandson he'd be for me. A sympathetic giggle behind me told me that Michael, on the back seat, had heard and relished the jest.

We had left the gates of Aussolas about half a mile behind when, at the corner of a by-road, Flurry pulled up. A short squat figure arose from the black shadow of a furze bush and came out into the moonlight, swinging its arms like a cabman and cursing audibly.

'Oh murdher, oh murdher, Misther Flurry! What kept ye at all? 'Twould perish the crows to be waiting here the way I am these two hours—'

'Ah, shut your mouth, Slipper!' said Flurry, who, to my surprise, had turned back the rug and was taking off his driving coat, 'I couldn't help it. Come on, Yeates, we've got to get out here.'

'What for?' I asked, in not unnatural bewilderment.

'It's all right. I'll tell you as we go along,' replied my companion, who was already turning to follow Slipper up the by-road. 'Take the trap on, Michael, and wait at the River's Cross.' He waited for me to come up with him, and then put his hand on my arm. 'You see, Major, this is the way it is. My grandmother's given me that colt right enough, but if I waited for her to send him over to me I'd never see a hair of his tail. So I just thought that as we were over here we might as well take him back with us, and maybe you'll give us a help with him; he'll not be altogether too handy for a first go off.'

I was staggered. An infant in arms could scarcely have failed to discern the fishiness of the transaction, and I begged Mr. Knox not to put himself to this trouble on my account, as I had no doubt I could find a horse for my friend elsewhere. Mr. Knox assured me that it was no trouble at all, quite the contrary, and that, since his grandmother had given him the colt, he saw no reason why he should not take him when he wanted him; also, that if I didn't want him he'd be glad enough to keep him himself; and finally, that I wasn't the chap to go back on a friend, but I was welcome to drive back to Shreelane with Michael this minute if I liked.

Of course I yielded in the end. I told Flurry I should lose my job over the business, and he said I could then marry his grandmother, and the discussion was abruptly closed by the necessity of following Slipper over a locked five-barred gate.

Our pioneer took us over about half a mile of country, knocking down stone gaps where practicable and scrambling over tall banks in the deceptive moonlight. We found ourselves at length in a field with a shed in one corner of it; in a dim group of farm buildings a little way off a light was shining.

'Wait here,' said Flurry to me in a whisper; 'the less noise the better. It's an open shed, and we'll just slip in and coax him out.'

Slipper unwound from his waist a halter, and my colleagues glided like spectres into the shadow of the shed, leaving me to meditate on my duties as Resident Magistrate, and on the questions that would be asked in the House by our local member when Slipper had given away the adventure in his cups.

In less than a minute three shadows emerged from the shed, where two had gone in. They had got the colt.

'He came out as quiet as a calf when he winded the sugar,' said Flurry; 'it was well for me I filled my pockets from grandmamma's sugar basin.'

He and Slipper had a rope from each side of the colt's head; they took him quickly across a field towards a gate. The colt stepped daintily between them over the moonlit grass; he snorted occasionally, but appeared on the whole amenable.

The trouble began later, and was due, as trouble often is, to the beguilements of a short cut. Against the maturer judgment of Slipper, Flurry insisted on following a route that he assured us he knew as well as his own pocket, and the consequence was that in about five minutes I found myself standing on top of a bank hanging on to a rope, on the other end of which the colt dangled and danced, while Flurry, with the other rope, lay prone in the ditch, and Slipper administered to the bewildered colt's hind quarters such chastisement as could be ventured on.

I have no space to narrate in detail the atrocious difficulties and disasters of the short cut. How the colt set to work to buck, and went away across a field, dragging the faithful Slipper, literally *ventre à terre*, after him, while I picked myself in ignominy out of a briar patch, and Flurry cursed himself black in the face. How we were attacked by ferocious cur dogs, and I lost my eye-glass; and how, as we neared the River's Cross, Flurry espied the police patrol on the road, and we all hid behind a rick of turf while I realised in fullness what an exceptional ass I was, to have been beguiled into an enterprise that involved hiding with Slipper from the Royal Irish Constabulary.

Let it suffice to say that Trinket's infernal offspring was finally handed over on the high road to Michael and Slipper, and Flurry drove me home in a state of mental and physical overthrow.

I saw nothing of my friend Mr. Knox for the next couple of days, by the end of which time I had worked up a high polish on my misgivings, and had determined to tell him that under no circumstances would I have anything to say to his grandmother's birthday present. It was like my usual luck that, instead of writing a note to this effect, I thought it would be good for my liver to walk across the hills to Tory Cottage and tell Flurry so in person.

It was a bright, blustery morning, after a muggy day. The feeling of spring was in the air, the daffodils were already in bud, and crocuses showed purple in the grass on either side of the avenue. It was only a couple of miles to Tory Cottage by the way across the hills; I walked fast, and it was barely twelve o'clock when I saw its pink walls and clumps of evergreens below me. As I looked down at it the chiming of Flurry's hounds in the kennels came to me on the wind; I stood still to listen, and could almost have sworn that I was hearing again the clash of Magdalen bells, hard at work on May morning.

The path that I was following led downwards through a larch plantation to Flurry's back gate. Hot wafts from some hideous cauldron at the other side of a wall apprised me of the vicinity of the kennels and their cuisine, and the fir-trees round were hung with gruesome and unknown joints. I thanked heaven that I was not a master of hounds, and passed on as quickly as might be to the hall door.

I rang two or three times without response; then the door opened a couple of inches and was instantly slammed in my face. I heard the hurried paddling of bare feet on oil-cloth, and a voice, 'Hurry, Bridgie, hurry! There's quality at the door!'

Bridgie, holding a dirty cap on with one hand, presently arrived and informed me that she believed Mr. Knox was out about the place. She seemed perturbed, and she cast scared glances down the drive while speaking to me.

I knew enough of Flurry's habits to shape a tolerably direct course for his whereabouts. He was, as I had expected, in the training paddock, a field behind the stable yard, in which he had put up practice jumps for his horses. It was a good-sized field with clumps of furze in it, and Flurry was standing near one of these with his hands in his pockets, singularly unoccupied. I supposed that he was prospecting for a place to put up another jump. He did not see me coming, and turned with a start as I spoke to him. There was a queer expression of mingled guilt and what I can only describe as divilment in his grey eyes as he greeted me. In my dealings with Flurry Knox, I have since formed the habit of sitting tight, in a general way, when I see that expression.

'Well, who's coming next, I wonder!' he said, as he shook hands with me; it's not ten minutes since I had two of your d—d peelers here searching the whole place for my grandmother's colt!'

'What!' I exclaimed, feeling cold all down my back; 'do you mean the police have got hold of it?'

'They haven't got hold of the colt anyway,' said Flurry, looking sideways at me from under the peak of his cap, with the glint of the sun in his eye. 'I got word in time before they came.'

'What do you mean?' I demanded; 'where is he? For heaven's sake
don't tell me you've sent the brute over to my place!'

'It's a good job for you I didn't,' replied Flurry, 'as the police are on
their way to Shreelane this minute to consult you about it. *You!*' He gave
utterance to one of his short diabolical fits of laughter. 'He's where they'll
not find him, anyhow. Ho ho! It's the funniest hand I ever played!'

'Oh yes, it's devilish funny, I've no doubt,' I retorted, beginning to lose
my temper, as is the manner of many people when they are frightened;
'but I give you fair warning that if Mrs. Knox asks me any questions
about it, I shall tell her the whole story.'

'All right,' responded Flurry; 'and when you do, don't forget to tell her
how you flogged the colt out on to the road over her own bounds ditch.'

'Very well,' I said hotly, 'I may as well go home and send in my
papers. They'll break me over this—'

'Ah, hold on, Major,' said Flurry soothingly, 'it'll be all right. No one
knows anything. It's only on spec the old lady sent the bobbies here. If
you'll keep quiet it'll all blow over.'

'I don't care,' I said, struggling hopelessly in the toils; 'if I meet your
grandmother, and she asks me about it, I shall tell her all I know.'

'Please God you'll not meet her! After all, it's not once in a blue moon
that she—' began Flurry. Even as he said the words his face changed.
'Holy fly!' he ejaculated, 'isn't that her dog coming into the field? Look
at her bonnet over the wall! Hide, hide for your life!' He caught me by
the shoulder and shoved me down among the furze bushes before I
realised what had happened.

'Get in there! I'll talk to her.'

I may as well confess that at the mere sight of Mrs. Knox's purple
bonnet my heart had turned to water. In that moment I knew what it
would be like to tell her how I, having eaten her salmon, and capped her
quotations, and drunk her best port, had gone forth and helped to steal
her horse. I abandoned my dignity, my sense of honour; I took the furze
prickles to my breast and wallowed in them.

Mrs. Knox had advanced with vengeful speed; already she was in high
altercation with Flurry at no great distance from where I lay; varying
sounds of battle reached me, and I gathered that Flurry was not – to put
it mildly – shrinking from that economy of truth that the situation
required.

'Is it that curby, long-backed brute? You promised him to me long
ago, but I wouldn't be bothered with him!'

The old lady uttered a laugh of shrill derision. 'Is it likely I'd promise
you my best colt? And still more, is it likely that you'd refuse him if I
did?'

'Very well, ma'am.' Flurry's voice was admirably indignant. 'Then I
suppose I'm a liar and a thief.'

'I'd be more obliged to you for the information if I hadn't known it before,' responded his grandmother with lightning speed; 'if you swore to me on a stack of Bibles you knew nothing about my colt I wouldn't believe you! I shall go straight to Major Yeates and ask his advice. I believe *him* to be a gentleman, in spite of the company he keeps!'

I writhed deeper into the furze bushes, and thereby discovered a sandy rabbit run, along which I crawled, with my cap well over my eyes, and the furze needles stabbing me through my stockings. The ground shelved a little, promising profounder concealment, but the bushes were very thick, and I laid hold of the bare stem of one to help my progress. It lifted out of the ground in my hand, revealing a freshly cut stump. Something snorted, not a yard away; I glared through the opening, and was confronted by the long, horrified face of Mrs. Knox's colt, mysteriously on a level with my own.

Even without the white diamond on his forehead I should have divined the truth; but how in the name of wonder had Flurry persuaded him to couch like a woodcock in the heart of a furze brake? For a full minute I lay as still as death for fear of frightening him, while the voices of Flurry and his grandmother raged on alarmingly close to me. The colt snorted, and blew long breaths through his wide nostrils, but he did not move. I crawled an inch or two nearer, and after a few seconds of cautious peering I grasped the position. They had buried him.

A small sandpit among the furze had been utilised as a grave; they had filled him in up to his withers with sand, and a few furze bushes, artistically disposed around the pit, had done the rest. As the depth of Flurry's guile was revealed, laughter came upon me like a flood; I gurgled and shook apoplectically, and the colt gazed at me with serious surprise, until a sudden outburst of barking close to my elbow administered a fresh shock to my tottering nerves.

Mrs. Knox's woolly dog had tracked me into the furze, and was now baying the colt and me with mingled terror and indignation. I addressed him in a whisper, with perfidious endearments, advancing a crafty hand towards him the while, made a snatch for the back of his neck, missed it badly, and got him by the ragged fleece of his hind quarters as he tried to flee. If I had flayed him alive he could hardly have uttered a more deafening series of yells, but, like a fool, instead of letting him go, I dragged him towards me, and tried to stifle the noise by holding his muzzle. The tussle lasted engrossingly for a few seconds, and then the climax of the nightmare arrived.

Mrs. Knox's voice, close behind me, said, 'Let go my dog this instant, sir! Who are you—'

Her voice faded away, and I knew that she also had seen the colt's head.

I positively felt sorry for her. At her age there was no knowing what effect the shock might have on her. I scrambled to my feet and confronted her.

'Major Yeates!' she said. There was a deathly pause. 'Will you kindly tell me,' said Mrs. Knox slowly, 'am I in Bedlam, or are you? And *what is that?*'

She pointed to the colt, and that unfortunate animal, recognising the voice of his mistress, uttered a hoarse and lamentable whinny. Mrs. Knox felt around her for support, found only furze prickles, gazed speechlessly at me, and then, to her eternal honour, fell into wild cackles of laughter.

So, I may say, did Flurry and I. I embarked on my explanation and broke down; Flurry followed suit and broke down too. Overwhelming laughter held us all three, disintegrating our very souls. Mrs. Knox pulled herself together first.

'I acquit you, Major Yeates, I acquit you, though appearances are against you. It's clear enough to me you've fallen among thieves.' She stopped and glowered at Flurry. Her purple bonnet was over one eye. 'I'll thank you, sir,' she said, 'to dig out that horse before I leave this place. And when you've dug him out you may keep him. I'll be no receiver of stolen goods!'

She broke off and shook her fist at him. 'Upon my conscience, Tony, I'd give a guinea to have thought of it myself!'

A Sea of Headwaiters

GERALD DURRELL

Gerald Durrell and his wife, Jacquie, set out to spend eight months in Argentina to collect more animals for their zoo in Jersey. Once arrived in Buenos Aires, they decided on a trip to Patagonia . . .

The plains of Patagonia are boundless, for they are scarcely passable, and hence unknown; they bear the stamp of having lasted, as they are now, for ages, and there appears no limit to their duration through future time.

CHARLES DARWIN: THE VOYAGE OF H.M.S. BEAGLE.

WE SET OFF FOR THE SOUTH in the pearly grey dawn light of what promised to be a perfect day. The streets were empty and echoing, and the dew-drenched parks and squares had their edges frothed with great piles of fallen blooms from the *palo borracho* and jacaranda trees, heaps of glittering flowers in blue, yellow and pink.

On the outskirts of the city we rounded a corner and came upon the first sign of life we had seen since we had started, a covey of dustmen indulging in their early morning ballet. This was such an extraordinary sight that we drove slowly behind them for some way in order to watch. The great dust-cart rumbled down the centre of the road at a steady five miles an hour, and standing in the back, up to his knees in rubbish, stood the emptier. Four other men loped alongside the cart like wolves, darting off suddenly into dark doorways to reappear with dustbins full of trash balanced on their shoulders. They would run up alongside the cart and throw the dustbin effortlessly into the air, and the man on the cart would catch it and empty it and throw it back, all in one fluid movement. The timing of this was superb, for as the empty dustbin was hurtling downwards a full one would be sailing up. They would pass in mid air, and the full bin would be caught and emptied. Sometimes there would be four dustbins in the air at once. The whole action was performed in silence and with incredible speed.

Soon we left the edge of the city, just stirring to wakefulness, and sped out into the open countryside, golden in the rising sun. The early morning air was chilly, and Dicky had dressed for the occasion. He was wearing a long tweed overcoat and white gloves, and his dark, bland eyes and neat, butterfly-shaped moustache peered out from under a ridiculous deerstalker hat which he wore, he explained to me, in order to 'keep the ears heated.' Sophie and Marie crouched in strange prenatal postures in the back of the Land-Rover, on top of our mountainous pile of equipment, most of which, they insisted, had been packed in boxes with knife-like edges. Jacquie and I sat next to Dicky in the front seat, a map spread out across our laps, our heads nodding, as we endeavoured to work out our route. Some of the places we had to pass through were delightful: Chascomus, Dolores, Necochea, Tres Arroyos, and similar delicious names that slid enticingly off the tongue. At one point we passed through two villages, within a few miles of each other, one called 'The Dead Christian' and the other 'The Rich Indian.' Marie's explanation of this strange nomenclature was that the Indian was rich because he killed the Christian, and had stolen all his money, but attractive though this story was, I felt it could not be the right one.

For two days we sped through the typical landscape of the Pampa, flat golden grassland in which the cattle grazed knee-deep; occasional clumps of eucalyptus trees, with their bleached and peeling trunks like leprous limbs; small, neat *estancias*, gleaming white in the shade of huge, carunculated *ombù* trees, that stood massively and grimly on their enormous squat trunks. In places the neat fences that lined the road were almost obliterated under a thick cloak of convolvulus, hung with electric-blue flowers the size of saucers, and every third or fourth fence-post would have balanced upon it the strange, football-like nest of an oven-bird. It was a lush, prosperous and well-fed-looking landscape that only just escaped being monotonous. Eventually, in the evening of the third day, we lost our way, and so we pulled in to the side of the road and argued over the map. Our destination was a town called Carmen de Patagones, on the north bank of the Rio Negro. I particularly wanted to spend the night here, because it was a town that Darwin had stayed in for some time during the voyage of the *Beagle*, and I was interested to see how it had changed in the last hundred years. So, in spite of near-mutiny on the part of the rest of the expedition, who wanted to stop at the first suitable place we came to, we drove on. As it turned out it was all we could have done anyway, for we did not pass a single habitation until we saw gleaming ahead of us a tiny cluster of feeble lights. Within ten minutes we were driving cautiously through the cobbled streets of Carmen de Patagones, lit by pale, trembling street-lights. It was two o'clock in the morning, and every house was blank-faced and tightly shuttered. Our chances of finding anyone who could direct us to a hostelry were remote, and we certainly needed direction, for each house looked exactly like the ones on each side of it, and there was no indication as to whether it was a hotel or a private habitation. We stopped in the main square of the town and were arguing tiredly and irritably over this problem when suddenly, under one of the street lights, appeared an angel of mercy, in the shape of a tall, slim policeman clad in an immaculate uniform, his belt and boots gleaming. He saluted smartly, bowed to the female members of the party, and with old-world courtesy directed us up some side-roads to where he said we should find an hotel. We came to a great gloomy house, heavily shuttered, with a massive front door that would have done justice to a cathedral. We beat a sharp tattoo on its weather-beaten surface and waited patiently. Ten minutes later there was still no response from the inhabitants, and so Dicky, in desperation, launched an assault on the door that would, if it had succeeded, have awakened the dead. But as he lashed out at the door it swung mysteriously open under his assault, and displayed a long, dimly-lit passageway, with doors along each side, and a marble staircase leading to the upper floors. Dead tired and extremely hungry we were in no mood to consider other people's property, so we marched into the echoing hall like an invading army. We stood there and shouted '¡Holà¡' until the hotel rang with our shouts, but there was no response.

'I think, Gerry, that sometime they are all deceased,' said Dicky gravely.

'Well, if they are I suggest we spread out and find ourselves some beds,' I said.

So we climbed the marble staircase and found ourselves three bedrooms, with beds made up, by the simple expedient of opening every door in sight. Eventually, having found a place to sleep, Dicky and I went downstairs to see if the hotel boasted of any sanitary arrangements. The first door we threw open in our search led us into a dim bedroom in which was an enormous double-bed hung with an old-fashioned canopy. Before we could back out of the room a huge figure surged out from under the bedclothes like a surfacing whale, and waddled towards us. It turned out to be a colossal woman, clad in a flowing flannel nightie, who must have weighed somewhere in the neighbourhood of fifteen stone. She came out, blinking, into the hallway, pulling on a flowing kimono of bright green covered with huge pink roses, so the effect was rather as if one of the more exotic floral displays of the Chelsea Flower Show had suddenly taken on a life of its own. Over her ample bosoms spread two long streamers of grey hair which she flicked deftly over her shoulder as she did up her kimono, smiling at us with sleepy goodwill.

'Buenas noches,' she said politely.

'Buenas noches, señora,' we replied, not to be outdone in good manners at that hour of the morning.

'¿Hablo con la patrona?' inquired Dicky.

'*Si, si, señor,*' she said, smiling broadly, '*¿que queres?*'

Dicky apologized for our late arrival, but *la patrona* waved away our apologies. Was it possible, Dicky asked, for us to have some sandwiches and coffee? Why not? inquired *la patrona*. Further, said Dicky, we were in urgent need of a lavatory, and could she be so kind as to direct us to it. With great good humour she led us to a small tiled room, showed us how to pull the plug, and stood there chatting amiably while Dicky and I relieved the pangs of nature. Then she puffed and undulated her way down to the kitchen and cut us a huge pile of sandwiches and made a steaming mug of coffee. Having assured herself that there was nothing further she could do for our comfort, she waddled off to bed.

The next morning, having breakfasted, we did a rapid tour of the town. As far as I could see, apart from the introduction of electricity, it had changed very little since Darwin's day, and so we left and sped down a hill and across the wide iron bridge that spanned the rusty red waters of the Rio Negro. We rattled across the bridge from the Province of Buenos Aires to the Province of Chubut, and by that simple action of crossing a river we entered a different world.

Gone were the lush green plains of the Pampa, and in their place was an arid waste stretching away as far as the eye could see on each side of the dusty road, a uniform pelt of grey-green scrub composed of plants about three feet high, each armed with a formidable array of thorns and spikes. Nothing appeared to live in this dry scrub, for when we stopped there was no bird or insect song, only the whispering of the wind through the thorn scrub in this monochromatic Martian landscape, and the only moving thing apart from ourselves was the giant plume of dust we trailed behind the vehicle. This was terribly tiring country to drive in. The road, deeply rutted and potholed, unrolled straight ahead to the horizon, and after a few hours this monotony of scene numbed one's brain, and one would suddenly drop off to sleep, to be awoken by the vicious scrunch of the wheels as the Land-Rover swerved off into the brittle scrub.

The evening before we were due to reach Deseado this happened on a stretch of road which, unfortunately, had recently been rained upon, so that the surface had turned into something resembling high-grade glue. Dicky, who had been driving for a long time, suddenly nodded off behind the wheel, and before anyone could do anything sensible, both Land-Rover and trailer had skidded violently into the churned-up mud at the side of the road, and settled there snugly, wheels spinning like mad. Reluctantly we got out into the bitter chill of the evening wind, and in the dim sunset light set to work to unhitch the trailer and then push it and the Land-Rover separately out of the mud. Then, our feet and hands frozen, the five of us crouched in the shelter of the Land-Rover and watched the sunset, passing from hand to hand a bottle of Scotch which I had been keeping for just such an emergency.

On every side of us the scrubland stretched away, dark and flat, so that you got the impression of being in the centre of a gigantic plate. The sky had become suffused with green as the sun sank, and then, unexpectedly, turned to a very pale powder-blue. A tattered mass of clouds on the western horizon suddenly turned black, edged delicately with flame-red, and resembled a great armada of Spanish galleons waging a fierce sea-battle across the sky, drifting towards each other, turned into black silhouette by the fierce glare from their cannons. As the sun sank lower and lower the black of the clouds became shot and mottled with grey, and the sky behind them became striped with green, blue and pale red. Suddenly our fleet of galleons disappeared, and in its place was a perfect archipelago of islands strung out across the sky in what appeared to be a placid, sunset-coloured sea. The illusion was perfect: you could pick out the tiny, white rimmed coves in the rocky, indented shoreline, the occasional long, white beach; the dangerous shoal of rocks formed by a wisp of cloud at the entrance to a safe anchorage; the curiously-shaped mountains inland covered with a tattered pelt of evening-dark forest. We sat there, the whisky warming our bodies, watching enraptured the geography of this archipelago unfold. We each of us chose an island which appealed to us, on which we would like to spend a holiday, and stipulated what the hotel on each of our islands would have to provide in the way of civilized amenities.

'A very, *very* big bath, and very deep,' said Marie.

'No, a nice hot shower and a comfortable chair,' said Sophie.

'Just a bed,' said Jacquie, 'a large feather bed.'

'A bar that serves real ice with its drinks,' I said dreamily.

Dicky was silent for a moment. Then he glanced down at his feet, thickly encrusted with rapidly drying mud.

'I must have a man to clean my feets,' he said firmly.

'Well, I doubt whether we'll get any of that at Deseado,' I said gloomily, 'but we'd better press on.'

When we drove into Deseado at ten o'clock the next morning, it became immediately obvious that we could not expect any such luxuries as feather beds, ice in the drinks, or even a man to clean our feets. It was the most extraordinarily dead-looking town I had ever been in. It resembled the set for a rather bad Hollywood cowboy film, and gave the impression that its inhabitants (two thousand, according to the guide-book) had suddenly packed up and left it alone to face the biting winds and scorching sun. The empty, rutted streets between the blank-faced houses were occasionally stirred by the wind, which produced half-hearted dust-devils, that swirled up for a moment and then collapsed tiredly to the ground. As we drove slowly into what we imagined to be the centre of the town we saw only a dog, trotting briskly about his affairs, and a child, crouched in the middle of a road, absorbed in some mysterious game of childhood. Then, swinging the Land-Rover round a corner, we were startled to see a man on horseback, clopping slowly along the road with the subdued air of one who is the sole survivor of a catastrosphe. He pulled up and greeted us politely, but without interest, when we stopped, and directed us to the only two hotels in the place. As these turned out to be opposite each other and both equally unprepossessing from the outside, we chose one by tossing a coin and made our way inside.

In the bar we found the proprietor, who, with the air of one who had just suffered a terrible bereavement, reluctantly admitted that he had accommodation, and led us through dim passages to three small, grubby rooms. Dicky, his deer-stalker on the back of his head, stood in the centre of his room, pulling off his white gloves, surveying the sagging bed and its grey linen with a cat-like fastidiousness.

'You know what, Gerry?' he said with conviction. 'This is the stinkiest hotel I ever dream.'

'I hope you never dream of a stinkier one,' I assured him.

Presently we all repaired to the bar to have a drink and await the arrival of one Captain Giri, whom I had an introduction to, a man who knew all about the penguin colonies of Puerto Deseado. We sat round a small table, sipping our drinks and watching the other inhabitants of the bar with interest. For the most part they seemed to consist of very old men, with long, sweeping moustaches, whose brown faces were seamed and stitched by the wind. They sat in small groups, crouched over their tiny tumblers of cognac or wine with a dead air, as though they were hibernating there in this dingy bar, staring hopelessly into the bottoms of their glasses, wondering when the wind would die down, and knowing it would not. Dicky, delicately smoking a cigarette, surveyed the smoke-blackened walls, the rows of dusty bottles, and the floor with its twenty-year-layer of dirt well trodden into its surface.

'What a bar, eh?' he said to me.

'Not very convivial, is it?'

'It is so old . . . it has an air of old,' he said staring about him. 'You know, Gerry, I bet it is so old that even the flies have beards.'

Then the door opened suddenly, a blast of cold air rushed into the bar, the old men looked up in a flat-eyed, reptilian manner, and through the door strode Captain Giri. He was a tall, well-built man with blond hair, a handsome, rather aesthetic face and the most vivid and candid blue eyes I had ever seen. Having introduced himself he sat down at our table and looked round at us with such friendliness and good humour in his child-like eyes that the dead atmosphere of the bar dropped away, and we suddenly found ourselves becoming alive and enthusiastic. We had a drink, and then Captain Giri produced a large roll of charts and spread them on the table, while we pored over them.

'Penguins,' said the Captain meditatively, running his forefinger over the chart. 'Now, down here is the best colony . . . by far the best and biggest, but I think that that is too far for you, is it not?'

'Well, it is a bit,' I admitted. 'We didn't want to go that far south if we could avoid it. It's a question of time, really. I had hoped that there would be a reasonable colony within fairly easy reach of Deseado.'

'There is, there is,' said the Captain, shuffling the charts like a conjuror and producing another one from the pile. 'Now, here, you see, at this spot . . . it's about four hours' drive from Deseado . . . all along this bay here.'

'That's wonderful,' I said enthusiastically, 'just the right distance.'

'There is only one thing that worries me,' said the Captain, turning troubled blue eyes on to me. 'Are there enough birds there for what you want . . . for your photography?'

'Well,' I said doubtfully, 'I want a fair number. How many are there in this colony?'

'At a rough estimate I should say a million,' said Captain Giri. 'Will that be enough?'

I gaped at him. The man was not joking. He was seriously concerned that a million penguins might prove to be too meagre a quantity for my purpose.

'I think I can make out with a million penguins,' I said. 'I should be able to find one or two photogenic ones among that lot. Tell me, are they all together, or scattered about?'

'Well, there are about half or three-quarters concentrated *here*,' he said, stabbing at the chart. 'And the rest are distributed all along the bay *here*.'

'Well, that seems perfect to me. Now what about somewhere to camp?'

'Ah!' said Captain Giri. 'That is the difficulty. Now, just here is the *estancia* of a friend of mine, Señor Huichi. He is not on the *estancia* at the moment. But if we went to see him he might let you stay there. It is, you see, about two kilometres from the main colony, so it would be a good place for you to stay.'

'That would be wonderful,' I said enthusiastically 'When could we see Señor Huichi?'

The Captain consulted his watch and made a calculation.

'We can go and see him now, if you would like,' he said.

'Right!' I said, finishing my drink. 'Let's go.'

Huichi's house was on the outskirts of Deseado, and Huichi himself, when Captain Giri introduced us, was a man I took an instant liking to. Short, squat, with a weather-browned face, he had very dark hair, heavy black eyebrows and moustache, and dark brown eyes that were kind and humorous, with crow's feet at the corners. In his movements and his speech he had an air of quiet, unruffled confidence about him that was very reassuring. He stood silently while Giri explained our mission, occasionally glancing at me, as if summing me up. Then he asked a couple of questions, and, finally, to my infinite relief, he held out his hand to me and smiled broadly.

'Señor Huichi has agreed that you shall use his *estancia*,' said Giri, 'and he is going to accompany you himself, so as to show you the best places for penguins.'

'That is very kind of Señor Huichi . . . we are most grateful,' I said.

'Could we leave tomorrow afternoon, after I have seen my friend off on the plane?'

'¿*Si, si, como no?*' said Huichi when this had been translated to him. So we arranged to meet him on the morrow, after an early lunch, when we had seen Dicky off on the plane that was to take him to Buenos Aires.

So, that evening we sat in the depressing bar of our hotel, sipping our drinks and contemplating the forlorn fact that the next day Dicky would be leaving us. He had been a charming and amusing companion, who had put up with discomfort without complaint, and had enlivened our flagging spirits throughout the trip with jokes, fantastically phrased remarks, and lilting Argentine songs. We were going to miss him, and he was equally depressed at the thought of leaving us just when the trip was starting to get interesting. In a daring fit of *joie de vivre* the hotel proprietor had switched on a small radio, strategically placed on a shelf between two bottles of brandy. This now blared out a prolonged and mournful tango of the more cacophonous sort. We listened to it in silence until the last despairing howls had died away.

'What is the translation of that jolly little piece?' I asked Marie.

'It is a man who has discovered that his wife has T.B.,' she explained. 'He has lost his job and his children are starving. His wife is dying. He is very sad, and he asks the meaning of life.'

The radio launched itself into another wailing air that sounded almost identical with the first. When it had ended I raised my eyebrows inquiringly at Marie.

'That is a man who has just discovered that his wife is unfaithful,' she translated moodily. 'He has stabbed her. Now he is to be hung, and his children will be without mother or father. He is very sad and he asks the meaning of life.'

A third refrain rent the air. I looked at Marie. She listened attentively for a moment, then shrugged.

'The same,' she said tersely.

We got up in a body and went to bed.

Early the next morning Marie and I drove Dicky out to the airstrip, while Sophie and Jacquie went round the three shops in Deseado to buy necessary supplies for our trip out to Huichi's *estancia*. The airstrip consisted of a more or less level strip of ground on the outskirts of the town, dominated by a moth-eaten-looking hangar, whose loose boards flapped and creaked in the wind. The only living things were three ponies, grazing forlornly. Twenty minutes after the plane had been due in there was still no sign of her, and we began to think that Dicky would have to stay with us after all. Then along the dusty road from the town came bustling a small van. It stopped by the hangar, and from inside appeared two very official-looking men in long khaki coats. They examined the wind-sock with a fine air of concentration, stared up into the sky, and consulted each other with frowning faces. Then they looked at their watches and paced up and down.

'They must be mechanics,' said Dicky.

'They certainly look very official,' I admitted.

'Hey! Listen!' said Dicky, as a faint drone made itself heard. 'She is arrive.'

The plane came into view as a minute speck on the horizon that rapidly grew bigger and bigger. The two men in khaki coats now came into their own. With shrill cries they ran out on to the airstrip and proceeded to drive away the three ponies, who, up till then had been grazing placidly in the centre of what now turned out to be the runway. There was one exciting moment just as the plane touched down, when we thought that one of the ponies wqas going to break back, but one of the khaki-clad men, launched himself forward and grabbed it by the mane at the last minute. The plane bumped and shuddered to a halt, and the two men left their equine charges and produced, from the depths of the hangar, a flimsy ladder on wheels which they set against the side of the plane. Apparently Dicky was the only passenger to be picked up in Deseado.

Dicky wrung my hand.

'Gerry,' he said, 'you will do for me one favour, yes?'

'Of course, Dicky,' I said, 'anything at all.'

'See that there is no bloody bastard horses in the way when we go up, eh?' he said earnestly, and then strode off to the plane, the flaps of his deer-stalker flopping to and fro in the wind.

The plane roared off, the ponies shambled back on to the runway, and we turned the blunt snout of the Land-Rover back towards the town.

We picked up Huichi at a little after twelve, and he took over the wheel of the Land-Rover. I was heartily glad of this, for we had only travelled a couple of miles from Deseado when we branched off the road on to something so vague that it could hardly be dignified with the term of track. Occasionally this would disappear altogether, and, if left to myself, I would have been utterly lost, but Huichi would aim the Land-Rover at what appeared to be an impenetrable thicket of thorn bushes, and we would tear through it, the thorns screaming along the sides of the vehicle like so many banshees, and there, on the further side, the faint wisp of track would start again. At other points the track turned into what appeared to be the three-feet-deep bed of an extinct river, exactly the same width as the Land-Rover, so we were driving cautiously along with two wheels on one bank – as it were – and two wheels on the other. Any slight miscalculation here and the vehicle could have fallen into the trough and become hopelessly stuck.

Gradually, as we got nearer and nearer to the sea, the landscape underwent a change. Instead of being flat it became gently undulating, and here and there the wind had rasped away the topsoil and exposed large areas of yellow and rust-red gravel, like sores on the furry pelt of the land. These small desert-like areas seemed to be favoured by that curious animal, the Patagonian hare, for it was always on these brilliant expanses of gravel that we found them, sometimes in pairs, sometimes in small groups of three or four. They were strange creatures, that looked as though they had been put together rather carelessly. They had blunt, rather hare-like faces, small, neat, rabbit-shaped ears, neat forequarters with slender forelegs. But the hindquarters were large and muscular in comparison, with powerful hind-legs. The most attractive part of their anatomy was their eyes, which were large, dark and lustrous, with a thick fringe of eyelashes. They would lie on the gravel, sunning themselves, gazing aristocratically down their blunt noses, looking like miniature Trafalgar Square lions. They would let us approach fairly close, and then suddenly their long lashes would droop over their eyes seductively, and with amazing speed they would bounce into a sitting position. They would turn their heads and gaze at us for one brief moment; and then they would launch themselves at the heat-shimmered horizon in a series of gigantic bounding leaps, as if they were on springs, the black and white pattern on their behinds showing up like a retreating target.

Presently, towards evening, the sun sank lower and in is slanting rays the landscape took on new colours. The low growth of thorn scrub became purple, magenta and brown, and the areas of gravel were slashed with scarlet, rust, white and yellow. As we scrunched our way across one such multi-coloured area of gravel we noticed a black blob in the exact centre of the expanse, and driving closer to it we discovered it was a huge tortoise, heaving himself over the hot terrain with the grim determination of a glacier. We stopped and picked him up, and the reptile, horrified by such an unexpected meeting, urinated copiously. Where he could have found, in that desiccated land, sufficient moisture to produce this lavish defensive display was a mystery. However, we christened him Ethelbert, put him in the back of the Land-Rover and drove on.

Presently, in the setting sun, the landscape heaved itself up into a series of gentle undulations, and we switchbacked over the last of these and out on to what at first looked like the level bed of an ancient lake. It lay encircled by a ring of low hills, and was, in fact, a sort of miniature dust-bowl created by the wind, which had carried the sand from the shore behind the hills and deposited it here in a thick, choking layer that had killed off the vegetation. As we roared across this flat area, spreading a fan of white dust behind us, we saw, in the lee of the further hills, a cluster of green trees, the first we had seen since leaving Deseado. As we drew nearer we could see that this little oasis of trees was surrounded by a neat white fence, and in the centre, sheltered by the trees, stood a neat wooden house, gaily painted in bright blue and white.

Huichi's two peons came to meet us, two wild-looking characters dressed in *bombachas* and tattered shirts, with long black hair and dark, flashing eyes. They helped us unload our gear and carry it into the house, and then, while we unpacked and washed, they went with Huichi to kill a sheep and prepare an *asado* in our honour. At the bottom of the slope on which the house was built, Huichi had prepared a special *asado* ground. An *asado* needs a fierce fire, and with the biting and continuous wind that blew in Patagonia you had to be careful unless you wanted to see your entire fire suddenly lifted into the air and blown away to set fire to the tinder-dry scrub for miles around. In order to guard against this Huichi had planted, at the bottom of the hill, a great square of cypress trees. These had been allowed to grow up to a height of some twelve feet, and had then had their tops lopped off, with the result that they had grown very bushy. They had been planted so close together in the first place that now their branches entwined, and formed an almost impenetrable hedge. Then Huichi had carved a narrow passage-way into the centre of this box of cypress, and had there chopped out a room, some twenty feet by twelve. This was the *asado* room, for, protected by the thick walls of cypress, you could light a fire without danger.

By the time we had washed and changed, and the sheep had been killed and stripped, it was dark; we made our way down to the *asado* room, where one of the peons had already kindled an immense fire. Near it a great stake had been stuck upright in the ground, on this a whole sheep, slit open like an oyster, had been spitted. We lay on the ground around the fire and drank red wine while waiting for our meal to cook.

I have been to many *asados* in the Argentine, but that first one at Huichi's *estancia* will always remain in my mind as the most perfect. The wonderful smell of burning brushwood, mingling with the smells of roasting meat, the pink and orange tongues of flame lighting up the green cypress walls of the shelter, and the sound of the wind battering ferociously against these walls and then dying to a soft sigh as it became entangled and sapped of its strength in the mesh of branches, and above us the night sky, trembling with stars, lit by a fragile chip of moon. To gulp a mouthful of soft, warm red wine, and then to lean forward and slice a fragrant chip of meat from the brown, bubbling carcase in front of you, dunk it in the fierce sauce of vinegar, garlic and red pepper, and then stuff it, nut-sweet and juicy, into your mouth, seemed one of the most satisfying actions of my life.

Presently, when our attacks on the carcase became more desultory, Huichi took a gulp of wine, wiped his mouth with the back of his hand, and beamed at me across the red, pulsating embers of the fire, lying like a great sunset on the ground.

'¿*Mañana*,' he said, smiling, 'we go to the *pinguinos*¿'

'*Si, si*,' I responded sleepily, leaning forward in sheer greed to detach another strip of crackling skin from the cooling remains of the sheep, '*mañana* the *pinguinos*.'

Early the next morning, while it was still dark, I was awoken by Huichi moving around the kitchen, whistling softly to himself, clattering the coffee-pot and cups, trying to break in on our slumbers gently. My immediate reaction was to snuggle down deeper under the pile of soft, warm, biscuit-coloured guanaco skins that covered the enormous double-bed in which Jacquie and I were ensconced. Then, after a moment's meditation, I decided that if Huichi was up I ought to be up as well; in any case, I knew I should have to get up in order to rout the others out. So, taking a deep breath, I threw back the bed-clothes and leapt nimbly out of bed. I have rarely regretted an action more: it was rather like coming freshly from a boiler-room and plunging into a mountain stream. With chattering teeth I put on all the clothes I could find, and hobbled out into the kichen. Huichi smiled and nodded at me, and then, in the most understanding manner, poured two fingers of brandy into a large cup, filled it up with steaming coffee and handed it to me. Presently, glowing with heat, I took off one of my three pullovers, and took a malicious delight in making the rest of the party get out of bed.

We set off eventually, full of brandy and coffee, in the pale daffodil-yellow dawn light and headed towards the place where the penguins were to be found. Knots of blank-faced sheep scuttled across the nose of the Land-Rover as we drove along, their fleeces wobbling as they ran, and at one point we passed a long, shallow dew-pond, caught in a cleft between the gentle undulation of hills, and six flamingoes were feeding at its edge, pink as cyclamen buds. We drove a quarter of an hour or so, and then Huichi swung the Land-Rover off the main track and headed across country, up a gentle slope of land. As we came to the top of the rise, he turned and grinned at me.

'*Ahora,*' he said, '*ahora los pinguinos.*'

Then we reached the top of the slope and there was the penguin colony.

Ahead of us the low, brown scrub petered out, and in its place was a great desert of sun-cracked sand. This was separated from the sea beyond by a crescent-shaped ridge of white sand-dunes, very steep and some two hundred feet high. It was in this desert area, protected from the sea wind by the encircling arm of the dunes, that the penguins had created their city. As far as the eye could see on every side the ground was pock-marked with nesting burrows, some a mere half-hearted scrape in the sand, some several feet deep. These craters made the place look like a small section of the moon's surface seen through a powerful telescope. In among these craters waddled the biggest collection of penguins I had ever seen, like a sea of pigmy headwaiters, solemnly shuffling to and fro as if suffering from fallen arches due to a lifetime of carrying overloaded trays. Their numbers were prodigious, stretching to the furthermost horizon where they twinkled black and white in the heat haze. It was a breath-taking sight. Slowly we drove through the scrub until we reached the edge of this gigantic honeycomb of nest burrows and then we stopped and got out of the Land-Rover.

We stood and watched the penguins, and they stood and watched us with immense respect and interest. As long as we stayed near the vehicle they showed no fear. The greater proportion of birds were, of course, adult; but each nesting burrow contained one or two youngsters, still wearing their baby coats of down, who regarded us with big, melting dark eyes, looking rather like plump and shy debutantes clad in outsize silver-fox furs. The adults, sleek and neat in their black and white suits, had red wattles round the base of their beaks, and bright, predatory street-pedlar eyes. As you approached them they would back towards their burrows, twisting their heads from side to side in a warning display, until sometimes they would be looking at you completely upside down. If you approached too close they would walk backwards into their burrows and gradually disappear, still twisting their heads vigorously. The babies, on the other hand, would let you get within about four feet of them, and then their nerve would break and they would turn and dive into the burrow, so that their great fluffy behinds and frantically flapping feet was all that could be seen of them.

At first the noise and movement of the vast colony was confusing. As a background to the continuous whispering of the wind was the constant peeting of the youngsters, and the loud prolonged, donkey-like bray of the adults, standing up stiff and straight, flippers spread wide, beaks pointing at the blue sky as they brayed joyfully and exultingly. To begin with you did not know where to look first, and the constant movement of the adults and young seemed to be desultory and without purpose. Then after a few hours of getting used to being amongst such a huge assemblage of birds, a certain pattern seemed to emerge. The first thing that became obvious was that most of the movement in the colony was due to adult birds. A great number stood by the nest burrows, obviously doing sentry duty with the young, while among them vast numbers of other birds passed to and fro, some making their way towards the sea, others coming from it. The distant sand-dunes were freckled with the tiny plodding figures of penguins, either climbing the steep slopes or sliding down them. This constant trek to and fro to the sea occupied a large portion of the penguins' day, and it was such a tremendous feat that it deserves to be described in detail. By carefully watching the colony, day by day, during the three weeks we lived among it, we discovered that this is what happened.

Early in the morning one of the parent birds (either male or female) would set out towards the sea, leaving its mate in charge of the nestlings. In order to get to the sea the bird had to cover about a mile and a half of the most gruelling and difficult terrain imaginable. First they had to pick their way through the vast patchwork of nesting burrows that made up the colony, and when they reached the edge of this – the suburbs, as it were – they were faced by the desert area, where the sand was caked and split by the sun into something resembling a gigantic jig-saw puzzle. The sand in this area would, quite early in the day, get so hot that it was painful to touch, and yet the penguins would plod dutifully across it, pausing frequently for a rest, as though in a trance. This used to take them about an hour. But, when they reached the other side of the desert they were faced with another obstacle, the sand-dunes. These towered over the diminutive figures of the birds like a snow-white chain of Himalayan mountains, two hundred feet high, their steep sides composed of fine, loose shifting sand. We found it difficult enough to negotiate these dunes, so it must have been far worse for such an ill-equipped bird as a penguin.

When they reached the base of the dunes they generally paused for about ten minutes to have a rest. Some just sat there, brooding, while others fell forwards on to their tummies and lay there panting. Then when they had rested, they would climb sturdily to their feet and start the ascent. Gathering themselves, they would rush at the slope, obviously hoping to get the worst of the climb over as quickly as possible. But this rapid climb would peter out about a quarter of the way up; their progress would slow down, and they would pause to rest more often. As the gradient grew steeper and steeper they would eventually be forced to flop down on their bellies, and tackle the slope that way, using their flippers to assist them in the climb. Then, with one final, furious burst of speed, they would triumphantly reach the top, where they would stand up straight, flap their flippers in delight, and then flop down on to their tummies for a ten-minute rest. They had reached the half-way mark and, lying there on the knife-edge top of the dune, they would see the sea, half a mile away, gleaming coolly and enticingly. But they had still to descend the other side of the dune, across a quarter of a mile of scrub-land and then several hundred yards of shingle beach before they reached the sea.

Going down the dune, of course, presented no problem to them, and they accomplished this in two ways, both equally amusing to watch. Either they would walk down, starting very sedately and getting quicker and quicker the steeper the slope became, until they were galloping along in the most undignified way, or else they would slide down on their tummies, using their wings and feet to propel their bodies over the surface of the sand exactly as if they were swimming. With either method they reached the bottom of the dune in a small avalanche of fine sand, and they would get to their feet, shake themselves, and set off grimly through the scrub towards the beach. But it was the last few hundred yards of beach that seemed to make them suffer most. There was the sea, blue, glittering, lisping seductively on the shore, and to get to it they had to drag their tired bodies over the stony beach, where the pebbles scrunched and wobbled under their feet, throwing them off balance. But at last it was over, and they ran the last few feet to the edge of the waves in a curious crouching position, then suddenly straightened up and plunged into the cool water. For ten minutes or so they twirled and ducked in a shimmer of sun ripples, washing the dust and sand from their heads and wings, fluttering their hot, sore feet in the water in ecstasy, whirling and bobbing, disappearing beneath the water, and popping up again like corks. Then, thoroughly refreshed, they would set about the stern task of fishing, undaunted by the fact that they would have to face that difficult journey once again before the food they caught could be delivered to their hungry young.

Once they had plodded their way – full of fish – back over the hot terrain to the colony, they would have to start on the hectic job of feeding their ravenous young. This feat resembled a cross between a boxing- and an all-in wrestling-match, and was fascinating and amusing to watch. There was one family that lived in a burrow close to the spot where we parked the Land-Rover each day, and both the parent birds and their young got so used to our presence that they allowed us to sit and film them at a distance of about twenty feet, so we could see every detail of the feeding process very clearly. Once the parent bird reached the edge of the colony it had run the gauntlet of several thousand youngsters before it reached its own nest-burrow and babies. All these youngsters were convinced that, by launching themselves at the adult bird in a sort of tackle, they could get it to regurgitate the food it was carrying. So the adult had to avoid the attacks of these fat, furry youngsters by dodging to and fro like a skilful centre-forward on a football field. Generally the parent would end up at its nest-burrow, still hotly pursued by two or three strange chicks, who were grimly determined to make it produce food. When it reached home the adult would suddenly lose patience with its pursuers, and, rounding on them, would proceed to beat them up in no uncertain fashion, pecking at them so viciously that large quantities of the babies' fluff would be pecked away, and float like thistle-down across the colony.

Having routed the strange babies, it would then turn its attention to its own chicks, who were by now attacking it in the same way as the others had done, uttering shrill wheezing cries of hunger and impatience. It would squat down at the entrance to the burrow and stare at its feet pensively, making motions like someone trying to stifle an acute attack of hiccups. On seeing this the youngsters would work themselves into a frenzy of delighted anticipation, uttering their wild, wheezing cries, flapping their wings frantically, pressing themselves close to the parent bird's body, and stretching up their beaks and clattering them against the adult's. This would go on for perhaps thirty seconds, when the parent would suddenly – with an expression of relief – regurgitate vigorously, plunging its beak so deeply into the gaping mouths of the youngsters that you felt sure it would never be able to pull its head out again. The babies, satisfied and apparently not stabbed from stem to stern by the delivery of the first course, would squat down on their plump behinds and meditate for a while, and their parent would seize the opportunity to have a quick wash and brush up, carefully preening its breast-feathers, picking minute pieces of dirt off its feet, and running its beak along its wings with a clipper-like motion. Then it would yawn, bending forward like someone attempting to touch his toes, wings stretched out straight behind, beak gaping wide. Then it would sink into the trance-like state that its babies had attained some minutes earlier. All would be quiet for five minutes or so, and then suddenly the parent would start its strange hiccupping motions again, and pandemonium would break out immediately. The babies would rouse themselves from their digestive reverie and hurl themselves at the adult, each trying its best to get its beak into position first. Once more each of them in turn would be apparently stabbed to the heart by the parent's beak, and then once more they would sink back into somnolence.

The parents and young who occupied this nest-burrow where we filmed the feeding process were known, for convenient reference, as the Joneses. Quite close to the Joneses' establishment was another burrow that contained a single, small and very undernourished-looking chick whom we called Henrietta Vacanttum. Henrietta was the product of an unhappy home-life. Her parents were, I suspected, either dim-witted or just plain idle, for they took twice as long as any other penguins to produce food for Henrietta, and then only in such minute quantities that she was always hungry. An indication of her parents' habits was the slovenly nest-burrow, a mere half-hearted scrape, scarcely deep enough to protect Henrietta from any inclement weather, totally unlike the deep, carefully dug villa-residence of the Jones family. So it was not surprising that Henrietta had a big-eyed, half-starved, ill-cared-for look about her that made us feel very sorry for her. She was always on the look-out for food, and as the Jones parents had to pass her front door on their way to their own neat burrow, she always made valiant attempts to get them to regurgitate before they reached home.

These efforts were generally in vain, and all Henrietta got for her pains was a severe pecking that made her fluff come out in great clouds. She would retreat, disgruntled, and with anguished eye watch the two disgustingly fat Jones babies wolfing down their food. But one day, by accident, Henrietta discovered a way to pinch the Jones family's food without any unpleasant repercussions. She would wait until the parent Jones had started the hiccupping movements as a preliminary to regurgiation, and the baby Joneses were frantically gyrating round, flapping their wings and wheezing, and then, at the crucial moment, she would join the group, carefully approaching the parent bird from behind. Then, wheezing loudly, and opening her beak wide, she would thrust her head either over the adult's shoulder, as it were, or under its wing, but still carefully maintaining her position behind the parent so that she should not be recognized. The parent Jones, being harried by its gaping-mouthed brood, its mind fully occupied with the task of regurgitating a pint of shrimps, did not seem to notice the introduction of a third head into the general mêlé that was going on around it. And when the final moment came it would plunge its head into the first gaping beak that was presented, with the slightly desperate air of an aeroplane passenger seizing his little brown paper bag at the onset of the fiftieth air-pocket. Only when the last spasm had died away, and the parent Jones could concentrate on external matters, would it realize that it had been feeding a strange offspring, and then Henrietta had to be pretty nifty on her great, flat feet to escape the wrath. But even if she did not move quickly enough, and received a beating up for her iniquity, the smug look on her face seemed to argue that it was worth it.

In the days when Darwin had visited this area there had still been the remnants of the Patagonian Indian tribes left, fighting a losing battle against extermination by the settlers and soldiers. These Indians were described as being uncouth and uncivilized and generally lacking in any quality that would qualify them for a little Christian charity. So they vanished, like so many animal species when they come into contact with the beneficial influences of civilization, and no one, apparently, mourned their going. In various museums up and down Argentina you can see a few remains of their crafts (spears, arrows, and so on) and inevitably a large and rather gloomy picture purporting to depict the more unpleasant side of the Indians' character, their lechery. In every one of these pictures there was shown a group of long-haired wild-looking Indians on prancing wild steeds, and the leader of the troupe inevitably had clasped across his saddle a white woman in a diaphanous garment, whose mammary development would give any modern film star pause for thought. In every museum the picture was almost the same, varying only in the number of Indians shown, and the chest expansion of their victim. Fascinating though these pictures were, the thing that puzzled me was that there was never a companion piece to show a group of civilized white men galloping off with a voluptuous Indian girl, and yet this had happened as frequently (if not more frequently) than the rape of white women. It was a curious and interesting sidelight on history. But nevertheless these spirited but badly-painted portraits of abduction had one interesting feature. They were obviously out to give the worst possible impression of the Indians, and yet all they succeeded in doing was in impressing you with a wild and rather beautiful people, and filling you with a pang of sorrow that they were no longer in existence. So, when we got down into Patagonia I searched eagerly for relics of these Indians, and questioned everyone for stories about them. The stories, unfortunately, were much of a muchness and told me little, but when it came to relics, it turned out, I could not have gone to a better place than the penguin metropolis.

One evening, when we had returned to the *estancia* after a hard day's filming and were drinking *maté* round the fire, I asked Señor Huichi – *via* Marie – if there had been many Indian tribes living in those parts. I phrased my questions delicately, for I had been told that Huichi had Indian blood in him, and I was not sure whether this was a thing he was proud of or not. He smiled his slow and gentle smile, and said that on and around his *estancias* had been one of the largest concentrations of Indians in Patagonia, in fact, he went on, the place where the penguins lived still yielded evidence of their existence. What sort of evidence, I asked eagerly. Huichi smiled again, and, getting to his feet he disappeared into his darkened bedroom. I heard him pull a box out from under his bed, and he returned carrying it in his hands and placed it on the table. He removed the lid and tipped the contents out on to the white tablecloth, and I gasped.

I had seen, as I say, various relics in the museums, but nothing to compare with this; for Huichi tumbled out on to the table a rainbow-coloured heap of stone objects that were breathtaking in their colouring and beauty. There were arrow-heads ranging from delicate, fragile-looking ones the size of your little fingernail, to ones the size of an egg. There were spoons made by slicing in half and carefully filing down big sea-shells; there were long, curved stone scoops for removing the edible molluscs from their shells; there were spearheads with razor-sharp edges; there were the balls for the *boleadoras*, round as billiard-balls, with a shallow trough running round their equators, as it were, which took the thong from which they hung; these were so incredibly perfect that one could hardly believe that such precision could be achieved without a machine. Then there were the purely decorative articles: the shells neatly pierced for ear-rings, the necklace made of beautifully matched green, milky stone rather like jade, the seal-bone that had been chipped and carved into a knife that was obviously more ornamental than useful. The pattern on it was simple arrangements of lines, but carved with great precision.

I sat poring over these objects delightedly. Some of the arrowheads were so small it seemed impossible that anyone could create them by crude chipping, but hold them up to the light and you could see where the delicate wafers of stone had been chipped away. What was more incredible still was that each of these arrowheads, however small, had a minutely serrated edge to give it a bite and sharpness. As I was examining the articles I was suddenly struck by their colouring. On the beaches near the penguins almost all the stones were brown or black; to find attractively coloured ones you had to search. And yet every arrowhead, however small, every spearhead, in fact every piece of stone that had been used had obviously been picked for its beauty. I arranged all the spear- and arrowheads in rows on the tablecloth, and they lay there gleaming like the delicate leaves from some fabulous tree. There were red ones with a darker vein of red, like dried blood; there were green ones covered with a fine tracery of white; there were blue-white ones, like mother-of-pearl; and yellow and white ones covered with a freckling of blurred patterns in blue or black where the earth's juices had stained the stone. Each piece was a work of art, beautifully shaped, carefully and minutely chipped, edged and polished, constructed out of the most beautiful piece of stone the maker could find. You could see they had been made with love. And these, I reminded myself, were made by the barbarous, uncouth, savage and utterly uncivilized Indians for whose passing no one appeared to be sorry.

Huichi seemed delighted that I should display such obvious interest and admiration for his relics, and he went back into the bedroom and unearthed another box. This one contained an extraordinary weapon carved from stone: it was like a small dumb-bell. The central shaft which connected the two great, misshapen balls of stone fitted easily into the palm of your hand, so that then you had a great ball of stone above and below your fist. As the whole thing weighed about three pounds it was a fearsome weapon, capable of splitting a man's skull like a puffball. The next item in the box – which

Huichi reverently unwrapped from a sheet of tissue paper – looked as though, in fact, it had been treated with this stone club. It was an Indian skull, white as ivory, with a great splinter-edged gaping hole across the top of the cranium.

Huichi explained that over the years, whenever his work had taken him to the corner of the *estancia* where the penguins lived, he had searched for Indian relics. He said that the Indians had apparently used that area very extensively, for what particular purpose no one was quite sure. His theory was that they had used the great flat area where the penguins now nested as a sort of arena, where the young men of the tribe practised shooting with bow and arrow, spear-throwing, and the art of entangling their quarry's legs with the *boleadoras*. On the other side of the great sand-dunes, he said, were to be found huge piles of empty sea-shells. I had noticed these great, white heaps of shells, some covering an area of a quarter of an acre and about three feet thick, but I had been so engrossed in my filming of the penguins that I had only given them a passing thought. Huchi's theory was that this had been a sort of holiday resort, as it were, the Margate of the Indians. They had come down there to feed on the succulent and plentiful shellfish, to find stones on the shingle beach from which to make their weapons, and a nice flat area on which to practise with these weapons. What other reason would there be for finding these great piles of empty shells, and, scattered over the sand-dune and shingle patches, such a host of arrow- and spear-heads, broken necklaces, and the occasional crushed skull? I must say Huichi's idea seemed to me to be a sensible one, though I suppose a professional archaeologist would have found some method of disproving it. I was horrified at the thought of the number of delicate and lovely arrowheads that must have been splintered and crushed beneath the Land-Rover wheels as we had gaily driven to and fro over the penguin town. I resolved that the next day when we had finished filming we would search for arrowheads.

As it happened, the next day we had only about two hours' decent sunshine suitable for filming, and so the rest of the time we spent crawling over the sand-dunes in curious prenatal postures, searching for arrowheads and other Indian left-overs. I very soon discovered that it was not nearly as easy as it seemed. Huichi, after years of practice, could spot things with uncanny accuracy from a great distance.

'*Esto, una.*' he would say, smiling, pointing with the toe of his shoe at a huge pile of shingle. I would glare at the area indicated, but could see nothing but unworked bits of rock.

'*Esto,*' he would say again, and bending down pick up a beautiful leaf-shaped arrowhead that had been within five inches of my hand. Once it had been pointed out, of course, it became so obvious that you wondered how you had missed it. Gradually, during the course of the day, we improved, and our pile of finds started mounting, but Huichi still took a mischievous delight in wandering erect behind me as I crawled laboriously across the dunes, and, as soon as I thought I had sifted an area thoroughly, he would stoop down and find three arrowheads which I had somehow missed. This happened with such monotonous regularity that I began to wonder, under the influence of an aching back and eyes full of sand, whether he was not palming the arrowheads, like a conjuror, and pretending to find them just to pull my leg. But then my unkind doubts were dispelled, for he suddenly leant forward and pointed at an area of shingle I was working over.

'*Esto*,' he said, and leaning down, pointed out to me a minute area of yellow stone protruding from under a pile of shingle. I gazed at it unbelievingly. Then I took it gently between my fingers and eased from under the shingle a superb yellow arrowhead with a meticulously serrated edge. There had been approximately a quarter of an inch of the side of the arrowhead showing, and yet Huichi had spotted it.

However, it was not long before I got my own back on him. I was making my way over a sand-dune towards the next patch of shingle, when my toe scuffed up something that gleamed white. I bent down and picked it up, and to my astonishment found I was holding a beautiful harpoon-head about six inches long, magnificently carved out of fur seal bone. I called to Huichi, and when he saw what I had found his eyes widened. He took it from me gently and wiped the sand off it, and then turned it over and over in his hands, smiling with delight. He explained that a harpoon-head like this was one of the rarest things you could find. He had only ever found one, and that had been so crushed that it had not been worth saving. Ever since he had been looking, without success, for a perfect one to add to his collection.

Presently it was getting towards evening, and we were all scattered about the sand-dunes hunched and absorbed in our task. I rounded a spur of sand and found myself in a tiny valley between the high dunes, a valley decorated with two or three wizened and carunculated trees. I paused to light a cigarette and ease my aching back. The sky was turning pink and green as it got towards sunset time, and apart from the faint whisper of the sea and the wind it was silent and peaceful. I walked slowly up the little valley, and suddenly I noticed a slight movement ahead of me. I small, very hairy armadillo was scuttling along the top of the dunes like a clockwork toy, intent on his evening search for food. I watched him until he disappeared over the dunes and then walked on. Under one of the bushes I was surprised to see a pair of penguins, for they did not usually choose this fine sand to dig their nest burrows in. But this pair had chosen this valley for some reason of their own, and had scraped and scrabbled a rough hole in which squatted a single fur-coated chick. The parents castanetted their beaks at me and twisted their heads upside down, very indignant that I should disturb their solitude. I watched them for a moment, and then I noticed something half hidden in the pile of sand which they had dug out to form their nest. It was something smooth and white. I went forward and, despite the near hysterics of the penguins, I scraped away the sand. There lying in front of me was a perfect Indian skull, which the birds must have unearthed.

I sat down with the skull on my knee and smoked another cigarette while

I contemplated it. I wondered what sort of a man this vanished Indian had been. I could imagine him, squatting on the shore, carefully and cleverly chipping minute flakes off a piece of stone to make one of the lovely arrow-heads that now squeaked and chuckled in my pocket. I could imagine him, with his fine brown face and dark eyes, his hair hanging to his shoulders, his rich brown guanaco skin cloak pulled tight about him as he sat very straight on a wild, unshod horse. I gazed into the empty eye-sockets of the skull and wished fervently that I could have met the man who had produced anything as beautiful as those arrowheads. I wondered if I ought to take the skull back to England with me and give it a place of honour in my study, sur-rounded by his artistic products. But then I looked around, and decided against it. The sky was now a vivid dying blue, with pink and green thumb-smudges of cloud. The wind made the sand trickle down in tiny rivulets that hissed gently. The strange, witch-like bushes creaked pleas-antly and musically. I felt that the Indian would not mind sharing his last resting place with the creatures of what had once been his country, the pen-guins and the armadillos. So I dug a hole in the sand and placing the skull in it I gently covered it over. When I stood up in the rapidly gathering gloom the whole area seemed steeped in sadness, and the presence of the vanished Indians seemed very close. I could almost believe that, if I looked over my shoulder quickly, I would see one on horseback, silhouetted against the col-oured sky. I shrugged this feeling off as fanciful, and walked back towards the Land-Rover.

As we rattled and bumped our way back in the dusk towards the *estancia*, Huichi, talking to Marie, said very quietly:

'You know, *señorita*, that place always seems to be sad. I feel the Indians there very much. They are all around you, their ghosts, and one feels sorry for them because they do not seem to be happy ghosts.'

This had been my feeling exactly.

Before we left the next day I gave Huichi the harpoon-head I had found. It broke my heart to part with it, but he had done so much for us that it seemed very small return for his kindness. He was delighted, and I know that it is now reverently wrapped in tissue-paper in the box beneath his bed, not too far from where it ought to be, buried on the great shining dunes, feel-ing only the shifting sand as the penguins thump solidly overhead.

Stumberleap

HENRY WILLIAMSON

WHEN I WAS A LITTLE BOY at school, I was indifferent to nearly all my lessons, including Geography. I remember the drawing of maps (but not the maps) and the putting-in of capes, rivers, bays, and mountains; the dull lists of towns and places I had to learn by heart; and what things, usually of commerce, the places were 'noted for'. It was dreary work, for usually I was thinking of other things – of how, if they would choose me for the team, I would kick a goal for my House, amid cheers, as the whistle blew; of a steam engine or an electric motor in a catalogue; of a raft to be made of boxes and provisioned by free samples, and steered by a compass out of a Christmas party cracker, with which I should set out on an exploration (I didn't know where); but most often I thought of the wild animals and birds – especially the birds – of the fields and woods I knew. And any reference I found, in any of the lesson books, to a bird or animal – it must be an English one! – how my mind took hold of it, and dreamed on it, as a green weed takes hold and dreams on a brick wall in the smoke of London. There was, I remember, but one green and living plant in all the waste of the big Geography book we 'did lessons from', and that was a paragraph against a map of south-western England, which said that Exmoor was 'noted for' the wild red deer, because it was the only place in all England and Wales where the red deer had survived in their wild ways. I think I used to hunt a red stag every Geography lesson, with a bow and arrow; I was a mighty hunter, although really my arms were very thin, and I was no good at boxing. And now I am more or less grown up: and perhaps in some school a little boy dreams of the wild red deer which Exmoor is 'noted for'; and here is a story of a stag for him, which is as true as my small knowledge of Stumberleap can make of it. It is not a quarter as good as the proper *Story of a Red*

Deer, which Sir John Fortescue told me he wrote during a fortnight's holiday to please a small boy; but Sir John was bred in the country of the deer and saw them as a child on his native moor, while I saw them only in the Geography book.

Now if the dull Geography book is still in misuse, which I hope is not so, it will be wrong, for it said that the red deer roam wild in but one part of England and Wales, on the high and tameless tract called Exmoor; whereas in Wales is a wooded hill overlooking the Severn Sea, and in the wood lives a wild stag who sometimes gazes across many miles of water to the dim blue moor of his birth. That book will be right again one day, perhaps before it can be corrected; for a stag's life is as a tree's, whose lost branches measure its years; and the last antlers have grown and dropped from the stag's head. He is a solitary, and this is his story.

The hound Deadlock nearly died in the last chase of the stag, but eleven thorns fastened his wound until I brought him to the farmhouse, where he grew well within a fortnight. But his pace was gone from him; and he was drafted to the otter hunters who walk in the valleys.

First I must tell you a little about the life of 'the girt old stag of Stumberleap Wood', as he was called by the farmer. Several times I saw him, before the stag-hunting season, once in the Badgeworthy valley in June, when his coat was glowing ruddy-gold, for he was fat with young corn and roots plundered from moorland farms.

And during the rutting season I saw him coming down from the hills before an October gale, driving a herd of hinds. Three young male deer followed the herd, and sometimes one would approach too near a hind, when Stumberleap would charge back and the young deer would race away. The old stag was gaunt with sinew and muscle, in shape of body not unlike a donkey, but taller; the hair of his flanks was shaggy with mud, and he was thin with so much travelling and fighting. They say on the moor that at such a time a stag's blood is black and poisonous, and that he eats nothing for weeks. The grey gale fell upon the valley, the oaks shuddered in the rainy wind, and as I crouched under a rock Stumberleap was seen against the sky. His head was thrown back as he roared a challenge to any other stag that might be in the goyal. Then bending his neck he dug his antlers into the boggy ground and tore up grasses and sods, which the wind flung away. Again he bellowed. So brazen was the note above the wind that terror entered into me, and fearing lest when he crossed my scent he might charge back and drive the brow-point through my body into the trunk which sheltered me, I climbed the tree. The bark was rough with lichen, and I scrambled along a branch in order to watch as another bellow had answered Stumberleap. Immediately he roared back, and trotted forward, and, while I sat on the creaking bough, a strange stag came forward to meet him. The points of the stranger's antlers made the outline of a crown, whereas Stumberleap's was a forked head. Both stags jumped round feinting for an opening to stab and point. While the gale passed over the sombre moor they thrust and drew back to watch, but suddenly Stumberleap leapt up, and plunged down his head, and the horns clashed. With fury they wrestled and swayed, breaking the soft leaf-mould at the hill's edge with their slot, until the crown-headed stag (who for three days and nights had hardly eaten or slept, for every breeze that drew across his nostrils had made him more feverish to travel and seek the hinds of his rivals) was so buffeted that he was thrown down the slope. Again the antlers clashed, and a young hind stole back from the herd and butted him in the flank. She had been conquered by Stumberleap, and loved him. The stranger seemed to lose strength, and after a minute he backed away and ran into the undergrowth. Stumberleap threw up his head, stretched his thick neck, and bellowed; then rose on his hind legs and sniffed. I saw the instant alertness in the fine eyes of the head upheld. He scented man. The deer were gone, and the rain and the wind blurred all things in my sight.

Stumberleap must have been hunted many times before that October, as he had possessed all his rights – the points called brow, bay, and tray – some years previously, at the age of five years. Until his sixth year he was not called a stag, but a male red deer, and as such not warrantable or worthy of being chased. Every April his antlers began to grow, and every following March they dropped off, and then Stumberleap hid himself in a wood, and avoided all deer, the horns started to grow again soon afterwards, when blood and nerves rushed up the two beams (which were soft and tender, and gave him pain when anything touched them) and formed the points known as 'brow, bay, tray, and three-point-top'. Six points came on each beam at the beginning of his sixth year of life, and were fully formed towards the end of August, when the horn became hard, and the protecting skin, or 'velvet', cracked and peeled off. His horns itched, and Stumberleap travelled to the fir-trees growing on the high ground above the sea, and rubbed his antlers against the trunks and branches to ease the itch. Many of these trees were dead, the bark having been ringed by stags in former summers, so that the sap could not rise, and they withered.

He grew bigger with the years, and took only the best food – he sought the buds of the ash and beech in March, and crunched the leaves of the ivy. In the early summer he roamed far into the green valleys below the heather moor, and wherever he went he pillaged crops, orchards, and gardens, exercising the rights of his race which roamed there thousands of years before the soil was tilled and sown by man. For the red deer were of more ancient lineage than any other creatures on Exmoor. Many races of the chief hunter, man, had lived there, and the red deer had remained. Their instincts were uncorrupt, and came pure from the earth-spirit, which had given them fleetness and grace, and a pride of race that prevented them mating with the tame fallow deer of the parks. Exmoor is a true child of her mother the earth, and her abiding pride is the tall red deer.

And now, in the twentieth century, while another human civilization was decaying, some of the farmers made straw-stuffed dummies in their own image, and placed them in the beech-hedges guarding the root-crops, to frighten the wild red deer! Stumberleap ignored the oddmedodds as he walked down the rows, biting a turnip, often pulling it up and throwing it over his shoulder, to tear off the juicy flake between his teeth. Sometimes he and other stags would ruin a whole field in a night, but the hinds were not so destructive, for their necks were not so strong, nor were they so impatient. Cornfields he 'used', tearing mouthfuls of the golden ears, while the hinds wasted hardly a berry. To keep out the wild red deer the farmers put wires on the stone banks, fixed with tarred stakes, but Stumberleap easily leapt over the obstacles, although they kept out the hinds, which preferred to scramble up a bank or through a beech-tree hedge.

But most of all Stumberleap liked the acorns which fell from the oaks in autumn. He swallowed them without munching, as many as he could find. He bolted apples until his paunch was filled. At seven years of age the points of his antlers were thirteen, and in his fifteenth year he carried fifteen points, and three offers (which were little knobs on the beam, as though points had offered to grow there). His head was an 'imperial', or, as the harbourer described him, he was 'brow, bay, tray, five p'n-tap, four p'n-tap'. Five top-points on one beam, four on the other.

Many of his sons had been killed, but Stumberleap lived, because he was cunning and knew the waters. He lived through so many seasons that no one knew his age; but one morning in September, when the brown heather-bells of the commons were dry and honeyless, and a golden haze brimmed the goyals and lay lightly on the hills, he was dozing under his favourite oak-tree, unaware that a keen-eyed man had seen that his slot on the deer-path led into Stumberleap Wood, and not out again.

The man was the harbourer. He was the huntsman's secret agent. He had not seen the stag for a week, yet he knew where he had been, where he had drunk, and what he had eaten. Indeed, he did not need to see the stag, for he could read easily his comings and goings. His nose and eyes were almost as keen as a wild animal's, and his clothes were the hues of the moor.

He knew 'the girt old stag of Stumberleap Wood' by his slot, or hoof-print. A hind's slot was smaller, and had only a slight cleft between the two halves of the hoof, whereas that of the matured stag was square, the halves were longer and more pointed. For the last three sunrisings the harbourer had gone to the soiling-pit of Stumberleap – where every

155

dawn before going home the stag went to drink and bathe–and 'made good' his slot.

In July the stag had returned to Stumberleap Wood, and the harbourer had seen in a goyal several trunks of rowan-tree and alder with their bark ringed, the work of a stag with itching antlers, desiring to rub off the velvet from the new hardening horn. During August he had come occasionally to the soiling-pit, which was made by the cutting of turf during previous summers. The water looked black with old dead heather roots. He read the slot of stag, hind, staggart, pricket, or calf as easily as he knew trees by their leaves.

September came, and a meet was fixed at Stumberleap Farm, a mile away and below the wood, built on the ridge which rose between two valleys, called the Globe. The day before the meet the harbourer did not go near the wood, but he went to the soiling-pit in the early morning and slurred with his boot all slot imprints. At sunrise next morning he saw the fresh slot of 'the girt old stag of Stumberleap Wood', with those of a staggart, or younger male deer. Then he walked to a young ash-tree on the way from the pit to the wood. The tree was a perpetual cripple. Not only were its four sapling-trunks gnawn, but all its younger branches, which had striven to grow, were maimed. And every May its leaf-shoots were cut. The harbourer glanced at one new spray, and turned back downhill. He had seen what he wanted—stag's teeth had hastily torn at one spray in passing: he had not been hungry: therefore he had torn it when going to his layer, or bed, after the night's feeding.

The harbourer hurried to the farmhouse, where with the grooms he ate a hearty breakfast of eggs, bacon, hog's-pudding, and fried bread, washed down with a quart of mulled ale. Afterwards the ease of legs drying before a fire, while he waited for huntsman and tufters.

Stumberleap farm was a long stone building roofed with slate. Bright yellow lichens spread in patches over the walls and roof. Starlings sang upon great square chimney tuns, in the cracks of which grew ferns of wall-rue and hart's tongue. On the top of each tun two slabs of shale were mortared in the form of a triangle, to cut the winds which in winter would pour down the chimneys. Beeches and pines surrounded the cluster of house, barns, and shippen. One of the beech trees was hollow and had held the nest of a brown owl every spring for half a century. On a thick branch parallel with the ground a rope swing was tied, and the farm children played here, swinging from the same branch from which, it has been said, their great-great-great-great-grandfather was hanged after a raid by the robbers of Hoccombe-goyal.*

In one of the stable buildings six hunters had been in stall for more than an hour. Now, at ten o'clock in the morning, grooms in shirt-sleeves

*Mistakenly (some declare) called Doone Valley.

and unhitched braces were finally polishing bits and stirrup irons, and unrolling bandages from tails and canons. There was the clack and stamp of shoes on the brick floor. These were the spare mounts of the Master and the two hunt servants. In the stall of another building stood a clipped Exmoor pony, with old grass-champ on its dull nickel bit, carrying a saddle with irons and buckles rusted by the moor mists of many seasons. It had been born on the moor, and driven with its dam into Bampton Pony Fair fifteen Septembers since, and purchased by the farmer for a guinea. The farmer had carried it away under his arm, squealing and kicking, but since its fifth year it had carried him many thousands of miles, and eaten many apples from the paunches of stags for whom the mort blast had sounded.

At half-past ten, the time of the meet, over a hundred people had come to the farm. Hunters neighed, men and women smiled and chatted, moved about greeting friends; pink and black and tweed coats made gay colour in the field behind the farm. The sun of a fair September morning dropped its gold into dewy freshness of the valley. In blinding spikes and splashes of light it moved up the southern sky, above the sombre moor whose summit undulated with the four curves of Dunkery's cloud-high crest. Seen from the Globe, the moor's outline against blue space was like the back of a monster petrified in the fires of earth's creation, showing black bristles singed almost to the roots; westwards the last paw-stroke of the dying monster had made claw-rips in the steep slope of Lucott Ridge.

The people on Dunkery Beacon, tiny as singed bristles, saw the horsemen waiting on the Globe a mile and a half below them. Black and scarlet specks moved by the farm, near one of the barns in which, pacing restlessly the clean straw, sitting moodily on haunches, throwing up heads and occasionally 'singing', the hounds were shut. Five couple of tufters had already gone with the huntsman and his whipper-in. Already they were approaching Stumberleap, and while the mournful 'singing' of a hound made the male starlings on the roof listen in order to imitate, the harbourer took the huntsman to the path where that morning the stag had entered the wood after his night's feeding. The tufters were old hounds, wise and trusty, and their job was to make Stumberleap break covert. The trees grew in the sides of the goyal, which diminished in depth and width until it ended half-way up the great slope, grown with heather and whortleberry, which stretched up to the crest. The watchers on the Globe saw a red speck on a grey horse cantering through the bracken along the farther edge of the wooded goyal. This was the whipper-in, who was to watch where the stag would run. Then they heard the horn faintly singing. So did the stag, where he lay in dread of the return of a fly whose wing-whirr he had just heard—a red-bearded bot-fly that was circling with almost inaudible flight above his head, ready to dart into his nostril, and squirt a drop of fluid containing maggots, which would hook themselves to the skin before he could sneeze out their parent. When he heard the horn he pressed his chin on the ground, and waited. He knew what the horn meant.

A hound whimpered in the wood, but the stag did not move. He listened. The bot-fly settled on the long shaggy hairs of his upper neck, and washed its silvery face; for Stumberleap was not breathing. The stag heard the voice of the huntsman and the more abrupt cries of the whipper-in farther away. Then a hound threw its tongue, and jumped forward, followed by other tufters. Stumberleap jumped up and one of his top-points furrowed the bark of a branch above his thrown-up head. One hound made as if to run in upon him, but stopped, remembering.

When the huntsman came up he encouraged hounds with his horn and voice, and the ten tongues clamoured about him. Stumberleap kicked at one, and drew from it a yelp of pain. The others pressed upon him, he sank slightly upon his haunches, quivered as he pressed all his strength into his muscles, and sprang over hounds and away among the trees. *Forrards!* cried the huntsman, and at the sound the harbourer, waiting at the edge of the wood, cantered to a place where it was possible to observe the going away.

Stumberleap, however, did not mean to leave the wood. With a clattering of horn against twigs and small branches he ran swiftly to the bed of the staggart. The male deer, four years old, bore only six points on his antlers. Since the previous winter he had followed Stumberleap wherever he went, feeding with him, soiling in the same pit, and lying near him by day. Now the old stag came to him and he sprang up, but would not leave his layer. Stumberleap reared up on his hind legs, then plunged down his head, and his antlers rattled against the antlers of the staggart. For a few seconds only they fought, and then the staggart, overmastered by his sire and terrified by the approaching clamour, turned and ran away. The tufters running the line of Stumberleap came to the bed, hesitated, and catching the scent on the wind, pursued the staggart.

The huntsman heard him crashing through the bushes, and stood up in his stirrups to get a better view. He did not think that it was the stag, and a glance told him that the hounds were pursuing the wrong deer. He called, and the whipper-in galloped along the ferny edge of the wood, crying the name of the hounds as the wrist-power of his curling thong cracked off the lash into the air. They were called off, and the huntsman took them back to the stag. They roused him and drove him up the wood, but he returned again, and for more than an hour he refused to leave. He was trying to wind another deer, in order to force it to run for him. He found none, and at last, followed everywhere and unable to shake off pursuit, he made for the bracken outside the wood. Short repeated notes of the horn twanged through the trees, and at this signal the whipper-in cantered forward to a place whence he could observe. Hardly had he checked when Stumberleap broke out of the wood, and in a lurching canter set off over the heather. On the crest he stopped, looked back for a moment, and was gone.

Without delay the huntsman returned to Stumberleap Farm, and the prolonged notes of his horn echoed in the goyals. At once the groups of men and horses around the stone buildings began to agitate. Farmers mounted their moor ponies, taller and sleeker hunters capered and whinnied, bowler-hatted grooms in black coats cross-braced with spare stirrup-leathers held bridles and threw up into saddles ladies in habits of brown, grey, and blue. Girths were finally inspected and reins laid flat on necks—"Steady, old mare, steady!" Pedestrians dodged dancing hoofs, and the farm wife looked on, bidding her children keep close to the threshold. Mournful singing of hounds changed to eager chorus as the rain-rotted wooden doors of the barn were pulled open, and the 'girt dogs' immediately pushed through. The pack trotted under ash-trees and the gold-blotched shade was transferred to heads and backs, tiger-like. A cowman, whose face, arms, and collarless neck were brown as old leather, said to the farmer's wife: "The girt old zstag of Zstumberleap Wood be zsparking now, a' reckons," which meant that the stag was away, fleet as the brilliant pinewood spark that shoots out of the hearth and vanishes.

The cowman was not entirely right. When the pack was laid on to the line from Stumberleap Wood the Stag was three miles away, travelling easy and untroubled on his native moor, slanting up the goyal-sides with the ease of clouds in the blue sky over him, the halves of his slot spreading wide at each thrust.

He determined to cross the moor to the pool in the water he knew so well. He traversed a common where the wiry stems of ling and bell-heather grew with furze and bushes of whortleberry. Behind him was silence. He ran at the biggest furze bushes, gauging height and length and scarcely checking before rising up and over with the ease of tense strength, clearing the spikes with forelegs tucked back; so faultless his eye that not a spike was touched by foreslot polished and black. He hoped by the jumps to break the line of his scent. A light landing, and on again, over the common to a goyal, a deep narrow groove in whose turfy sides boulders were embedded, on which lizards and vipers were basking. His passing made them hide, and he went down until he came to the shady bottom where a small stream tumbled and bubbled over a clear brown stony bed. He lay in a pool, lapping the cold water, and then rolled, kicking his legs and tapping the stones with his antlers. He rejoiced in the soiling, then rose and shook himself, listened, and went in a slant up the coombeside. At the edge he met the sun again, and fled swiftly, while the blackcock crouched at the terse thuds of his feet. Sheep with curled horns stared at him, soon to be left behind. The ground rose steadily to the line of the sky more than two miles away, but there was another coombe between, into which he descended. He ran in shallow water up to the stream's end among rushes and red-withering grass and rusty-filmed bog-water, where a curlew flapped up crying with bubbly sweetness, *cur-leek, cur-leek*. He never paused, but ran over tussocks of coarse grass and wild cotton plant to the summit, just under which was a bank of stone and earth six feet high. There was a slight break near a gate, but he avoided it, and choosing the highest part, slowed to a trot, tautened sinew and muscle pressed his hind legs under him, and jumped. Miles away one of the watchers on the Beacon saw through glasses a speck rise out of the darkness into a mist of light, and vanish again.

Stumberleap was now travelling over high ground where in some years the winter snows lie beyond April, it is so high and cold under the sky. He turned south, and cantered down the long rough tawny slope until he came to where the sparse heather rooted itself in a soil of dry grains which once were rock. Its stems were blackened by the summer sun, and twisted with the struggle to hold the life-water. Whitish lumps of hard marble-like stone lay in the sandy patches; the everlasting wind would one day make them dust. Across the treeless place he ran, over patches of scree shining like sun-sores, and going down into a goyal where grew thorns grey and hoary as though with hair, for everywhere the lichens clung to their branches. The thorns grew close, and Stumberleap knew it would be hard going for the hounds – whose feet were not horny like his own slot – and that the thorns would wound nose and pad. For half a mile he ran the bed of a stream, on the banks of which bracken grew under ash and holly-trees. Again he drank and soiled, afterwards lurching down the water while trout darted zigzag from his shape to hide in still caves under the brown boulders. Leaving the water before a footbridge made of a thrown tree, he climbed the steep side of the goyal again, bursting through bushes to delay pursuit, and crossed a further goyal. Loping up to high ground once more, he looked back before trotting on at a slackening pace.

He disturbed a herd of deer which was resting with heads to leeward. Some of the hinds had calves with them, and when they saw Stumberleap they sprang out of the gorse and bracken and ran away, knowing that he was being hunted. Stumberleap tried to mingle with them, but was shunned. For half an hour he followed the herd, then turning away he made for the retreat where always before he had hid unseen. He ran in a loop of many miles. The sun of the afternoon was hotter in the goyals than at noon, and the air was thickening.

A motor coach was making a cloud of dust less than a quarter of a mile away as Stumberleap crossed a road. The driver stopped, and the people in it stood up and gazed . They decided to wait and watch the hunt go by, but after ten minutes, when no one appeared, the coach drove on. It had gone a mile along the narrow lumpy road when they met the huntsman, and by their timely information the pack was saved twelve miles of the loop, and laid on again where the stag had crossed the road. Huntsman and whip mounted second horses. The long-drawn file of hounds ran silently. Behind them a string of riders coiled over miles of moorland. Some horses had been bogged, others gone lame, or lost their way, or were dead-beat. Sixteen and a half couple of hounds loped into the heather. They ran mute, without fatigue, without haste. And Stumberleap, topping a ridge by a tumulus, half a league distant as the blackcock flies (but a league by running) heard the thin echo of the horn. His heart pounded, his tongue dripped.

And the hounds ran on, mute and inevitable as the hours that passed. The sun of September became an orb of larger and duller gold rolling down to the sea, which could be seen grey and remote from the breezy hill. The wind had changed, and now was blowing from the south-west, from the headland dark blue beyond the remote sea. Above the headland, and travelling in ponderous silence towards the moor, was a black and ragged cloud, and others came after it, bringing the friendly deluge that washes scent from earth and air. Stumberleap knew that the south-west gale was coming. His sinews and muscles had lost their tension, no longer did he fly five-barred gates and banks. But he was nearing the refuge which had saved him many times before. He descended another goyal, and entering the stream at the bottom, drank and soiled, and rose refreshed. Upon the opposite bank he leapt, bounded along beside the water for a hundred yards, suddenly sprang sideways into the stream again, and ran on down. Trees grew here, and magpies scolded as he passed. For two miles he ran the bed of the stream, until he came to a pool near the ruined hut-circle of a primitive tribe. Into the pool he sank all but his head, and waited in the shadow of a rowan-tree that grew over it. So still was he that a pair of grey thrushes flew to the tree and began to swallow the scarlet berries. About fifty yards away a man was lying so still that neither thrushes nor stag knew he was there. The man never moved. The water made its music, the winged hum of flies sounded under the oaks, and all was quiet for a time.

From where I lay I could see the reflection of ripples gliding on his ears and antlers. For hours I had loitered in that sweet shady place, lying on my back and watching the flakes of sky between the oak leaves, waiting for Stumberleap. He had hidden there before. After a while, far above me on the sunlit height of the hill, I heard the thin gleaming note of the horn. The stag heard it also, for his head moved, and a ripple spread across the dark pool. Later the voice of either whip or huntsman floated down, and I knew that the hounds were coming to the stream. Minute after minute passed. A jay flew to drink, and his smoke-grey eye saw the larger brown eye of the stag; he screeched to other jays because the staring eye was unusual and might be dangerous. Two jays came at once, and perched on the lower branches of the rowan-tree, leaned

161

forward and screeched. I showed myself. A jay saw me, warned his friends with a quicker note, and the three flew away. Again I lay down, and the minutes passed, until near me a voice said: *Hold up, you!* to a horse slipping on its haunches down the incline. Sound carries far in the coombes on a still day, and the wind was above the coombe. Hearing the voice, Stumberleap bent back his head, so that all of him was concealed by the water except his nose and the brow and bay points of his antlers. The ripples from the movement had hardly worn away, when a black-and-white hound named Deadlock ran down the bank with nose to ground, followed by other hounds. The pack had divided, and were casting down the banks to find where the stag had quit the water.

Last of all came a straggler, who nosed about among the dead bracken, and seeing me came and placed a thick white paw on my coat. He was a young hound, and I imagined by his callow look that it was his first season, possibly his first chase. I spoke to him, and he struck me with his paw, while his stern wagged like a flag. Again he struck my coat, so droll a look on his face that I knew he was begging for food. Where he had learnt to beg, in what household his puppyhood had been so pleasantly passed, I do not know. I gave him a biscuit, and after eating it he pressed his muzzle on my knee and gazed into my face with limpid eyes, the whites of which were of that tint of blue usually seen in the young eyes of the higher mammals, and most beautiful in children.

When the whipper-in trotted past on sweating mare I ordered the hound, in the usual phrase used to a rioter to 'get on to him', which was altogether a despicable betrayal of the creature's trust. The whip rated Credulous, and stung his hindquarters with his lash, so that the young hound yelped and ran away.

For half an hour Stumberleap lay in the pool, only his nose above water. Hounds had gone downstream a mile and a half; and two horsemen had followed after them. When it was quiet the jays flew back to the rowan-tree and peered at him, for his head was no longer held under the water. I heard them screaming as I returned upstream, and so did the huntsman, who was posted on the hill above. The harsh cries of the jays continued hardly without interval.

The huntsman rode down and saw Stumberleap. He blew short notes on the horn, and I heard the whip's high voice recalling hounds. Good-bye, Stumberleap, I thought; you've had a very pleasant life, and all things have to die, and if it hadn't been for the hunt you would probably have been shot or trapped before you were a month old. The pack pressed upon him, and Stumberleap swam downstream to shallower water where he might use his horns, but other hounds were there, baying in triumph and seeking to pull him down by the legs. Against the high bank, which the winter floods had carved, he stood at bay, the tragic head held high and ready to rip hound or man who dared go near. But no hound dared run within the slashing area of his antlers. I saw the huntsman loosen the long knife in its sheath under his left arm, before he walked into the water with two men, to wade across the stream. The current pressed against them, soaking red coat-tails and white breeches, and filling black top-boots. The two men hoped to get behind the stag with the looped thongs to hold back the head for the huntsman's quick stab in the throat; and the spirit of Stumberleap would roam the shining hills beyond the quest of stars.

Water dropped from the rough hairs of the stag's neck, but his eyes did not flinch. They strained down at the hounds. The two men felt their way step by step over the slippery stones to the opposite bank, fixing their sight on the eyes staring down. With loops ready to cast they edged nearer the stag, while the huntsman approached in front, to hold its gaze. Several hounds swam between him, and Guardsman bared his teeth to seize a knee. A couple named Darnel and Prudence swam with Guardsman, and then another couple. The whipper-in called them back, while the two men patiently climbed on hands and knees up the bank, one on either flank. They meant to twist their thongs round the top points which almost touched his back Now they were off their knees, and crouching; step by step they moved, until one made a sudden grab for the beam. He shouted to the other man, who had grasped the other antler and was about to put all his weight on it when with a movement of great power and swiftness, Stumberleap plunged his head between his forefeet, hurling both men into the water. Without pausing he flung up his head, rose on hind legs, and struck down at the huntsman, missing him with his slot, but knocking him over with a glancing blow of his shoulder. Then he was across the stream, and through the oaks, the jays screeching at stag, hounds, and men.

Down the valley echoed the full-throated music of the pack. Hounds scrambled out of the water and pursued. Huntsman picked himself up, and his screaming cheer went after them. He floundered to the bank and remounted.

Another rider appeared, with battered hat, on a horse whose flanks were covered with flattened froth. Wearily man and beast forded the stream and followed up the hill at a walk. Then came a riderless horse, that had rid itself of saddle. It was not sweating – its rider must have been lost hours ago. Should I . . . ? The rolling music diminished as the pack reached the wooded crest and went on over the hill. The horse did not run from me. I patted its neck, felt its withers; it waited quietly. I scrambled on its back, pressed my calves in, and off we cantered, up through the trees, across a heathery common, past stone hut-circles around which wild cattle were staring, for Stumberleap had gone among them in order to destroy scent. The sunshine dulled, clouds covered the sun. The south-west wind made a running hiss in the heather and whortleberry bushes. After a mile he had gained a lead of five hundred yards, but after two miles he ran not so fast. Down another goyal side and a brake of furze; he sprang into its centre, causing a hind who had been drowsing there with her calf to press her chin on the gound. The stag lay down and panted. With her nose the hind nuzzled the calf, which lay silently beside her. She heard hounds, and telling her little one to follow, she ran out of the brake and down the coombe. Deadlock led the pack (with the exception of the deserter Credulous) after the fresh scent, while the hind, who bore no protecting antlers on her smaller head, repeatedly glanced back at her pursuers. The legs of the calf went so fast during the first mile that very soon he grew tired, and the hind stopped, placed her head under his ribs, and tossed him several feet into a patch of bracken wherein he immediately settled himself and lay still. The hind ran on, and the pack followed her scent up the coombeside, passing the calf who held his breath and never moved. She ran swifter than Stumberleap had ever run, and returned in a wide circle to a point near the furze brake out of which he had turned her. Twice she ran to meet the hounds, swinging round and away again when they were almost upon her. Or she may have known that it was not yet the season of hind-hunting, and that the red-coat on horseback, viewing her, would protect her. She overran her starting point, describing roughly the figure 6 inverted, and seeing the huntsman, doubled back along the shank of the figure and stopped at the bushes where Stumberleap was resting. Then the huntsman knew that the stag was lying low in the brake. He and the whipper-in stopped hounds off the hind; Deadlock alone had to be lashed. Several times before a stag had been found in the covert. Hounds were capped into it. *Tally Ho! Yoi, yoi, then, pull'm down, yoi, yoi!*

Deadlock alone barred his way, and as the hound leapt at him, Stumberleap lowered his head and one of the uplashing points ripped him open, and with a howl the hound began to twist in a spiral, and lick his wound. Stumberleap leapt over him and crashed away through the bushes. The wind was rising, an ondrifting pallor made trees and hill-lines hard and distinct. Clouds massy and black were closing upon the moor, and before them wheeled a flock of gulls that had come from the sea. Their forlorn cries came sadly from the heights. Already the headland behind them was invisible, and half the sea of Bideford Bay was blurred in the driven grey slats of the storm. Hounds needed neither cap nor cheer nor horn. Up the goyal side went Stumberleap, not slanting up in his easy long-striding lurch, but straight up the steep side with a slow and heavy action. He staggered over the skyline, a long file of silent hounds pursuing him. Over the common from which the coast of Wales could be seen across the Severn Sea; over the road bridge under which lay the narrow gauge railway to Lynton, down the road for half a mile, over heath again and down a thread of water to a river. Hounds making the distance smaller, the hounds which had run nearly fifty miles and were still going. Moisture running from his eyes made them smaller; blood sometimes blackened his sight. His heart was throwing his legs about, the storm was still afar, although the clouds were above, and a great moaning was coming across the moor. A whirling greyness was between the four remaining horsemen and the pack, and the weary rider in the battered hat had been blown from the saddle by the gale which was hurling itself across Woolhanger.

Down the stony bed of the shallow river ran Stumberleap, past an inn, before which a group of people stood, watching the dark of the travelling storm, and the hard grey precipice-edges of the thunder clouds. A flash which stilled speech, a waiting for the reverberation, someone counting *one–two–three–four* .. a voice asking suddenly *What was that?* The baying of hounds! The man who was counting the seconds to calculate the distance of the lightning had counted *seven* when thunder broke upon them. Nearly two miles away. When the last stupendous tumbling of sound had ceased, they listened. They had motored to the meet on the Globe that morning, and the last they had seen of the chase were the tiny figures on horseback toiling up by the five clawmarks in the slope rising in Lucott moor. Yes, that was a hound! Six and a half hours from the lay on at Stumberleap Wood! Listen. Only a straying seagull wailing as the wind hurled it overhead, while the gale tore at the trees on the hill, and then the storm crashed upon them – *boom*, the wind screamed around the Hunters Inn, and the rain instantly beat down the swirling dust cloud.

The sea was less than a mile away. The river flowed below a towering cleave, tameless and unclimbable, its sides grey and smooth with loose flakes of shale. All things in the cleave were hidden as the hounds of the storm bayed across sky. The wind's thong whirled, the lash of the lightning cracked, the hills resounded with the hoofs of the thunder. Far behind on the moor the horsemen rode in a bluish mist of ground lightning which flicked and swished about them, seeming to curl in lashes of light about the huntsman's horn; icy thorns of driven rain pricked necks and ears; horses swung and swirled as though in a flood.

Fed by a hundred torrents, the river rose many feet, and when the storm ceased an hour later a muddy stain was spread in the sea at its mouth. Beyond the stain, swimming in the rolling waves, was Stumberleap, and after him, fifteen and a half couple of staghounds.

Just before dawn the bracken ceased to shake; the wind betook itself off the moor when a golden scarecrow rose in the east. Seeing the scarecrow the puppy-hound Credulous, who all night had been shivering miserably in the wet bracken because the nearness of the hind, threw up his head and bayed. This mournful noise made more fearful the hind who, all the nigt, had been shivering miserably because the nearness of Credulous had prevented her from returning to her calf. The little creature had been quiet in the bracken ever since she had tossed him there. Credulous tottered towards the golden scarecrow, which was the waning moon, and blundered upon the calf, who was cold and frightened. Credulous was so very pleased to find himself no longer alone that he licked its soft head, whined to it, struck it with his paw, and curled himself up beside it. He slept for several hours. When he left the calf it was reluctantly to follow a human voice. So the hind had her calf again, and Credulous had breakfast with me in a farmhouse where Deadlock twitched in sleep because of the stitches in the skin of his belly.

A fortnight later he was well and back at kennels, among the remaining twenty-four couples. Fifteen days previously nearly thirty couple of hounds had lain at night on the straw-strewn zinc benches above the red-tiled floors, and eaten cold porridge and chopped horseflesh once a day. The pack that had chased the old stag of Stumberleap Wood never ate again in the kennel yard; indeed, when the carcasses of these hounds were eventually washed by the tides into Cardiff harbour, fish were eating them.

The Dog That Bit People
JAMES THURBER

PROBABLY NO ONE MAN should have as many dogs in his life as I have had, but there was more pleasure than distress in them for me except in the case of an Airedale named Muggs. He gave me more trouble than all the other fifty-four or five put together, although my moment of keenest embarrassment was the time a Scotch terrier named Jeannie, who had just had six puppies in the clothes closet of a fourth floor apartment in New York, had the unexpected seventh and last at the corner of Eleventh Street and Fifth Avenue during a walk she had insisted on taking. Then, too, there was the prize-winning French poodle, a great big black poodle – none of your little, untroublesome white miniatures – who got sick riding in the rumble seat of a car with me on her way to the Greenwich Dog Show. She had a red rubber bib tucked around her throat and, since a rain storm came up when we were halfway through the Bronx, I had to hold over her a small green umbrella, really more of a parasol. The rain beat down fearfully and suddenly the driver of the car drove into a big garage, filled with mechanics. It happened so quickly that I forgot to put the umbrella down and I will always remember, with sickening distress, the look of incredulity mixed with hatred that came over the face of the particular hardened garage man that came over to see what we wanted, when he took a look at me and the poodle. All garage men, and people of that intolerant stripe, hate poodles with their curious hair cut, especially the pom-poms that you got to leave on their hips if you expect the dogs to win a prize.

But the Airedale, as I have said, was the worst of all my dogs. He really wasn't my dog, as a matter of fact: I came home from a vacation one summer to find that my brother Roy had bought him while I was away. A big, burly, choleric dog, he always acted as if he thought I wasn't one of the family. There was a slight advantage in being one of the family, for he didn't bite the family as often as he bit strangers. Still, in the years that we had him he bit everybody but mother, and he made a pass at her once but missed. That was during the month when we suddenly had mice, and Muggs refused to do anything about them. Nobody ever had mice exactly like the mice we had that month. They acted like pet mice, almost like mice somebody had trained. They were so friendly that one night when mother entertained at dinner the Frir-aliras, a club she and my father had belonged to for twenty years, she put down a lot of little dishes with food in them on the pantry floor so that the mice would be satisfied with that and wouldn't come into the dining room. Muggs stayed out in the pantry with the mice, lying on the floor, growling to himself – not at the mice, but about all the people in the next room that he would have liked to get at. Mother slipped out into the pantry once to see how everything was going. Everything was going fine. It made her so mad to see Muggs lying there, oblivious of the mice – they came running up to her – that she slapped him and he slashed at her, but didn't make it. He was sorry immediately, mother said. He was always sorry, she said, after he bit someone, but we could not understand how she figured this out. He didn't act sorry.

Mother used to send a box of candy every Christmas to the people the Airedale bit. The list finally contained forty or more names. Nobody could understand why we didn't get rid of the dog. I didn't understand it very well myself, but we didn't get rid of him. I think that one or two people tried to poison Muggs – he acted poisoned once in a while – and old Major Moberly fired at him once with his service revolver near the Seneca Hotel in East Broad Street – but Muggs lived to be almost eleven years old and even when he could hardly get around he bit a Congressman who had called to see my father on business. My mother had never liked the Congressman – she said the signs of his horoscope showed he couldn't be trusted (he was Saturn with the moon in Virgo) – but she sent him a box of candy that Christmas. He sent it right back, probably because he suspected it was trick candy. Mother persuaded herself it was all for the best that the dog had bitten him, even though father lost an important business association because of it. 'I wouldn't be associated with such a man,' mother said, 'Muggs could read him like a book.'

We used to take turns feeding Muggs to be on his good side, but that didn't always work. He was never in a very good humour, even after a meal. Nobody knew exactly what was the matter with him, but whatever it was it made him irascible, especially in the mornings. Roy never felt very well in the morning, either, especially before breakfast, and once when he came downstairs and found that Muggs had moodily chewed up the morning paper he hit him in the face with a grapefruit and then jumped up on the dining room table, scattering dishes and silverware and spilling the coffee. Muggs' first free leap carried him all the way across the table and into a brass fire screen in front of the gas grate, but he was back on his feet in a moment and in the end he got Roy and gave him a pretty vicious bite in the leg. Then he was all over it; he never bit anyone more than once at a time. Mother always mentioned that as an argument in his favour; she said he had a quick temper but that he didn't hold a grudge. She was forever defending him. I think she liked him because he wasn't well. 'He's not strong,' she would say, pityingly, but that was inaccurate; he may not have been well but he was terribly strong.

One time my mother went to the Chittenden Hotel to call on a woman mental healer who was lecturing in Columbus on the subject of 'Harmonious Vibrations'. She wanted to find out if it was possible to get harmonious vibrations into a dog. 'He's a large tan-coloured Airedale,' mother explained. The woman said that she had never treated a dog but she advised my mother to hold the thought that he did not bite and would not bite. Mother was holding the thought the very next morning when Muggs got the ice-man but she blamed that slip-up on the ice-man. 'If you didn't think he would bite you, he wouldn't,' mother told him. He stomped out of the house in a terrible jangle of vibrations.

One morning when Muggs bit me slightly, more or less in passing, I reached down and grabbed his short stumpy tail and hoisted him into the air. It was a foolhardy thing to do and the last time I saw my mother, about six months ago, she said she didn't know what possessed me. I don't either, except that I was pretty mad. As long as I held the dog off the floor by his tail he couldn't get at me, but he twisted and jerked so, snarling all the time, that I realized I couldn't hold him that way very long. I carried him to the kitchen and flung him onto the floor and shut the door on him just as he crashed against it. But I forgot about the backstairs. Muggs went up the backstairs and down the frontstairs and had me cornered in the living room. I managed to get up onto the mantelpiece above the fireplace, but it gave way and came down with a tremendous crash, throwing a large marble clock, several vases, and myself heavily to the floor. Muggs was so alarmed by the racket that when I picked myself up he had disappeared. We couldn't find him anywhere, although we whistled and shouted, until old Mrs. Detweiler called after dinner that night. Muggs had bitten her once, in the leg, and she came into the living room only after we assured her that Muggs had run away. She had just seated herself when, with a great growling and scratching of claws, Muggs emerged from under a davenport where he had been quietly hiding all the time, and bit her again. Mother examined the bite and put arnica on it and told Mrs. Detweiler that it was only a bruise. 'He just bumped you,' she said. But Mrs. Detweiler left the house in a nasty state of mind.

Lots of people reported our Airedale to the police but my father held a municipal office at the time and was on friendly terms with the police.

Even so, the cops had been out a couple of times – once when Muggs bit Mrs. Rufus Sturtevant and again when he bit Lieutenant-Governor Malloy – but mother told them that it hadn't been Muggs' fault but the fault of the people who were bitten. 'When he starts for them, they scream,' she explained, 'and that excites him.' The cops suggested that it might be a good idea to tie the dog up, but mother said that it mortified him to be tied up and that he wouldn't eat when he was tied up.

Muggs at his meals was an unusual sight. Because of the fact that if you reached toward the floor he would bite you, we usually put his food plate on top of an old kitchen table with a bench alongside the table. Muggs would stand on the bench and eat. I remember that my mother's Uncle Horatio, who boasted that he was the third man up Missionary Ridge, was splutteringly indignant when he found out that we fed the dog on a table because we were afraid to put his plate on the floor. He said he wasn't afraid of any dog that ever lived and that he would put the dog's plate on the floor if we would give it to him. Roy said that if Uncle Horatio had fed Muggs on the ground just before the battle he would have been the first man up Missionary Ridge. Uncle Horatio was furious. 'Bring him in! Bring him in now!' he shouted. 'I'll feed the – – on the floor!' Roy was all for giving him a chance, but my father wouldn't hear of it. He said that Muggs had already been fed. 'I'll feed him again!' bawled Uncle Horatio. We had quite a time quieting him.

In his last year Muggs used to spend practically all of his time outdoors. He didn't like to stay in the house for some reason or other – perhaps it held too many unpleasant memories for him. Anyway, it was hard to get him to come in and as a result the garbage man, the iceman, and the laundryman wouldn't come near the house. We had to haul the garbage down to the corner, take the laundry out and bring it back, and meet the iceman a block from home. After this had gone on for some time we hit on an ingenious arrangement for getting the dog in the house so that we could lock him up while the gas meter was read, and so on. Muggs was afraid of only one thing, an electrical storm. Thunder and lightning frightened him out of his senses (I think he thought a storm had broken the day the mantelpiece fell). He would rush into the house and hide under a bed or in a clothes closet. So we fixed up a thunder machine out of a long narrow piece of sheet iron with a wooden handle on one end. Mother would shake this vigorously when she wanted to get Muggs into the house. It made an excellent imitation of thunder, but I suppose it was the most roundabout system for running a household that was ever devised. It took a lot out of mother.

A few months before Muggs died, he got to 'seeing things'. He would rise slowly from the floor, growling low, and stalk stiff-legged and menacing toward nothing at all. Sometimes the Thing would be just a little to the right or left of a visitor. Once a Fuller Brush salesman got hysterics. Muggs came wandering into the room like Hamlet following

170

his father's ghost. His eyes were fixed on a spot just to the left of the Fuller Brush man, who stood it until Muggs was about three slow, creeping paces from him. Then he shouted. Muggs wavered on past him into the hallway grumbling to himself but the Fuller man went on shouting. I think mother had to throw a pan of cold water on him before he stopped. That was the way she used to stop us boys when we got into fights.

Muggs died quite suddenly one night. Mother wanted to bury him in the family lot under a marble stone with some such inscription as 'Flights of angels sing thee to thy rest' but we persuaded her it was against the law. In the end we just put up a smooth board above his grave along a lonely road. On the board I wrote with an indelible pencil 'Cave Canem'. Mother was quite pleased with the simple classic dignity of the old Latin epitaph.

The Bull That Thought

RUDYARD KIPLING

WESTWARD FROM A TOWN by the Mouths of the Rhône, runs a road so mathematically straight, so barometrically level, that it ranks among the world's measured miles and motorists use it for records.

I had attacked the distance several times, but always with a Mistral blowing, or the unchancy cattle of those parts on the move. But once, running from the East, into a high-piled, almost Egyptian, sunset, there came a night which it would have been sin to have wasted. It was warm with the breath of summer in advance; moonlit till the shadow of every rounded pebble and pointed cypress wind-break lay solid on that vast flat-floored waste; and my Mr. Leggatt, who had slipped out to make sure, reported that the road-surface was unblemished.

'*Now*,' he suggested, 'we might see what she'll do under strict road-conditions. She's been pullin' like the Blue de Luxe all day. Unless I'm all off, it's her night out.'

We arranged the trial for after dinner – thirty kilometres as near as might be; and twenty-two of them without even a level crossing.

There sat beside me at table d'hôte an elderly, bearded Frenchman wearing the rosette of by no means the lowest grade of the Legion of Honour, who had arrived in a talkative Citroën. I gathered that he had spent much of his life in the French Colonial Service in Annam and Tonquin. When the war came, his years barring him from the front line, he had supervised Chinese wood-cutters who, with axe and dynamite, deforested the centre of France for trench-props. He said my chauffeur had told him that I contemplated an experiment. He was interested in cars – had admired mine – would, in short, be greatly indebted to me if I permitted him to assist as an observer. One could not well refuse; and, knowing my Mr. Leggatt, it occurred to me there might also be a bet in the background.

While he went to get his coat, I asked the proprietor his name. 'Voiron – Monsieur André Voiron,' was the reply. 'And his business?' 'Mon Dieu! He is Voiron! He is all those things, there!' The proprietor waved his hands at brilliant advertisements on the dining-room walls, which declared that Voiron Frères dealt in wines, agricultural implements, chemical manures, provisions and produce throughout that part of the globe.

He said little for the first five minutes of our trip, and nothing at all for the next ten – it being, as Leggatt had guessed, Esmeralda's night out. But, when her indicator climbed to a certain figure and held there for three blinding kilometres, he expressed himself satisfied, and proposed to me that we should celebrate the event at the hotel. 'I keep yonder,' said he, 'a wine on which I should value your opinion.'

On our return, he disappeared for a few minutes, and I heard him rumbling in a cellar. The proprietor presently invited me to the dining-room, where, beneath one frugal light, a table had been set with local dishes of renown. There was, too, a bottle beyond most known sizes, marked black on red, with a date. Monsieur Voiron opened it, and we drank to the health of my car. The velvety, perfumed liquor, between fawn and topaz, neither too sweet nor too dry, creamed in its generous glass. But I knew no wine composed of the whispers of angels' wings, the breath of Eden and the foam and pulse of Youth renewed. So I asked what it might be.

'It is champagne,' he said gravely.

'Then what have I been drinking all my life?'

'If you were lucky, before the War, and paid thirty shillings a bottle, it is possible you may have drunk one of our better-class *tisanes*.'

'And where does one get this?'

'Here, I am happy to say. Elsewhere, perhaps, it is not so easy. We growers exchange these real wines among ourselves.'

I bowed my head in admiration, surrender, and joy. There stood the most ample bottle, and it was not yet eleven o'clock. Doors locked and shutters banged throughout the establishment. Some last servant yawned on his way to bed. Monsieur Voiron opened a window and the moonlight flooded in from a small pebbled court outside. One could almost hear the town of Chambres breathing in its first sleep. Presently, there was a thick noise in the air, the passing of feet and hooves, lowings, and a stifled bark or two. Dust rose over the courtyard wall, followed by the strong smell of cattle.

'They are moving some beasts,' said Monsieur Voiron, cocking an ear. 'Mine, I think. Yes, I hear Christophe. Our beasts do not like automobiles – so we move at night. You do not know our country – the Crau, here, or the Camargue? I was – I am now, again – of it. All France is good;

but this is the best.' He spoke, as only a Frenchman can, of his own loved part of his own lovely land.

'For myself, if I were not so involved in all these affairs' – he pointed to the advertisements – 'I would live on our farm with my cattle, and worship them like a Hindu. You know our cattle of the Camargue, Monsieur? No? It is not an acquaintance to rush upon lightly. There are no beasts like them. They have a mentality superior to that of others. They graze and they ruminate, by choice, facing our Mistral, which is more than some automobiles will do. Also they have in them the potentiality of thought – and when cattle think – I have seen what arrives.'

'Are they so clever as all that?' I asked idly.

'Monsieur, when your sportif chauffeur camouflaged your limousine so that she resembled one of your Army lorries, I would not believe her capacities. I bet him – ah – two to one – she would not touch ninety kilometres. It was proved that she could. I can give you no proof, but will you believe me if I tell you what a beast who thinks can achieve?'

'After the War,' said I spaciously, 'everything is credible.'

'That is true! Everything inconceivable has happened; but still we learn nothing and we believe nothing. When I was a child in my father's house – before I became a Colonial Administrator – my interest and my affection were among our cattle. We of the old rock live here – have you seen? – in big farms like castles. Indeed, some of them may have been Saracenic. The barns group round them – great white-walled barns, and yards solid as our houses. One gate shuts all. It is a world apart; an administration of all that concerns beasts. It was there I learned something about cattle. You see, they are our playthings in the Camargue and the Crau. The boy measures his strength against the calf that butts him in play among the manure-heaps. He moves in and out among the cows, who are – not so amiable. He rides with the herdsmen in the open to shift the herds. Sooner or later, he meets as bulls the little calves that knocked him over. So it was with me – till it became necessary that I should go to our Colonies.' He laughed. 'Very necessary. That is a good time in youth, Monsieur, when one does these things which shock our parents. Why is it always Papa who is so shocked and has never heard of such things – and Mamma who supplies the excuses? . . . And when my brother – my elder who stayed and created the business – begged me to return and help him, I resigned my Colonial career gladly enough. I returned to our own lands, and my well-loved, wicked white and yellow cattle of the Camargue and the Crau. My Faith, I could talk of them all night, for this stuff unlocks the heart, without making repentance in the morning. . . . Yes! It was after the War that this happened. There was a calf, among Heaven knows how many of ours – a bull-calf – an infant indistinguishable from his companions. He was sick, and he had been taken up with his mother into the big farmyard at home with us.

Naturally the children of our herdsmen practised on him from the first. It is in their blood. The Spaniards make a cult of bull-fighting. Our little devils down here bait bulls as automatically as the English child kicks or throws balls. This calf would chase them with his eyes open, like a cow when she hunts a man. They would take refuge behind our tractors and wine-carts in the centre of the yard: he would chase them in and out as a dog hunts rats. More than that, he would study their psychology, his eyes in their eyes. Yes, he watched their faces to divine which way they would run. He himself, also, would pretend sometimes to charge directly at a boy. Then he would wheel right or left – one could never tell – and knock over some child pressed against a wall who thought himself safe. After this, he would stand over him, knowing that his companions must come to his aid; and when they were all together, waving their jackets across his eyes and pulling his tail, he would scatter them – how he would scatter them! He could kick, too, sideways like a cow. He knew his ranges as well as our gunners, and he was as quick on his feet as our Carpentier. I observed him often. Christophe – the man who passed just now – our chief herdsman, who had taught me to ride with our beasts when I was ten – Christophe told me that he was descended from a yellow cow of those days that had chased us once into the marshes. "He kicks just like her," said Christophe. "He can side-kick as he jumps. Have you seen, too, that he is not deceived by the jacket when a boy waves it? He uses it to find the boy. They think they are feeling him. He is feeling them always. He thinks, that one." I had come to the same conclusion. Yes – the creature was a thinker along the lines necessary to his sport; and he was a humorist also, like so many natural murderers. One knows the type among beasts as well as among men. It possesses a curious truculent mirth – almost indecent but infallibly significant—'

Monsieur Voiron replenished our glasses with the great wine that went better at each descent.

'They kept him for some time in the yards to practise upon. Naturally he became a little brutal; so Christophe turned him out to learn manners among his equals in the grazing lands, where the Camargue joins the Crau. How old was he then? About eight or nine months, I think. We met again a few months later – he and I. I was riding one of our little half-wild horses, along a road of the Crau, when I found myself almost unseated. It was he! He had hidden himself behind a wind-break till we passed, and had then charged my horse from behind. Yes, he had deceived even my little horse! But I recognized him. I gave him the whip across the nose, and I said: "Apis, for this thou goest to Arles! It was unworthy of thee, between us two." But that creature had no shame. He went away laughing, like an Apache. If he had dismounted me, I do not think it is I who would have laughed – yearling as he was.'

'Why did you want to send him to Arles?' I asked.

'For the bull-ring. When your charming tourists leave us, we institute our little amusements there. Not a real bullfight, you understand, but young bulls with padded horns, and our boys from hereabouts and in the city go to play with them. Naturally, before we send them we try them in our yards at home. So we brought up Apis from his pastures. He knew at once that he was among the friends of his youth – he almost shook hands with them – and he submitted like an angel to padding his horns. He investigated the carts and tractors in the yards, to choose his lines of defence and attack. And then – he attacked with an *élan*, and he defended with a tenacity and forethought that delighted us. In truth, we were so pleased that I fear we trespassed upon his patience. We desired him to repeat himself, which no true artist will tolerate. But he gave us fair warning. He went out to the centre of the yard, where there was some dry earth; he knelt down and – you have seen a calf whose horns fret him thrusting and rooting into a bank? He did just that, very deliberately, till he had rubbed the pads off his horns. Then he rose, dancing on those wonderful feet that tinkled, and he said: "Now, my friends, the buttons are off the foils. Who begins?" We understood. We finished at once. He was turned out again on the pastures till it should be time to amuse them at our little metropolis. But, some time before he went to Arles – yes, I think I have it correctly – Christophe, who had been out on the Crau, informed me that Apis had assassinated a young bull who had given signs of developing into a rival. That happens, of course, and our herdsmen should prevent it. But Apis had killed in his own style – at dusk, from the ambush of a wind-break – by an oblique charge from behind which knocked the other over. He had then disembowelled him. All very possible, *but* – the murder accomplished – Apis went to the bank of a wind-break, knelt, and carefully, as he had in our yard, cleaned his horns in the earth. Christophe, who had never seen such a thing, at once borrowed (do you know, it is most efficacious when taken that way?) some Holy Water from our little chapel in those pastures, sprinkled Apis (whom it did not affect), and rode in to tell me. It was obvious that a thinker of that bull's type would also be meticulous in his toilette; so, when he was sent to Arles, I warned our consignees to exercise caution with him. Happily, the change of scene, the music, the general attention, and the meeting again with old friends – all our bad boys attended – agreeably distracted him. He became for the time a pure *farceur* again; but his wheelings, his rushes, his rat-huntings were more superb than ever. There was in them now, you understand, a breadth of technique that comes of reasoned art, and, above all, the passion that arrives after experience. Oh, he had learned, out there on the Crau! At the end of his little turn, he was, according to local rules, to be handled in all respects except for the sword, which was a stick, as a professional bull who must die. He was manoeuvred into, or he posed himself in, the proper attitude; made his rush; received the point on his shoulder and then – turned about and cantered towards the door by which he had entered the arena. He said to the world: "My friends, the representation is ended. I thank you for your applause. I go to repose myself." But our Arlesians, who are – not so clever as some, demanded an encore, and Apis was headed back again. We others from this country, we knew what would happen. He went to the centre of the ring, kneeled, and, slowly, with full parade, plunged his horns alternately in the dirt till the pads came off. Christophe shouts: "Leave him alone, you straight-nosed imbeciles! Leave him before you must." But they required emotion; for Rome has always debauched her loved Provincia with bread and circuses. It was given. Have you, Monsieur, ever seen a servant, with pan and broom, sweeping round the base-board of a room? In a half-minute Apis has them all swept out and over the barrier. Then he demands once more that the door shall be opened to him. It is opened and he retires as though – which, truly, is the case – loaded with laurels.'

Monsieur Voiron refilled the glasses, and allowed himself a cigarette, which he puffed for some time.

'And afterwards?' I said.

'I am arranging it in my mind. It is difficult to do it justice. Afterwards – yes, afterwards – Apis returned to his pastures and his mistresses and I to my business. I am no longer a scandalous old "sportif" in shirt-sleeves howling encouragement to the yellow son of a cow. I revert to Voiron Frères – wines, chemical manures, *et cetera*. And next year, through some chicane which I have not the leisure to unravel, and also, thanks to our patriarchal system of paying our older men out of the increase of the herds, old Christophe possesses himself of Apis. Oh, yes, he proves it through descent from a certain cow that my father had given his father before the Republic. Beware, Monsieur, of the memory of the illiterate man! An ancestor of Christophe had been a soldier under our Soult against your Beresford, near Bayonne. He fell into the hands of Spanish guerrillas. Christophe and his wife used to tell me the details on certain Saints' Days when I was a child. Now, as compared with our recent war, Soult's campaign and retreat across the Bidassoa—'

'But did you allow Christophe just to annex the bull?' I demanded.

'You do not know Christophe. He had sold him to the Spaniards before he informed me. The Spaniards pay in coin – douros of very pure silver. Our peasants mistrust our paper. You know the saying: "A thousand francs paper; eight hundred metal, and the cow is yours." Yes, Christophe sold Apis, who was then two and a half years old, and to Christophe's knowledge thrice at least an assassin.'

'How was that?' I said.

'Oh, his own kind only; and always, Christophe told me, by the same oblique rush from behind, the same sideways overthrow, and the same swift disembowelment, followed by this levitical cleaning of the horns. In human life he would have kept a manicurist – this Minotaur. And so,

Apis disappears from our country. That does not trouble me. I know in due time I shall be advised. Why? Because, in this land, Monsieur, not a hoof moves between Berre and the Saintes Maries without the knowledge of specialists such as Christophe. The beasts are the substance and the drama of their lives to them. So when Christophe tells me, a little before Easter Sunday, that Apis makes his début in the bull-ring of a small Catalan town on the road to Barcelona, it is only to pack my car and trundle there across the frontier with him. The place lacked importance and manufactures, but it had produced a matador of some reputation, who was condescending to show his art in his native town. They were even running one special train to the place. Now our French railway system is only execrable, but the Spanish—'

'You went down by road, didn't you?' said I.

'Naturally. It was not too good. Villamarti was the matador's name. He proposed to kill two bulls for the honour of his birthplace. Apis, Christophe told me, would be his second. It was an interesting trip, and that little city by the sea was ravishing. Their bull-ring dates from the middle of the seventeenth century. It is full of feeling. The ceremonial too – when the horsemen enter and ask the Mayor in his box to throw down the keys of the bull-ring – that was exquisitely conceived. You know, if the keys are caught in the horseman's hat, it is considered a good omen. They were perfectly caught. Our seats were in the front row beside the gates where the bulls enter, so we saw everything.

'Villamarti's first bull was not too badly killed. The second matador, whose name escapes me, killed his without distinction – a foil to Villamarti. And the third, Chisto, a laborious, middle-aged professional who had never risen beyond a certain dull competence, was equally of the background. Oh, they are as jealous as the girls of the Comédie Française, these matadors! Villamarti's troupe stood ready for his second bull. The gates opened, and we saw Apis, beautifully balanced on his feet, peer coquettishly round the corner, as though he were at home. A picador – a mounted man with the long lance-goad – stood near the barrier on his right. He had not even troubled to turn his horse, for the capeadors – the men with the cloaks – were advancing to play Apis – to feel his psychology and intentions, according to the rules that are made for bulls who do not think. . . . I did not realize the murder before it was accomplished! The wheel, the rush, the oblique charge from behind, the fall of horse and man were simultaneous. Apis leaped the horse, with whom he had no quarrel, and alighted, all four feet together (it was enough), between the man's shoulders, changed his beautiful feet on the carcass, and was away, pretending to fall nearly on his nose. Do you follow me? In that instant, by that stumble, he produced the impression that his adorable assassination was a mere bestial blunder. Then, Monsieur, I began to comprehend that it was an artist we had to deal with. He did not stand over the body to draw the rest of the troupe. He chose to reserve that trick. He let the attendants bear out the dead, and went on to amuse himself among the capeadors. Now to Apis, trained among our children in the yards, the cloak was simply a guide to the boy behind it. He pursued, you understand, the person, not the propaganda – the proprietor, not the journal. If a third of our electors of France were as wise, my friend! . . . But it was done leisurely, with humour and a touch of truculence. He romped after one man's cloak as a clumsy dog might do, but I observed that he kept the man on his terrible left side. Christophe whispered to me: "Wait for his mother's kick. When he has made the fellow confident it will arrive." It arrived in the middle of a gambol. My God! He lashed out in the air as he frisked. The man dropped like a sack, lifted one hand a little towards his head, and – that was all. So you see, a body was again at his disposition; a second time the cloaks ran up to draw him off, but, a second time, Apis refused his grand scene. A second time he acted that his murder was accident and – he convinced his audience! It was as though he had knocked over a bridge-gate in the marshes by mistake. Unbelievable? I saw it.'

The memory sent Monsieur Voiron again to the champagne; and I accompanied him.

'But Apis was not the sole artist present. They say Villamarti comes of a family of actors. I saw him regard Apis with a new eye. He, too, began to understand. He took his cloak and moved out to play him before they should bring on another picador. He had his reputation. Perhaps Apis knew it. Perhaps Villamarti reminded him of some boy with whom he had practised at home. At any rate Apis permitted it – up to a certain point; but he did not allow Villamarti the stage. He cramped him throughout. He dived and plunged clumsily and slowly, but always with menace and always closing in. We could see that the man was conforming to the bull – not the bull to the man; for Apis was playing him towards the centre of the ring, and, in a little while – I watched his face – Villamarti knew it. But I could not fathom the creature's motive. "Wait," said old Christophe. "He wants that picador on the white horse yonder. When he reaches his proper distance he will get him. Villamarti is his cover. He used me once that way." And so it was, my friend! With the clang of one of our own Seventy-fives, Apis dismissed Villamarti with his chest – breasted him over – and had arrived at his objective near the barrier. The same oblique charge; the head carried low for the sweep of the horns; the immense sideways fall of the horse, broken-legged and half-paralysed; the senseless man on the ground, and – behold Apis between them, backed against the barrier – his right covered by the horse; his left by the body of the man at his feet. The simplicity of it! Lacking the carts and tractors of his early parade-grounds he, being a genius, had extemporized with the materials at hand, and dug himself in. The troupe closed up again, their left wing broken by the kicking horse, their right immobilized by the man's body which Apis bestrode with significance.

Villamarti almost threw himself between the horns, but – it was more
an appeal than an attack. Apis refused him. He held his base. A picador
was sent at him – necessarily from the front, which alone was open. Apis
charged – he who, till then, you realize, had not used the horn! The
horse went over backwards, the man half beneath him. Apis halted,
hooked him under the heart, and threw him to the barrier. We heard his
head crack, but he was dead before he hit the wood. There was no
demonstration from the audience. They, also, had begun to realize this
Foch among bulls! The arena occupied itself again with the dead. Two
of the troupe irresolutely tried to play him – God knows in what hope!
– but he moved out to the centre of the ring. "Look!" said Christophe.
"Now he goes to clean himself. That always frightened me." He knelt
down; he began to clean his horns. The earth was hard. He worried at
it in an ecstasy of absorption. As he laid his head along and rattled his
ears, it was as though he were interrogating the Devils themselves upon
their secrets, and always saying impatiently: "Yes, I know that – and
that – and *that*! Tell me more – *more*!' In the silence that covered us, a
woman cried: "He digs a grave! Oh, Saints, he digs a grave!" Some others
echoed this – not loudly – as a wave echoes in a grotto of the sea.

'And when his horns were cleaned, he rose up and studied poor
Villamarti's troupe, eyes in eyes, one by one, with the gravity of an equal
in intellect and the remote and merciless resolution of a master in his art.
This was more terrifying than his toilette.'

'And they – Villamarti's men?' I asked.

'Like the audience, were dominated. They had ceased to posture, or
stamp, or address insults to him. They conformed to him. The two other
matadors stared. Only Chisto, the oldest, broke silence with some call or
other, and Apis turned his head towards him. Otherwise he was isolated,
immobile – sombre – meditating on those at his mercy. Ah!

'For some reason the trumpet sounded for the *banderillas* – those gay
hooked darts that are planted in the shoulders of bulls who do not think,
after their neck-muscles are tired by lifting horses. When such bulls feel
the pain, they check for an instant, and, in that instant, the men step
gracefully aside. Villamarti's banderillero answered the trumpet mechanically – like one condemned. He stood out, poised the darts and stammered
the usual patter of invitation. . . . And after? I do not assert that Apis
shrugged his shoulders, but he reduced the episode to its lowest elements,
as could only a bull of Gaul. With his truculence was mingled always
– owing to the shortness of his tail – a certain Rabelaisian abandon,
especially when viewed from the rear. Christophe had often commented
upon it. Now, Apis brought that quality into play. He circulated round
that boy, forcing him to break up his beautiful poses. He studied him
from various angles, like an incompetent photographer. He presented to
him every portion of his anatomy except his shoulders. At intervals he
feigned to run in upon him. My God, he was cruel! But his motive was

obvious. He was playing for a laugh from the spectators which should synchronize with the fracture of the human morale. It was achieved. The boy turned and ran towards the barrier. Apis was on him before the laugh ceased; passed him; headed him – what do I say? – herded him off to the left, his horns beside and a little in front of his chest: he did not intend him to escape into a refuge. Some of the troupe would have closed in, but Villamarti cried: "If he wants him he will take him. Stand!" They stood. Whether the boy slipped or Apis nosed him over I could not see. But he dropped, sobbing. Apis halted like a car with four brakes, struck a pose, smelt him very completely and turned away. It was dismissal more ignominious than degradation at the head of one's battalion. The representation was finished. Remained only for Apis to clear his stage of the subordinate characters.

'Ah! His gesture then! He gave a dramatic start – this Cyrano of the Camargue – as though he was aware of them for the first time. He moved. All their beautiful breeches twinkled for an instant along the top of the barrier. He held the stage alone! But Christophe and I, we trembled! For, observe, he had now involved himself in a stupendous drama of which he only could supply the third act. And, except for an audience on the razor-edge of emotion, he had exhausted his material. Molière himself – we have forgotten, my friend, to drink to the health of that great soul – might have been at a loss. And Tragedy is but a step behind Failure. We could see the four or five Civil Guards, who are sent always to keep order, fingering the breeches of their rifles. They were but waiting a word from the Mayor to fire on him, as they do sometimes at a bull who leaps the barrier among the spectators. They would, of course, have killed or wounded several people – but that would not have saved Apis.'

Monsieur Voiron drowned the thought at once, and wiped his beard.

'At that moment Fate – the Genius of France, if you will – sent to assist in the incomparable finale, none other than Chisto, the eldest, and I should have said (but never again will I judge!) the least inspired of all; mediocrity itself, but at heart – and it is the heart that conquers always, my friend – at heart an artist. He descended stiffly into the arena, alone and assured. Apis regarded him, his eyes in his eyes. The man took stance, with his cloak, and called to the bull as to an equal: "Now, Señor, we will show these honourable caballeros something together." He advanced thus against this thinker who at a plunge – a kick – a thrust – could, we all knew, have extinguished him. My dear friend, I wish I could convey to you something of the unaffected bonhomie, the humour, the delicacy, the consideration bordering on respect even, with which Apis, the supreme artist, responded to this invitation. It was the Master, wearied after a strenuous hour in the atelier, unbuttoned and at ease with some not inexpert but limited disciple. The telepathy was instantaneous between them. And for good reason! Christophe said to me:

"All's well. That Chisto began among the bulls. I was sure of it when I heard him call just now. He has been a herdsman. He'll pull it off." There was a little feeling and adjustment, at first, for mutual distances and allowances.

'Oh, yes! And here occurred a gross impertinence of Villamarti. He had, after an interval, followed Chisto – to retrieve his reputation. My Faith! I can conceive the elder Dumas slamming his door on an intruder precisely as Apis did. He raced Villamarti into the nearest refuge at once. He stamped his feet outside it, and he snorted: "Go! I am engaged with an artist." Villamarti went – his reputation left behind for ever.

'Apis returned to Chisto saying: "Forgive the interruption. I am not always master of my time, but you were about to observe, my dear confrère . . .?" Then the play began. Out of compliment to Chisto, Apis chose as his objective (every bull varies in this respect) the inner edge of the cloak – that nearest to the man's body. This allows but a few millimetres clearance in charging. But Apis trusted himself as Chisto trusted him, and, this time, he conformed to the man, with inimitable judgement and temper. He allowed himself to be played into the shadow or the sun, as the delighted audience demanded. He raged enormously; he feigned defeat; he despaired in statuesque abandon, and thence flashed into fresh paroxysms of wrath – but always with the detachment of the true artist who knows he is but the vessel of an emotion whence others, not he, must drink. And never once did he forget that honest Chisto's cloak was to him the gauge by which to spare even a hair on the skin. He inspired Chisto too. My God! His youth returned to that meritorious beef-sticker – the desire, the grace, and the beauty of his early dreams. One could almost see that girl of the past for whom he was rising, rising to these present heights of skill and daring. It was his hour too – a miraculous hour of dawn returned to gild the sunset. All he knew was at Apis' disposition. Apis acknowledged it with all that he had learned at home, at Arles and in his lonely murders on our grazing-grounds. He flowed round Chisto like a river of death – round his knees, leaping at his shoulders, kicking just clear of one side or the other of his head; behind his back, hissing as he shaved by; and once or twice – inimitable! – he reared wholly up before him while Chisto slipped back from beneath the avalanche of that instructed body. Those two, my dear friend, held five thousand people dumb with no sound but of their breathings – regular as pumps. It was unbearable. Beast and man realized together that we needed a change of note – a détente. They relaxed to pure buffoonery. Chisto fell back and talked to him outrageously. Apis pretended he had never heard such language. The audience howled with delight. Chisto slapped him; he took liberties with his short tail, to the end of which he clung while Apis pirouetted; he played about him in all postures; he had become the herdsman again – gross, careless, brutal, but comprehending. Yet Apis was always the more consummate clown. All that time (Christophe and I saw it) Apis drew off towards the gates of the *toril* where so many bulls enter but – have you ever heard of one that returned? *We* knew that Apis knew that as he had saved Chisto, so Chisto would save him. Life is sweet to us all; to the artist who lives many lives in one, sweetest. Chisto did not fail him. At the last, when none could laugh any longer, the man threw his cape across the bull's back, his arm round his neck. He flung up a hand at the gate, as Villamarti, young and commanding but *not* a herdsman, might have raised it, and he cried: "Gentlemen, open to me and my honourable little donkey." They opened – I have misjudged Spaniards in my time! – those gates opened to the man and the bull together, and closed behind them. And then? From the Mayor to the Guardia Civil they went mad for five minutes, till the trumpets blew and the fifth bull rushed out – an unthinking black Andalusian. I suppose some one killed him. My friend, my very dear friend, to whom I have opened my heart, I confess that I did not watch. Christophe and I, we were weeping together like children of the same Mother. Shall we drink to Her?'

The Pacing Mustang

ERNEST THOMPSON SETON

JO CALONE THREW DOWN his saddle on the dusty ground, turned his horses loose, and went clanking into the ranch-house.

'Nigh about chuck time?' he asked.

'Seventeen minutes,' said the cook glancing at the Waterbury, with the air of a train-starter, though this show of precision had never yet been justified by events.

'How's things on the Perico?' said Jo's pard.

'Hotter'n hinges,' said Jo. 'Cattle seem O.K.; lots of calves.'

'I seen that bunch o' mustangs that waters at Antelope Springs; couple o' colts along; one little dark one, a fair dandy; a born pacer. I run them a mile or two, and he led the bunch, an' never broke his pace. Cut loose, an' pushed them jest for fun, an' darned if I could make him break.'

'You didn't have no reefreshments along?' said Scarth, incredulously.

'That's all right, Scarth. You had to crawl on our last bet, an' you'll get another chance soon as you're man enough.'

'Chuck,' shouted the cook, and the subject was dropped. Next day the scene of the round-up was changed, and the mustangs were forgotten.

A year later the same corner of New Mexico was worked over by the roundup, and again the mustang bunch was seen. The dark colt was now a black yearling, with thin, clean legs and glossy flanks; and more than one of the boys saw with his own eyes this oddity – the mustang was a born pacer.

Jo was along, and the idea now struck him that that colt was worth having. To an Easterner this thought may not seem startling or original, but in the West, where an unbroken horse is worth $5, and where an ordinary saddlehorse is worth $15 or $20, the idea of a wild mustang being desirable property does not occur to the average cowboy, for mustangs are hard to catch, and when caught are merely wild animal prisoners, perfectly useless and untamable to the last. Not a few of the cattle-owners make a point of shooting all mustangs at sight, for they are not only useless cumberers of the feeding-grounds, but commonly lead away domestic horses, which soon take to the wild life and are thenceforth lost.

Wild Jo Calone knew a 'bronk right down to subsoil.' 'I never seen a white that wasn't soft, nor a chestnut that wasn't nervous, nor a bay that wasn't good if broke right, nor a black that wasn't hard as nails, an' full of old Harry. All a black bronk wants is claws to be wus'n Daniel's hull outfit of lions.'

Since then a mustang is worthless vermin, and a black mustang ten times worse than worthless, Jo's pard 'didn't see no sense in Jo's wantin' to corral the yearling,' as he now seemed intent on doing. But Jo got no chance to try that year.

He was only a cow-puncher on $25 a month, and tied to hours. Like most of the boys, he always looked forward to having a ranch and an outfit of his own. His brand, the hogpen, of sinister suggestion, was already registered at Santa Fé, but of horned stock it was borne by a single old cow, so as to give him a legal right to put his brand on any maverick (or unbranded animal) he might chance to find.

Yet each fall, when paid off, Jo could not resist the temptation to go to town with the boys and have a good time 'while the stuff held out.' So that his property consisted of little more than his saddle, his bed, and his old cow. He kept on hoping to make a strike that would leave him well fixed with a fair start, and when the thought came that the Black Mustang was his mascot, he only needed a chance to 'make the try.'

The roundup circled down to the Canadian River, and back in the fall by the Don Carlos Hills, and Jo saw no more of the Pacer, though he heard of him from many quarters, for the colt, now a vigorous, young horse, rising three, was beginning to be talked of.

Antelope Springs is in the middle of a great level plain. When the water is high it spreads into a small lake with a belt of sedge around it; when it is low there is a wide flat of black mud, glistening white with alkali in places, and the spring a water-hole in the middle. It has no flow or outlet and yet is fairly good water, the only drinking-place for many miles.

This flat, or prairie as it would be called farther north, was the favorite feeding-ground of the Black Stallion, but it was also the pasture of many herds of range horses and cattle. Chiefly interested was the 'L cross F' outfit. Foster, the manager and part owner, was a man of enterprise. He believed it would pay to handle a better class of cattle and horses on the range, and one of his ventures was ten half-blooded mares, tall, clean-limbed, deer-eyed creatures, that made the scrub cow-ponies look like pitiful starvelings of some degenerate and quite different species.

One of these was kept stabled for use, but the nine, after the weaning of their colts, managed to get away and wandered off on the range.

A horse has a fine instinct for the road to the best feed, and the nine mares drifted, of course, to the prairie of Antelope Springs, twenty miles to the southward. And when, later that summer Foster went to round them up, he found the nine indeed, but with them and guarding them with an air of more than mere comradeship was a coal-black stallion, prancing around and rounding up the bunch like an expert, his jet-black coat a vivid contrast to the golden hides of his harem.

The mares were gentle, and would have been easily driven homeward but for a new and unexpected thing. The Black Stallion became greatly aroused. He seemed to inspire them too with his wildness, and flying this way and that way drove the whole band at full gallop where he would. Away then went, and the little cow-ponies that carried the men were easily left behind.

This was maddening, and both men at last drew their guns and sought a chance to drop that 'blasted stallion.' But no chance came that was not 9 to 1 of dropping one of the mares. A long day of manoeuvring made no change. The Pacer, for it was he, kept his family together and disappeared among the southern sandhills. The cattlemen on their jaded ponies set out for home with the poor satisfaction of vowing vengeance for their failure on the superb cause of it.

One of the most aggravating parts of it was that one or two experiences like this would surely make the mares as wild as the Mustang, and there seemed to be no way of saving them from it.

Scientists differ on the power of beauty and prowess to attract female admiration among the lower animals, but whether it is admiration or the prowess itself, it is certain that a wild animal of uncommon gifts soon wins a large following from the harems of his rivals. And the great Black Horse, with his inky mane and tail and his green-lighted eyes, ranged through all that region and added to his following from many bands till not less than a score of mares were in his 'bunch.' Most were merely humble cow-ponies turned out to range, but the nine great mares were there, a striking group by themselves. According to all reports, this bunch was always kept rounded up and guarded with such energy and jealousy that a mare, once in it, was a lost animal so far as man was concerned, and the ranchmen realized soon that they had gotten on the range a mustang that was doing them more harm than all other sources of loss put together.

It was December, 1893. I was new in the country, and was setting out from the ranch-house on the Pinavetitos, to go with a wagon to the Canadian River. As I was leaving, Foster finished his remark by: 'And if you get a chance to draw a bead on that accursed mustang, don't fail to drop him in his tracks.'

This was the first I had heard of him, and as I rode along I gathered from Burns, my guide, the history that has been given. I was full of curiosity to see the famous three-year-old, and was not a little disappointed on the second day when we came to the prairie on Antelope Springs and saw no sign of the Pacer or his band.

But on the next day, as we crossed the Alamosa Arroyo, and were rising to the rolling prairie again, Jack Burns, who was riding on ahead, suddenly dropped flat on the neck of his horse, and swung back to me in the wagon, saying:

'Get out your rifle, here's that - stallion.'

I seized my rifle, and hurried forward to a view over the prairie ridge. In the hollow below was a band of horses, and there at one end was the Great Black Mustang. He had heard some sound of our approach, and was not unsuspicious of danger. There he stood with head and tail erect, and nostrils wide, an image of horse perfection and beauty, as noble an animal as ever ranged the plains, and the mere notion of turning that magnificent creature into a mass of carrion was horrible. In spite of Jack's exhortation to 'shoot quick,' I delayed, and threw open the breach, whereupon he, always hot and hasty, swore at my slowness, growled, 'Gi' me that gun,' and as he seized it I turned the muzzle up, and *accidentally* the gun went off.

Instantly the herd below was all alarm, the great black leader snorted and neighed and dashed about. And the mares bunched, and away all went in a rumble of hoofs, and a cloud of dust.

The Stallion careered now on this side, now on that, and kept his eye on all and led and drove them far away. As long as I could see I watched, and never once did he break his pace.

Jack made Western remarks about me and my gun, as well as that mustang, but I rejoiced in the Pacer's strength and beauty, and not for all the mares in the bunch would I have harmed his glossy hide.

There are several ways of capturing wild horses. One is by creasing – that is, grazing the animal's nape with a rifle-ball so that he is stunned long enough for hobbling.

'Yes! I seen about a hundred necks broke trying it, but I never seen a mustang creased yet,' was Wild Jo's critical remark.

Sometimes, if the shape of the country abets it, the herd can be driven into a corral; sometimes with extra fine mounts they can be run down, but by far the commonest way, paradoxical as it may seem, is to *walk* them down.

The fame of the Stallion that never was known to gallop was spreading. Extraordinary stories were told of his gait, his speed, and his wind, and when old Montgomery of the 'triangle-bar' outfit came out plump at Well's Hotel in Clayton, and in presence of witnesses said he'd give one thousand dollars cash for him safe in a box-car, providing the stories were true, a dozen young cow-punchers were eager to cut loose and win the purse, as soon as present engagements were up. But Wild Jo had had his eye on this very deal for quite a while; there was no time to lose, so ignoring present contracts he rustled all night to raise the necessary equipment for the game.

By straining his already overstrained credit, and taxing the already overtaxed generosity of his friends, he got together an expedition consisting of twenty good saddle-horses, a mess-wagon, and a fortnight's stuff for three men – himself, his 'pard,' Charley, and the cook.

Then they set out from Clayton, with the avowed intention of walking down the wonderfully swift wild horse. The third day they arrived at Antelope Springs, and as it was about noon they were not surprised to see the black Pacer marching down to drink with all his band behind him. Jo kept out of sight until the wild horses each and all had drunk their fill, for a thirsty animal always travels better than one laden with water.

Jo then rode quietly forward. The Pacer took alarm at half a mile, and led his band away out of sight on the soapweed mesa to the southeast. Jo followed at a gallop till he once more sighted them, then came back and instructed the cook, who was also teamster, to make for Alamosa Arroyo in the south. Then away to the southeast he went after the mustangs. After a mile or two he once more sighted them, and walked his horse quietly till so near that they again took alarm and circled away to the south. An hour's trot, not on the trail, but cutting across to where they ought to go, brought Jo again in close sight. Again he walked quietly toward the herd, and again there was the alarm and flight. And so they passed the afternoon, but circled ever more and more to the south, so that when the sun was low they were, as Jo had expected, not far from Alamosa Arroyo. The band was again close at hand, and Jo, after starting them off, rode to the wagon, while his pard, who had been taking it easy, took up the slow chase on a fresh horse.

After supper the wagon moved on to the upper ford of the Alamosa, as arranged, and there camped for the night.

Meanwhile, Charley followed the herd. They had not run so far as at first, for their pursuer made no sign of attack, and they were getting used to his company. They were more easily found, as the shadows fell, on account of a snow-white mare that was in the bunch. A young moon in the sky now gave some help, and relying on his horse to choose the path, Charley kept him quietly walking after the herd, represented by that ghost-white mare, till they were lost in the night. He then got off, unsaddled and picketed his horse, and in his blanket quickly went to sleep.

At the first streak of dawn he was up, and within a short half-mile, thanks to the snowy mare, he found the band. At his approach, the shrill neigh of the Pacer bugled his troop into a flying squad. But on the first mesa they stopped, and faced about to see what this persistent follower was, and what he wanted. For a moment or so they stood against the sky to gaze, and then deciding that he knew him as well as he wished to, that black meteor flung his mane on the wind, and led off at his tireless, even swing, while the mares came streaming after.

Away they went, circling now to the west, and after several repetitions of this same play, flying, following, and overtaking, and flying again, they passed, near noon, the old Apache look-out, Buffalo Bluff. And here, on watch, was Jo. A long thin column of smoke told Charley to come to camp, and with a flashing pocket-mirror he made response.

Jo, freshly mounted, rode across, and again took up the chase, and back came Charley to camp to eat and rest, and then move on up stream.

All that day Jo followed, and managed, when it was needed, that the herd should keep the great circle, of which the wagon cut a small chord. At sundown he came to Verde Crossing, and there was Charley with a fresh horse and food, and Jo went on in the same calm, dogged way. All the evening he followed, and far into the night, for the wild herd was now getting somewhat used to the presence of the harmless strangers, and were more easily followed; moreover, they were tiring out with perpetual travelling. They were no longer in the good grass country, they were not grain-fed like the horses on their track, and above all, the slight but continuous nervous tension was surely telling. It spoiled their appetites, but made them very thirsty. They were allowed, and as far as possible encouraged, to drink deeply at every chance. The effect of large quantities of water on a running animal is well known; it tends to stiffen the limbs and spoil the wind. Jo carefully guarded his own horse against such excess, and both he and his horse were fresh when they camped that night on the trail of the jaded mustangs.

At dawn he found them easily close at hand, and though they ran at first they did not go far before they dropped into a walk. The battle seemed nearly won now, for the chief difficulty in the 'walk-down' is to keep track of the herd the first two or three days when they are fresh.

All that morning Jo kept in sight, generally in close sight, of the band. About ten o'clock, Charley relieved him near José Peak and that day the mustangs walked only a quarter of a mile ahead with much less spirit than the day before and circled now more north again. At night Charley was supplied with a fresh horse and followed as before.

Next day the mustangs walked with heads held low, and in spite of the efforts of the Black Pacer at times they were less than a hundred yards ahead of their pursuer.

The fourth and fifth days passed the same way, and now the herd was nearly back to Antelope Springs. So far all had come out as expected. The chase had been in a great circle with the wagon following a lesser circle. The wild herd was back to its starting-point, worn out; and the hunters were back, fresh and on fresh horses. The herd was kept from drinking till late in the afternoon and then driven to the Springs to swell themselves with a perfect water gorge. Now was the chance for the skilful ropers on the grain-fed horses to close in, for the sudden heavy drink was ruination, almost paralysis, of wind and limb, and it would be easy to rope and hobble them one by one.

There was only one weak spot in the programme, the Black Stallion, the cause of the hunt, seemed made of iron, that ceaseless swinging pace seemed as swift and vigorous now as on the morning when the chase began. Up and down he went rounding up the herd and urging them on by voice and example to escape. But they were played out. The old white mare that had been such help in sighting them at night, had dropped out hours ago, dead beat. The half-bloods seemed to be losing all fear of the horsemen, the band was clearly in Jo's power. But the one who was the prize of all the hunt seemed just as far as ever out of reach.

Here was a puzzle. Jo's comrades knew him well and would not have been surprised to see him in a sudden rage attempt to shoot the Stallion down. But Jo had no such mind. During that long week of following he had watched the horse all day at speed and never once had he seen him gallop.

The horseman's adoration of a noble horse had grown and grown, till now he would as soon have thought of shooting his best mount as firing on that splendid beast.

Jo even asked himself whether he would take the handsome sum that was offered for the prize. Such an animal would be a fortune in himself to sire a race of pacers for the track.

But the prize was still at large – the time had come to finish up the hunt. Jo's finest mount was caught. She was a mare of Eastern blood, but raised on the plains. She never would have come into Jo's possession but for a curious weakness. The loco is a poisonous weed that grows in these regions. Most stock will not touch it; but sometimes an animal tries it and becomes addicted to it. It acts somewhat like morphine, but the animal, though sane for long intervals, has always a passion for the herb and finally dies mad. A beast with the craze is said to be locoed. And Jo's best mount had a wild gleam in her eye that to an expert told the tale.

But she was swift and strong and Jo chose her for the grand finish of the chase. It would have been an easy matter now to rope the mares, but was no longer necessary. They could be separated from their black leader and driven home to the corral. But that leader still had the look of untamed strength. Jo, rejoicing in a worthy foe, went bounding forth to try the odds. The lasso was flung on the ground and trailed to take out every kink, and gathered as he rode into neatest coils across his left palm. Then putting on the spur the first time in that chase he rode straight for the Stallion a quarter of a mile beyond. Away he went, and away went Jo, each at his best, while the fagged-out mares scattered right and left and let them pass. Straight across the open plain the fresh horse went at its hardest gallop, and the Stallion, leading off, still kept his start and kept his famous swing.

It was incredible, and Jo put on more spur and shouted to his horse, which fairly flew, but shortened up the space between by not a single inch. For the Black One whirled across the flat and up and passed a soapweed mesa and down across a sandy treacherous plain, then over a grassy stretch where prairie dogs barked, then hid below, and on came Jo, but there to see, could he believe his eyes, the Stallion's start grown longer still, and Jo began to curse his luck, and urge and spur his horse until the poor uncertain brute got into such a state of nervous fright, her eyes began to roll, she wildly shook her head from side to side, no longer picked her ground – a badger-hole received her foot and down she went, and Jo went flying to the earth. Though badly bruised, he gained his feet and tried to mount his crazy beast. But she, poor brute, was done for – her off fore-leg hung loose.

There was but one thing to do. Jo loosed the cinch, put Lightfoot out of pain, and carried back the saddle to the camp. While the Pacer steamed away till lost to view.

This was not quite defeat, for all the mares were manageable now, and Jo and Charley drove them carefully to the 'L cross F' corral and claimed a good reward. But Jo was more than ever bound to own the Stallion. He had seen what stuff he was made of, he prized him more and more, and only sought to strike some better plan to catch him.

The cook on that trip was Bates – Mr. Thomas Bates, he called himself at the post-office where he regularly went for the letters and remittance which never came. Old Tom Turkeytrack, the boys called him, from his cattlebrand, which he said was on record at Denver, and which, according to his story, was also borne by countless beef and saddle stock on the plains of the unknown North.

When asked to join the trip as a partner, Bates made some sarcastic remarks about horses not fetching $12 a dozen, which had been literally true within the year, and he preferred to go on a very meagre salary. But no one who once saw the Pacer going had failed to catch the craze. Turkeytrack experienced the usual change of heart. He now wanted to own that mustang. How this was to be brought about he did not clearly see till one day there called at the ranch that had 'secured his services,' as he put it, one, Bill Smith, more usually known as Horseshoe Billy, from his cattle-brand. While the excellent fresh beef and bread and the vile coffee, dried peaches and molasses were being consumed, he of the horseshoe remarked, in tones which percolated through a huge stop-gap of bread:

'Wall, I seen that thar Pacer to-day, nigh enough to put a plait in his tail.'

'What, you didn't shoot?'

'No, but I come mighty near it.'

'Don't you be led into no sich foolishness,' said a 'double-bar H' cow-puncher at the other end of the table. 'I calc'late that maverick 'ill carry my brand before the moon changes.'

'You'll have to be pretty spry or you'll find a "triangle dot" on his weather side when you get there.'

'Where did you run acrost him?'

'Wall, it was like this; I was riding the flat by Antelope Springs and I sees a lump on the dry mud inside the rush belt. I knowed I never seen that before, so rides up, thinking it might be some of our stock, an' seen it was a horse lying plumb flat. The wind was blowing like-from him to me, so I rides up close and seen it was the Pacer, dead as a mackerel. Still, he didn't look swelled or cut, and there wa'n't no smell, an' I didn't know what to think till I seen his ear twitch off a fly and then I knowed he was sleeping. I gits down me rope and coils it, and seen it was old and pretty shaky in spots, and me saddle a single cinch, an' me pony about 700 again a 1,200 lbs. stallion, an' I sez to meself, sez I: "'Tain't no use, I'll only break me cinch and git throwed an' lose me saddle." So I hits the saddle-horn a crack with the hondu, and I wish't you'd a seen that mustang. He lept six foot in the air an' snorted like he was shunting cars. His eyes fairly bugged out an' he lighted out lickety split for California, and he orter be there about now if he kep' on like he started – and I swear he never made a break the hull trip.'

The story was not quite so consecutive as given here. It was much punctuated by present engrossments, and from first to last was more or less infiltrated through the necessaries of life, for Bill was a healthy young man without a trace of false shame. But the account was complete and everyone believed it, for Billy was known to be reliable. Of all those who heard, old Turkeytrack talked the least and probably thought the most, for it gave him a new idea.

During his after-dinner pipe he studied it out and deciding that he could not go it alone, he took Horseshoe Billy into his council and the result was a partnership in a new venture to capture the Pacer; that is, the $5,000 that was now said to be the offer for him safe in a box-car.

Antelope Springs was still the usual watering-place of the Pacer. The water being low left a broad belt of dry black mud between the sedge and the spring. At two places this belt was broken by a well-marked trail made by the animals coming to drink. Horses and wild animals usually kept to these trails, though the horned cattle had no hesitation in taking a short cut through the sedge.

In the most used of these trails the two men set to work with shovels and digged a pit 15 feet long, 6 feet wide and 7 feet deep. It was a hard twenty hours work for them as it had to be completed between the Mustang's drinks, and it began to be very damp work before it was finished. With poles, brush, and earth it was then cleverly covered over and concealed. And the men went to a distance and hid in pits made for the purpose.

About noon the Pacer came, alone now since the capture of his band. The trail on the opposite side of the mud belt was little used, and old Tom, by throwing some fresh rushes across it, expected to make sure that the Stallion would enter by the other, if indeed he should by any caprice try to come by the unusual path.

What sleepless angel is it watches over and cares for the wild animals? In spite of all reasons to take the usual path, the Pacer came along the other. The suspicious-looking rushes did not stop him; he walked calmly to the water and drank. There was only one way now to prevent utter failure; when he lowered his head for the second draft which horses always take, Bates and Smith quit their holes and ran swiftly toward the trail behind him, and when he raised his proud head Smith sent a revolver-shot into the ground behind him.

Away went the Pacer at his famous gait straight to the trap. Another second and he would be into it. Already he is on the trail, and already they feel they have him, but the Angel of the wild things is with him, that incomprehensible warning comes, and with one mighty bound he clears the fifteen feet of treacherous ground and spurns the earth as he fades away unharmed, never again to visit Antelope Springs by either of the beaten paths.

Wild Jo never lacked energy. He meant to catch that Mustang, and when he learned that others were bestirring themselves for the same purpose he at once set about trying the best untried plan he knew – the plan by which the coyote catches the fleeter jackrabbit, and the mounted Indian the far swifter antelope – the old plan of the relay chase.

The Canadian River on the south, its affluent, the Piñavetitos Arroyo, on the northeast, and the Don Carlos Hills with the Ute Creek Cañon on the west, formed a sixty-mile triangle that was the range of the Pacer. It was believed that he never went outside this, and at all times Antelope Springs was his headquarters. Jo knew this country well, all the water-holes and cañon crossings as well as the ways of the Pacer.

If he could have gotten fifty good horses he could have posted them to advantage so as to cover all points, but twenty mounts and five good riders were all that proved available.

The horses, grain-fed for two weeks before, were sent on ahead; each man was instructed now to play his part and sent to his post the day before the race. On the day of the start Jo with his wagon drove to the plain of Antelope Springs and, camping far off in a little draw, waited.

At last he came, that coal-black Horse, out from the sand-hills at the south, alone as always now, and walked calmly down to the Springs and circled quite around it to sniff for any hidden foe. Then he approached where there was no trail at all and drank.

Jo watched and wished he would drink a hogshead. But the moment that he turned and sought the grass Jo spurred his steed. The Pacer heard the hoofs, then saw the running horse, and did not want a nearer view but led away. Across the flat he went down to the south, and kept the famous swinging gait that made his start grow longer. Now through the sandy dunes he went, and steadying to an even pace he gained considerably and Jo's too-laden horse plunged through the sand and sinking fetlock deep, he lost at every bound. Then came a level stretch where the runner seemed to gain, and then a long decline where Jo's horse dared not run his best, so lost again at every step.

But on they went, and Jo spared neither spur nor quirt. A mile – a mile – and another mile, and the far-off rock at Arriba loomed up ahead.

And there Jo knew fresh mounts were held, and on they dashed. But the night-black mane out level on the breeze ahead was gaining more and more.

Arriba Cañon reached at last, the watcher stood aside, for it was not wished to turn the race, and the Stallion passed – dashed down, across and up the slope, with that unbroken pace, the only one he knew.

And Jo came bounding on his foaming steed, and leaped on the waiting mount, then urged him down the slope and up upon the track, and on the upland once more drove in the spurs, and raced and raced, and raced, but not a single inch he gained.

Ga-lump, ga-lump, ga-lump with measured beat he went – an hour – an hour, and another hour – Arroyo Alamosa just ahead with fresh relays, and Jo yelled at his horse and pushed him on and on. Straight for the place the Black One made, but on the last two miles some strange foreboding turned him to the left, and Jo foresaw escape in this, and pushed his jaded mount at any cost to head him off, and hard as they had raced this was the hardest race of all, with gasps for breath and leather squeaks at every straining bound. Then cutting right across, Jo seemed to gain, and drawing his gun he fired shot after shot to toss the dust, and so turned the Stallion's head and forced him back to take the crossing to the right.

Down they went. The Stallion crossed and Jo sprang to the ground. His horse was done, for thirty miles had passed in the last stretch, and Jo himself was worn out. His eyes were burnt with flying alkali dust. He was half blind so he motioned to his 'pard' to 'go ahead and keep him straight for Alamosa ford.'

Out shot the rider on a strong, fresh steed, and away they went – up and down on the rolling plain – the Black Horse flecked with snowy foam. His heaving ribs and noisy breath showed what he felt – but on and on he went.

And Tom on Ginger seemed to gain, then lose and lose, when in an hour the long decline of Alamosa came. And there a freshly mounted lad took up the chase and turned it west, and on they went past towns of prairie dogs, through soapweed tracts and cactus brakes by scores, and pricked and wrenched rode on. With dust and sweat the Black was now a dappled brown, but still he stepped the same. Young Carrington, who followed, had hurt his steed by pushing at the very start, and spurred and urged him now to cut across a gulch at which the Pacer shied. Just one misstep and down they went.

The boy escaped, but the pony lies there yet, and the wild Black Horse kept on.

This was close to old Gallego's ranch where Jo himself had cut across refreshed to push the chase. Within thirty minutes he was again scorching the Pacer's trail.

Far in the west the Carlos Hills were seen, and there Jo knew fresh men and mounts were waiting, and that way the indomitable rider tried to turn the race, but by a sudden whim, of the inner warning born perhaps - the Pacer turned. Sharp to the north he went, and Jo, the skilful wrangler, rode and rode and yelled and tossed the dust with shots, but down a gulch the wild black meteor streamed and Jo could only follow. Then came the hardest race of all; Jo, cruel to the Mustang, was crueller to his mount and to himself, The sun was hot, the scorching plain was dim in shimmering heat, his eyes and lips were burnt with sand and salt, and yet the chase sped on. The only chance to win would be if he could drive the Mustang back to Big Arroyo Crossing. Now almost for the first time he saw signs of weakening in the Black. His mane and tail were not just quite so high, and his short half mile of start was down by more than half, but still he stayed ahead and paced and paced and paced.

An hour and another hour, and still they went the same. But they turned again, and night was near when big Arroyo ford was reached - full twenty miles. But Jo was game, he seized the waiting horse. The one he left went gasping to the stream and gorged himself with water till he died.

Then Jo held back in hopes the foaming Black would drink. But he was wise; he gulped a single gulp, splashed through the stream and then passed on with Jo at speed behind him. And when they last were seen the Black was on ahead just out of reach and Jo's horse bounding on.

It was morning when Jo came to camp on foot. His tale was briefly told: - eight horses dead - five men worn out - the matchless Pacer safe and free.

"Taint possible; it can't be done. Sorry I didn't bore his hellish carcass through when I had the chance,' said Jo, and gave it up.

Old Turkeytrack was cook on this trip. He had watched the chase with as much interest as anyone, and when it failed he grinned into the pot and said: 'That mustang's mine unless I'm a darned fool.' Then falling back on Scripture for a precedent, as was his habit, he still addressed the pot:

'Reckon the Philistines tried to run Samson down and they got done up, an' would a stayed done ony for a nat'ral weakness on his part. An' Adam would a loafed in Eden yit ony for a leetle failing which we all onderstand. An' it aint $5000 I'll take for him nuther.'

Much persecution had made the Pacer wilder than ever. But it did not drive him away from Antelope Springs. That was the only drinking-place with absolutely no shelter for a mile on every side to hide an enemy. Here he came almost every day about noon, and after thoroughly spying the land approached to drink.

His had been a lonely life all winter since the capture of his harem, and of this old Turkeytrack was fully aware. The old cook's chum had a nice little brown mare which he judged would serve his ends, and taking a pair of the strongest hobbles, a spade, a spare lasso, and a stout post he mounted the mare and rode away to the famous Springs.

A few antelope skimmed over the plain before him in the early freshness of the day. Cattle were lying about in groups, and the loud, sweet song of the prairie lark was heard on every side. For the bright snowless winter of the mesas was gone and the springtime was at hand. The grass was greening and all nature seemed turning to thoughts of love.

It was in the air, and when the little brown mare was picketed out to graze she raised her nose from time to time to pour forth a long shrill whinny that surely was her song, if song she had, of love.

Old Turkeytrack studied the wind and the lay of the land. There was the pit he had labored at, now opened and filled with water that was rank with drowned prairie dogs and mice. Here was the new trail the animals were forced to make by the pit. He selected a sedgy clump near some smooth, grassy ground, and first firmly sunk the post, then dug a hole large enough to hide in, and spread his blanket in it. He shortened up the little mare's tether, till she could scarcely move; then on the ground between he spread his open lasso, tying the long end to the post, then covered the rope with dust and grass, and went into his hiding-place.

About noon, after long waiting, the amorous whinny of the mare was answered from the high ground, away to the west, and there, black against the sky, was the famous Mustang.

Down he came at that long swinging gait, but grown crafty with much pursuit, he often stopped to gaze and whinny, and got answer that surely touched his heart. Nearer he came again to call, then took alarm, and paced all around in a great circle to try the wind for his foes, and seemed in doubt. The Angel whispered 'Don't go.' But the brown mare called again. He circled nearer still, and neighed once more, and got reply that seemed to quell all fears, and set his heart aglow.

Nearer still he pranced, till he touched Solly's nose with his own, and finding her as responsive as he well could wish, thrust aside all thoughts of danger, and abandoned himself to the delight of conquest, until, as he pranced around, his hind legs for a moment stood within the evil circle of the rope. One deft sharp twitch, the noose flew tight, and he was caught.

A snort of terror and a bound in the air gave Tom the chance to add the double hitch. The loop flashed up the line, and snake-like bound those mighty hoofs.

Terror lent speed and double strength for a moment, but the end of the rope was reached, and down he went a captive, a hopeless prisoner at last. Old Tom's ugly, little crooked form sprang from the pit to complete the mastering of the great glorious creature whose mighty strength had proved as nothing when matched with the wits of a little old man. With snorts and desperate bounds of awful force the great beast dashed and struggled to be free; but all in vain. The rope was strong.

The second lasso was deftly swung, and the forefeet caught, and then with a skilful move the feet were drawn together, and down went the raging Pacer to lie a moment later 'hog-tied' and helpless on the ground. There he struggled till worn out, sobbing great convulsive sobs while tears ran down his cheeks.

Tom stood by and watched, but a strange revulsion of feeling came over the old cowpuncher. He trembled nervously from head to foot, as he had not done since he roped his first steer, and for a while could do nothing but gaze on his tremendous prisoner. But the feeling soon passed away. He saddled Delilah, and taking the second lasso, roped the great horse about the neck, and left the mare to hold the Stallion's head, while he put on the hobbles. This was soon done, and sure of him now old Bates was about to loose the ropes, but on a sudden thought he stopped. He had quite forgotten, and had come unprepared for something of importance. In Western law the Mustang was the property of the first man to mark him with his brand; how was this to be done with the nearest branding-iron twenty miles away?

Old Tom went to his mare, took up her hoofs one at a time, and examined each shoe. Yes! one was a little loose; he pushed and pried it with the spade, and got it off. Buffalo chips and kindred fuel were plentiful about the plain, so a fire was quickly made, and he soon had one arm of the horse-shoe red hot, then holding the other wrapped in his sock he rudely sketched on the left shoulder of the helpless mustang a turkeytrack, his brand, the first time really that it had ever been used. The Pacer shuddered as the hot iron seared his flesh, but it was quickly done, and the famous Mustang Stallion was a maverick no more.

Now all there was to do was to take him home. The ropes were loosed, the Mustang felt himself freed, thought he was free, and sprang to his feet only to fall as soon as he tried to take a stride. His forefeet were strongly tied together, his only possible gait a shuffling walk, or else a desperate labored bounding with feet so unnaturally held that within a few yards he was inevitably thrown each time he tried to break away. Tom on the light pony headed him off again and again, and by dint of driving, threatening, and manoeuvring, contrived to force his foaming, crazy captive northward toward the Piñavetitos Cañon. But the wild horse would not drive, would not give in. With snorts of terror or of rage and maddest bounds, he tried and tried to get away. It was one long cruel fight; his glossy sides were thick with dark foam, and the foam was stained with blood. Countless hard falls and exhaustion that a long day's chase was powerless to produce were telling on him; his straining bounds first this way and then that, were not now quite so strong, and the spray he snorted as he gasped was half a spray of blood. But his captor, relentless, masterful and cool, still forced him on. Down the slope toward the cañon they had come, every yard a fight, and now they were at the head of the draw that took the trail down to the only crossing of the cañon, the northmost limit of the Pacer's ancient range.

From this the first corral and ranch-house were in sight. The man rejoiced, but the Mustang gathered his remaining strength for one more desperate dash. Up, up the grassy slope from the trail he went, defied the swinging, slashing rope and the gunshot fired in air, in vain attempt to turn his frenzied course. Up, up and on, above the sheerest cliff he dashed then sprang away into the vacant air, down – down – two hundred downward feet to fall, and land upon the rocks below, a lifeless wreck – but free.

Tobermory

SAKI

IT WAS A CHILL, RAIN-WASHED afternoon of a late August day, that
indefinite season when partridges are still in security or cold storage, and
there is nothing to hunt – unless one is bounded on the north by the
Bristol Channel, in which case one may lawfully gallop after fat red
stags. Lady Blemley's house-party was not bounded on the north by the
Bristol Channel, hence there was a full gathering of her guests round the
tea-table on this particular afternoon. And, in spite of the blankness of
the season and the triteness of the occasion, there was no trace in the
company of that fatigued restlessness which means a dread of the pianola
and a subdued hankering for auction bridge. The undisguised open-
mouthed attention of the entire party was fixed on the homely negative
personality of Mr. Cornelius Appin. Of all her guests, he was the one
who had come to Lady Blemley with the vaguest reputation. Some one
had said he was 'clever', and he had got his invitation in the moderate
expectation on the part of his hostess, that some portion at least of his
cleverness would be contributed to the general entertainment. Until
tea-time that day she had been unable to discover in what direction, if
any, his cleverness lay. He was neither a wit nor a croquet champion,
a hypnotic force nor a begetter of amateur theatricals. Neither did his
exterior suggest the sort of man in whom women are willing to pardon
a generous measure of mental deficiency. He had subsided into mere Mr.
Appin, and the Cornelius seemed a piece of transparent baptismal bluff.
And now he was claiming to have launched on the world a discovery
beside which the invention of gunpowder, of the printing-press, and of
steam locomotion were inconsiderable trifles. Science had made bewildering strides in many directions during recent decades, but this thing

seemed to belong to the domain of miracle rather than to scientific achievement.

'And do you really ask us to believe,' Sir Wilfrid was saying, 'that you have discovered a means for instructing animals in the art of human speech, and that dear old Tobermory has proved your first successful pupil?'

'It is a problem at which I have worked for the last seventeen years,' said Mr. Appin, 'but only during the last eight or nine months have I been rewarded with glimmerings of success. Of course I have experimented with thousands of animals, but latterly only with cats, those wonderful creatures which have assimilated themselves so marvellously with our civilization while retaining all their highly developed feral instincts. Here and there among cats one comes across an outstanding superior intellect, just as one does among the ruck of human beings, and when I made the acquaintance of Tobermory a week ago I saw at once that I was in contact with a "Beyond-cat" of extraordinary intelligence. I had gone far along the road to success in recent experiments; with Tobermory, as you call him, I have reached the goal.'

Mr. Appin concluded his remarkable statement in a voice which he strove to divest of a triumphant inflection. No one said 'Rats,' though Clovis's lips moved in a monosyllabic contortion, which probably invoked those rodents of disbelief.

'And do you mean to say,' asked Miss Resker, after a slight pause, 'that you have taught Tobermory to say and understand easy sentences of one syllable?'

'My dear Miss Resker,' said the wonder-worker patiently, 'one teaches little children and savages and backward adults in that piecemeal fashion; when one has once solved the problem of making a beginning with an animal of highly developed intelligence one has no need for those halting methods. Tobermory can speak our language with perfect correctness.'

This time Clovis very distinctly said, 'Beyond-rats!' Sir Wilfrid was more polite, but equally sceptical.

'Hadn't we better have the cat in and judge for ourselves?' suggested Lady Blemley.

Sir Wilfrid went in search of the animal, and the company settled themselves down to the languid expectation of witnessing some more or less adroit drawing-room ventriloquism.

In a minute Sir Wilfrid was back in the room, his face white beneath its tan and his eyes dilated with excitement.

'By Gad, it's true!'

His agitation was unmistakably genuine, and his hearers started forward in a thrill of awakened interest.

Collapsing into an arm-chair he continued breathlessly: 'I found him dozing in the smoking-room, and called out to him to come for his tea. He blinked at me in his usual way, and I said, "Come on, Toby; don't keep us waiting"; and, by Gad! he drawled out in a most horribly natural voice that he'd come when he dashed well pleased! I nearly jumped out of my skin!'

Appin had preached to absolutely incredulous hearers; Sir Wilfrid's statement carried instant conviction. A Babel-like chorus of startled exclamation arose, amid which the scientist sat mutely enjoying the first fruit of his stupendous discovery.

In the midst of the clamour Tobermory entered the room and made his way with velvet tread and studied unconcern across to the group seated round the tea-table.

A sudden hush of awkwardness and constraint fell on the company. Somehow there seemed an element of embarrassment in addressing on equal terms a domestic cat of acknowledged mental ability.

'Will you have some milk, Tobermory?' asked Lady Blemley in a rather strained voice.

'I don't mind if I do,' was the response, couched in a tone of even indifference. A shiver of suppressed excitement went through the listeners, and Lady Blemley might be excused for pouring out the saucerful of milk rather unsteadily.

'I'm afraid I've spilt a good deal of it,' she said apologetically.

'After all, it's not my Axminster,' was Tobermory's rejoinder.

Another silence fell on the group, and then Miss Resker, in her best district-visitor manner, asked if the human language had been difficult to learn. Tobermory looked squarely at her for a moment and then fixed his gaze serenely on the middle distance. It was obvious that boring questions lay outside his scheme of life.

'What do you think of human intelligence?' asked Mavis Pellington lamely.

'Of whose intelligence in particular?' asked Tobermory coldly.

'Oh, well, mine for instance,' said Mavis, with a feeble laugh.

'You put me in an embarrassing position,' said Tobermory, whose tone and attitude certainly did not suggest a shred of embarrassment. 'When your inclusion in this house-party was suggested Sir Wilfrid protested that you were the most brainless woman of his acquaintance, and that there was a wide distinction between hospitality and the care of the feeble-minded. Lady Blemley replied that your lack of brain-power was the precise quality which had earned you your invitation, as you were the only person she could think of who might be idiotic enough to buy their old car. You know, the one they call "The Envy of Sisyphus," because it goes quite nicely up-hill if you push it.'

Lady Blemley's protestations would have had greater effect if she had not casually suggested to Mavis only that morning that the car in question would be just the thing for her down at her Devonshire home.

Major Barfield plunged in heavily to effect a diversion.

'How about your carryings-on with the tortoise-shell puss up at the stables, eh?'

The moment he had said it every one realized the blunder.

'One does not usually discuss these matters in public,' said Tobermory frigidly. 'From a slight observation of your ways since you've been in this house I should imagine you'd find it inconvenient if I were to shift the conversation on to your own little affairs.'

The panic which ensued was not confined to the Major.

'Would you like to go and see if cook has got your dinner ready?' suggested Lady Blemley hurriedly, affecting to ignore the fact that it wanted at least two hours to Tobermory's dinner-time.

'Thanks,' said Tobermory, 'not quite so soon after my tea. I don't want to die of indigestion.'

'Cats have nine lives, you know,' said Sir Wilfrid heartily.

'Possibly,' answered Tobermory; 'but only one liver.'

'Adelaide!' said Mrs. Cornett, 'do you mean to encourage that cat to go out and gossip about us in the servants' hall?'

The panic had indeed become general. A narrow ornamental balustrade ran in front of most of the bedroom windows at the Towers, and it was recalled with dismay that this had formed a favourite promenade for Tobermory at all hours, whence he could watch the pigeons – and heaven knew what else besides. If he intended to become reminiscent in his present outspoken strain the effect would be something more than disconcerting. Mrs. Cornett, who spent much time at her toilet table, and whose complexion was reputed to be of a nomadic though punctual disposition, looked ill at ease as the Major. Miss Scrawen, who wrote fiercely sensuous poetry and led a blameless life, merely displayed irritation; if you are methodical and virtuous in private you don't necessarily want every one to know it. Bertie van Tahn, who was so depraved at seventeen that he had long ago given up trying to be any worse, turned a dull shade of gardenia white, but he did not commit the error of dashing out of the room like Odo Finsberry, a young gentleman who was understood to be reading for the Church and who was possibly disturbed at the thought of scandals he might hear concerning other people. Clovis had the presence of mind to maintain a composed exterior; privately he was calculating how long it would take to procure a box of fancy mice through the agency of the *Exchange and Mart* as a species of hush-money.

Even in a delicate situation like the present, Agnes Resker could not endure to remain too long in the background.

'Why did I ever come down here?' she asked dramatically.

Tobermory immediately accepted the opening.

'Judging by what you said to Mrs. Cornett on the croquet-lawn yesterday, you were out for food. You described the Blemleys as the dullest people to stay with that you knew, but said they were clever enough to employ a first-rate cook; otherwise they'd find it difficult to get any one to come down a second time.'

'There's not a word of truth in it! I appeal to Mrs. Cornett—' exclaimed the discomfited Agnes.

'Mrs. Cornett repeated your remark afterwards to Bertie van Tahn,' continued Tobermory, 'and said, "That woman is a regular Hunger Marcher; she'd go anywhere for four square meals a day," and Bertie van Tahn said—'

At this point the chronicle mercifully ceased. Tobermory had caught a glimpse of the big yellow Tom from the Rectory working his way through the shrubbery towards the stable wing. In a flash he had vanished through the open French window.

With the disappearance of his too brilliant pupil Cornelius Appin found himself beset by a hurricane of bitter upbraiding, anxious inquiry, and frightened entreaty. The responsibility for the situation lay with him, and he must prevent matters from becoming worse. Could Tobermory impart his dangerous gift to other cats? was the first question he had to answer. It was possible, he replied, that he might have initiated his intimate friend the stable puss into his new accomplishment, but it was unlikely that his teaching could have taken a wider range as yet.

'Then,' said Mrs. Cornett, 'Tobermory may be a valuable cat and a great pet; but I'm sure you'll agree, Adelaide, that both he and the stable cat must be done away with without delay.'

'You don't suppose I've enjoyed the last quarter of an hour, do you?' said Lady Blemley bitterly. 'My husband and I are very fond of Tobermory – at least, we were before this horrible accomplishment was infused into him; but now, of course, the only thing is to have him destroyed as soon as possible.'

'We can put some strychnine in the scraps he always gets at dinner-time,' said Sir Wilfrid, 'and I will go and drown the stable cat myself. The coachman will be very sore at losing his pet, but I'll say a very catching form of mange has broken out in both cats and we're afraid of it spreading to the kennels.'

'But my great discovery!' expostulated Mr. Appin; 'after all my years of research and experiment—'

'You can go and experiment on the short-horns at the farm, who are under proper control,' said Mrs. Cornett, 'or the elephants at the Zoological Gardens. They're said to be highly intelligent, and they have this recommendation, that they don't come creeping about our bedrooms and under chairs, and so forth.'

An archangel ecstatically proclaiming the Millennium, and then finding that it clashed unpardonably with Henley and would have to be indefinitely postponed, could hardly have felt more crestfallen than Cornelius Appin at the reception of his wonderful achievement. Public opinion, however, was against him – in fact, had the general voice been consulted on the subject it is probable that a strong minority vote would have been in favour of including him in the strychnine diet.

Defective train arrangements and a nervous desire to see matters brought to a finish prevented an immediate dispersal of the party, but dinner that evening was not a social success. Sir Wilfrid had had rather a trying time with the stable cat and subsequently with the coachman. Agnes Resker ostentatiously limited her repast to a morsel of dry toast, which she bit as though it were a personal enemy; while Mavis Pellington maintained a vindictive silence throughout the meal. Lady Blemley kept up a flow of what she hoped was conversation, but her attention was fixed on the doorway. A plateful of carefully dosed fish scraps was in readiness on the sideboard, but sweets and savoury and dessert went their way, and no Tobermory appeared either in the dining-room or kitchen.

The sepulchral dinner was cheerful compared with the subsequent vigil in the smoking-room. Eating and drinking had at least supplied a distraction and cloak to the prevailing embarrassment. Bridge was out of the question in the general tension of nerves and tempers, and after Odo Finsberry had given a lugubrious rendering of 'Mélisande in the Wood' to a frigid audience, music was tacitly avoided. At eleven the servants went to bed, announcing that the small window in the pantry had been left open as usual for Tobermory's private use. The guests read steadily through the current batch of magazines, and fell back gradually on the 'Badminton Library' and bound volumes of *Punch*. Lady Blemley made periodic visits to the pantry, returning each time with an expression of listless depression which forestalled questioning.

At two o'clock Clovis broke the dominating silence.

'He won't turn up tonight. He's probably in the local newpaper office at the present moment, dictating the first instalment of his reminiscences. Lady What's-her-name's book won't be in it. It will be the event of the day.'

Having made this contribution to the general cheerfulness, Clovis went to bed. At long intervals the various members of the house-party followed his example.

The servants taking round the early tea made a uniform announcement in reply to a uniform question. Tobermory had not returned.

Breakfast was, if anything, a more unpleasant function than dinner had been, but before its conclusion the situation was relieved. Tobermory's corpse was brought in from the shrubbery, where a gardener had just discovered it. From the bites on his throat and the yellow fur which coated his claws it was evident that he had fallen in unequal combat with the big Tom from the Rectory.

By midday most of the guests had quitted the Towers, and after lunch Lady Blemley had sufficiently recovered her spirits to write an extremely nasty letter to the Rectory about the loss of her valuable pet.

Tobermory had been Appin's one successful pupil, and he was destined to have no successor. A few weeks later an elephant in the Dresden Zoological Garden, which had shown no previous signs of irritability, broke loose and killed an Englishman who had apparently been teasing it. The victim's name was variously reported in the papers as Oppin and Eppelin, but his front name was faithfully rendered Cornelius.

'If he was trying German irregular verbs on the poor beast,' said Clovis, 'he deserved all he got.'

Pig-Hoo-o-o-o-ey!

P. G. WODEHOUSE

THANKS TO THE PUBLICITY given to the matter by *The Bridgnorth, Shifnal, and Albrighton Argus* (with which is incorporated *The Wheat-Growers' Intelligencer and Stock Breeders' Gazetteer*), the whole world to-day knows that the silver medal in the Fat Pigs class at the eighty-seventh annual Shropshire Agricultural Show was won by the Earl of Emsworth's black Berkshire sow, Empress of Blandings.

Very few people, however, are aware how near that splendid animal came to missing the coveted honour.

Now it can be told.

This brief chapter of Secret History may be said to have begun on the night of the eighteenth of July, when George Cyril Wellbeloved (twenty-nine), pig-man in the employ of Lord Emsworth, was arrested by Police-Constable Evans of Market Blandings for being drunk and disorderly in the tap-room of the Goat and Feathers. On July the nineteenth, after first offering to apologize, then explaining that it had been his birthday, and finally attempting to prove an alibi, George Cyril was very properly jugged for fourteen days without the option of a fine.

On July the twentieth, Empress of Blandings, always hitherto a hearty and even a boisterous feeder, for the first time on record declined all nourishment. And on the morning of July the twenty-first, the veterinary surgeon called in to diagnose and deal with this strange asceticism, was compelled to confess to Lord Emsworth that the thing was beyond his professional skill.

Let us just see, before proceeding, that we have got these dates correct:

July 18. – Birthday Orgy of Cyril Wellbeloved.
July 19. – Incarceration of Ditto.
July 20. – Pig Lays off the Vitamins.

July 21. – Veterinary Surgeon Baffled.

Right.

The effect of the veterinary surgeon's announcement on Lord Emsworth was overwhelming. As a rule, the wear and tear of our complex modern life left this vague and amiable peer unscathed. So long as he had sunshine, regular meals, and complete freedom from the society of his younger son Frederick, he was placidly happy. But there were chinks in his armour, and one of these had been pierced this morning. Dazed by the news he stood at the window of the great library of Blandings Castle, looking out with unseeing eyes.

As he stood there, the door opened. Lord Emsworth turned; and having blinked once or twice, as was his habit when confronted suddenly with anything, recognized in the handsome and imperious looking woman who had entered, his sister, Lady Constance Keeble. Her demeanour, like his own, betrayed the deepest agitation.

'Clarence,' she cried, 'an awful thing has happened!'

Lord Emsworth nodded dully. 'I know. He's just told me.'

'What! Has he been here?'

'Only this moment left.'

'Why did you let him go? You must have known I would want to see him.'

'What good would that have done?'

'I could at least have assured him of my sympathy,' said Lady Constance stiffly.

'Yes, I suppose you could,' said Lord Emsworth, having considered the point. 'Not that he deserves any sympathy. The man's an ass.'

'Nothing of the kind. A most intelligent young man, as young men go.'

'Young? Would you call him young? Fifty, I should have said, if a day.'

'Are you out of your senses? Heacham fifty?'

'Not Heacham. Smithers.'

As frequently happened to her when in conversation with her brother, Lady Constance experienced a swimming sensation.

'Will you kindly tell me, Clarence, in a few simple words, what you imagine we are talking about?'

'I'm talking about Smithers. Empress of Blandings is refusing her food, and Smithers says he can't do anything about it. And he calls himself a vet!'

'Then you haven't heard? Clarence, a dreadful thing has happened. Angela has broken off her engagement to Heacham.'

'And the Agricultural Show on Wednesday week!'

'What on earth has that got to do with it?' demanded Lady Constance, feeling a recurrence of the swimming sensation.

'What has it got to do with it?' said Lord Emsworth warmly. 'My champion sow, with less than ten days to prepare herself for a most searching examination in competition with all the finest pigs in the county, starts refusing her food—'

'Will you stop maundering on about your insufferable pig and give your attention to something that really matters? I tell you that Angela – your niece Angela – has broken off her engagement to Lord Heacham and expresses her intention of marrying that hopeless ne'er-do-well, James Belford.'

'The son of old Belford, the parson?'

'Yes.'

'She can't. He's in America.'

'He is not in America. He is in London.'

'No,' said Lord Emsworth, shaking his head sagely. 'You're wrong. I remember meeting his father two years ago out on the road by Meeker's twenty-acre field, and he distinctly told me the boy was sailing for America next day. He must be there by this time.'

'Can't you understand? He's come back.'

'Oh? Come back? I see. Come *back?*'

'You know there was once a silly sentimental sort of affair between him and Angela; but a year after he left she became engaged to Heacham and I thought the whole thing was over and done with. And now it seems she met this young man Belford when she was in London last week, and it has started all over again. She tells me she has written to Heacham and broken the engagement.'

There was a silence. Brother and sister remained for a space plunged in thought. Lord Emsworth was the first to speak.

'We've tried acorns,' he said. 'We've tried skim milk. And we've tried potato-peel. But, no, she won't touch them.'

Conscious of two eyes raising blisters on his sensitive skin, he came to himself with a start.

'Absurd! Ridiculous! Preposterous!' he said, hurriedly. 'Breaking the engagement? Pooh! Tush! What nonsense! I'll have a word with that young man. If he thinks he can go about the place playing fast and loose with my niece and jilting her without so much as a—'

'Clarence!'

Lord Emsworth blinked. Something appeared to be wrong, but he could not imagine what. It seemed to him that in his last speech he had struck just the right note – strong, forceful, dignified.

'Eh?'

'It is Angela who has broken the engagement.'

'Oh, Angela?'

'She is infatuated with this man Belford. And the point is, what are we to do about it?'

Lord Emsworth reflected.

'Take a strong line,' he said firmly. 'Stand no nonsense. Don't send 'em a wedding-present.'

There is no doubt that, given time, Lady Constance would have found and uttered some adequately corrosive comment on this imbecile suggestion; but even as she was swelling preparatory to giving tongue, the door opened and a girl came in.

She was a pretty girl, with fair hair and blue eyes which in their softer moments probably reminded all sorts of people of twin lagoons slumbering beneath a southern sky. This, however, was not one of those moments. To Lord Emsworth, as they met his, they looked like something out of an oxy-acetylene blow-pipe; and, as far as he was capable of being disturbed by anything that was not his younger son Frederick, he was disturbed. Angela, it seemed to him, was upset about something; and he was sorry. He liked Angela.

To ease a tense situation, he said:

'Angela, my dear, do you know anything about pigs?'

The girl laughed. One of those sharp, bitter laughs which are so unpleasant just after breakfast.

'Yes, I do. You're one.'

'Me?'

'Yes, you. Aunt Constance says that, if I marry Jimmy, you won't let me have my money.'

'Money? Money?' Lord Emsworth was mildly puzzled. 'What money? You never lent me any money.'

Lady Constance's feelings found vent in a sound like an overheated radiator.

'I believe this absent-mindedness of yours is nothing but a ridiculous pose, Clarence. You know perfectly well that when poor Jane died she left you Angela's trustee.'

'And I can't touch my money without your consent till I'm twenty-five.'

'Well, how old are you?'

'Twenty-one.'

'Then what are you worrying about?' asked Lord Emsworth, surprised. 'No need to worry about it for another four years. God bless my soul, the money is quite safe. It is in excellent securities'

Angela stamped her foot. An unladylike action, but how much better than kicking an uncle with it, as her lower nature prompted.

'I have told Angela,' explained Lady Constance, 'that, while we naturally cannot force her to marry Lord Heacham, we can at least keep her money from being squandered by this wastrel on whom she proposes to throw herself away.'

'He isn't a wastrel. He's got quite enough money to marry me on, but he wants some capital to buy a partnership in a—'

'He is a wastrel. Wasn't he sent abroad because—'

'That was two years ago. And since then—'

'My dear Angela, you may argue until—'

'I'm not arguing. I'm simply saying that I'm going to marry Jimmy, if we both have to starve in the gutter.'

'What gutter?' asked his lordship, wrenching his errant mind away from thoughts of acorns.

'Any gutter.'

'Now, please listen to me, Angela.'

It seemed to Lord Emsworth that there was a frightful amount of conversation going on. He had the sensation of having become a mere bit of flotsam upon a tossing sea of female voices. Both his sister and his niece appeared to have much to say, and they were saying it simultaneously and *fortissimo*. He looked wistfully at the door.

It was smoothly done. A twist of the handle, and he was beyond those voices where there was peace. Galloping gaily down the stairs, he charged out into the sunshine.

His gaiety was not long-lived. Free at last to concentrate itself on the really serious issues of life, his mind grew sombre and grim. Once more there descended upon him the cloud which had been oppressing his soul before all this Heacham-Angela-Belford business began. Each step that took him nearer to the sty where the ailing Empress resided seemed a heavier step than the last. He reached the sty; and, draping himself over the rails, peered moodily at the vast expanse of pig within.

For, even though she had been doing a bit of dieting of late, Empress of Blandings was far from being an ill-nourished animal. She resembled a captive balloon with ears and a tail, and was as nearly circular as a pig can be without bursting. Nevertheless, Lord Emsworth, as he regarded her, mourned and would not be comforted. A few more square meals under her belt, and no pig in all Shropshire could have held its head up in the Empress's presence. And now, just for lack of those few meals, the supreme animal would probably be relegated to the mean obscurity of an 'Honourably Mentioned'. It was bitter, bitter.

He became aware that somebody was speaking to him; and, turning, perceived a solemn young man in riding breeches.

'I say,' said the young man.

Lord Emsworth, though he would have preferred solitude, was relieved to find that the intruder was at least one of his own sex. Women are apt to stray off into side-issues, but men are practical and can be relied on to stick to the fundamentals. Besides, young Heacham probably kept pigs himself and might have a useful hint or two up his sleeve.

'I say, I've just ridden over to see if there was anything I could do about this fearful business.'

'Uncommonly kind and thoughtful of you, my dear fellow,' said Lord Emsworth, touched. 'I fear things look very black.'

'It's an absolute mystery to me.'

'To me, too.'

'I mean to say, she was all right last week.'

'She was all right as late as the day before yesterday.'

'Seemed quite cherry and chirpy and all that.'

'Entirely so.'

'And then this happens – out of a blue sky, as you might say.'

'Exactly. It is insoluble. We have done everything possible to tempt her appetite.'

'Her appetite? Is Angela ill?'

'Angela? No, I fancy not. She seemed perfectly well a few minutes ago.'

'You've seen her this morning, then? Did she say anything about this fearful business?'

'No. She was speaking about some money.'

'It's all so dashed unexpected.'

'Like a bolt from the blue,' agreed Lord Emsworth. 'Such a thing has never happened before. I fear the worst. According to the Wolff-Lehmann feeding standards, a pig, if in health, should consume daily nourishment amounting to fifty-seven thousand eight hundred calories, these to consist of proteins four pounds five ounces, carbohydrates twenty-five pounds—'

'What has that got to do with Angela?'

'Angela?'

'I came to find out why Angela has broken off our engagement.'

Lord Emsworth marshalled his thoughts. He had a misty idea that he had heard something mentioned about that. It came back to him.

'Ah, yes, of course. She has broken off the engagement, hasn't she? I believe it is because she is in love with someone else. Yes, now that I recollect, that was distinctly stated. The whole thing comes back to me quite clearly. Angela has decided to marry someone else. I knew there was some satisfactory explanation. Tell me, my dear fellow, what are your views on linseed meal?'

'What do you mean, linseed meal?'

'Why, linseed meal,' said Lord Emsworth, not being able to find a better definition. 'As a food for pigs.'

'Oh, curse all pigs!'

'What!' There was a sort of astounded horror in Lord Emsworth's voice. He had never been particularly fond of young Heacham, for he was not a man who took much to his juniors, but he had not supposed him capable of anarchistic sentiments like this. 'What did you say?'

'I said, "Curse all pigs!" You keep talking about pigs. I'm not interested in pigs. I don't want to discuss pigs. Blast and damn every pig in existence!'

Lord Emsworth watched him, as he strode away, with an emotion that was partly indignation and partly relief – indignation that a landowner and a fellow son of Shropshire could have brought himself to utter such words, and relief that one capable of such utterance was not going to marry into his family. He had always in his woollen-headed way been very fond of his niece Angela, and it was nice to think that the child had such solid good sense and so much cool discernment. Many girls of her age would have been carried away by the glamour of young Heacham's position and wealth; but she, divining with an intuition beyond her years that he was unsound on the subject of pigs, had drawn back while there was still time and refused to marry him.

A pleasant glow suffused Lord Emsworth's bosom, to be frozen out a few moments later as he perceived his sister Constance bearing down upon him. Lady Constance was a beautiful woman, but there were times when the charm of her face was married by a rather curious expression; and from nursery days onward his lordship had learned that this expression meant trouble. She was wearing it now.

'Clarence,' she said, 'I have had enough of this nonsense of Angela and young Belford. The thing cannot be allowed to go drifting on. You must catch the two o'clock train to London.'

'What! Why?'

'You must see this man Belford and tell him that, if Angela insists on marrying him, she will not have a penny for four years. I shall be greatly surprised if that piece of information does not put an end of the whole business.'

Lord Emsworth scratched meditatively at the Empress's tank-like back. A mutinous expression was on his mild face.

'Don't see why she shouldn't marry the fellow,' he mumbled.

'Marry James Belford?'

'I don't see why not. Seems fond of him and all that.'

'You never have had a grain of sense in your head, Clarence. Angela is going to marry Heacham.'

'Can't stand that man. All wrong about pigs.'

'Clarence, I don't wish to have any more discussion and argument. You will go to London to the two o'clock train. You will see Mr. Belford. And you will tell him about Angela's money. Is that quite clear?'

'Oh, all right,' said his lordship moodily. 'All right, all right.'

The emotions of the Earl of Emsworth, as he sat next day facing his luncheon-guest, James Bartholomew Belford, across a table in the main dining-room of the Senior Conservative Club, were not of the liveliest and most agreeable. It was bad enough to be in London at all on such a day of golden sunshine. To be charged, while there, with the task of blighting the romance of two young people for whom he entertained a warm regard was unpleasant to a degree.

For, now that he had given the matter thought, Lord Emsworth recalled that he had always liked this boy Belford. A pleasant lad, with, he remembered now, a healthy fondness for that rural existence which so appealed to himself. By no means the sort of fellow who, in the very presence and hearing of Empress of Blandings, would have spoken disparagingly and with oaths of pigs as a class. It occurred to Lord Emsworth, as it has occurred to so many people, that the distribution of money in this world is all wrong. Why should a man like pig-despising Heacham have a rent roll that ran into the tens of thousands, while this very deserving youngster had nothing?

These thoughts not only saddened Lord Emsworth – they embarrassed him. He hated unpleasantness, and it was suddenly borne in upon him that, after he had broken the news that Angela's bit of capital was locked up and not likely to get loose, conversation with his young friend during the remainder of lunch would tend to be somewhat difficult.

He made up his mind to postpone the revelation. During the meal, he decided, he would chat pleasantly of this and that; and then, later, while bidding his guest good-bye, he would spring the thing on him suddenly and dive back into the recesses of the club.

Considerably cheered at having solved a delicate problem with such adroitness, he started to prattle.

'The gardens at Blandings,' he said, 'are looking particularly attractive this summer. My head-gardener, Angus McAllister, is a man with whom I do not always find myself seeing eye to eye, notably in the matter of hollyhocks, on which I consider his views subversive to a degree; but there is no denying that he understands roses. The rose garden—'

'How well I remember that rose garden,' said James Belford, sighing slightly and helping himself to brussels sprouts. 'It was there that Angela and I used to meet on summer mornings.'

Lord Emsworth blinked. This was not an encouraging start, but the Emsworths were a fighting clan. He had another try.

'I have seldom seen such a blaze of colour as was to be witnessed these during the month of June. Both McAllister and I adopted a very strong policy with the slugs and plant lice, with the result that the place was a mass of flourishing Damasks and Ayrshires and—'

'Properly to appreciate roses,' said James Belford, 'you want to see them as a setting for a girl like Angela. With her fair hair gleaming against the green leaves she makes a rose garden seem a veritable Paradise.'

'No doubt,' said Lord Emsworth. 'No doubt. I am glad you liked my rose garden. At Blandings, of course, we have the natural advantage of loamy soil, rich in plant food and humus; but, as I often say to McAllister, and on this point we have never had the slightest disagreement, loamy soil by itself is not enough. You must have manure. If every autumn a liberal mulch of stable manure is spread upon the beds and the coarser parts removed in the spring before the annual forking—'

'Angela tells me,' said James Belford, 'that you have forbidden our marriage.'

Lord Emsworth choked dismally over his chicken. Directness of this kind, he told himself with a pang of self-pity, was the sort of thing young Englishmen picked up in America. Diplomatic circumlocution flourished only in a more leisurely civilization, and in those energetic and forceful surroundings you learned to Talk Quick and Do It Now, and all sorts of uncomfortable things.

'Er – well, yes, now you mention it, I believe some informal decision of that nature was arrived at. You see, my dear fellow, my sister Constance feels rather strongly—'

'I understand. I suppose she thinks I'm a sort of prodigal.'

'No, no, my dear fellow. She never said that. Wastrel was the term she employed.'

'Well, perhaps I did start out in business on those lines. But you can take it from me that when you find yourself employed on a farm in Nebraska belonging to an applejack-nourished patriarch with strong views on work and a good vocabulary, you soon develop a certain liveliness.'

'Are you employed on a farm?'

'I was employed on a farm.'

'Pigs?' said Lord Emsworth in a low, eager voice.

'Among other things.'

Lord Emsworth gulped. His fingers clutched at the table-cloth.

'Then perhaps, my dear fellow, you can give me some advice. For the last two days my prize sow, Empress of Blandings, has declined all nourishment. And the Agricultural Show is on Wednesday week. I am distracted with anxiety.'

James Belford frowned thoughtfully.

'What does your pig-man say about it?'

'My pig-man was sent to prison two days ago. Two days!' For the first time the significance of the coincidence struck him. 'You don't think that can have anything to do with the animal's loss of appetite?'

'Certainly. I imagine she is missing him and pining away because he isn't there.'

Lord Emsworth was surprised. He had only a distant acquaintance with George Cyril Wellbeloved, but from what he had seen of him he had not credited him with this fatal allure.

'She probably misses his afternoon call.'

Again his lordship found himself perplexed. He had had no notion that pigs were such sticklers for the formalities of social life.

'His call?'

'He must have had some special call that he used when he wanted her to come to dinner. One of the first things you learn on a farm is hog-calling. Pigs are temperamental. Omit to call them, and they'll starve rather than put on the nose-bag. Call them right, and they will follow you to the ends of the earth with their mouths watering.'

'God bless my soul! Fancy that.'

'A fact, I assure you. These calls vary in different parts of America. In Wisconsin, for example, the words 'Poig, Poig, Poig" bring home – in both the literal and the figurative sense – the bacon. In Illinois, I believe they call "Burp, Burp, Burp", while in Iowa the phrase "Kus, Kus, Kus" is preferred. Proceeding to Minnesota, we find "Peega, Peega, Peega" or, alternatively, "Oink, Oink, Oink," whereas in Milwaukee, so largely inhabited by those of German descent, you will hear the good old Teuton "Komm Schweine, Komm Schweine." Oh, yes there are all sorts of pig-calls, from the Massachusetts "Phew, Phew, Phew" to the "Loo-ey, Loo-ey, Loo-ey" of Ohio, not counting various local devices such as beating on tin cans with axes or rattling pebbles in a suit-case. I knew a man out in Nebraska who used to call his pigs by tapping on the edge of the trough with his wooden leg.'

'Did he, indeed?'

'But a most unfortunate thing happened. One evening, hearing a woodpecker at the top of a tree, they started shinning up it; and when the man came out he found them all lying there in a circle with their necks broken.'

'This is no time for joking,' said Lord Emsworth, pained.

'I'm not joking. Solid fact. Ask anybody out there.'

Lord Emsworth placed a hand to his throbbing forehead.

'But if there is this wide variety, we have no means of knowing which call Wellbeloved . . .'

'Ah,' said James Belford, 'but wait. I haven't told you all. There is a master-word.'

'A what?'

'Most people don't know it, but I had it straight from the lips of Fred Patzel, the hog-calling champion of the Western States. What a man! I've known him to bring pork chops leaping from their plates. He informed me that, no matter whether an animal has been trained to answer to the Illinois "Burp" or the Minnesota "Oink", it will always give immediate service in response to this magic combination of syllables. It is to the pig world what the Masonic grip is to the human. "Oink" in Illinois or "Burp" in Minnesota, and the animal merely raises its eyebrows and stares coldly. But go to either State and call "Pig-hoo-oo-ey!" . . .'

The expression on Lord Emsworth's face was that of a drowning man who sees a lifeline.

'Is that the master-word of which you spoke?'

'That's it.'

'Pig—?'

'—hoo-oo-ey.'

'Pig-hoo-o-ey?'

'You haven't got it right. The first syllable should be short and staccato, the second long and rising into a falsetto, high but true.'

'Pig-hoo-o-o-ey.'

'Pig-hoo-o-o-ey.'

'Pig-hoo-o-o-ey!' yodelled Lord Emsworth, flinging his head back and giving tongue in a high, penetrating tenor which caused ninety-three Senior Conservatives, lunching in the vicinity, to congeal into living statues of alarm and disapproval.

'More body to the "hoo,"' advised James Belford.

'Pig-hoo-o-o-o-ey!'

The Senior Conservative Club is one of the few places in London where lunchers are not accustomed to getting music with their meals. White-whiskered financiers gazed bleakly at bald-headed politicians, as if asking silently what was to be done about this. Bald-headed politicians stared back at white-whiskered financiers, replying in the language of the eye that they did not know. The general sentiment prevailing was a vague determination to write to the Committee about it.

'Pig-hoo-o-o-o-ey!' carolled Lord Emsworth. And, as he did so, his eye fell on the clock over the mantelpiece. Its hands pointed to twenty minutes to two.

He started convulsively. The best train in the day for Market Blandings was the one which left Paddington station at two sharp. After that there was nothing till the five-five.

He was not a man who often thought; but when he did, to think was with him to act. A moment later he was scudding over the carpet, making for the door that led to the broad staircase.

Throughout the room which he had left, the decision to write in strong terms to the Committee was now universal; but from the mind, such as it was, of Lord Emsworth the past, with the single exception of the word "Pig-hoo-o-o-o-ey!" had been completely blotted.

Whispering the magic syllables, he sped to the cloakroom and retrieved his hat. Murmuring them over and over again, he sprang into a cab. He was still repeating them as the train moved out of the station; and he would doubtless have gone on repeating them all the way to Market Blandings, had he not, as was his invariable practice when travelling by rail, fallen asleep after the first ten minutes of the journey.

The stopping of the train at Swindon Junction woke him with a start. He sat up, wondering, after his usual fashion on these occasions, who and where he was. Memory returned to him, but a memory that was, alas, incomplete. He remembered his name. He remembered that he was on his way home from a visit to London. But what it was that you said to a pig when inviting it to drop in for a bite of dinner he had completely forgotten.

It was the opinion of Lady Constance Keeble, expressed verbally during dinner in the brief intervals when they were alone, and by means of silent telepathy when Beach, the butler, was adding his dignified presence to the proceedings, that her brother Clarence, in his expedition to London to put matters plainly to James Belford had made an outstanding idiot of himself.

There had been no need whatever to invite the man Belford to lunch; but, having invited him to lunch, to leave him sitting, without having clearly stated that Angela would have no money for four years, was the act of a congenital imbecile. Lady Constance had been aware ever since their childhood days that her brother had about as much sense as a—

Here Beach entered, superintending the bringing-in of the savoury, and she had been obliged to suspend her remarks.

This sort of conversation is never agreeable to a sensitive man, and his lordship had removed himself from the danger zone as soon as he could manage it. He was now seated in the library, sipping port and straining a brain which Nature had never intended for hard exercise in an effort to bring back that word of magic of which his unfortunate habit of sleeping in trains had robbed him.

'Pig—'

He could remember as far as that; but of what avail was a single syllable? Besides, weak as his memory was, he could recall that the whole gist or nub of the thing lay in the syllable that followed. The 'pig' was a mere preliminary.

Lord Emsworth finished his port and got up, He felt restless, stifled. The summer night seemed to call to him like some silver-voiced swineherd calling to his pig. Possibly, he thought, a breath of fresh air might stimulate his brain-cells. He wandered downstairs; and, having dug a shocking old slouch hat out of the cupboard where he hid it to keep his sister Constance from impounding and burning it, he strode heavily out into the garden.

He was pottering aimlessly to and fro in the parts adjacent to the rear of the castle when there appeared in his path a slender female form. He recognized it without pleasure. Any unbiased judge would have said that his niece Angela, standing there in the soft pale light, looked like some dainty spirit of the Moon. Lord Emsworth was not an unbiased judge. To him Angela merely looked like Trouble. The march of civilization has given the modern girl a vocabulary and an ability to use it which her grandmother never had. Lord Emsworth would not have minded meeting Angela's grandmother a bit.

'Is that you, my dear?' he said nervously.

'Yes.'

'I didn't see you at dinner.'

'I didn't want any dinner. The food would have choked me. I can't eat.'

'It's precisely the same with my pig,' said his lordship. 'Young Belford tells me—'

Into Angela's queenly disdain there flashed a sudden animation. 'Have you seen Jimmy? What did he say?'

'That's just what I can't remember. It began with the word "Pig"—'

'But after he had finished talking about you, I mean. Didn't he say anything about coming down here?'

'Not that I remember.'

'I expect you weren't listening. You've got a very annoying habit, Uncle Clarence,' said Angela maternally, "of switching your mind off and just going blah when people are talking to you. It gets you very much disliked on all sides. Didn't Jimmy say anything about me?'

'I fancy so. Yes, I am nearly sure he did.'

'Well, what?'

'I cannot remember.'

There was a sharp clicking noise in the darkness. It was caused by Angela's upper front teeth meeting her lower front teeth; and was followed by a sort of wordless exclamation. It seemed only too plain that the love and respect which a niece should have for an uncle were in the present instance at a very low ebb.

'I wish you wouldn't do that,' said Lord Emsworth plaintively.

'Do what?'

'Make clicking noises at me.'

'I will make clicking noises at you. You know perfectly well, Uncle Clarence, that you are behaving like a bohunkus.'

'A what?'

'A bohunkus,' explained his niece coldly, 'is a very inferior sort of worm. Not the kind of worm that you see on lawns, which you can respect, but a really degraded species.'

'I wish you would go in, my dear,' said Lord Emsworth. 'The night air may give you a chill.'

'I won't go in. I came out here to look at the moon and think of Jimmy. What are you doing out here, if it comes to that?'

'I came here to think. I am greatly exercised about my pig, Empress of Blandings. For two days she refused her food, and young Belford says she will not eat until she hears the proper call or cry. He very kindly taught it to me, but unfortunately I have forgotten it.'

'I wonder you had the nerve to ask Jimmy to teach you pig-calls, considering the way you're treating him.'

'But—'

'Like a leper, or something. And all I can say is that, if you remember this call of his, and it makes the Empress eat, you ought to be ashamed of yourself if you still refuse to let me marry him.'

'My dear,' said Lord Emsworth earnestly, 'if through young Belford's instrumentality Empress of Blandings is induced to take nourishment once more, there is nothing I will refuse him – nothing.'

'Honour bright?'

'I give you my solemn word.'

'You won't let Aunt Constance bully you out of it?'

Lord Emsworth drew himself up.

'Certainly not,' he said proudly. 'I am always ready to listen to your Aunt Constance's views, but there are certain matters where I claim the right to act according to my own judgment.' He paused and stood musing. 'It began with the word "Pig"—'

From somewhere near at hand music made itself heard. The servants' hall, its day's labours ended, was refreshing itself with the housekeeper's gramophone. To Lord Emsworth the strains were merely an additional annoyance. He was not fond of music. It reminded him of his younger son Frederick, a flat but persevering songster both in and out of the bath.

'Yes: I can distinctly recall as much as that. Pig – Pig—'

'WHO—'

Lord Emsworth leaped in the air. It was as if an electric shock had been applied to his person.

'WHO stole my heart away?' howled the gramophone. 'WHO—'

The peace of the summer night was shattered by a triumphant shout. 'Pig-HOO-o-o-o-ey!'

A window opened. A large, bald head appeared. A dignified voice spoke.

'Who is there? Who is making that noise?'

'Beach!' cried Lord Emsworth. 'Come out here at once.'

'Very good, your lordship.'

And presently the beautiful night was made still more lovely by the added attraction of the butler's presence.

'Beach, listen to this.'

'Very good, your lordship.'

'Pig-hoo-o-o-o-ey!' "

'Very good, your lordship.'

'Now you do it.'

'I, your lordship?'

'Yes, It's a way you call pigs.'

'I do not call pigs, your lordship,' said the butler coldly.

'What do you want Beach to do it for?' asked Angela.

'Two heads are better than one. If we both learn it, it will not matter should I forget it again.'

'By Jove, yes! Come on, Beach. Push it over the thorax,' urged the girl eagerly. 'You don't know it, but this is a matter of life and death. At-a-boy, Beach! Inflate the lungs and go to it.'

It had been the butler's intention, prefacing his remarks with the statement that he had been in service at the castle for eighteen years, to explain frigidly to Lord Emsworth that it was not his place to stand in the moonlight practising pig-calls. If, he would have gone on to add, his lordship saw the matter from a different angle, then it was his, Beach's painful duty to tender his resignation, to become effective one month from that day.

But the intervention of Angela made this impossible to a man of chivalry and heart. A paternal fondness for the girl, dating from the days when he had stooped to enacting – and very convincingly, too, for his was a figure that lent itself to the impersonation – the *role* of a hippopotamus for her childish amusement, checked the words he would have uttered. She was looking at him with bright eyes, and even the rendering of pig-noises seemed a small sacrifice to make for her sake.

'Very good, your lordship,' he said in a low voice, his face pale and set in the moonlight. 'I shall endeavour to give satisfaction. I would merely advance the suggestion, your lordship, that we move a few steps farther away from the vicinity of the servants' hall. If I were to be overheard by any of the lower domestics, it would weaken my position as a disciplinary force.'

'What chumps we are!' cried Angela, inspired. 'The place to do it is outside the Empress's sty. Then, if it works, we'll see it working.'

Lord Emsworth found this a little abstruse, but after a moment he got it.

'Angela,' he said, 'You are a very intelligent girl. Where you get your brains from, I don't know. Not from my side of the family.'

The bijou residence of the Empress of Blandings looked very snug and attractive in the moonlight. But beneath even the beautiful things of life there is always an underlying sadness. This was supplied in the present instance by a long, low trough, only too plainly full to the brim of succulent mash and acorns. The fast, obviously, was still in progress.

The sty stood some considerable distance from the castle walls, so that there had been ample opportunity for Lord Emsworth to rehearse his little company during the journey. By the time they had ranged themselves against the rails, his two assistants were letter-perfect.

'Now,' said his lordship.

There floated out upon the summer night a strange composite sound that sent the birds roosting in the trees above shooting off their perches like rockets. Angela's clear soprano rang out like the voice of the village blacksmith's daughter. Lord Emsworth contributed a reedy tenor. And the bass notes of Beach probably did more to startle the birds than any other one item in the programme.

They paused and listened. Inside the Empress's boudoir there sounded the movement of a heavy body. There was an inquiring grunt. The next moment the sacking that covered the doorway was pushed aside, and the noble animal emerged.

'Now!' said Lord Emsworth again.

Once more that musical cry shattered the silence of the night. But it brought no responsive movement from Empress of Blandings. She stood there motionless, her nose elevated, her ears hanging down, her eyes everywhere but on the trough where, by rights, she should now have been digging in and getting hers. A chill disappointment crept over Lord Emsworth, to be succeeded by a gust of petulant anger.

'I might have known it,' he said bitterly. 'That young scoundrel was deceiving me. He was playing a joke on me.'

'He wasn't,' cried Angela indignantly. 'Was he, Beach?'

'Not knowing the circumstances, Miss, I cannot venture an opinion.'

'Well, why has it no effect, then?' demanded Lord Emsworth.

'You can't expect it to work right away. We've got her stirred up, haven't we? She's thinking it over, isn't she? Once more will do the trick. Ready, Beach?'

'Quite ready, miss.'

'Then when I say three. And this time, Uncle Clarence, do please for goodness' sake not yowl like you did before. It was enough to put any pig off. Let it come out quite easily and gracefully. Now, then, one, two – three!'

The echoes died away. And as they did so a voice spoke.

'Community singing?'

'Jimmy!' cried Angela, whisking round.

'Hullo, Angela. Hullo, Lord Emsworth. Hullo, Beach.'

'Good evening, sir. Happy to see you once more.'

'Thanks. I'm spending a few days at the Vicarage with my father. I got down here by the five-five.'

Lord Emsworth cut peevishly in upon these civilities.

'Young man,' he said, 'what do you mean by telling me that my pig would respond to that cry? It does nothing of the kind.'

'You can't have done it right.'

'I did it precisely as you instructed me. I have had, moreover, the assistance of Beach here and my niece Angela—'

'Let's hear a sample.'

Lord Emsworth cleared his throat. 'Pig-hoo-o-o-o-ey!'

James Belford shook his head.

'Nothing like it,' he said. 'You want to begin the "Hoo" in a low minor of two quarter notes in four-four time. From this build gradually to a higher note, until at last the voice is soaring in full crescendo, reaching F sharp on the natural scale and dwelling for two retarded half-notes, then breaking into a shower of accidental grace-notes.'

'God bless my soul!' said Lord Emsworth, appalled. 'I shall never be able to do it.'

'Jimmy will do it for you,' said Angela. 'Now that he's engaged to me, he'll be one of the family and always popping about here. He can do it every day till the show is over.'

James Belford nodded.

'I think that would be the wisest plan. It is doubtful if an amateur could ever produce real results. You need a voice that has been trained on the open prairie and that has gathered richness and strength from competing with tornadoes. You need a manly, wind-scorched voice with a suggestion in it of the crackling of corn husks and the whisper of evening breezes in the fodder. Like this!'

Resting his hands on the rail before him, James Belford swelled before their eyes like a young balloon. The muscles on his cheek-bones stood out, his forehead became corrugated, his ears seemed to shimmer. Then, at the very height of the tension, he let it go like, as the poet beautifully puts it, the sound of a great Amen.

'Pig-HOOOOO-OOO-OOO-O-O-ey!'

They looked at him, awed. Slowly, fading off across hill and dale, the vast bellow died away. And suddenly, as it died, another, softer sound succeeded it. A sort of gulpy, gurgly, plobby, squishy, woffle-some sound, like a thousand eager men drinking soup in a foreign restaurant. And, as he heard it, Lord Emsworth uttered a cry of rapture.

The Empress was feeding.

The Hound of the Baskervilles

SIR ARTHUR CONAN DOYLE

The violent and mysterious death of Sir Charles Baskerville brings Sherlock Holmes and Dr. Watson to Grimpen in Yorkshire. Reports of a wild hound on the moors and the further death of an ex-convict, Selden, complicate the puzzle before it draws to its eery conclusion . . .

SIR HENRY WAS MORE pleased than surprised to see Sherlock Holmes, for he had for some days been expecting that recent events would bring him down from London. He did raise his eyebrows, however, when he found that my friend had neither any luggage nor any explanations for its absence. Between us we soon supplied his wants, and then over a belated supper we explained to the Baronet as much of our experience as it seemed desirable that he should know. But first I had the unpleasant duty of breaking the news of Selden's death to Barrymore and his wife. To him it may have been an unmitigated relief, but she wept bitterly in her apron. To all the world he was the man of violence, half animal and half demon; but to her he always remained the little wilful boy of her own girlhood, the child who had clung to her hand. Evil indeed is the man who has not one woman to mourn him.

'I've been moping in the house all day since Watson went off in the morning,' said the Baronet. 'I guess I should have some credit, for I have kept my promise. If I hadn't sworn not to go about alone I might have had a more lively evening, for I had a message from Stapleton asking me over there.'

'I have no doubt that you would have had a more lively evening,' said

Holmes, drily. 'By the way, I don't suppose you appreciate that we have been mourning over you as having broken your neck?'

Sir Henry opened his eyes. 'How was that?'

'This poor wretch was dressed in your clothes. I fear your servant who gave them to him may get into trouble with the police.'

'That is unlikely. There was no mark on any of them, so far as I know.'

'That's lucky for him – in fact, it's lucky for all of you, since you are all on the wrong side of the law in this matter. I am not sure that as a conscientious detective my first duty is not to arrest the whole household. Watson's reports are most incriminating documents.'

'But how about the case?' asked the Baronet. 'Have you made anything out of the tangle? I don't know that Watson and I are much the wiser since we came down.'

'I think that I shall be in a position to make the situation rather more clear to you before long. It has been an exceedingly difficult and most complicated business. There are several points upon which we still want light – but it is coming, all the same.'

'We've had one experience, as Watson has no doubt told you. We heard the hound on the moor, so I can swear that it is not all empty superstition. I had something to do with dogs when I was out West, and I know one when I hear one. If you can muzzle that one and put him on a chain I'll be ready to swear you are the greatest detective of all time.'

'I think I will muzzle him and chain him all right if you will give me your help.'

'Whatever you tell me to do I will do.'

'Very good; and I will ask you also to do it blindly, without always asking the reason.'

'Just as you like.'

'If you will do this I think the chances are that our little problem will soon be solved. I have no doubt—'

He stopped suddenly and stared fixedly up over my head into the air. The lamp beat upon his face, and so intent was it and so still that it might have been that of a clear-cut classical statue, a personification of alertness and expectation.

'What is it?' we both cried.

I could see as he looked down that he was repressing some internal emotion. His features were still composed, but his eyes shone with amused exultation.

'Excuse the admiration of a connoisseur,' said he, as he waved his hand towards the line of portraits which covered the opposite wall. 'Watson won't allow that I know anything of art, but that is mere jealousy, because our views upon the subject differ. Now, these are a really very fine series of portraits.'

'Well, I'm glad to hear you say so,' said Sir Henry, glancing with some surprise at my friend. 'I don't pretend to know much about these things, and I'd be a better judge of a horse or a steer than of a picture. I didn't know that you found time for such things.'

'I know what is good when I see it, and I see it now. That's a Kneller, I'll swear, that lady in the blue silk over yonder, and the stout gentleman with the wig ought to be a Reynolds. They are all family portraits, I presume?'

'Every one.'

'Do you know the names?'

'Barrymore has been coaching me in them, and I think I can say my lessons fairly well.'

'Who is the gentleman with the telescope?'

'That is Rear-Admiral Baskerville, who served under Rodney in the West Indies. The man with the blue coat and the roll of paper is Sir William Baskerville, who was Chairman of Committees of the House of Commons under Pitt.'

'And this Cavalier opposite to me – the one with the black velvet and the lace?'

'Ah, you have a right to know about him. That is the cause of all the mischief, the wicked Hugo, who started the Hound of the Baskervilles. We're not likely to forget him.'

I gazed with interest and some surprise upon the portrait.

'Dear me!' said Holmes, 'he seems a quiet, meek-mannered man enough, but I daresay that there was a lurking devil in his eyes. I had pictured him as a more robust and ruffianly person.'

'There's no doubt about the authenticity, for the name and the date, 1647, are on the back of the canvas.'

Holmes said little more, but the picture of the old roysterer seemed to have a fascination for him, and his eyes were continually fixed upon it during supper. It was not until later, when Sir Henry had gone to his room, that I was able to follow the trend of his thoughts. He led me back into the banqueting-hall, his bedroom candle in his hand, and he held it up against the time-stained portrait on the wall.

'Do you see anything there?'

I looked at the broad plumed hat, the curling love-locks, the white lace collar, and the straight, severe face which was framed between them. It was not a brutal countenance, but it was prim, hard, and stern, with a firm-set, thin-lipped mouth, and a coldly intolerant eye.

'Is it like anyone you know?'

'There is something of Sir Henry about the jaw.'

'Just a suggestion, perhaps. But wait an instant!' He stood upon a chair, and holding up the light in his left hand he curved his right arm over the broad hat and round the long ringlets.

'Good heavens!' I cried, in amazement.

The face of Stapleton had sprung out of the canvas.

'Ha, you see it now. My eyes have been trained to examine faces and not their trimmings. It is the first quality of a criminal investigator that he should see through a disguise.'

'But this is marvellous. It might be his portrait.'

'Yes, it is an interesting instance of a throw-back, which appears to be both physical and spiritual. A study of family portraits is enough to convert a man to the doctrine of reincarnation. The fellow is a Baskerville – that is evident.'

'With designs upon the succession.'

'Exactly. This chance of the picture has supplied us with one of our most obvious missing links. We have him, Watson, we have him, and I dare swear that before tomorrow night he will be fluttering in our net as helpless as one of his own butterflies. A pin, a cork, and a card, and we add him to the Baker Street collection!' He burst into one of his rare fits of laughter as he turned away from the picture. I have not heard him laugh often, and it has always boded ill to somebody.

I was up betimes in the morning, but Holmes was afoot earlier still, for I saw him as I dressed coming up the drive.

'Yes, we should have a full day to-day,' he remarked, and he rubbed his hands with the joy of action. 'The nets are all in place, and the drag is about to begin. We'll know before the day is out whether we have caught our big, lean-jawed pike, or whether he has got through the meshes.'

'Have you been on the moor already?'

'I have sent a report from Grimpen to Princetown as to the death of Selden. I think I can promise that none of you will be troubled in the matter. And I have also communicated with my faithful Cartwright, who would certainly have pined away at the door of my hut as a dog does at his master's grave if I had not set his mind at rest about my safety.'

'What is the next move?'

'To see Sir Henry. Ah, here he is!'

'Good morning, Holmes,' said the Baronet. 'You look like a general who is planning a battle with his chief of the staff.'

'That is the exact situation. Watson was asking for orders.'

'And so do I.'

'Very good. You are engaged, as I understand, to dine with our friends the Stapletons to-night.'

'I hope that you will come also. They are very hospitable people, and I am sure that they would be very glad to see you.'

'I fear that Watson and I must go to London.'

'To London?'

'Yes, I think that we should be more useful there at the present juncture.'

The Baronet's face perceptibly lengthened.

'I hoped that you were going to see me through this business. The Hall and the moor are not very pleasant places when one is alone.'

'My dear fellow, you must trust me implicitly and do exactly what I tell you. You can tell your friends that we should have been happy to have come with you, but that urgent business required us to be in town. We hope very soon to return to Devonshire. Will you remember to give them that message?'

'If you insist upon it.'

'There is no alternative, I assure you.'

I saw by the Baronet's clouded brow that he was deeply hurt by what he regarded as our desertion.

'When do you desire to go?' he asked, coldly.

'Immediately after breakfast. We will drive in to Coombe Tracey, but Watson will leave his things as a pledge that he will come back to you. Watson, you will send a note to Stapleton to tell him that you regret that you cannot come.'

'I have a good mind to go to London with you,' said the Baronet. 'Why should I stay here alone?'

'Because it is your post of duty. Because you gave me your word that you would do as you were told, and I tell you to stay.'

'All right, then, I'll stay.'

'One more direction! I wish you to drive to Merripit House. Send back your trap, however, and let them know that you intend to walk home.'

'To walk across the moor?'

'Yes.'

'But that is the very thing which you have so often cautioned me not to do.'

'This time you may do it with safety. If I had not every confidence in your nerve and courage I would not suggest it, but it is essential that you should do it.'

'Then I will do it.'

'And as you value your life do not go across the moor in any direction save along the straight path which leads from Merripit House to the Grimpen Road, and is your natural way home.'

'I will do just what you say.'

'Very good. I should be glad to get away as soon after breakfast as possible, so as to reach London in the afternoon.'

I was much astounded by this programme, though I remembered that Holmes had said to Stapleton on the night before that his visit would terminate next day. It had not crossed my mind, however, that he would wish me to go with him, nor could I understand how we could both be absent at a moment which he himself declared to be critical. There was nothing for it, however, but implicit obedience; so we bade good-bye to our rueful friend, and a couple of hours afterwards we were at the station of Coombe Tracey and had dispatched the trap upon its return journey. A small boy was waiting upon the platform.

'Any orders, sir?'

'You will take this train to town, Cartwright. The moment you arrive you will send a wire to Sir Henry Baskerville, in my name, to say that if he finds the pocket-book which I have dropped he is to send it by registered post to Baker Street.'

'Yes, sir.'

'And ask at the station office if there is a message for me.'

The boy returned with a telegram, which Holmes handed to me. It ran: 'Wire received. Coming down with unsigned warrant. Arrive five-forty. – LESTRADE.

'That is in answer to mine of this morning. He is the best of the professionals, I think, and we may need his assistance. Now, Watson, I think that we cannot employ our time better than by calling upon your acquaintance, Mrs. Laura Lyons.'

His plan of campaign was beginning to be evident. He would use the Baronet in order to convince the Stapletons that we were really gone, while we should actually return at the instant when we were likely to be needed. That telegram from London, if mentioned by Sir Henry to the Stapletons, must remove the last suspicions from their minds. Already I seemed to see our nets drawing closer round that lean-jawed pike.

Mrs. Laura Lyons was in her office, and Sherlock Holmes opened his interview with a frankness and directness which considerably amazed her.

'I am investigating the circumstances which attended the death of the late Sir Charles Baskerville,' said he. 'My friend here, Dr. Watson, has informed me of what you have communicated, and also of what you have withheld in connection with that matter.'

'What have I withheld?' she asked, defiantly.

'You have confessed that you asked Sir Charles to be at the gate at ten o'clock. We know that that was the place and hour of his death. You have withheld what the connection is between these events.'

'There is no connection.'

'In that case the coincidence must indeed be an extraordinary one. But I think that we shall succeed in establishing a connection after all. I wish to be perfectly frank with you, Mrs. Lyons. We regard this case as one of murder, and the evidence may implicate not only your friend Mr. Stapleton, but his wife as well.'

The lady sprang from her chair.

'His wife!' she cried.

'The fact is no longer a secret. The person who has passed for his sister is really his wife.'

Mrs. Lyons had resumed her seat. Her hands were grasping the arms of her chair, and I saw that the pink nails had turned white with the pressure of her grip.

'His wife!' she said, again. 'His wife! He was not a married man.'

Sherlock Holmes shrugged his shoulders.

'Prove it to me! Prove it to me! And if you can do so—!' The fierce flash of her eyes said more than any words.

'I have come prepared to do so,' said Holmes, drawing several papers from his pocket. 'Here is a photograph of the couple taken in York four years ago. It is indorsed "Mr. and Mrs. Vandeleur," but you will have no difficulty in recognising him, and her also, if you know her by sight. Here are three written descriptions by trustworthy witnesses of Mr. and Mrs. Vandeleur, who at that time kept St. Oliver's private school. Read them, and see if you can doubt the identity of these people.'

She glanced at them, and then looked up at us with the set, rigid face of a desperate woman.

'Mr. Holmes,' she said, 'this man had offered me marriage on condition that I could get a divorce from my husband. He has lied to me, the villain, in every conceivable way. Not one word of truth has he ever told me. And why – why? I imagined that all was for my own sake. But now I see that I was never anything but a tool in his hands. Why should I preserve faith with him who never kept any with me? Why should I try to shield him from the consequences of his own wicked acts? Ask me what you like, and there is nothing which I shall hold back. One thing I swear to you, and that is, that when I wrote the letter I never dreamed of any harm to the old gentleman, who had been my kindest friend.'

'I entirely believe you, madam,' said Sherlock Holmes. 'The recital of these events must be very painful to you, and perhaps it will make it easier if I tell you what occurred, and you can check me if I make any material mistake. The sending of this letter was suggested to you by Stapleton?'

'He dictated it.'

'I presume that the reason he gave was that you would receive help from Sir Charles for the legal expenses connected with your divorce?'

'Exactly.'

'And then after you had sent the letter he dissuaded you from keeping the appointment?'

'He told me that it would hurt his self-respect that any other man should find the money for such an object, and that though he was a poor man himself he would devote his last penny to removing the obstacles which divided us.'

'He appears to be a very consistent character. And then you heard nothing until you read the reports of the death in the paper?'

'No.'

'And he made you swear to say nothing about your appointment with Sir Charles?'

'He did. He said that the death was a very mysterious one, and that I should certainly be suspected if the facts came out. He frightened me into remaining silent.'

'Quite so. But you had your suspicions?'

She hesitated and looked down.

'I knew him,' she said. 'But if he had kept faith with me I should always have done so with him.'

'I think that on the whole you have had a fortunate escape,' said Sherlock Holmes. 'You have had him in your power and he knew it, and yet you are alive. You have been walking for some months very near to the edge of a precipice. We must wish you good morning now, Mrs. Lyons, and it is probable that you will very shortly hear from us again.'

'Our case becomes rounded off, and difficulty after difficulty thins away in front of us,' said Holmes, as we stood waiting for the arrival of the express from town. 'I shall soon be in the position of being able to put into a single connected narrative one of the most singular and sensational crimes of modern times. Students of criminology will remember the analogous incidents in Grodno, in Little Russia, in the year '66, and of course there are the Anderson murders in North Carolina, but this case possesses some features which are entirely its own. Even now we have no clear case against this very wily man. But I shall be very much surprised if it is not clear enough before we go to bed this night.'

The London express came roaring into the station, and a small, wiry bulldog of a man had sprung from a first-class carriage. We all three shook hands, and I saw at once from the reverential way in which Lestrade gazed at my companion that he had learned a good deal since the days when they had first worked together. I could well remember the scorn which the theories of the reasoner used then to excite in the practical man.

'Anything good?' he asked.

'The biggest thing for years,' said Holmes. 'We have two hours before we need think of starting. I think we might employ it in getting some dinner, and then, Lestrade, we will take the London fog out of your throat by giving you a breath of the pure night air of Dartmoor. Never been there? Ah, well, I don't suppose you will forget your first visit.'

One of Sherlock Holmes's defects – if, indeed, one may call it a defect – was that he was exceedingly loth to communicate his full plans to any other person until the instant of their fulfilment. Partly it came no doubt from his own masterful nature, which loved to dominate and surprise those who were around him. Partly also from his professional caution, which urged him never to take any chances. The result, however, was very trying for those who were acting as his agents and assistants. I had often suffered under it, but never more so than during that long drive in the darkness. The great ordeal was in front of us; at last we were about to make our final effort, and yet Holmes had said nothing, and I could only surmise what his course of action would be. My nerves thrilled with anticipation when at last the cold wind upon our faces and the dark, void spaces on either side of the narrow road told me that we were back upon the moor once again. Every stride of the horses and every turn of the wheels was taking us nearer to our supreme adventure.

Our conversation was hampered by the presence of the driver of the hired wagonette, so that we were forced to talk of trivial matters when our nerves were tense with emotion and anticipation. It was a relief to me, after that unnatural restraint, when we at last passed Frankland's house and knew that we were drawing near to the Hall and to the scene of action. We did not drive up to the door, but got down near the gate of the avenue. The wagonette was paid off and ordered to return to Temple Coombe forthwith, while we started to walk to Merripit House.

'Are you armed, Lestrade?'

The little detective smiled.

'As long as I have my trousers I have a hip-pocket, and as long as I have my hip-pocket I have something in it.'

'Good! My friend and I are also ready for emergencies.'

'You're mighty close about this affair, Mr. Holmes. What's the game now?'

'A waiting game.'

'My word, it does not seem a very cheerful place,' said the detective, with a shiver, glancing round him at the gloomy slopes of the hill and at the huge lake of fog which lay over the Grimpen Mire. 'I see the lights of a house ahead of us.'

'That is Merripit House and the end of our journey. I must request you to walk on tiptoe and not to talk above a whisper.'

We moved cautiously along the track as if we were bound for the house, but Holmes halted us when we were about two hundred yards from it.

'This will do,' said he. 'These rocks upon the right make an admirable screen.'

'We are to wait here?'

'Yes, we shall make our little ambush here. Get into this hollow, Lestrade. You have been inside the house, have you not, Watson? Can you tell the position of the rooms? What are those latticed windows at this end?'

'I think they are the kitchen windows.'

'And the one beyond, which shines so brightly?'

'That is certainly the dining-room.'

'The blinds are up. You know the lie of the land best. Creep forward quietly and see what they are doing – but for Heaven's sake don't let them know that they are watched!'

I tip-toed down the path and stooped behind the low wall which surrounded the stunted orchard. Creeping in its shadow I reached a point whence I could look straight through the uncurtained window.

There were only two men in the room, Sir Henry and Stapleton. They sat with their profiles towards me on either side of the round table. Both of them were smoking cigars, and coffee and wine were in front of them. Stapleton was talking with animation, but the Baronet looked pale and distrait. Perhaps the thought of that lonely walk across the ill-omened moor was weighing heavily upon his mind.

As I watched them Stapleton rose and left the room, while Sir Henry filled his glass again and leaned back in his chair, puffing at his cigar. I heard the creak of a door and the crisp sound of boots upon gravel. The steps passed along the path on the other side of the wall under which I crouched. Looking over, I saw the naturalist pause at the door of an out-house in the corner of the orchard. A key turned in a lock, and as he passed in there was a curious scuffling noise from within. He was only a minute or so inside, and then I heard the key turn once more and he passed me and re-entered the house. I saw him rejoin his guest, and I crept quietly back to where my companions were waiting to tell them what I had seen.

'You say, Watson, that the lady is not there?' Holmes asked, when I had finished my report.

'No.'

'Where can she be, then, since there is no light in any other room except the kitchen?'

'I cannot think where she is.'

I have said that over the great Grimpen Mire there hung a dense, white fog. It was drifting slowly in our direction and banked itself up like a wall on that side of us, low, but thick and well defined. The moon shone on it, and it looked like a great shimmering icefield, with the heads of the distant tors as rocks borne upon its surface. Holmes's face was turned towards it, and he muttered impatiently as he watched its sluggish drift.

'It's moving towards us, Watson.'

'Is that serious?'

'Very serious, indeed – the one thing upon earth which could have disarranged my plans. He can't be very long, now. It is already ten o'clock. Our success and even his life may depend upon his coming out before the fog is over the path.'

The night was clear and fine above us. The stars shone cold and bright, while a half-moon bathed the whole scene in a soft, uncertain light. Before us lay the dark bulk of the house, its serrated roof and bristling chimneys hard outlined against the silver-spangled sky. Broad bars of golden light from the lower windows stretched across the orchard and the moor. One of them was suddenly shut off. The servants had left the kitchen. There only remained the lamp in the dining-room where the two men, the murderous host and the unconscious guest, still chatted over their cigars.

Every minute that white woolly plain which covered one half of the moor was drifting closer and closer to the house. Already the first thin wisps of it were curling across the golden square of the lighted window. The farther wall of the orchard was already invisible, and the trees were standing out of a swirl of white vapour. As we watched it the fog-wreaths came crawling round both corners of the house and rolled slowly into one dense bank, on which the upper floor and the roof floated like a strange ship upon a shadowy sea. Holmes struck his hand passionately upon the rock in front of us, and stamped his feet in his impatience.

'If he isn't out in a quarter of an hour the path will be covered. In half an hour we won't be able to see our hands in front of us.'

'Shall we move farther back upon higher ground?'

'Yes, I think it would be as well.'

So as the fog-bank flowed onwards we fell back before it until we were half a mile from the house, and still that dense white sea, with the moon silvering its upper edge, swept slowly and inexorably on.

'We are going too far,' said Holmes. 'We dare not take the chance of his being overtaken before he can reach us. At all costs we must hold our ground where we are.' He dropped on his knees and clapped his ear to the ground. 'Thank Heaven, I think that I hear him coming.'

A sound of quick steps broke the silence of the moor. Crouching among the stones we stared intently at the silver-tipped bank in front of us. The steps grew louder, and through the fog, as through a curtain, there stepped the man whom we were awaiting. He looked round him in surprise as he emerged into the clear, star-lit night. Then he came swiftly along the path, passed close to where we lay, and went on up the long slope behind us. As he walked he glanced continually over either shoulder, like a man who is ill at ease.

'Hist!' cried Holmes, and I heard the sharp click of a cocking pistol. 'Look out! It's coming!'

There was a thin, crisp, continuous patter from somewhere in the heart of that crawling bank. The cloud was within fifty yards of where we lay, and we glared at it, all three, uncertain what horror was about to break from the heart of it. I was at Holmes's elbow, and I glanced for an instant at his face. It was pale and exultant, his eyes shining brightly in the moonlight. But suddenly they started forward in a rigid, fixed stare, and his lips parted in amazement. At the same instant Lestrade gave a yell of terror and threw himself face downwards upon the ground. I sprang to my feet, my inert hand grasping my pistol, my mind paralyzed by the dreadful shape which had sprung out upon us from the shadows of the fog. A hound it was, an enormous coal-black hound, but not such a hound as mortal eyes have ever seen. Fire burst from its open mouth, its eyes glowed with a smouldering glare, its muzzle and hackles and dewlap were outlined in flickering flame. Never in the delirious dream of a disordered brain could anything more savage, more appalling, more hellish be conceived than that dark form and savage face which broke upon us out of the wall of fog.

With long bounds the huge black creature was leaping down the track, following hard upon the footsteps of our friend. So paralyzed were we by the apparition that we allowed him to pass before we had recovered our nerve. Then Holmes and I both fired together, and the creature gave a hideous howl, which showed that one at least had hit him. He did not pause, however, but bounded onwards. Far away on the path we saw Sir Henry looking back, his face white in the moonlight, his hands raised in horror, glaring helplessly at the frightful thing which was hunting him down.

But that cry of pain from the hound had blown all our fears to the winds. If he was vulnerable he was mortal, and if we could wound him we could kill him. Never have I seen a man run as Holmes ran that night. I am reckoned fleet of foot, but he outpaced me as much as I outpaced the little professional. In front of us as we flew up the track we heard scream after scream from Sir Henry and the deep roar of the hound. I was in time to see the beast spring upon its victim, hurl him to the ground, and worry at his throat. But the next instant Holmes had emptied five barrels of his revolver into the creature's flank. With a last howl of agony and a vicious snap in the air it rolled upon its back, four feet pawing furiously, and then fell limp upon its side. I stooped, panting, and pressed my pistol to the dreadful, shimmering head, but it was useless to pull the trigger. The giant hound was dead.

Sir Henry lay insensible where he had fallen. We tore away his collar, and Holmes breathed a prayer of gratitude when we saw that there was no sign of a wound and that the rescue had been in time. Already our friend's eyelids shivered and he made a feeble effort to move. Lestrade thrust his brandy-flask between the Baronet's teeth, and two frightened eyes were looking up at us.

'My God!' he whispered. 'What was it? What, in Heaven's name, was it?'

'It's dead, whatever it is,' said Holmes. 'We've laid the family ghost once and for ever.'

In mere size and strength it was a terrible creature which was lying stretched before us. It was not a pure bloodhound and it was not a pure mastiff; but it appeared to be a combination of the two – gaunt, savage, and as large as a small lioness. Even now, in the stillness of death, the huge jaws seemed to be dripping with a bluish flame and the small, deep-set, cruel eyes were ringed with fire. I placed my hand upon the glowing muzzle, and as I held them up my own fingers smouldered and gleamed in the darkness.

'Phosphorus,' I said.

'A cunning preparation of it,' said Holmes, sniffing at the dead animal. 'There is no smell which might have interfered with his power of scent. We owe you a deep apology, Sir Henry, for having exposed you to this fright. I was prepared for a hound, but not for such a creature as this. And the fog gave us little time to receive him.'

'You have saved my life.'

'Having first endangered it. Are you strong enough to stand?'

'Give me another mouthful of that brandy and I shall be ready for anything. So! Now, if you will help me up. What do you propose to do?'

'To leave you here. You are not fit for further adventures to-night. If you will wait, one or other of us will go back with you to the Hall.'

He tried to stagger to his feet; but he was still ghastly pale and trembling in every limb. We helped him to a rock, where he sat shivering with his face buried in his hands.

'We must leave you now,' said Holmes. 'The rest of our work must be done, and every moment is of importance. We have our case, and now we only want our man.

'It's a thousand to one against our finding him at the house,' he continued, as we retraced our steps swiftly down the path. 'Those shots must have told him that the game was up.'

'We were some distance off, and this fog may have deadened them.'

'He followed the hound to call him off – of that you may be certain. No, no, he's gone by this time! But we'll search the house and make sure.'

The front door was open, so we rushed in and hurried from room to room, to the amazement of a doddering old manservant, who met us in the passage. There was no light save in the dining-room, but Holmes caught up the lamp and left no corner of the house unexplored. No sign could we see of the man whom we were chasing. On the upper floor, however, one of the bedroom doors was locked.

'There's someone in here,' cried Lestrade. 'I can hear a movement. Open this door!'

A faint moaning and rustling came from within. Holmes struck the door just over the lock with the flat of his foot and it flew open. Pistol in hand, we all three rushed into the room.

But there was no sign within it of that desperate and defiant villain whom we expected to see. Instead we were faced by an object so strange and so unexpected that we stood for a moment staring at it in amazement.

The room had been fashioned into a small museum, and the walls were lined by a number of glass-topped cases full of that collection of butterflies and moths the formation of which had been the relaxation of this complex and dangerous man. In the centre of this room there was an upright beam, which had been placed at some period as a support for the old, worm-eaten balk of timber which spanned the roof. To this post a figure was tied, so swathed and muffled in the sheets which had been used to secure it that one could not for the moment tell whether it was that of a man or a woman. One towel passed round the throat and was secured at the back of the pillar. Another covered the lower part of the face, and over it two dark eyes – eyes full of grief and shame and a dreadful questioning – stared back at us. In a minute we had torn off the gag, unswathed the bonds, and Mrs. Stapleton sank upon the floor in front of us. As her beautiful head fell upon her chest I saw the clear red weal of a whiplash across her neck.

'The brute!' cried Holmes. 'Here, Lestrade, your brandy-bottle! Put her in the chair! She has fainted from ill-usage and exhaustion.'

She opened her eyes again.

'Is he safe?' she asked. 'Has he escaped?'

'He cannot escape us, madam.'

'No, no, I did not mean my husband. Sir Henry? Is he safe?'

'Yes.'

'And the hound?'

'It is dead.'

She gave a long sigh of satisfaction.

'Thank God! Thank God! Oh, this villain! See how he has treated me!' She shot her arms out from her sleeves, and we saw with horror that they we all mottled with bruises. 'But this is nothing – nothing! It is my mind and soul that he has tortured and defiled. I could endure it all, ill-usage, solitude, a life of deception, everything, as long as I could still cling to the hope that I had his love, but now I know that in this also I have been his dupe and his tool.' She broke into passionate sobbing as she spoke.

'You bear him no good will, madam,' said Holmes. 'Tell us then where we shall find him. If you have ever aided him in evil, help us now and so atone.'

'There is but one place where he can have fled,' she answered. 'There is an old tin mine on an island in the heart of the Mire. It was there that he kept his hound and there also he had made preparations so that he might have a refuge. That is where he would fly.'

The fog-bank lay like white wool against the window. Holmes held the lamp towards it.

'See,' said he. 'No one could find his way into the Grimpen Mire to-night.'

She laughed and clapped her hands. Her eyes and teeth gleamed with fierce merriment.

'He may find his way in, but never out,' she cried. 'How can he see the guiding wands to-night? We planted them together, he and I, to mark the pathway through the Mire. Oh, if I could only have plucked them out to-day. Then indeed you would have had him at your mercy!'

It was evident to us that all pursuit was in vain until the fog had lifted. Meanwhile we left Lestrade in possession of the house while Holmes and I went back with the Baronet to Baskerville Hall. The story of the Stapletons could no longer be withheld from him, but he took the blow bravely when he learned the truth about the woman whom he had loved. But the shock of the night's adventures had shattered his nerves, and before morning he lay delirious in a high fever, under the care of Dr. Mortimer. The two of them were destined to travel together round the world before Sir Henry had become once more the hale, hearty man that he had been before he became master of that ill-omened estate.

And now I come rapidly to the conclusion of this singular narrative, in which I have tried to make the reader share those dark fears and vague surmises which clouded our lives so long, and ended in so tragic a manner. On the morning after the death of the hound the fog had lifted and we were guided by Mrs. Stapleton to the point where they had found a pathway through the bog. It helped us to realize the horror of this woman's life when we saw the eagerness and joy with which she laid us on her husband's track. We left her standing upon the thin peninsula of firm, peaty soil which tapered out into the widespread bog. From the end of it a small wand planted here and there showed where the path zigzagged from tuft to tuft of rushes among those green scummed pits and foul quagmires which barred the way to the stranger. Rank reeds and lush, slimy water-plants sent an odour of decay and a heavy miasmatic vapour into our faces, while a false step plunged us more than once thigh-deep into the dark, quivering mire, which shook for yards in soft undulations around our feet. Its tenacious grip plucked at our heels as we walked, and when we sank into it it was as if some malignant hand were tugging us down into those obscene depths, so grim and purposeful was the clutch in which it held us. Once only we saw a trace that someone had passed that perilous way before us. From amid a tuft of cotton-grass which bore it up out of the slime some dark thing was projecting. Holmes sank to his waist as he stepped from the path to seize it, and had we not been there to drag him out he could never have set his foot upon firm land again. He held an old black boot in the air. 'Meyers, Toronto,' was printed on the leather inside.

'It is worth a mud bath,' said he. 'It is our friend Sir Henry's missing boot.'

'Thrown there by Stapleton in his flight.'

'Exactly. He retained it in his hand after using it to set the hound upon his track. He fled when he knew the game was up, still clutching it. And he hurled it away at this point of his flight. We know at least that he came so far in safety.'

But more than that we were never destined to know, though there was much which we might surmise. There was no chance of finding footsteps in the mire, for the rising mud oozed swiftly in upon them, but as we at last reached firmer ground beyond the morass we all looked eagerly for them.

But no slightest sign of them ever met our eyes. If the earth told a true story, then Stapleton never reached that island of refuge towards which he struggled through the fog upon that last night. Somewhere in the heart of the great Grimpen Mire, down in the foul slime of the huge morass which had sucked him in, this cold and cruel-hearted man is for ever buried.

Many traces we found of him in the bog-girt island where he had hid his savage ally. A huge driving-wheel and a shaft half-filled with rubbish showed the position of an abandoned mine. Beside it were the crumbling remains of the cottages of the miners, driven away no doubt by the foul reek of the surrounding swamp. In one of these a staple and chain with a quantity of gnawed bones showed where the animal had been confined. A skeleton with a tangle of brown hair adhering to it lay among the *débris*.

'A dog!' said Holmes. 'By Jove, a curly-haired spaniel. Poor Mortimer will never see his pet again. Well, I do not know that this place contains any secret which we have not already fathomed. He could hide his hound, but he could not hush its voice, and hence came those cries which even in daylight were not pleasant to hear. On an emergency he could keep the hound in the out-house at Merripit, but it was always a risk, and it was only on the supreme day, which he regarded as the end of all his efforts, that he dared to do it. This paste in the tin is no doubt the luminous mixture with which the creature was daubed. It was suggested, of course, by the story of the family hell-hound, and by the desire to frighten old Sir Charles to death. No wonder the poor wretch of a convict ran and screamed, even as our friend did, and as we ourselves might have done, when he saw such a creature bounding through the darkness of the moor upon his track. It was a cunning device, for, apart from the chance of driving your victim to his death, what peasant would venture to inquire too closely into such a creature should he get sight of it, as many have done, upon the moor? I said it in London, Watson, and I say it again now, that never yet have we helped to hunt down a more dangerous man than he who is lying yonder' – he swept his long arm towards the huge mottled expanse of green-splotched bog which stretched away until it merged into the russet slopes of the moor.

It was the end of November, and Holmes and I sat, upon a raw and foggy night, on either side of a blazing fire in our sitting-room in Baker Street. My friend was in excellent spirits over the success which had attended a succession of difficult and important cases, so that I was able to induce him to discuss the details of the Baskerville mystery. I had waited patiently for the opportunity, for I was aware that he would never permit cases to overlap, and that his clear and logical mind would not be drawn from its present work to dwell upon memories of the past. Sir Henry and Dr. Mortimer were, however, in London, on their way to that long voyage which had been recommended for the restoration of his shattered nerves. They had called upon us that very afternoon, so that it was natural that the subject should come up for discussion.

'The whole course of events,' said Holmes, 'from the point of view of the man who called himself Stapleton was simple and direct, although to us, who had no means in the beginning of knowing the motives of his actions and could only learn part of the facts, it all appeared exceedingly complex. I have had the advantage of two conversations with Mrs. Stapleton, and the case has now been so entirely cleared up that I am not aware that there is anything which has remained a secret to us. You will find a few notes upon the matter under the heading B in my indexed list of cases.'

'Perhaps you would kindly give me a sketch of the course of events from memory.'

'Certainly, though I cannot guarantee that I carry all the facts in my mind. Intense mental concentration has a curious way of blotting out what has passed. So far as the case of the Hound goes, however, I will give you the course of events as nearly as I can, and you will suggest anything which I may have forgotten.

'My inquiries show beyond all question that the family portrait did not lie, and that this fellow was indeed a Baskerville. He was a son of that Rodger Baskerville, the younger brother of Sir Charles, who fled with a sinister reputation to South America, where he was said to have died unmarried. He did, as a matter of fact, marry, and had one child, this fellow, whose real name is the same as his father. He married Beryl Garçia, one of the beauties of Costa Rica, and, having purloined a considerable sum of public money, he changed his name to Vandeleur and fled to England, where he established a school in the east of Yorkshire. His reason for attempting this special line of business was that he had struck up an acquaintance with a consumptive tutor upon the voyage home, and that he had used this man's ability to make the undertaking a success. Fraser, the tutor, died, however, and the school which had begun well sank from disrepute into infamy. The Vandeleurs found it convenient to change their name to Stapleton, and he brought the remains of his fortune, his schemes for the future, and his taste for entomology to the south of England. I learn at the British Museum that he was a recognised authority upon the subject, and that the name of Vandeleur has been permanently attached to a certain moth which he had, in his Yorkshire days, been the first to describe.

'We now come to that portion of his life which has proved to be of such intense interest to us. The fellow had evidently made inquiry, and found that only two lives intervened between him and a valuable estate. When he went to Devonshire his plans were, I believe, exceedingly hazy, but that he meant mischief from the first is evident from the way in which he took his wife with him in the character of his sister. The idea of using her as a decoy was clearly already in his mind, though he may not have been certain how the details of his plot were to be arranged. He meant in the end to have the estate, and he was ready to use any tool or run any risk for that end. His first act was to establish himself as near to his ancestral home as he could, and his second was to cultivate a friendship with Sir Charles Baskerville and with the neighbours.

'The Baronet himself told him about the family hound, and so prepared the way for his own death. Stapleton, as I will continue to call him, knew that the old man's heart was weak and that a shock would kill him. So much he had learned from Dr. Mortimer. He had heard also that Sir Charles was superstitious and had taken this grim legend very seriously. His ingenious mind instantly suggested a way by which the Baronet could be done to death, and yet it would be hardly possible to bring home the guilt to the real murderer.

'Having conceived the idea he proceeded to carry it out with considerable finesse. An ordinary schemer would have been content to work with a savage hound. The use of artificial means to make the creature diabolical was a flash of genius upon his part. The dog he bought in London from Ross and Mangles, the dealers in Fulham Road. It was the strongest and most savage in their possession. He brought it down by the North Devon line and walked a great distance over the moor so as to get it home without exciting any remarks. He had already on his insect hunts learned to penetrate the Grimpen Mire, and so had found a safe hiding-place for the creature. Here he kennelled it and waited his chance.

'But it was some time coming. The old gentleman could not be decoyed outside of his grounds at night. Several times Stapleton lurked about with his hound, but without avail. It was during these fruitless quests that he, or rather his ally, was seen by peasants, and that the legend of the demon dog received a new confirmation. He had hoped that his wife might lure Sir Charles to his ruin, but here she proved unexpectedly independent. She would not endeavour to entangle the old gentleman in a sentimental attachment which might deliver him over to his enemy. Threats and even, I am sorry to say, blows refused to move her. She would have nothing to do with it, and for a time Stapleton was at a deadlock.

'He found a way out of his difficulties through the chance that Sir Charles, who had conceived a friendship for him, made him the minister of his charity in the case of this unfortunate woman, Mrs. Laura Lyons. By representing himself as a single man he acquired complete influence over her, and he gave her to understand that in the event of her obtaining a divorce from her husband he would marry her. His plans were suddenly brought to a head by his knowledge that Sir Charles was about to leave the Hall on the advice of Dr. Mortimer, with whose opinion he himself pretended to coincide. He must act at once, or his victim might get beyond his power. He therefore put pressure upon Mrs. Lyons to write this letter, imploring the old man to give her an interview on the evening before his departure for London. He then, by a specious argument, prevented her from going, and so had the chance for which he had waited.

'Driving back in the evening from Coombe Tracey he was in time to get his hound, to treat it with his infernal paint, and to bring the beast round to the gate at which he had reason to expect that he would find the old gentleman waiting. The dog, incited by its master, sprang over the wicket-gate and pursued the unfortunate Baronet, who fled screaming down the Yew Alley. In that gloomy tunnel it must indeed have been a dreadful sight to see that huge black creature, with its flaming jaws and blazing eyes, bounding after its victim. He fell dead at the end of the alley from heart disease and terror. The hound had kept upon the grassy border while the Baronet had run down the path, so that no track but the man's was visible. On seeing him lying still the creature had probably approached to sniff at him, but finding him dead had turned away again. It was then that it left the print which was actually observed by Dr. Mortimer. The hound was called off and hurried away to its lair in the Grimpen Mire, and a mystery was left which puzzled the authorities, alarmed the countryside, and finally brought the case within the scope of our observation.

'So much for the death of Sir Charles Baskerville. You perceive the devilish cunning of it, for really it would be almost impossible to make a case against the real murderer. His only accomplice was one who could never give him away, and the grotesque, inconceivable nature of the device only served to make it more effective. Both of the women concerned in the case, Mrs. Stapleton and Mrs. Laura Lyons, were left with a strong suspicion against Stapleton. Mrs. Stapleton knew that he had designs upon the old man, and also of the existence of the hound. Mrs. Lyons knew neither of these things, but had been impressed by the death occurring at the time of an uncancelled appointment which was only known to him. However, both of them were under his influence, and he had nothing to fear from them. The first half of his task was successfully accomplished, but the more difficult still remained.

'It is possible that Stapleton did not know of the existence of an heir in Canada. In any case he would very soon learn it from his friend Dr. Mortimer, and he was told by the latter all details about the arrival of Henry Baskerville. Stapleton's first idea was that this young stranger from Canada might possibly be done to death in London without coming down to Devonshire at all. He distrusted his wife ever since she had refused to help him in laying a trap for the old man, and he dared not leave her long out of his sight for fear he should lose his influence over her. It was for this reason that he took her to London with him. They lodged, I find, at the Mexborough Private Hotel, in Craven Street, which was actually one of those called upon by my agent in search of evidence. Here he kept his wife imprisoned in her room while he, disguised in a beard, followed Dr. Mortimer to Baker Street and afterwards to the station and to the Northumberland Hotel. His wife had some inkling of his plans; but she had such a fear of her husband – a fear founded upon brutal ill-treatment – that she dare not write to warn the man whom she knew to be in danger. If the letter should fall into Stapleton's hands her own life would not be safe. Eventually, as we know, she adopted the expedient of cutting out the words which would form the message, and addressing the letter in a disguised hand. It reached the Baronet, and gave him the first warning of his danger.

'It was very essential for Stapleton to get some article of Sir Henry's attire so that, in case he was driven to use the dog, he might always have the means of setting him upon his track. With characteristic promptness and audacity he set about this at once, and we cannot doubt that the boots or chambermaid of the hotel was well bribed to help his in his design. By chance, however, the first boot which was procured for him was a new one and, therefore, useless for his purpose. He then had it returned and obtained another – a most instructive incident, since it proved conclusively to my mind that we were dealing with a real hound, as no other supposition could explain this anxiety to obtain an old boot and this indifference to a new one. The more *outré* and grotesque an incident is the more carefully it deserves to be examined, and the very point which appears to complicate a case is, when duly considered and scientifically handled, the one which is most likely to elucidate it.

'Then we had the visit from our friends next morning, shadowed always by Stapleton in the cab. From his knowledge of our rooms and of my appearance, as well as from his general conduct, I am inclined to think that Stapleton's career of crime has been by no means limited to this single Baskerville affair. It is suggestive that during the last three years there have been four considerable burglaries in the West Country, for none of which was any criminal ever arrested. The last of these, at Folkestone Court, in May, was remarkable for the cold-blooded pistolling of the page, who surprised the masked and solitary burglar. I cannot doubt that Stapleton recruited his waning resources in this fashion, and that for years he has been a desperate and dangerous man.

'We had an example of his readiness of resource that morning when he got away from us so successfully, and also of his audacity in sending back my own name to me through the cabman. From that moment he understood that I had taken over the case in London, and that therefore there was no chance for him there. He returned to Dartmoor and awaited the arrival of the Baronet.'

'One moment!' said I. 'You have, no doubt, described the sequence of events correctly, but there is one point which you have left unexplained. What became of the hound when its master was in London?'

'I have given some attention to this matter and it is undoubtedly of importance. There can be no question that Stapleton had a confidant, though it is unlikely that he ever placed himself in his power by sharing all his plans with him. There was an old manservant at Merripit House, whose name was Anthony. His connection with the Stapletons can be traced for several years, as far back as the schoolmastering days, so that he must have been aware that his master and mistress were really husband and wife. This man has disappeared and has escaped from the country. It is suggestive that Anthony is not a common name in England, while Antonio is so in all Spanish or Spanish-American countries. The man, like Mrs. Stapleton herself, spoke good English, but with a curious lisping accent. I have myself seen this old man cross the Grimpen Mire by the path which Stapleton had marked out. It is very probable, therefore, that in the absence of his master it was he who cared for the hound, though he may never have known the purpose for which the beast was used.

'The Stapletons then went down to Devonshire, whither they were soon followed by Sir Henry and you. One word now as to how I stood myself at that time. It may possibly recur to your memory that when I examined the paper upon which the printed words were fastened I made a close inspection for the water-mark. In doing so I held it within a few inches of my eyes, and was conscious of a faint smell of the scent known as white jessamine. There are seventy-five perfumes, which it is very necessary that a criminal expert should be able to distinguish from each other, and cases have more than once within my own experience depended upon their prompt recognition. The scent suggested the presence of a lady, and already my thoughts began to turn towards the Stapletons. Thus I had made certain of the hound, and had guessed at the criminal before ever we went to the West Country.

'It was my game to watch Stapleton. It was evident, however, that I could not do this if I were with you, since he would be keenly on his guard. I deceived everybody therefore, yourself included, and I came down secretly when I was supposed to be in London. My hardships were not so great as you imagined, though such trifling details must never interfere with the investigation of a case. I stayed for the most part at Coombe Tracey, and only used the hut upon the moor when it was necessary to be near the scene of action. Cartwright had come down with me, and in his disguise as a country boy he was of great assistance to me. I was dependent upon him for food and clean linen. When I was watching Stapleton Cartwright was frequently watching you, so that I was able to keep my hand upon all the strings.

'I have already told you that your reports reached me rapidly, being forwarded instantly from Baker Street to Coombe Tracey. They were of great service to me, and especially that one incidentally truthful piece of biography of Stapleton's. I was able to establish the identity of the man and the woman, and knew at last exactly how I stood. The case had been considerably complicated through the incident of the escaped convict and the relations between him and the Barrymores. This also you cleared up in a very effective way, though I had already come to the same conclusions from my own observations.

'By the time that you discovered me upon the moor I had a complete knowledge of the whole business, but I had not a case which could go to a jury. Even Stapleton's attempt upon Sir Henry that night which ended in the death of the unfortunate convict did not help us much in proving murder against our man. There seemed to be no alternative but to catch him red-handed, and to do so we had to use Sir Henry, alone and apparently unprotected, as a bait. We did so, and at the cost of a severe shock to our client we succeeded in completing our case and driving Stapleton to his destruction. That Sir Henry should have been exposed to this is, I must confess, a reproach to my management of the case, but we had no means of foreseeing the terrible and paralyzing spectacle which the beast presented, nor could we predict the fog which enabled him to burst upon us at such short notice. We succeeded in our object at a cost which both the specialist and Dr. Mortimer assure me will be a temporary one. A long journey may enable our friend to recover not only from his shattered nerves, but also from his wounded feelings. His love for the lady was deep and sincere, and to him the saddest part of all this black business was that he should have been deceived by her.

'It only remains to indicate the part which she had played throughout. There can be no doubt that Stapleton exercised an influence over her which may have been love or may have been fear, or very possibly both, since they are by no means incompatible emotions. It was, at least, absolutely effective. At his command she consented to pass as his sister, though he found the limits of his power over her when he endeavoured to make her the direct accessory to murder. She was ready to warn Sir Henry so far as she could without implicating her husband, and again and again she tried to do so. Stapleton himself seems to have been capable of jealousy, and when he saw the Baronet paying court to the lady, even though it was part of his own plan, still he could not help interrupting with a passionate outburst that revealed the fiery soul which his self-contained manner so cleverly concealed. By encouraging the intimacy he made it certain that Sir Henry would frequently come to Merripit House and that he would sooner or later get the opportunity which he desired. On the day of the crisis, however, his wife turned suddenly against him. She had learned something of the death of the convict, and she knew that the hound was being kept in the out-house on the evening that Sir Henry was coming to dinner. She taxed her husband with his intended crime, and a furious scene followed, in which he showed her for the first time that she had a rival in his love. Her fidelity turned in an instant to bitter hatred and he saw that she would betray him. He tied her up, therefore, that she might have no chance of warning Sir Henry, and he hoped, no doubt, that when the whole countryside put down the Baronet's death to the curse of his family, as they certainly would do, he could win his wife back to accept an accomplished fact, and to keep silent upon what she knew. In this I fancy that in any case he made a miscalculation, and that, if we had not been there, his doom would none the less have been sealed. A woman of Spanish blood does not condone such an injury so lightly. And now, my dear Watson, without referring to my notes, I cannot give you a more detailed account of this curious case. I do not know that anything essential has been left unexplained.'

'He could not hope to frighten Sir Henry to death as he had done the old uncle with his bogie hound.'

'The beast was savage and half-starved. If its appearance did not frighten its victim to death, at least it would paralyze the resistance which might be offered.'

'No doubt. There only remains one difficulty. If Stapleton came into the succession, how could he explain the fact that he, the heir, had been living unannounced under another name so close to the property? How could he claim it without causing suspicion and inquiry?'

'It is a formidable difficulty, and I fear that you ask too much when you expect me to solve it. The past and the present are within the field of my inquiry, but what a man may do in the future is a hard question to answer. Mrs. Stapleton has heard her husband discuss the problem on several occasions. There were three possible courses. He might claim the property from South America, establish his identity before the British authorities there, and so obtain the fortune without ever coming to England at all; or he might adopt an elaborate disguise during the short time that he need be in London; or, again, he might furnish an accomplice with the proofs and papers, putting him in as heir, and retaining a claim upon some proportion of his income. We cannot doubt from what we know of him that he would have found some way out of the difficulty. And now, my dear Watson, we have had some weeks of severe work, and for one evening, I think, we may turn our thoughts into more pleasant channels. I have a box for "Les Huguenots." Have you heard the De Reszkes? Might I trouble you then to be ready in half an hour, and we can stop at Marcini's for a little dinner on the way?'

It Shouldn't Happen to a Vet
JAMES HERRIOT

IT WAS WHEN I WAS PLODDING up Mr. Kay's field for the ninth time that it began to occur to me that this wasn't going to be my day. For some time now I had been an L.V.I., the important owner of a little certificate informing whosoever it may concern that James Herriot M.R.C.V.S. was a Local Veterinary Inspector of the Ministry of Agriculture and Fisheries. It meant that I was involved in a lot of routine work like clinical examinations and tuberculin testing. It also highlighted something which I had been suspecting for some time – the Dales farmers' attitude to time was different from my own.

It had been all right when I was calling on them to see a sick animal; they were usually around waiting for me and the beast would be confined in some building when I arrived. It was very different, however, when I sent them a card saying I was coming to inspect their dairy cows or test their herd. It stated quite clearly on the card that the animals must be assembled indoors and that I would be there at a certain time and I planned my day accordingly; fifteen minutes or so for a clinical and anything up to several hours for a test depending on the size of the herd. If I was kept waiting for ten minutes at every clinical while they got the cows in from the field it means simply that after six visits I was running an hour late.

So when I drove up to Mr. Kay's farm for a tuberculin test and found his cows tied up in their stalls I breathed a sigh of relief. We were through them in no time at all and I thought I was having a wonderful start to the day when the farmer said he had only half a dozen young heifers to do to complete the job. It was when I left the buildings and saw the group of shaggy roans and reds grazing contentedly at the far end of a large field that I felt the old foreboding.

'I thought you'd have them inside, Mr. Kay,' I said apprehensively.

Mr. Kay tapped out his pipe on to his palm, mixed the sodden dottle with a few strands of villainous looking twist and crammed it back into the bowl. 'Nay, nay,' he said, puffing appreciatively, 'Ah didn't like to put them in on a grand 'ot day like this. We'll drive them up to that little house.' He pointed to a tumbledown grey-stone barn at the summit of the long, steeply sloping pasture and blew out a cloud of choking smoke. 'Won't take many minutes.'

At his last sentence a cold hand clutched at me. I'd heard these dreadful words so many times before. But maybe it would be all right this time. We made our way to the bottom of the field and got behind the heifers.

'Cush, cush!' cried Mr. Kay.

'Cush, cush!' I added encouragingly, slapping my hands against my thighs.

The heifers stopped pulling the grass and regarded us with mild interest, their jaws moving lazily, then in response to further cries they began to meander casually up the hill. We managed to coax them up to the door of the bar but there they stopped. The leader put her head inside for a moment then turned suddenly and made a dash down the hill. The others followed suit immediately and though we danced about and waved our arms they ran past us as if we weren't there. I looked thoughtfully at the young beasts thundering down the slope, their tails high, kicking up their heels like mustangs; they were enjoying this new game.

Down the hill once more and again the slow wheedling up to the door and again the sudden breakaway. This time one of them tried it on her own and as I galloped vainly to and fro trying to turn her the others charged with glee through the gap and down the slope again.

It was a long, steep hill and as I trudged up for the third time with the sun blazing on my back I began to regret being so conscientious about my clothes; in the instructions to the new L.V.I.'s the Ministry had been explicit that they expected us to be properly attired to carry out our duties. I had taken it to heart and rigged myself out in the required uniform but I realised now that a long oilskin coat and wellingtons was not an ideal outfit for the job in hand. The sweat was trickling into my eyes and my shirt was beginning to cling to me.

When, for the third time, I saw the retreating backs careering joyously down the hill, I thought it was time to do something about it.

'Just a minute,' I called to the farmer, 'I'm getting a bit warm.'

I took off the coat, rolled it up and placed it on the grass well away from the barn. And as I made a neat pile of my syringe, the box of tuberculin, my calipers, scissors, notebook and pencil, the thought kept intruding that I was being cheated in some way. After all, Ministry work was easy – any practitioner would tell you that. You didn't have to get up in the middle of the night, you had nice set hours and you never really had to exert yourself. In fact it was money for old rope – a pleasant relaxation from the real thing. I wiped my streaming brow and stood for a few seconds panting gently – this just wasn't fair.

We started again and at the fourth visit to the barn I thought we had won because all but one of the heifers strolled casually inside. But that last one just wouldn't have it. We cushed imploringly, waved and even got near enough to poke at its rump but it stood in the entrance regarding the interior with deep suspicion. Then the heads of its mates began to reappear in the doorway and I knew we had lost again; despite my frantic dancing and shouting they wandered out one by one before joining again in their happy downhill dash. This time I found myself galloping down after them in an agony of frustration.

We had another few tries during which the heifers introduced touches of variation by sometimes breaking away half way up the hill or occasionally trotting round the back of the barn and peeping at us coyly from behind the old stones before frisking to the bottom again.

After the eighth descent I looked appealingly at Mr. Kay who was relighting his pipe calmly and didn't appear to be troubled in any way. My time schedule was in tatters but I don't think he had noticed that we had been going on like this for about forty minutes.

'Look, we're getting nowhere,' I said. 'I've got a lot of other work waiting for me. Isn't there anything more we can do?'

The farmer stamped down the twist with his thumb, drew deeply and pleasurably a few times then looked at me with mild surprise. 'Well, let's see. We could bring dog out but I don't know as he'll be much good. He's nobbut a young 'un.'

He sauntered back to the farmhouse and opened a door. A shaggy cur catapulted out, barking in delight, and Mr. Kay brought him over to the field. 'Get away by!' he cried gesturing towards the cattle who had resumed their grazing and the dog streaked behind them. I really began to hope as we went up the hill with the hairy little figure darting in, nipping at the heels, but at the barn the rot set in again. I could see the heifers beginning to sense the inexperience of the dog and one of them managed to kick him briskly under the chin as he came in. The little animal yelped and his tail went down. He stood uncertainly, looking at the beasts, advancing on him now, shaking their horns threateningly, then he seemed to come to a decision and slunk away. The young cattle went after him at increasing speed and in a moment I was looking at the extraordinary spectacle of the dog going flat out down the hill with the heifers drumming close behind him. At the foot he disappeared under a gate and we saw him no more.

Something seemed to give way in my head. 'Oh God,' I yelled, 'we're never going to get these damn things tested! I'll just have to leave them. I don't know what the Ministry is going to say, but I've had enough!'

The farmer looked at me ruminatively. He seemed to recognise that

I was at breaking point. 'Aye, it's no good,' he said, tapping his pipe out on his heel. 'We'll have to get Sam.'

'Sam?'

'Aye, Sam Broadbent. Works for me neighbour. He'll get 'em in all right.'

'How's he going to do that?'

'Oh, he can imitate a fly.'

For a moment my mind reeled. 'Did you say imitate a fly?'

'That's right. A warble fly, tha knows. He's a bit slow is t'lad but by gaw he can imitate a fly. I'll go and get him – he's only two fields down the road.'

I watched the farmer's retreating back in disbelief then threw myself down on the ground. At any other time I would have enjoyed lying there on the slope with the sun on my face and the grass cool against my sweating back; the air was still and heavy with the fragrance of clover and when I opened my eyes the gentle curve of the valley floor was a vision of peace. But my mind was a turmoil. I had a full day's Ministry work waiting for me and I was an hour behind time already. I could picture the long succession of farmers waiting for me and cursing me heartily. The tension built in me till I could stand it no longer; I jumped to me feet and ran down to the gate at the foot. I could see along the road from there and was relieved to find that Mr. Kay was on his way back.

Just behind him a large, fat man was riding slowly on a very small bicycle, his heels on the pedals, his feet and knees sticking out at right angles. Tufts of greasy black hair stuck out at random from under a kind of skull cap which looked like an old bowler without the brim.

'Sam's come to give us a hand,' said Mr. Kay with an air of quiet triumph.

'Good morning,' I said and the big man turned slowly and nodded. The eyes in the round, unshaven face were vacant and incurious and I decided that Sam did indeed look a bit slow. I found it difficult to imagine how he could possibly be of any help.

The heifers, standing near by, watched with languid interest as we came through the gate. They had obviously enjoyed every minute of the morning's entertainment and it seemed they were game for a little more fun if we so desired; but it was up to us, of course – they weren't worried either way.

Sam propped his bicycle against the wall and paced solemnly forward. He made a circle of his thumb and forefinger and placed it to his lips. His cheeks worked as though he was getting everything into place then he took a deep breath. And, from nowhere it seemed came a sudden swelling of angry sound, a vicious humming and buzzing which made me look round in alarm for the enraged insect zooming in for the kill.

The effect on the heifers was electric. Their superior air vanished and was replaced by a rigid anxiety; then, as the noise increased in volume, they turned and charged up the hill. But it wasn't the carefree frolic of before – no tossing heads, waving tails and kicking heels; this time they kept shoulder to shoulder in a frightened block.

Mr. Kay and I, trotting on either side, directed them yet again up to the building where they formed a group, looking nervously around them.

We had to wait for a short while for Sam to arrive. He was clearly a one-pace man and ascended the slope unhurriedly. At the top he paused to regain his breath, fixed the animals with a blank gaze and carefully adjusted his fingers against his mouth. A moment's tense silence then the humming broke out again, even more furious and insistent than before.

The heifers knew when they were beaten. With a chorus of startled bellows they turned and rushed into the building and I crashed the half door behind them; I stood leaning against it unable to believe my troubles were over. Sam joined me and looked into the dark interior. As if to finally establish his mastery he gave a sudden sharp blast, this time without his fingers, and his victims huddled still closer against the far wall.

A few minutes later, after Sam had left us, I was happily clipping and injecting the necks. I looked up at the farmer. 'You know, I can still hardly believe what I saw there. It was like magic. That chap has a wonderful gift.'

Mr. Kay looked over the half door and I followed his gaze down the grassy slope to the road. Sam was riding away and the strange black headwear was just visible, bobbing along the top of the wall.

'Aye, he can imitate a fly all right. Poor awd lad, it's t'only thing he's good at.'

Hurrying away from Mr. Kay's to my second test I reflected that if I had to be more than an hour late for an appointment it was a lucky thing that my next call was at the Hugills. The four brothers and their families ran a herd which, with cows, followers and calves must have amounted to nearly two hundred and I had to test the lot of them; but I knew that my lateness wouldn't bring any querulous remarks on my head because the Hugills had developed the Dales tradition of courtesy to an extraordinary degree. The stranger within their gates was treated like royalty.

As I drove into the yard I could see everybody leaving their immediate tasks and advancing on me with beaming faces. The brothers were in the lead and they stopped opposite me as I got out of the car, and I thought as I always did that I had never seen such healthy-looking men. Their ages ranged from Walter, who was about sixty, down through Thomas and Fenwick to William, the youngest, who would be in his late forties, and I should say their average weight would be about fifteen stones. They weren't fat, either, just huge, solid men with bright red, shining faces and clear eyes.

William stepped forward from the group and I knew what was coming;

this was always his job. He leaned forward, suddenly solemn, and looked into my face.

'How are you today, sorr?' he asked.

'Very well, thank you, Mr. Hugill,' I replied.

'Good!' said William fervently, and the other brothers all repeated 'Good, good, good,' with deep satisfaction.

William took a deep breath. 'And how is Mr. Farnon?'

'Oh, he's very fit, thanks.'

'Good!' Then the rapid fire of the responses from behind him: 'Good, good, good.'

William hadn't finished yet. He cleared his throat. 'And how is young Mr. Farnon?'

'In really top form.'

'Good!' But this time William allowed himself a gentle smile and from behind him came a few dignified ho-ho's. Walter closed his eyes and his great shoulders shook silently. They all knew Tristan.

William stepped back into line, his appointed task done and we all went into the byre. I braced myself as I looked at the low row of backs, the tails swishing at the flies. There was some work ahead here.

'Sorry I'm so late,' I said, as I drew the tuberculin into the syringe. 'I was held up at the last place. It's difficult to forecast how long these tests will take.'

All four brothers replied eagerly. 'Aye, you're right, sorr. It's difficult. It IS difficult. You're right, you're right, it's difficult.' They went on till they had thrashed the last ounce out of the statement.

I finished filling the syringe, got out my scissors and began to push my way between the first two cows. It was a tight squeeze and I puffed slightly in the stifling atmosphere.

'It's a bit warm in here,' I said.

Again the volley of agreement. 'You're right, sorr. Aye, it's warm. It IS warm. You're right. It's warm. It's warm. Aye, you're right.' This was all delivered with immense conviction and vigorous nodding of heads as though I had made some incredible discovery; and as I looked at the grave, intent faces still pondering over my brilliant remark, I could feel my tensions beginning to dissolve. I was lucky to work here. Where else but in the high country of Yorkshire would I meet people like these?

I pushed along the cow and got hold of its ear, but Walter stopped me with a gentle cough.

'Nay, Mr. Herriot, you won't have to look in the ears. I have all t'numbers wrote down.'

'Oh, that's fine. It'll save us a lot of time.' I had always found scratching the wax away to find ear tattoos an overrated pastime. And it was good to hear that the Hugills were attending to the clerical side; there was a section in the Ministry form which said: 'Are the herd records in good order?' I always wrote 'Yes,' keeping my fingers crossed as I thought of the scrawled figures on the backs of old bills, milk recording sheets, anything.

'Aye,' said Walter. 'I have 'em all set down proper in a book.'

'Great! Can you go and get it, then?'

'No need, sorr, I have it 'ere.' Walter was the boss, there was no doubt about it. They all seemed to live in perfect harmony but when the chips were down Walter took over automatically. He was the organiser, the acknowledge brains of the outfit. The battered trilby which he always wore in contrast with the others' caps gave him an extra air of authority.

Everybody watched respectfully as he slowly and deliberately extracted a spectacle case from an inside pocket. He opened it and took out an old pair of steel-rimmed spectacles, blowing away fragments of the hay and corn chaff with which the interior of the case was thickly powdered. There was a quiet dignity and importance in the way he unhurriedly threaded the side pieces over his ears and stood grimacing slightly to work everything into place. Then he put his hand into his waistcoat pocket.

When he took it out he was holding some object but it was difficult to identify, being almost obscured by his enormous thumb. Then I saw that it was a tiny, black-covered miniature diary about two inches square – the sort of novelty people give each other at Christmas.

'Is that the herd record?' I asked.

'Yes, this is it. It's all set down in here.' Walter daintily flicked over the pages with a horny forefinger and squinted through his spectacles. 'Now that fust cow – she's number eighty-fower.'

'Splendid!' I said. 'I'll just check this one and then we can go by the book.' I peered into the ear. 'That's funny, I make it twenty-six.'

The brothers had a look. 'You're right, sorr, you're right. It IS twenty-six.'

Walter pursed his lips. 'Why, that's Bluebell's calf isn't it?'

'Nay,' said Fenwick, 'she's out of awd Buttercup.'

'Can't be,' mumbled Thomas. 'Awd Buttercup was sold to Tim Jefferson afore this 'un was born. This is Brenda's calf.'

William shook his head. 'Ah'm sure we got her as a heifer at Bob Ashby's sale.'

'All right,' I said, holding up a hand. 'We'll put in twenty-six.' I had to cut in. It was in no way an argument, just a leisurely discussion but it looked as if it could go on for some time. I wrote the number in my notebook and injected the cow. 'Now how about this next one?'

'Well ah DO know that 'un,' said Walter confidently, stabbing at an entry in the diary. 'Can't make no mistake, she's number five.'

I looked in the ear. 'Says a hundred and thirty seven here.'

It started again. 'She was bought in, wasn't she?' 'Nay, nay she's out of awd Dribbler.' 'Don't think so – Dribbler had nowt but bulls . . .'

I raised my hand again. 'You know, I really think it might be quicker to look in all the ears. Time's getting on.'

'Aye, you're right, sorr, it IS getting on.' Walter returned the herd record to his waistcoat pocket philosophically and we started the laborious business of clipping, measuring and injecting every animal, plus rubbing the inside of the ears with a cloth soaked in spirit to identify the numbers which had often faded to a few unrelated dots. Occasionally Walter referred to his tiny book. 'Ah, that's right, ninety-two. I thowt so. It's all set down here.'

Fighting with the loose animals in the boxes round the fold yard was like having a dirty Turkish bath while wearing oilskins. The brothers caught the big beasts effortlessly and even the strongest bullock grew quickly discouraged when it tried to struggle against those mighty arms. But I noticed one strange phenomenon: the men's fingers were so thick and huge that they often slipped out of the animals' noses through sheer immobility.

It took an awful long time but we finally got through. The last calf had a space clipped in his shaggy neck and bawled heartily as he felt the needle, then I was out in the sweet air throwing my coat in the car boot. I looked at my watch – three o'clock. I was nearly two hours behind my schedule now and already I was hot and weary, with skinned toes on my right foot where a cow had trodden and a bruised left instep caused by the sudden descent of Fenwick's size thirteen hobnails during a particularly violent mêlée. As I closed the boot and limped round to the car door I began to wonder a little about this easy Ministry work.

Walter loomed over me and inclined his head graciously. 'Come in and sit down and have a drink o' tea.'

'It's very kind of you and I wish I could, Mr Hugill. But I've got a long string of inspections waiting and I don't know when I'll get round them. I've fixed up far too many and I completely underestimated the time needed for your test. I really am an absolute fool.'

And the brothers intoned sincerely. 'Aye, you're right, sorr, you're right, you're right.'

Well, there was no more testing today, but ten inspections still to do and I should have been at the first one two hours ago. I roared off, feeling that little ball tightening in my stomach as it always did when I was fighting the clock. Gripping the wheel with one hand and exploring my lunch packet with the other, I pulled out a piece of Mrs. Hall's ham and egg pie and began to gnaw at it as I went along.

But I had gone only a short way when reason asserted itself. This was no good. It was an excellent pie and I might as well enjoy it. I pulled off the unfenced road on to the grass, switched off the engine and opened the windows wide. The farm back there was like an island of activity in the quiet landscape and now that I was away from the noise and the stuffiness of the buildings the silence and the emptiness enveloped me like a soothing blanket. I leaned my head against the back of the seat and looked out at the checkered greens of the little fields along the flanks of the hills; thrusting upwards between their walls till they gave way to the jutting rocks and the harsh brown of the heather which flooded the wild country above.

I felt better when I drove away and didn't particularly mind when the farmer at the first inspection greeted me with a scowl.

'This isn't one o'clock, Maister!' he snapped. 'My cows have been in all afternoon and look at the bloody mess they've made. Ah'll never get the place clean again!'

I had to agree with him when I saw the muck piled up behind the cows; it was one of the snags about housing animals in grass time. And the farmer's expression grew blacker as most of them cocked their tails as though in welcome and added further layers to the heaps.

'I won't keep you much longer,' I said briskly, and began to work my way down the row. Before the tuberculin testing scheme came into being, these clinical examinations were the only means of detecting tuberculous cows and I moved from animals to animal palpating the udders for any unusual induration. The routine examinations were known jocularly in the profession as 'bag-snatching' or 'cow-punching' and it was a job that soon got tedious.

I found the only way to stop myself going nearly mad with boredom was to keep reminding myself what I was there for. So when I came to a gaunt red cow with a pendulous udder I straightened up and turned to the farmer.

'I'm going to take a milk sample from this one. She's a bit hard in that left hind quarter.'

The farmer sniffed. 'Please yourself. There's nowt wrong with her but I suppose it'll make a job for somebody.'

Squirting milk from the quarter into a two ounce bottle, I thought about Siegfried's veterinary friend who always took a pint sample from the healthiest udder he could find to go with his lunchtime sandwiches.

I labelled the bottle and put it into the car. We had a little electric centrifuge at Skeldale House and tonight I would spin this milk and examine the sediment on a slide after staining by Ziehl-Neelsen. Probably I would find nothing but at times there was the strange excitement of peering down the microscope at a clump of bright red, iridescent T.B. bacilli. When that happened the cow was immediately slaughtered and there was always the thought that I might have lifted the death sentence from some child – the meningitis, the spinal and lung infections which were so common in those days.

Returning to the byre I finished the inspection by examining the wall in front of each cow.

The farmer watched me dourly. 'What you on with now?'

254

'Well, if a cow has a cough you can often find some spit on the wall.' I had, in truth, found more tuberculous cows this way than any other – by scraping a little sputum on to a glass slide and then staining it as for the milk.

The modern young vet just about never sees a T.B. cow, thank heavens, but 'screws' were all too common thirty years ago. There were very few in the high Pennines but in the low country on the plain you found them; the cows that 'weren't doing right', the ones with the soft, careful cough and slightly accelerated breathing. Often they were good milkers and ate well, but they were killers and I was learning to spot them. And there were the others, the big, fat, sleek animals which could still be riddled with the disease. They were killers of a more insidious kind and nobody could pick them out. It took the tuberculin test to do that.

At the next four places I visited, the farmers had got tired of waiting for me and had turned their cows out. They had all to be brought in from the field and they came slowly and reluctantly; there was nothing like the rodeo I had had with Mr. Kay's heifers but a lot more time was lost. The animals kept trying to turn back to the field while I sped around their flanks like a demented sheepdog; and as I panted to and fro each farmer told me the same thing – that cows only liked to come in at milking time.

Milking time did eventually come and I caught three of my herds while they were being milked, but it was after six when I came tired and hungry to my second last inspection. A hush hung over the place and after shouting my way round the buildings without finding anybody I walked over to the house.

'Is your husband in, Mrs. Bell?' I asked.

'No, he's had to go into t'village to get the horse shod but he won't be long before he's back. He's left cows in for you,' the farmer's wife replied.

That was fine. I'd soon get through this lot. I almost ran into the byre and started the old routine, feeling sick to death of the sight and smell of cows and fed up with pawing at their udders. I was working along almost automatically when I came to a thin, rangy cow with a narrow red and white face; she could be a crossed Shorthorn-Ayrshire. I had barely touched her udder when she lashed out with the speed of light and caught me just above the kneecap.

I hopped round the byre on one leg, groaning and swearing in my agony. It was some time before I was able to limp back to have another try and this time I scratched her back and cush-cushed her in a wheedling tone before sliding my hand gingerly between her legs. The same thing happened again only this time the sharp-edged cloven foot smacked slightly higher up my leg.

Crashing back against the wall, I huddled there, almost weeping with pain and rage. After a few minutes I reached a decision. To hell with her. If she didn't want to be examined she could take her luck. I had had enough for one day – I was in no mood for heroics.

Ignoring her, I proceeded down the byre till I had inspected the others. But I had to pass her on my way back and paused to have another look; and whether it was sheer stubbornness or whether I imagined she was laughing at me, I don't know, but I decided to have just one more go. Maybe she didn't like me coming from behind. Perhaps if I worked from the side she wouldn't mind so much.

Carefully I squeezed my way between her and her neighbour, gasping as the craggy pelvic bones dug into my ribs. Once in the space beyond, I thought, I would be free to do my job; and that was my big mistake. Because as soon as I had got there the cow went to work on me in earnest. Switching her back end round quickly to cut off my way of escape, she began to kick me systematically from head to foot. She kicked forward, reaching at times high on my chest as I strained back against the wall.

Since then I have been kicked by an endless variety of cows in all sorts of situation but never by such an expert as this one. There must be very few really venomous bovines and when one of them uses her feet it is usually an instinctive reaction to being hurt or frightened; and they kick blindly. But this cow measured me up before each blow and her judgement of distance was beautiful. And as she drove me further towards her head she was able to hook me in the back with her horns by way of variety. I am convinced she hated the human race.

My plight was desperate. I was completely trapped and it didn't help when the apparently docile cow next door began to get into the act by prodding me off with her horns as I pressed against her.

I don't know what made me look up, but there, in the thick wall of the byre was a hole about two feet square where some of the crumbling stone had fallen out. I pulled myself up with an agility that amazed me and as I crawled through head first a sweet fragrance came up to me. I was looking into a hay barn and, seeing a deep bed of finest clover just below I launched myself into space and did a very creditable roll in the air before landing safely on my back.

Lying there, bruised and breathless, with the front of my coat thickly patterned with claw marks I finally abandoned any lingering illusion I had had that Ministry work was a soft touch.

I was rising painfully to my feet when Mr. Bell strolled in. 'Sorry ah had to go out,' he said, looking me over with interest, 'But I'd just about given you up. You're 'ellish late.'

I dusted myself down and picked a few strands of hay from my hair. 'Yes, sorry about that. But never mind, I managed to get the job done.'

'But . . . were you havin' a bit of a kip, then?'

'No, not exactly. I had some trouble with one of your cows.' There wasn't much point in standing on my dignity. I told him the story.

Even the friendliest farmer seems to derive pleasure from a vet's discomfiture and Mr. Bell listened with an ever-widening grin of delight. By the time I had finished he was doubled up, beating his breeches knees with his hands.

'I can just imagine it. That Ayrshire cross! She's a right bitch. Picked her up cheap at market last spring and thought ah'd got a bargain, but ah soon found out. Took us a fortnight to get bugger tied up!'

'Well, I just wish I'd known,' I said, rather tight lipped.

The farmer looked up at the hole in the wall. 'And you crawled through ...' he went into another convulsion which lasted some time, then he took off his cap and wiped his eyes with the lining.

'Oh dear, oh dear,' he murmured weakly. 'By gaw, I wish I'd been here.'

My last call was just outside Darrowby and I could hear the church clock striking a quarter past seven as I got stiffly out of the car. After my easy day in the service of the government I felt broken in mind and body; I had to suppress a scream when I saw yet another long line of cows' backsides awaiting me. The sun was low, and dark thunder clouds piling up in the west had thrown the countryside into an eerie darkness; and in the old-fashioned, slit-windowed byre the animals looked shapeless and ill-defined in the gloom.

Right, no messing about. I was going to make a quick job of this and get off home; home to some food and an armchair. I had no further ambitions. So left hand on the root of the tail, right hand between the hind legs, a quick feel around and on to the next one. Eyes half closed, my mind numb, I moved from cow to cow going through the motions like a robot with the far end of the byre seeming like the promised land.

And finally here it was, the very last one up against the wall. Left hand on tail, right hand between legs ... At first my tired brain didn't take in the fact that there was something different here, but there was ... something vastly different. A lot of space and instead of the udder a deeply cleft, pendulous something with no teats anywhere.

I came awake suddenly and looked along the animal's side. A huge woolly head was turned towards me and two wide-set eyes regarded me enquiringly. In the dull light I could just see the gleam of the copper ring in the nose.

The farmer who had watched me in silence, spoke up.

'You're wasting your time there, young man. There's nowt wrong wi' HIS bag.'

The Country of the Houyhnhnms

JONATHAN SWIFT

First published in 1726 Gulliver's Travels was written as a scathing satirical attack on social and moral behaviour. A ship's surgeon, Lemuel Gulliver, is set ashore in a strange land inhabited by creatures of an innate and thought-provoking nobility . . .

I CONTINUED AT HOME with my Wife and Children about five Months in a very happy Condition, if I could have learned the Lesson of knowing when I was well. I left my poor Wife big with Child, and accepted an advantageous Offer made me to be Captain of the *Adventure*, a stout Merchant-man of 350 Tuns: For I understood Navigation well, and being grown weary of a Surgeon's Employment at Sea, which however I could exercise upon Occasion, I took a skilful young Man of that Calling, one *Robert Purefoy*, into my Ship. We set sail from *Portsmouth* upon the 7th Day of *September*, 1710; on the 14th we met with Captain *Pocock* of *Bristol*, at *Tenariff*, who was going to the Bay of *Campeachy*, to cut Logwood. On the 16th he was parted from us by a Storm: I heard since my Return, that his Ship foundered, and none escaped, but one Cabbin-Boy. He was an honest Man, and a good Sailor, but a little too positive in his own Opinions, which was the Cause of his Destruction, as it hath been of several others. For if he had followed my Advice, he might at this Time have been safe at home with his Family as well as my self.

I had several Men died in my Ship of Calentures, so that I was forced to get Recruits out of *Barbadoes*, and the *Leeward Islands*, where I touched by the Direction of the Merchants who employed me; which I had soon too much Cause to repent; for I found afterwards that most of them had been Buccaneers. I had fifty Hands on Board; and my Orders were, that I should trade with the *Indians* in the *South-Sea*, and make what Discoveries I could. These Rogues whom I had picked up, debauched my other Men, and they all formed a Conspiracy to seize the Ship and secure me; which they did one Morning, rushing into my Cabbin, and binding me Hand and Foot, threatening to throw me overboard, if I offered to stir. I told them, I was their Prisoner, and would submit. This they made me swear to do, and then unbound me, only fastening one of my Legs with a Chain near my Bed; and placed a Centry at my Door with his Piece charged, who was commanded to shoot me dead if I attempted my Liberty. They sent me down Victuals and Drink, and took the Government of the Ship to themselves. Their Design was to turn Pirates, and plunder the *Spaniards*, which they could not do, till they got more Men. But first they resolved to sell the Goods in the Ship, and then go to *Madagascar* for Recruits, several among them having died since my Confinement. They sailed many Weeks, and traded with the *Indians*; but I knew not what Course they took, being kept close Prisoner in my Cabbin, and expecting nothing less than to be murdered, as they often threatened me.

Upon the 9th Day of *May*, 1711, one *James Welch* came down to my Cabbin; and said he had Orders from the Captain to set me ashore. I expostulated with him, but in vain; neither would he so much as tell me who their new Captain was. They forced me into the Long-boat, letting me put on my best Suit of Cloaths, which were as good as new, and a small Bundle of Linnen, but no Arms except my Hanger; and they were so civil as not to search my Pockets, into which I conveyed what Money I had, with some other little Necessaries. They rowed about a League; and then set me down on a Strand. I desired them to tell me what Country it was: They all swore, they knew no more than my self, but said, that the Captain (as they called him) was resolved, after they had sold the Lading, to get rid of me in the first Place where they discovered Land. They pushed off immediately, advising me to make haste, for fear of being overtaken by the Tide; and bade me farewell.

In this desolate Condition I advanced forward, and soon got upon firm Ground, where I sat down on a Bank to rest my self, and consider what I had best to do. When I was a little refreshed, I went up into the Country, resolving to deliver my self to the first Savages I should meet; and purchase my Life from them by some Bracelets, Glass Rings, and other Toys, which Sailors usually provide themselves with in those Voyages, and whereof I had some about me: The Land was divided by long Rows of Trees, not regularly planted, but naturally growing; there was great Plenty of Grass, and several Fields of Oats. I walked very circumspectly for fear of being surprised, or suddenly shot with an Arrow from behind, or on either Side. I fell into a beaten Road, where I saw many Tracks of human Feet, and some of Cows, but most of Horses. At last I beheld several Animals in a Field, and one or two of the same Kind sitting in Trees. Their Shape was very singular, and deformed, which a little discomposed me, so that I lay down behind a Thicket to observe them better. Some of them coming forward near the Place where I lay, gave me an Opportunity of distinctly marking their Form. Their Heads and Breasts were covered with a thick Hair, some frizzled and others lank; they had Beards like Goats, and a long Ridge of Hair down their Backs, and the fore Parts of their Legs and Feet; but the rest of their Bodies were bare, so that I might see their Skins, which were of a brown Buff Colour. They had no Tails, nor any Hair at all on their Buttocks, except about the *Anus*; which, I presume Nature had placed there to defend them as they sat on the Ground; for this Posture they used, as well as lying down, and often stood on their hind Feet. They climbed high Trees, as nimbly as a Squirrel, for they had strong extended Claws before and behind, terminating on sharp Points, hooked. They would often spring, and bound, and leap with prodigious Agility. The Females were not so large as the Males; they had long lank Hair on their Heads, and only a Sort of Down on the rest of their Bodies, except about the *Anus*, and *Pudenda*. Their Dugs hung between their fore Feet, and often reached almost to the Ground as they walked. The Hair of both Sexes was of several Colours, brown, red, black and yellow. Upon the whole, I never beheld in all my Travels so disagreeable an Animal, or one against which I naturally conceived so strong an Antipathy. So that thinking I had seen enough, full of Contempt and Aversion, I got up and pursued the beaten Road, hoping it might direct me to the Cabbin of some *Indian*. I had not gone far when I met one of these Creatures full in my Way, and coming up directly to me. The ugly Monster, when he saw me, distorted several Ways every Feature of his Visage, and stared as at an Object he had never seen before; then approaching nearer, lifted up his fore Paw, whether out of Curiosity or Mischief, I could not tell: But I drew my Hanger, and gave him a good Blow with the flat Side of it; for I durst not strike him with the Edge, fearing the Inhabitants might be provoked against me, if they should come to know, that I had killed or maimed any of their Cattle. When the Beast felt the Smart, he drew back, and roared so loud, that a Herd of at least forty came flocking about me from the next Field, howling and making odious Faces; but I ran to the Body of a Tree, and leaning my Back against it, kept them off, by waving my Hanger. Several of this cursed Brood getting hold of the Branches behind, leaped up into the Tree, from whence they began to discharge their Excrements on my Head: However, I escaped pretty well, by sticking close to the Stem of the Tree, but was almost stifled with the Filth, which fell about me on every Side.

In the Midst of this Distress, I observed them all to run away on a sudden as fast as they could; at which I ventured to leave the Tree, and pursue the Road, wondering what it was that could put them into this Fright. But looking on my Left-Hand, I saw a Horse walking softly in the Field; which my Persecutors having sooner discovered, was the Cause of their Flight. The Horse started a little when he came near me, but soon recovering himself, looked full in my Face with manifest Tokens of Wonder: He viewed my Hands and Feet, walking round me several times. I would have pursued my Journey, but he placed himself directly in the Way, yet looking with a very mild Aspect, never offering the least Violence. We stood gazing at each other for some time; at last I took the Boldness, to reach my Hand towards his Neck, with a Design to stroak it; using the common Style and Whistle of Jockies when they are going to handle a strange Horse. But, this Animal seeming to receive my Civilities with Disdain, shook his Head, and bent his Brows, softly raising up his Left Fore-Foot to remove my Hand. Then he neighed three or four times, but in so different a Cadence, that I almost began to think he was speaking to himself in some Language of his own.

While He and I were thus employed, another Horse came up; who applying himself to the first in a very formal Manner, they gently struck each others Right Hoof before, neighing several times by Turns, and varying the Sound, which seemed to be almost articulate. They went some Paces off, as if it were to confer together, walking Side by Side, backward and forward, like Persons deliberating upon some Affair of Weight; but often turning their Eyes towards me, as it were to watch that I might not escape. I was amazed to see such Actions and Behaviour in Brute Beasts; and concluded with myself, that if the Inhabitants of this Country were endued with a proportionable Degree of Reason, they must needs be the wisest People upon Earth. This Thought gave me so much Comfort, that I resolved to go forward untill I could discover some House or Village, or meet with any of the Natives; leaving the two Horses to discourse together as they pleased. But the first, who was a Dapple-Grey, observing me to steal off, neighed after me in so expressive a Tone, that I fancied myself to understand what he meant; whereupon I turned back, and came near him, to expect his farther Commands; but concealing my Fear as much as I could; for I began to be in some Pain, how this Adventure might terminate; and the Reader will easily believe I did not much like my present Situation.

The two Horses came up close to me, looking with great Earnestness upon my Face and Hands. The grey Steed rubbed my Hat all round with his Right Fore-hoof, and discomposed it so much, that I was forced to adjust it better, by taking it off, and settling it again; whereat both he and his Companion (who was a brown Bay) appeared to be much surprized; the latter felt the Lappet of my Coat, and finding it to hang loose about me, they both looked with new Signs of Wonder. He stroked my Right Hand, seeming to admire the Softness, and Colour; but he squeezed it so hard between his Hoof and his Pastern, that I was forced to roar; after which they both touched me with all possible Tenderness. They were under great Perplexity about my Shoes and Stockings, which they felt very often, neighing to each other, and using various Gestures, not unlike those of a Philospher, when he would attempt to solve some new and difficult Phænomenon.

Upon the whole, the Behaviour of these Animals was so orderly and rational, so acute and judicious, that I at last concluded, they must needs be Magicians, who had thus metamorphosed themselves upon some Design; and seeing a Stranger in the Way, were resolved to divert themselves with him; or perhaps were really amazed at the Sight of a Man so very different in Habit, Feature and Complexion from those who might probably live in so remote a Climate. Upon the Strength of this Reasoning, I venture to address them in the following Manner: Gentlemen, if you be Conjurers, as I have good Cause to believe, you can understand any Language; therefore I make bold to let your Worships know, that I am a poor distressed *Englishman*, driven by his Misfortunes upon your Coast; and I entreat one of you, to let me ride upon his Back, as if he were a real Horse, to some House or Village, where I can be relieved. In return of which Favour, I will make you a Present of this Knife and Bracelet, (taking them out of my Pocket.) The two Creatures stood silent while I spoke, seeming to listen with great Attention; and when I had ended, they neighed frequently towards each other, as if they were engaged in serious Conversation. I plainly observed, that their Language expressed the Passions very well, and the Words might with little Pains be resolved into an Alphabet more easily than the *Chinese*.

I could frequently distinguish the Word *Yahoo*, which was repeated by each of them several times; and although it were impossible for me to conjecture what it meant, yet while the two Horses were busy in Conversation, I endeavoured to practice this Word upon my Tongue; and as soon as they were silent, I boldly pronounced *Yahoo* in a loud Voice, imitating, at the same time, as near as I could, the Neighing of a Horse; at which they were both visibly surprized, and the Grey repeated the same Word twice, as if he meant to teach me the right Accent, wherein I spoke after him as well as I could, and found myself perceivably to improve every time, although very far from any Degree of Perfection. Then the Bay tried me with a second Word, much harder to be pronounced; but reducing it to the *English Orthography*, may be spelt thus, *Houyhnhnm*. I did not succeed in this so well as the former, but after two or three farther Trials, I had better Fortune; and they both appeared amazed at my Capacity.

After some farther Discourse, which I then conjectured might relate to me, the two Friends took their Leaves, with the same Compliment of striking each other's Hoof; and the Grey made me Signs that I should walk before him; wherein I thought it prudent to comply, till I could find a better Director. When I offered to slacken my Pace, he would cry *Hhuun, Hhuun*; I guessed his Meaning, and gave him to understand, as well as I could, that I was weary, and not able to walk faster; upon which, he would stand a while to let me rest.

Having travelled about three Miles, we came to a long Kind of Building, made of Timber, stuck in the Ground, and wattled a-cross; the Roof was low, and covered with Straw. I now began to be a little comforted; and took out some Toys, which Travellers usually carry for Presents to the Savage *Indians* of *America* and other Parts, in hopes the People of the House would be thereby encouraged to receive me kindly. The Horse made me a Sign to go in first; it was a large Room with a smooth Clay Floor, and a Rack and Manger extending the whole Length on one Side. There were three Nags, and two Mares, not eating, but some of them sitting down upon their Hams, which I very much wondered at; but wondered more to see the rest employed in domestick Business: The last seemed but ordinary Cattle; however this confirmed my first Opinion, that a People who could so far civilize brute Animals, must needs excel in Wisdom all the Nations of the World. The Grey came in just after, and thereby prevented any ill Treatment, which the others might have given me. He neighed to them several times in a Style of Authority, and received Answers.

Beyond this Room there were three others, reaching the Length of the House, to which you passed through three Doors, opposite to each other, in the Manner of a Vista: We went through the second Room towards the third; here the Grey walked in first, beckoning me to attend: I waited in the second Room, and got ready my Presents, for the Master and Mistress of the House: They were two Knives, three Bracelets of false Pearl, a small Looking Glass and a Bead Necklace. The Horse neighed three or four Times, and I waited to hear some answers in a human Voice, but I heard no other Returns than in the same Dialect, only one of two a little shriller than his. I began to think that this House must belong to some Person of great Note among them, because there appeared so much Ceremony before I could gain Admittance. But, that a Man of Quality should be served all by Horses, was beyond my Comprehension. I feared my Brain was disturbed by my Sufferings and Misfortunes: I roused my self, and looked about me in the Room where I was left alone; this was furnished as the first, only after a more elegant Manner. I rubbed my Eyes often, but the same Objects still occurred. I pinched my Arms and Sides to awake my self, hoping I might be in a Dream. I then absolutely concluded, that all these Appearances could be nothing else but Necromancy and Magick. But I had no Time to pursue these Reflections; for the Grey Horse came to the Door, and made me a Sign to follow him into the third Room; where I saw a very comely Mare,

263

together with a Colt and Fole, sitting on their Haunches, upon Mats of Straw, not unartfully made, and perfectly neat and clean.

The Mare soon after my Entrance, rose from her Mat, and coming up close, after having nicely observed my Hands and Face, gave me a most contemptuous Look; then turning to the Horse, I heard the Word *Yahoo* often repeated betwixt them; the meaning of which Word I could not then comprehend, although it were the first I had learned to pronounce; but I was soon better informed, to my everlasting Mortification: For the Horse beckoning to me with his Head, and repeating the Word *Hhuun, Hhuun,* as he did upon the Road, which I understood was to attend him, led me out into a kind of Court, where was another Building at some Distance from the House. Here we entered, and I saw three of those detestable Creatures, which I first met after my landing, feeding upon Roots, and the Flesh of some Animals, which I afterwards found to be that of Asses and Dogs, and now and then a Cow dead by Accident or Disease. They were all tied by the Neck with strong Wyths, fastened to a Beam; they held their Food between the Claws of their fore Feet, and tore it with their Teeth.

The Master Horse ordered a Sorrel Nag, one of his Servants, to untie the largest of these Animals, and take him into a Yard. The Beast and I were brought close together; and our Countenances diligently compared, both by Master and Servant, who thereupon repeated several Times the Word *Yahoo*. My Horror and Astonishment are not to be described, when I observed, in this abominable Animal, a perfect human Figure; the Face of it indeed was flat and broad, the Nose depressed, the Lips large, and the Mouth wide: But these Differences are common to all savage Nations, where the Lineaments of the Countenance are distorted by the Natives suffering their Infants to lie grovelling on the Earth, or by carrying them on their Backs, nuzzling with their Face against the Mother's Shoulders. The Fore-feet of the *Yahoo* differed from my Hands in nothing else, but the Length of the Nails, the Coarseness and Brownness of the Palms, and the Hairiness on the Backs. There was the same Resemblance between our Feet, with the same Differences, which I knew very well, although the Horses did not, because of my Shoes and Stockings; the same in every Part of our Bodies, except as to Hairiness and Colour, which I have already described.

The great Difficulty that seemed to stick with the two Horses, was, to see the rest of my Body so very different from that of a *Yahoo*, for which I was obliged to my Cloaths, whereof they had no Conception: The Sorrel Nag offered me a Root, which he held (after their Manner, as we shall describe in its proper Place) between his Hoof and Pastern; I took it in my Hand, and having smelt it, returned it to him again as civilly as I could. He brought out of the *Yahoo's* Kennel a Piece of Ass's Flesh, but it smelt so offensively that I turned from it with loathing; he then threw it to the *Yahoo*, by whom it was greedily devoured. He afterwards shewed me a Wisp of Hay, and a Fettlock full of Oats; but I shook my Head, to signify that neither of these were Food for me. And indeed, I now apprehended, that I must absolutely starve, if I did not get to some of my own Species: For as to those filthy *Yahoos*, although there were few greater Lovers of Mankind, at that time, than myself; yet I confess I never saw any sensitive Being so detestable on all Accounts; and the more I came near them, the more hateful they grew, while I stayed in that Country. This the Master Horse observed by my Behaviour, and therefore sent the *Yahoo* back to his Kennel. He then put his Fore-hoof to his Mouth, at which I was much surprized, although he did it with Ease, and with a Motion that appear'd perfectural natural; and made other Signs to know what I would eat; but I could not return him such an Answer as he was able to apprehend; and if he had understood me, I did not see how it was possible to contrive any way for finding myself Nourishment. While we were thus engaged, I observed a Cow passing by; whereupon I pointed to her, and expressed a Desire to let me go and milk her. This had its Effect; for he led me back into the House, and ordered a Mare-servant to open a Room, where a good Store of Milk lay in Earthen and Wooden Vessels, after a very orderly and cleanly Manner. She gave me a large Bowl full, of which I drank very heartily, and found myself well refreshed.

About Noon I saw coming towards the House a Kind of Vehicle, drawn like a Sledge by four *Yahoos*. There was in it an old Steed, who seemed to be of Quality; he alighted with his Hind-feet forward, having by Accident got a Hurt in his Left Fore-foot. He came to dine with our Horse, who received him with great Civility. They dined in the best Room, and had Oats boiled in Milk for the second Course, which the old Horse eat warm, but the rest cold. Their Mangers were placed circular in the Middle of the Room, and divided into several Partitions, round which they sat on their Haunches upon Bosses of Straw. In the Middle was a large Rack with Angles answering to every Partition of the Manger. So that each Horse and Mare eat their own Hay, and their own Mash of Oats and Milk, with much Decency and Regularity. The Behaviour of the young Colt and Fole appeared very modest; and that of the Master and Mistress extremely chearful and complaisant to their Guest. The Grey ordered me to stand by him; and much Discourse passed between him and his Friend concerning me, as I found by the Stranger's often looking on me, and the frequent Repetition of the Word *Yahoo*.

I happened to wear my Gloves; which the Master Grey observing, seemed perplexed; discovering Signs of Wonder what I had done to my Fore-feet; he put his Hoof three or four times to them, as if he would signify, that I should reduce them to their former Shape, which I presently did, pulling off both my Gloves, and putting them into my Pocket. This occasioned farther Talk, and I saw the Company was pleased with my Behaviour, whereof I soon found the good Effects. I was ordered to speak the few Words I understood; and while they were at Dinner, the Master taught me the Names for Oats, Milk, Fire, Water, and some others; which I could readily pronounce after him; having from my Youth a great Facility in learning Languages.

When Dinner was done, the Master Horse took me aside, and by Signs and Words made me understand the Concern he was in, that I had nothing to eat. Oats in their Tongue are called *Hlunnh*. This Word I pronounced two or three times; for although I had refused them at first, yet upon second Thoughts, I considered that I could contrive to make a Kind of Bread, which might be sufficient with Milk to keep me alive, till I could make my Escape to some other Country, and to Creatures of my own Species. The Horse immediately ordered a white Mare-servant of his Family to bring me a good Quantity of Oats in a Sort of wooden Tray. These I heated before the Fire as well as I could, and rubbed them till the Husks came off, which I made a shift to winnow from the Grain; I ground and beat them between two Stones, then took Water, and made them into a Paste or Cake, which I toasted at the Fire, and eat warm with Milk. It was at first a very insipid Diet, although common enough in many Parts of *Europe*, but grew tolerable by Time; and having been often reduced to hard Fare in my Life, this was not the first Experiment I had made how easily Nature is satisfied. And I cannot but observe, that I never had one Hour's Sickness, while I staid in this Island. It is true, I sometimes made a shift to catch a Rabbet, or Bird, by Springes made of *Yahoos* Hairs; and I often gathered wholesome Herbs, which I boiled, or eat as Salades with my Bread; and now and then, for a Rarity, I made a little Butter, and drank the Whey. I was at first at a great Loss for Salt; but Custom soon reconciled the Want of it; and I am confident that the frequent Use of Salt among us is an Effect of Luxury, and was first introduced only as a Provocative to Drink; except where it is necessary for preserving of Flesh in long Voyages, or in Places remote from great Markets. For we observe no Animal to be fond of it but Man: And as to myself, when I left this Country, it was a great while before I could endure the Taste of it in any thing that I eat.

This is enough to say upon the Subject of my Dyet, wherewith other Travellers fill their Books, as if the Readers were personally concerned, whether we fare well or ill. However, it was necessary to mention this Matter, lest the World should think it impossible that I could find Sustenance for three Years in such a Country, and among such Inhabitants.

When it grew towards Evening, the Master Horse ordered a Place for me to lodge in; it was but Six Yards from the House, and separated from the Stable of the *Yahoos*. Here I got some Straw, and covering myself with my own Cloaths, slept very sound. But I was in a short time better accommodated, as the Reader shall know hereafter, when I come to treat more particularly about my Way of living.

My principal Endeavour was to learn the Language, which my Master (for so I shall henceforth call him) and his Children, and every Servant of his House were desirous to teach me. For they looked upon it as a Prodigy, that a brute Animal should discover such Marks of a rational Creature. I pointed to every thing, and enquired the Name of it, which I wrote down in my *Journal Book* when I was alone, and corrected my bad Accent, by desiring those of the Family to pronounce it often. In this Employment, a Sorrel Nag, one of the under Servants, was very ready to assist me.

In speaking, they pronounce through the Nose and Throat, and their Language approaches nearest to the *High Dutch* or *German*, of any I know in *Europe*; but is much more graceful and significant. The Emperor *Charles* V. made almost the same Observation, when he said, That if he were to speak to his Horse, it should be in *High Dutch*.

The Curiosity and Impatience of my Master were so great, that he spent many Hours of his Leisure to instruct me. He was convinced (as he afterwards told me) that I must be a *Yahoo*, but my Teachableness, Civility and Cleanliness astonished him; which were Qualities altogether so opposite to those Animals. He was most perplexed about my Cloaths, reasoning sometimes with himself, whether they were a Part of my Body; for I never pulled them off till the Family were asleep, and got them on before they waked in the Morning. My Master was eager to learn from whence I came; how I acquired those Appearances of Reason, which I discovered in all my Actions; and to know my Story from my own Mouth, which he hoped he should soon do by the great Proficiency I made in learning and pronouncing their Words and Sentences. To help my Memory, I formed all I learned into the *English* Alphabet, and writ the Words down with the Translations. This last, after some time, I ventured to do in my Master's Presence. It cost me much Trouble to explain to him what I was doing; for the Inhabitants have not the least Idea of Books or Literature.

In about ten Weeks time I was able to understand most of his Questions; and in three Months could give some tolerable Answers. He was extremely curious to know from what Part of the Country I came, and how I was taught to imitate a rational Creature; because the *Yahoos*, (whom he saw I exactly resembled in my Head, Hands and Face, that were only visible,) with some Appearance of Cunning, and the strongest Disposition to Mischief, were observed to be the most unteachable of all Brutes. I answered; that I came over the Sea, from a far Place, with many others of my own Kind, in a great hollow Vessel made of the Bodies of Trees: That, my Companions forced me to land on this Coast, and then left me to shift for myself. It was with some Difficulty, and by the Help of many Signs, that I brought him to understand me. He replied, That I must needs be mistaken, or that I *said the thing which was not.* (For they have no Word in their Language to express Lying or Falshood.) He knew it

was impossible that there could be a Country beyond the Sea, or that a
Parcel of Brutes could move a wooden Vessel whither they pleased upon
Water. He was sure no *Houyhnhnm* alive could make such a Vessel, or
would trust *Yahoos* to manage it.

The Word *Houyhnhnm*, in their Tongue, signifies a *Horse*; and in its
Etymology, *the Perfection of Nature*. I told my Master, that I was at a
Loss for Expression, but would improve as fast as I could; and hoped in
a short time I should be able to tell him Wonders: He was pleased to
direct his own Mare, his Colt and Fole, and the Servants of the Family
to take all Opportunities of instructing me; and every Day for two or
three Hours, he was at the same Pains himself: Several Horses and
Mares of Quality in the Neighbourhood came often to our House, upon
the Report spread of a wonderful *Yahoo*, that could speak like a
Houyhnhnm, and seemed in his Words and Actions to discover some
Glimmerings of Reason. These delighted to converse with me; they put
many Questions, and received such Answers, as I was able to return. By
all which Advantages, I made so great a Progress, that in five Months
from my Arrival, I understood whatever was spoke, and could express
myself tolerably well.

The *Houyhnhnms* who came to visit my Master, out of a Design of
seeing and talking with me, could hardly believe me to be a right *Yahoo*,
because my Body had a different Covering from others of my Kind. They
were astonished to observe me without the usual Hair or Skin, except on
my Head, Face and Hands: but I discovered that Secret to my Master,
upon an Accident, which happened about a Fortnight before.

I have already told the Reader, that every Night when the Family
were gone to Bed, it was my Custom to strip and cover myself with my
Cloaths: It happened one Morning early, that my Master sent for me,
by the Sorrel Nag, who was his Valet; when he came, I was fast asleep,
my Cloaths fallen off on one Side, and my Shirt above my Waste. I
awaked at the Noise he made, and observed him to deliver his Message
in some Disorder; after which he went to my Master, and in a great
Fright gave him a very confused Account of what he had seen: This I
presently discovered; for going as soon as I was dressed, to pay my
Attendance upon his Honour, he asked me the Meaning of what his
Servant had reported; that I was not the same Thing when I slept as I
appeared to be at other times; that his Valet assured him, some Part of
me was white, some yellow, at least not so white, and some brown.

I had hitherto concealed the Secret of my Dress, in order to distinguish
myself as much as possible, from that cursed Race of *Yahoos*; but now
I found it in vain to do so any longer. Besides, I considered that my
Cloaths and Shoes would soon wear out, which already were in a
declining Condition, and must be supplied by some Contrivance from the
Hides of *Yahoos*, or other Brutes; whereby the whole Secret would be
known. I therefore told my Master, that in the Country from whence I

came, those of my Kind always covered their Bodies with the Hairs of certain Animals prepared by Art, as well for Decency, as to avoid Inclemencies of Air both hot and cold; of which, as to my own Person I would give him immediate Conviction, if he pleased to command me; only desiring his Excuse, if I did not expose those Parts that Nature taught us to conceal. He said, my Discourse was all very strange, but especially the last Part; for he could not understand why Nature should teach us to conceal what Nature had given. That neither himself nor Family were ashamed of any Parts of their Bodies; but however I might do as I pleased. Whereupon, I first unbuttoned my Coat, and pulled it off. I did the same with my Waste-coat; I drew off my Shoes, Stockings and Breeches. I let my Shirt down to my Waste, and drew up the Bottom, fastening it like a Girdle about my Middle to hide my Nakedness.

My Master observed the whole Performance with great Signs of Curiosity and Admiration. He took up all my Cloaths in his Pastern, one Piece after another, and examined them diligently; he then stroaked my Body very gently, and looked round me several Times; after which he said, it was plain I must be a perfect *Yahoo*; but that I differed very much from the rest of my Species, in the Whiteness, and Smoothness of my Skin, my want of Hair in several Parts of my Body, the Shape and Shortness of my Claws behind and before, and my Affectation of walking continually on my two hinder Feet. He desired to see no more; and gave me leave to put on my Cloaths again, for I was shuddering with Cold.

I expressed my Uneasiness at his giving me so often the Appellation of *Yahoo*, an odious Animal, for which I had so utter an Hatred and Contempt. I begged he would forbear applying that Word to me, and take the same Order in his Family, and among his Friends whom he suffered to see me. I requested likewise, that the Secret of my having a false Covering to my Body might be known to none but himself, at least as long as my present Cloathing should last: For as to what the Sorrel Nag his Valet had observed, his Honour might command him to conceal it.

All this my Master very graciously consented to; and thus the Secret was kept till my Cloaths began to wear out, which I was forced to supply by several Contrivances, that shall hereafter be mentioned. In the mean Time, he desired I would go on with my utmost Diligence to learn their Language, because he was more astonished at my Capacity for Speech and Reason, than at the Figure of my Body, whether it were covered or no; adding, that he waited with some Impatience to hear the Wonders which I promised to tell him.

From thenceforward he doubled the Pains he had been at to instruct me; he brought me into all Company, and made them treat me with Civility, because, as he told them privately, this would put me into good Humour, and make me more diverting.

Every Day when I waited on him, beside the Trouble he was at in teaching, he would ask me several Questions concerning my self, which I answered as well as I could; and by those Means he had already received some general Ideas, although very imperfect. It would be tedious to relate the several Steps, by which I advanced to a more regular Conversation: But the first Account I gave of my self in any Order and Length, was to this Purpose:

That, I came from a very far Country, as I already had attempted to tell him, with about fifty more of my own Species; that we travelled upon the Seas, in a great hollow Vessel made of Wood, and larger than his Honour's House. I described the Ship to him in the best Terms I could; and explained by the Help of my Handkerchief displayed, how it was driven forward by the Wind. That, upon a Quarrel among us, I was set on Shoar on this Coast, where I walked forward without knowing whither, till he delivered me from the Persecution of those execrable *Yahoos.* He asked me, Who made the Ship, and how it was possible that the *Houyhnhnms* of my Country would leave it to the Management of Brutes? My Answer was, that I durst proceed no farther in my Relation, unless he would give me his Word and Honour that he would not be offended; and then I would tell him the Wonders I had so often promised. He agreed; and I went on by assuring him, that the Ship was made by Creatures like myself, who in all the Countries I had travelled, as well as in my own, were the only governing, rational Animals; and that upon my Arrival hither, I was as much astonished to see the *Houyhnhnms* act like rational Beings, as he or his Friends could be in finding some Marks of Reason in a Creature he was pleased to call a *Yahoo*; to which I owned my Resemblance in every Part, but could not account for their degenerate and brutal Nature. I said farther, That if good Fortune ever restored me to my native Country, to relate my Travels hither, as I resolved to do; every Body would believe that I *said the Thing which was not*; that I invented the Story out of my own Head: And with all possible Respect to Himself, his Family, and Friends, and under his Promise of not being offended, our Countrymen would hardly think it probable, that a *Houyhnhnm* should be the presiding Creature of a Nation, and a *Yahoo* the Brute.

Lady Into Fox

DAVID GARNETT

Tragedy strikes the lives of Richard and Silvia Tebrick when the latter is suddenly and mysteriously transformed – into a fox. Eventually, Mr. Tebrick has to bow sadly to the inevitable, and Silvia leaves their old home to build a new life in the wild . . .

ONE MORNING THE FIRST week in May, about four o'clock, when he was out waiting in the little copse, he sat down for a while on a tree stump, and when he looked up saw a fox coming towards him over the ploughed field. It was carrying a hare over its shoulder so that it was nearly all hidden from him. At last, when it was not twenty yards from him, it crossed over, going into the copse, when Mr. Tebrick stood up and cried out, 'Silvia, Silvia, is it you?'

The fox dropped the hare out of his mouth and stood looking at him, and then our gentleman saw at the first glance that this was not his wife. For whereas Mrs. Tebrick had been of a very bright red, this was a swarthier duller beast altogether, moreover it was a good deal larger and higher at the shoulder and had a great white tag to his brush. But the fox after the first instant did not stand for his portrait you may be sure, but picked up his hare and made off like an arrow.

Then Mr. Tebrick cried out to himself: 'Indeed I am crazy now! My affliction has made me lose what little reason I ever had. Here am I taking every fox I see to be my wife! My neighbours call me a madman and now I see that they are right. Look at me now, oh God! How foul a creature I am. I hate my fellows. I am thin and wasted by this consuming passion, my reason is gone and I feed myself on dreams.

Recall me to my duty, bring me back to decency, let me not become a beast likewise, but restore me and forgive me, Oh my Lord.'

With that he burst into scalding tears and knelt down and prayed, a thing he had not done for many weeks.

When he rose up he walked back feeling giddy and exceedingly weak, but with a contrite heart, and then washed himself thoroughly and changed his clothes, but his weakness increasing he lay down for the rest of the day, but read in the Book of Job and was much comforted.

For several days after this he lived very soberly, for his weakness continued, but every day he read in the bible, and prayed earnestly, so that his resolution was so much strengthened that he determined to overcome his folly, or his passion, if he could, and at any rate to live the rest of his life very religiously. So strong was this desire in him to amend his ways that he considered if he should not go to spread the Gospel abroad, for the Bible Society, and so spend the rest of his days.

Indeed he began a letter to his wife's uncle, the canon, and he was writing this when he was startled by hearing a fox bark.

Yet so great was this new turn he had taken that he did not rush out at once, as he would have done before, but stayed where he was and finished his letter.

Afterwards he said to himself that it was only a wild fox and sent by the devil to mock him, and that madness lay that way if he should listen. But on the other hand he could not deny to himself that it might have been his wife, and that he ought to welcome the prodigal. Thus he was torn between these two thoughts, neither of which did he completely believe. He stayed thus tormented with doubts and fears all night.

The next morning he woke suddenly with a start and on the instant heard a fox bark once more. At that he pulled on his clothes and ran out as fast as he could to the garden gate. The sun was not yet high, the dew thick everywhere, and for a minute or two everything was very silent. He looked about him eagerly but could see no fox, yet there was already joy in his heart.

Then while he looked up and down the road, he saw his vixen step out of the copse about thirty yards away. He called to her at once.

'My dearest wife! Oh, Silvia! You are come back!' and at the sound of his voice he saw her wag her tail, which set his last doubts at rest.

But then though he called her again, she stepped into the copse once more though she looked back at him over her shoulder as she went. At this he ran after her, but softly and not too fast lest he should frighten her away, and then looked about for her again and called to her when he saw her among the trees still keeping her distance from him. He followed her then, and as he approached so she retreated from him, yet always looking back at him several times.

He followed after her through the underwood up the side of the hill, when suddenly she disappeared from his sight, behind some bracken.

When he got there he could see her nowhere, but looking about him found a fox's earth, but so well hidden that he might have passed it by a thousand times and would never have found it unless he had made particular search at that spot.

But now, though he went on his hands and knees, he could see nothing of his vixen, so that he waited a little while wondering.

Presently he heard a noise of something moving in the earth, and so waited silently, then saw something which pushed itself into sight. It was a small sooty black beast, like a puppy. There came another behind it, then another and so on till there were five of them. Lastly there came his vixen pushing her litter before her, and while he looked at her silently, a prey to his confused and unhappy emotions, he saw that her eyes were shining with pride and happiness.

She picked up one of her youngsters then, in her mouth, and brought it to him and laid it in front of him, and then looked up at him very excited, or so it seemed.

Mr. Tebrick took the cub in his hands, stroked it and put it against his cheek. It was a little fellow with a smutty face and paws, with staring vacant eyes of a brilliant electric blue and a little tail like a carrot. When he was put down he took a step towards his mother and then sat down very comically.

Mr. Tebrick looked at his wife again and spoke to her, calling her a good creature. Already he was resigned and now, indeed, for the first time he thoroughly understood what had happened to her, and how far apart they were now. But looking first at one cub, then at another, and having them sprawling over his lap, he forgot himself, only watching the pretty scene, and taking pleasure in it. Now and then he would stroke his vixen and kiss her, liberties which she freely allowed him. He marvelled more than ever now at her beauty; for her gentleness with the cubs and the extreme delight she took in them seemed to him then to make her more lovely than before. Thus lying amongst them at the mouth of the earth he idled away the whole of the morning.

First he would play with one, then with another, rolling them over and tickling them, but they were too young yet to lend themselves to any other more active sport than this. Every now and then he would stroke his vixen, or look at her, and thus the time slipped away quite fast and he was surprised when she gathered her cubs together and pushed them before her into the earth, then coming back to him once or twice very humanly bid him 'Good-bye and that she hoped she would see him soon again, now he had found out the way.'

So admirably did she express her meaning that it would have been superfluous for her to have spoken had she been able, and Mr. Tebrick, who was used to her, got up at once and went home.

But now that he was alone, all the feelings which he had not troubled himself with when he was with her, but had, as it were, put aside till after his innocent pleasures were over, all these came swarming back to assail him in a hundred tormenting ways.

Firstly he asked himself: Was not his wife unfaithful to him, had she not prostituted herself to a beast? Could he still love her after that? But this did not trouble him so much as it might have done. For now he was convinced inwardly that she could no longer in fairness be judged as a woman, but as a fox only. And as a fox she had done no more than other foxes, indeed in having cubs and tending them with love, she had done well.

Whether in this conclusion Mr. Tebrick was in the right or not, is not for us here to consider. But I would only say to those who would censure him for a too lenient view of the religious side of the matter, that we have not seen the thing as he did, and perhaps if it were displayed before our eyes we might be led to the same conclusions.

This was, however, not a tenth part of the trouble in which Mr. Tebrick found himself. For he asked himself also: 'Was he not jealous?' And looking into his heart he found that he was indeed jealous, yes, and angry too, that now he must share his vixen with wild foxes. Then he questioned himself if it were not dishonourable to do so, and whether he should not utterly forget her and follow his original intention of retiring from the world, and see her no more.

Thus he tormented himself for the rest of that day, and by evening he had resolved never to see her again.

But in the middle of the night he woke up with his head very clear, and said to himself in wonder, 'Am I not a madman? I torment myself foolishly with fantastic notions. Can a man have his honour sullied by a beast? I am a man, I am immeasurably superior to the animals. Can my dignity allow of my being jealous of a beast? A thousand times no. Were I to lust after a vixen, I were a criminal indeed. I can be happy in seeing my vixen, for I love her, but she does right to be happy according to the laws of her being.'

Lastly, he said to himself what was, he felt, the truth of this whole matter:

'When I am with her I am happy. But now I distort what is simple and drive myself crazy with false reasoning upon it.'

Yet before he slept again he prayed, but though he had thought first to pray for guidance, in reality he prayed only that on the morrow he would see his vixen again and that God would preserve her, and her cubs too, from all dangers, and would allow him to see them often, so that he might come to love them for her sake as if he were their father, and that if this were a sin he might be forgiven, for he sinned in ignorance.

The next day or two he saw vixen and cubs again, though his visits were cut shorter, and these visits gave him such an innocent pleasure that very soon his notions of honour, duty and so on, were entirely forgotten, and his jealousy lulled asleep.

One day he tried taking with him the stereoscope and a pack of cards.

But though his Silvia was affectionate and amiable enough to let him put the stereoscope over her muzzle, yet she would not look through it, but kept turning her head to lick his hand, and it was plain to him that now she had quite forgotten the use of the instrument. It was the same too with the cards. For with them she was pleased enough, but only delighting to bite at them, and flip them about with her paws, and never considering for a moment whether they were diamonds or clubs, or hearts, or spades or whether the card was an ace or not. So it was evident that she had forgotten the nature of cards too.

Thereafter he only brought them things which she could better enjoy, that is sugar, grapes, raisins and butcher's meat.

Bye-and-bye, as the summer wore on, the cubs came to know him, and he them, so that he was able to tell them easily apart, and then he christened them. For this purpose he brought a little bowl of water, sprinkled them as if in baptism and told them he was their godfather and gave each of them a name, calling them Sorel, Kasper, Selwyn, Esther and Angelica.

Sorel was a clumsy little beast of a cheery and indeed puppyish disposition; Kasper was fierce, the largest of the five, even in his play he would always bite, and gave his godfather many a sharp nip as time went on. Esther was of a dark complexion, a true brunette and very sturdy; Angelica the brightest red and the most exactly like her mother; while Selwyn was the smallest cub, with a very prying, inquisitive and cunning temper, but delicate and undersized.

Thus Mr. Tebrick had a whole family now to occupy him, and, indeed, came to love them with very much of a father's love and partiality.

His favourite was Angelica (who reminded him so much of her mother in her pretty ways) because of a gentleness which was lacking in the others, even in their play. After her in his affections came Selwyn, whom he soon saw was the most intelligent of the whole litter. Indeed he was so much more quick-witted than the rest that Mr. Tebrick was led into speculating as to whether he had not inherited something of the human from his dam. Thus very early he learnt to know his name, and would come when he was called, and what was stranger still, he learnt the names of his brothers and sisters before they came to do so themselves.

Besides all this he was something of a young philosopher, for though his brother Kasper tyrannized over him he put up with it all with an unruffled temper. He was not, however, above playing tricks on the others, and one day when Mr. Tebrick was by, he made believe that there was a mouse in a hole some little way off. Very soon he was joined by Sorel, and presently by Kasper and Esther. When he had got them all digging, it was easy for him to slip away, and then he came to his godfather with a sly look, sat down before him, and smiled and then jerked his head over towards the others and smiled again and wrinkled his brows so that Mr. Tebrick knew as well as if he had spoken that the youngster was saying, 'Have I not made fools of them all?'

He was the only one that was curious about Mr. Tebrick: he made him take out his watch, put his ear to it, considered it and wrinkled up his brows in perplexity. On the next visit it was the same thing. He must see the watch again, and again think over it. But clever as he was, little Selwyn could never understand it, and if his mother remembered anything about watches it was a subject which she never attempted to explain to her children.

One day Mr. Tebrick left the earth as usual and ran down the slope to the road, when he was surprised to find a carriage waiting before his house and a coachman walking about near his gate. Mr. Tebrick went in and found that his visitor was waiting for him. It was his wife's uncle.

They shook hands, though the Rev. Canon Fox did not recognize him immediately, and Mr. Tebrick led him into the house.

The clergyman looked about him a good deal, at the dirty and disorderly rooms, and when Mr. Tebrick took him into the drawing room it was evident that it had been unused for several months, the dust lay so thickly on all the furniture.

After some conversation on indifferent topics Canon Fox said to him: 'I have called really to ask about my niece.'

Mr. Tebrick was silent for some time and then said:

'She is quite happy now.'

'Ah – indeed. I have heard she is not living with you any longer.'

'No. She is not living with me. She is not far away. I see her every day now.'

'Indeed. Where does she live?'

'In the woods with her children. I ought to tell you that she has changed her shape. She is a fox.'

The Rev. Canon Fox got up; he was alarmed, and everything Mr. Tebrick said confirmed what he had been led to expect he would find at Rylands. When he was outside, however, he asked Mr. Tebrick:

'You don't have many visitors now, eh?'

'No – I never see anyone if I can avoid it. You are the first person I have spoken to for months.'

'Quite right, too, my dear fellow. I quite understand – in the circumstances.' Then the cleric shook him by the hand, got into his carriage and drove away.

'At any rate,' he said to himself, 'there will be no scandal.' He was relieved also because Mr. Tebrick had said nothing about going abroad to disseminate the Gospel. Canon Fox had been alarmed by the letter, had not answered it, and thought that it was always better to let things be, and never to refer to anything unpleasant. He did not at all want to recommend Mr. Tebrick to the Bible Society if he were mad. His

eccentricities would never be noticed at Stokoe. Besides that, Mr. Tebrick
had said he was happy.

He was sorry for Mr. Tebrick too, and he said to himself that the
queer girl, his niece, must have married him because he was the first
man she had met. He reflected also that he was never likely to see her
again and said aloud, when he had driven some little way:

'Not an affectionate disposition,' then to his coachman: 'No, that's all
right. Drive on, Hopkins.'

When Mr. Tebrick was alone he rejoiced exceedingly in his solitary
life. He understood, or so he fancied, what it was to be happy, and that
he had found complete happiness now, living from day to day, careless
of the future, surrounded every morning by playful and affectionate little
creatures whom he loved tenderly, and sitting beside their mother, whose
simple happiness was the source of his own.

'True happiness,' he said to himself, 'is to be found in bestowing love;
there is no such happiness as that of the mother for her babe, unless I
have attained it in mine for my vixen and her children.'

With these feelings he waited impatiently for the hour on the morrow
when he might hasten to them once more.

When, however, he had toiled up the hillside, to the earth, taking
infinite precaution not to tread down the bracken, or make a beaten path
which might lead others to that secret spot, he found to his surprise that
Silvia was not there and that there were no cubs to be seen either. He
called to them, but it was in vain, and at last he laid himself on the mossy
bank beside the earth and waited.

For a long while, as it seemed to him, he lay very still, with closed
eyes, straining his ears to hear every rustle among the leaves, or any
sound that might be the cubs stirring in the earth.

At last he must have dropped asleep, for he woke suddenly with all
his senses alert, and opening his eyes found a full-grown fox within six
feet of him sitting on its haunches like a dog and watching his face with
curiosity. Mr. Tebrick saw instantly that it was not Silvia. When he
moved the fox got up and shifted his eyes, but still stood his ground, and
Mr. Tebrick recognized him then for the dog-fox he had seen once before
carrying a hare. It was the same dark beast with a large white tag to his
brush. Now the secret was out and Mr. Tebrick could see his rival before
him. Here was the real father of his god-children, who could be certain
of their taking after him, and leading over again his wild and rakish life.
Mr. Tebrick stared for a long time at the handsome rogue, who glanced
back at him with distrust and watchfulness patent in his face, but not
without defiance too, and it seemed to Mr. Tebrick as if there was also
a touch of cynical humour in his look, as if he said:

'By Gad! we two have been strangely brought together!'

And to the man, at any rate, it seemed strange that they were thus linked, and he wondered if the love his rival there bare to his vixen and his cubs were the same thing in kind as his own.

'We would both of us give our lives for theirs,' he said to himself as he reasoned upon it, 'we both of us are happy chiefly in their company. What pride this fellow must feel to have such a wife, and such children taking after him. And has he not reason for his pride? He lives in a world where he is beset with a thousand dangers. For half the year he is hunted, everywhere dogs pursue him, men lay traps for him or menace him. He owes nothing to another.'

But he did not speak, knowing that his words would only alarm the fox; then in a few minutes he saw the dog-fox look over his shoulder, and then he trotted off as lightly as a gossamer veil blown in the wind, and, in a minute or two more, back he comes with his vixen and the cubs all around him. Seeing the dog-fox thus surrounded by vixen and cubs was too much for Mr. Tebrick; in spite of all his philosophy a pang of jealousy shot through him. He could see that Silvia had been hunting with her cubs, and also that she had forgotten that he would come that morning, for she started when she saw him, and though she carelessly licked his hand, he could see that her thoughts were not with him.

Very soon she led her cubs into the earth, the dog-fox had vanished and Mr. Tebrick was again alone. He did not wait longer but went home.

Now was his peace of mind all gone, the happiness which he had flattered himself the night before he knew so well how to enjoy, seemed now but a fool's paradise in which he had been living. A hundred times this poor gentleman bit his lip, drew down his torvous brows, and stamped his foot, and cursed himself bitterly, or called his lady bitch. He could not forgive himself neither, that he had not thought of the damned dog-fox before, but all the while had let the cubs frisk round him, each one a proof that a dog-fox had been at work with his vixen. Yes, jealousy was now in the wind, and every circumstance which had been a reason for his felicity the night before was now turned into a monstrous feature of his nightmare. With all this Mr. Tebrick so worked upon himself that for the time being he had lost his reason. Black was white and white black, and he was resolved that on the morrow he would dig the vile brood of foxes out and shoot them, and so free himself at last from this hellish plague.

All that night he was in this mood, and in agony, as if he had broken in the crown of a tooth and bitten on the nerve. But as all things will have an ending so at last Mr. Tebrick, worn out and wearied by this loathed passion of jealousy, fell into an uneasy and tormented sleep.

After an hour or two the procession of confused and jumbled images which first assailed him passed away and subsided into one clear and powerful dream. His wife was with him in her own proper shape, walking as they had been on that fatal day before her transformation. Yet she was changed too, for in her face there were visible tokens of unhappiness, her face swollen with crying, pale and downcast, her hair hanging in disorder, her damp hands wringing a small handkerchief into a ball, her whole body shaken with sobs, and an air of long neglect about her person. Between her sobs she was confessing to him some crime which she had committed, but he did not catch the broken words, nor did he wish to hear them, for he was dulled by his sorrow. So they continued walking together in sadness as it were for ever, he with his arm about her waist, she turning her head to him and often casting her eyes down in distress.

At last they sat down, and he spoke, saying: 'I know they are not my children, but I shall not use them barbarously because of that. You are still my wife. I swear to you they shall never be neglected. I will pay for their education.'

Then he began turning over the names of schools in his mind. Eton would not do, nor Harrow, nor Winchester, nor Rugby . . . But he could not tell why these schools would not do for these children of hers, he only knew that every school he thought of was impossible, but surely one could be found. So turning over the names of schools he sat for a long while holding his dear wife's hand, till at length, still weeping, she got up and went away and then slowly he awoke.

But even when he had opened his eyes and looked about him he was thinking of schools, saying to himself that he must send them to a private academy, or even at the worst engage a tutor. 'Why, yes,' he said to himself, putting one foot out of bed, 'that is what it must be, a tutor, though even then there will be a difficulty at first.'

At those words he wondered what difficulty there would be and recollected that they were not ordinary children. No, they were foxes – mere foxes. When poor Mr. Tebrick had remembered this he was, as it were, dazed or stunned by the fact, and for a long time he could understand nothing, but at last burst into a flood of tears compassionating them and himself too. The awfulness of the fact itself, that his dear wife should have foxes instead of children, filled him with an agony of pity, and, at length, when he recollected the cause of their being foxes, that is that his wife was a fox also, his tears broke out anew, and he could bear it no longer but began calling out in his anguish, and beat his head once or twice against the wall, and then cast himself down on his bed again and wept and wept, sometimes tearing the sheets asunder with his teeth.

The whole of that day, for he was not to go to the earth till evening, he went about sorrowfully, torn by true pity for his poor vixen and her children.

At last when the time came he went again up to the earth, which he found deserted, but hearing his voice, out came Esther. But though he called the others by their names there was no answer, and something in the way the cub greeted him made him fancy she was indeed alone. She was truly rejoiced to see him, and scrambled up into his arms, and thence to his shoulder, kissing him, which was unusual in her (though natural enough in her sister Angelica). He sat down a little way from the earth fondling her, and fed her with some fish he had brought for her mother, which she ate so ravenously that he concluded she must have been short of food that day and probably alone for some time.

At last while he was sitting there Esther pricked up her ears, started up, and presently Mr. Tebrick saw his vixen come towards them. She greeted him very affectionately but it was plain had not much time to spare, for she soon started back whence she had come with Esther at her side. When they had gone about a rod the cub hung back and kept stopping and looking back to the earth, and at last turned and ran back home. But her mother was not to be fobbed off so, for she quickly overtook her child and gripping her by the scruff began to drag her along with her.

Mr. Tebrick, seeing then how matters stood, spoke to her, telling her he would carry Esther if she would lead, so after a little while Silvia gave her over, and then they set out on their strange journey.

Silvia went running on a little before while Mr. Tebrick followed after with Esther in his arms whimpering and struggling now to be free, and indeed, once she gave him a nip with her teeth. This was not so strange a thing to him now, and he knew the remedy for it, which is much the same as with others whose tempers run too high, that is a taste of it themselves. Mr. Tebrick shook her and gave her a smart little cuff, after which, though she sulked, she stopped her biting.

They went thus above a mile, circling his house and crossing the highway until they gained a small covert that lay with some waste fields adjacent to it. And by this time it was so dark that it was all Mr. Tebrick could do to pick his way, for it was not always easy for him to follow where his vixen found a big enough road for herself.

But at length they came to another earth, and by the starlight Mr. Tebrick could just make out the other cubs skylarking in the shadows.

Now he was tired, but he was happy and laughed softly for joy, and presently his vixen, coming to him, put her feet upon his shoulders as he sat on the ground, and licked him, and he kissed her back on the muzzle and gathered her in his arms and rolled her in his jacket and then laughed and wept by turns in the excess of his joy.

All his jealousies of the night before were forgotten now. All his desperate sorrow of the morning and the horror of his dream were gone. What if they were foxes? Mr. Tebrick found that he could be happy with them. As the weather was hot he lay out there all the night, first playing hide and seek with them in the dark till, missing his vixen and the cubs proving obstreperous, he lay down and was soon asleep.

He was woken up soon after dawn by one of the cubs tugging at his shoelaces in play. When he sat up he saw two of the cubs standing near him on their hind legs, wrestling with each other, the other two were playing hide and seek round a tree trunk, and now Angelica let go his laces and came romping into his arms to kiss him and say 'Good morning' to him, then worrying the points of his waistcoat a little shyly after the warmth of his embrace.

That moment of awakening was very sweet to him. The freshness of the morning, the scent of everything at the day's rebirth, the first beams of the sun upon a tree-top near, and a pigeon rising into the air suddenly, all delighted him. Even the rough scent of the body of the cub in his arms seemed to him delicious.

At that moment all human customs and institutions seemed to him nothing but folly; for said he, 'I would exchange all my life as a man for my happiness now, and even now I retain almost all of the ridiculous conceptions of a man. The beasts are happier and I will deserve that happiness as best I can.'

After he had looked at the cubs playing merrily, how, with soft stealth, one would creep behind another to bounce out and startle him, a thought came into Mr. Tebrick's head, and that was that these cubs were innocent, they were as stainless snow, they could not sin, for God had created them to be thus and they could break none of His commandments. And he fancied also that men sin because they cannot be as the animals.

Presently he got up full of happiness, and began making his way home when suddenly he came to a full stop and asked himself: 'What is going to happen to them?'

This question rooted him stockishly in a cold and deadly fear as if he had seen a snake before him. At last he shook his head and hurried on his path. Aye, indeed, what would become of his vixen and her children?

This thought put him into such a fever of apprehension that he did his best not to think of it any more, but yet it stayed with him all that day and for weeks after, at the back of his mind, so that he was not careless in his happiness as before, but as it were trying continually to escape his own thoughts.

This made him also anxious to pass all the time he could with his dear Silvia, and, therefore, he began going out to them for more of the daytime, and then he would sleep the night in the woods also as he had done that night; and so he passed several weeks, only returning to his house occasionally to get himself a fresh provision of food. But after a week or ten days at the new earth both his vixen and the cubs, too, got a new habit of roaming. For a long while back, as he knew, his vixen had been lying out alone most of the day, and now the cubs were all for doing the same thing. The earth, in short, had served its purpose and was now distasteful to them, and they would not enter it unless pressed with fear.

This new manner of their lives was an added grief to Mr. Tebrick, for sometimes he missed them for hours together, or for the whole day even, and not knowing where they might be was lonely and anxious. Yet his

Silvia was thoughtful for him too and would often send Angelica or another of the cubs to fetch him to their new lair, or come herself if she could spare the time. For now they were all perfectly accustomed to his presence, and had come to look on him as their natural companion, and although he was in many ways irksome to them by scaring rabbits, yet they always rejoiced to see him when they had been parted from him. This friendliness of theirs was, you may be sure, the source of most of Mr. Tebrick's happiness at this time. Indeed he lived now for nothing but his foxes, his love for his vixen had extended itself insensibly to include her cubs, and these were now his daily playmates so that he knew them as well as if they had been his own children. With Selwyn and Angelica indeed he was always happy; and they never so much as when they were with him. He was not stiff in his behaviour either, but had learnt by this time as much from his foxes as they had from him. Indeed never was there a more curious alliance than this or one with stranger effects upon both of the parties.

Mr. Tebrick now could follow after them anywhere and keep up with them too, and could go through a wood as silently as a deer. He learnt to conceal himself if ever a labourer passed by so that he was rarely seen, and never but once in their company. But what was most strange of all, he had got a way of going doubled up, often almost on all fours with his hands touching the ground every now and then, particularly when he went uphill.

He hunted with them too sometimes, chiefly by coming up and scaring rabbits towards where the cubs lay ambushed, so that the bunnies ran straight into their jaws.

He was useful to them in other ways, climbing up and robbing pigeons' nests for the eggs which they relished exceedingly, or by occasionally dispatching a hedgehog for them so they did not get the prickles in their mouths. But while on his part he thus altered his conduct, they on their side were not behindhand, but learnt a dozen human tricks from him that are ordinarily wanting in Reynard's education.

One evening he went to a cottager who had a row of skeps, and bought one of them, just as it was after the man had smothered the bees. This he carried to the foxes that they might taste the honey, for he had seen them dig out wild bees' nests often enough. The skep full was indeed a wonderful feast for them, they bit greedily into the heavy-scented comb, their jaws were drowned in the sticky flood of sweetness, and they gorged themselves on it without restraint. When they had crunched up the last morsel they tore the skep in pieces, and for hours afterwards they were happily employed in licking themselves clean.

That night he slept near their lair, but they left him and went hunting. In the morning when he woke he was quite numb with cold, and faint with hunger. A white mist hung over everything and the wood smelt of autumn.

He got up and stretched his cramped limbs, and then walked home-wards. The summer was over and Mr. Tebrick noticed this now for the first time and was astonished. He reflected that the cubs were fast growing up, they were foxes at all points, and yet when he thought of the time when they had been sooty and had blue eyes it seemed to him only yesterday. From that he passed to thinking of the future, asking himself as he had done once before what would become of his vixen and her children. Before the winter he must tempt them into the security of his garden, and fortify it against all the dangers that threatened them.

But though he tried to allay his fear with such resolutions he remained uneasy all that day. When he went out to them that afternoon he found only his wife Silvia there and it was plain to him that she too was alarmed, but alas, poor creature, she could tell him nothing, only lick his hands and face, and turn about pricking her ears at every sound.

'Where are your children, Silvia?' he asked her several times, but she was impatient of his questions, but at last sprang into his arms, flattened herself upon his breast and kissed him gently, so that when he departed his heart was lighter because he knew that she still loved him.

That night he slept indoors, but in the morning early he was awoken by the sound of trotting horses, and running to the window saw a farmer riding by very sprucely dressed. Could they be hunting so soon, he wondered, but presently reassured himself that it could not be a hunt already.

He heard no other sound till eleven o'clock in the morning when suddenly there was the clamour of hounds giving tongue and not so far off neither. At this Mr. Tebrick ran out of his house distracted and set open the gates of his garden, but with iron bars and wire at the top so the huntsmen could not follow. There was silence again; it seems the fox must have turned away, for there was no other sound of the hunt. Mr. Tebrick was now like one helpless with fear, he dared not go out, yet could not stay still at home. There was nothing that he could do, yet he would not admit this, so he busied himself in making holes in the hedges, so that Silvia (or her cubs) could enter from whatever side she came.

At last he forced himself to go indoors and sit down and drink some tea. While he was there he fancied he heard the hounds again; it was but a faint ghostly echo of their music, yet when he ran out of the house it was already close at hand in the copse above.

Now it was that poor Mr. Tebrick made his great mistake, for hearing the hounds almost outside the gate he ran to meet them, whereas rightly he should have run back to the house. As soon as he reached the gate he saw his wife Silvia coming towards him but very tired with running and just upon her the hounds. The horror of that sight pierced him, for ever afterwards he was haunted by those hounds – their eagerness, their desperate efforts to gain on her, and their blind lust for her came at odd moments to frighten him all his life. Now he should have run back, though it was already late, but instead he cried out to her, and she ran straight through the open gate to him. What followed was all over in a flash, but it was seen by many witnesses.

The side of Mr. Tebrick's garden there is bounded by a wall, about six feet high and curving round, so that the huntsmen could see over this wall inside. One of them indeed put his horse at it very boldly, which was risking his neck, and although he got over safe was too late to be of much assistance.

His vixen had at once sprung into Mr. Tebrick's arms, and before he could turn back the hounds were upon them and had pulled them down. Then at that moment there was a scream of despair heard by all the field that had come up, which they declared afterwards was more like a woman's voice than a man's. But yet there was no clear proof whether it was Mr. Tebrick or his wife who had suddenly regained her voice. When the huntsman who had leapt the wall got to them and had whipped off the hounds Mr. Tebrick had been terribly mauled and was bleeding from twenty wounds. As for his vixen she was dead, though he was still clasping her dead body in his arms.

Mr. Tebrick was carried into the house at once and assistance sent for, but there was no doubt now about his neighbours being in the right when they called him mad.

For a long while his life was despaired of, but at last he rallied, and in the end he recovered his reason and lived to be a great age, for that matter he is still alive.

A Cat in the Window

DEREK TANGYE

*After years of devout cat-hating, Derek Tangye is converted by
the arrival of Monty, a spirited and delightful feline character.*

NOT ONLY THE FOSTERS but others along the river bank kept a watch on
Monty. He was a talisman to the passers-by as he sat in the dining-room
window, hour after hour, waiting for our return. One autumn we spent
a month in Paris and when we got back we were looked at reproachfully
by those who had seen him day after day in the window. 'You should
have seen him late at night when the street lamp lit up his face,' said a
neighbour, 'he looked so mournful.' We hated to hear such remarks
because we felt we were in the wrong. Of course he had been well looked
after by his guardians but he had been very lonely. And yet what does
one do if ever one wishes to go away for a holiday with an easy conscience?
Deposit a cat at the vet and you may think it is safe but you cannot
possibly persuade yourself that the cat in such strange surroundings does
not believe it has been deserted and has been left in a prison. There
seems to be no answer except never to take a holiday.

Monty's big day in the dining-room window was Boat Race day. The
Boat Race party, as far as we were concerned, came round each year
much too quickly. An annual affair which had such raucous results as
a Boat Race party, is apt to dissolve in some mysterious way with its
predecessors. Time stands still. The guests have never left, or they are
always just arriving or saying goodbye. Hence my old friends Mr. and
Mrs. X are greeted by me at the door and I feel I am simultaneously
greeting them this year, last year and the year before. Ours used to be
a bottle party and as the Boat Race generally took place at some unearthly
hour in the morning, guests began to arrive with their bottles at 9 a.m.

The trouble with a bottle party is the stress it puts on the host and hostess who are inclined to greet their guests with graduated enthusiasm, according to the importance of the bottle. We had one guest who regularly brought a bottle of milk. I never found out whether this was a joke, for he consumed alcohol like everyone else; but I remember how our greeting became dimmer each year until it would have become extinct had we not departed for Cornwall.

The preparations, of course, began at the crack of dawn and as it was always a marathon day of festivity, large quantities of food were prepared to cope with late breakfasts, lunch, tea and those who still had the stamina to stay for supper. For Monty these preparations were a nuisance and this might be considered surprising because, with so much food about, one might have expected him to be the official taster. But he was never a greedy cat. He ate his requirements and no more, although like all of us he had certain favourite dishes, chopped pigs' liver, for instance, which he gobbled faster than others. He considered these preparations a nuisance, I think, because he wanted to get on with the party. He had a role to play, and it was a role which he enjoyed.

He would keep out of sight, the airing-cupboard was the ideal hiding-place, until he had the good sense to realize the towpath was waking up; shouts of small boys who without reason for loyalty to either University were violently partisan on behalf of one or other of the crews, odd couples booking places on the railings, then the appearance of hawkers with dark and light blue favours. There was a pleasant atmosphere of impending excitement, and it was now that Monty appeared and expected attention.

Both Jeannie and I were Cambridge supporters and before our first Boat Race party Jeannie had bought Monty a large light blue ribbon which she tied in a bow round his neck. I did not approve. I thought such a gesture was ostentatious and silly and I anticipated confidently that Monty would wriggle free from the encumbrance as soon as he had the chance. He did not do so. True the ribbon became more and more askew as the day wore on with the bow finishing up under his tummy, but this had nothing to do with any action on his part. It was the attention he received which caused that.

Hence the light blue ribbon became an annual ritual and invariably, after the bow had been tied, he would sit in the dining-room window staring with a lordly air at the crowds; and the crowds looking for a diversion until the race began, would call to him and shout to their friends about him. He adored this period of glory. So much on his own but now at last receiving his due. And when our guests arrived, a hundred or more packing the cottage, a cacophony of laughter and talk, cigarette smoke clouding the rooms, people sitting on the floor and the stairs, glasses everywhere, Jeannie and I rushing around with bottles and plates of cold food, Monty was as cool as a cucumber. He would stroll from room to room, pausing beside a guest when the praise was high, even deigning to jump on a lap, ignoring the cat haters, refusing with well-bred disgust any morsel dangled before him by some well-meaning admirer. He was unobtrusively sure of himself; and when the rackety day was over, when Jeannie and I had gone to bed feeling too tired to sleep and we put out a hand and touched him at the bottom of the bed, we both felt safe. Safe, I mean, from the tensions among which we lived.

Sometimes I wonder if we would ever have come to Cornwall had it not been for Monty. Decisions are often based on motives which are not obviously apparent, and cool intellects certainly would not believe that two people could change the mainspring of their life because of a cat. Such intellects, however, are free from turbulent emotions. They are the human version of the computer; to be envied, perhaps, because they are spared the distractions of light and shade. They can barge through life indifferent to the sensibilities of others because they have none themselves. Materialism in their view, is the only virtue.

Monty became a factor in our decision because he reflected, in his own fashion, stability. It did not matter how tired we were when we reached home, how irritated we might be by the day's conflict of personalities, how worried by inflated anxieties, how upset by apparent failures, Monty was solidly there to greet us. His presence, you might say, knocked sense back into us. He thus gave a clue to the kind of reward we might have if we exchanged our existing way of life for one that had a more enduring standard of values. We did not say this self-consciously at the time, too many other factors were involved; but on reflection I realize his example helped us to take the plunge.

The process of changing over from a city to a country life was spread over a year and more. We made several sorties to the cottage near Land's End during that time, and Monty was usually a companion. He appeared to be quite unconcerned by the long car journey except once, and that was my fault. I was naturally on guard against him jumping out of the car in a panic whenever on the route I had to slow down or stop; but there came a time when I exchanged my ordinary car for a Land Rover. A saloon car you could shut tight but a Land Rover with its canvas hood had potential gaps through which a determined cat might escape. I therefore bought him a basket and at the instant of leaving Mortlake I pushed him in it, banged down the lid and tied it, and set off. It was an appalling miscalculation. Instead of appreciating my action as a gesture towards his own safety, he took it as an insult. He was enraged. He clawed and spat and cried and growled. I was half way to Staines when the noise of his temper forced me to stop, and I gingerly lifted the lid up an inch. A pair of eyes of such fury blazed through the slit that I hastily banged down the lid again.

Now Jeannie was with me on this occasion and inevitably this incident developed an argument. She wanted to take him out of the basket. I was too scared that once allowed to be free there would be no holding him. My imagination saw him gashing us with his claws as he fought to escape, then away like a madman into the countryside. She, however, insisted that only the basket angered him and he would be his old gentle self as soon as he was let out. So the argument went on, past Staines, past Camberley, past Basingstoke; it was not until we reached the outskirts of Andover that I gave in. Monty was released and, with a look of disgust in my direction, the purrs began.

There was another occasion when he travelled as a stowaway on the night train from Paddington. Jeannie was always very proud of this exploit as she was the architect of its success. She was due to join me for the week-end and was dining at the Savoy before catching her sleeper when she suddenly decided she would like Monty to accompany her. She dashed back to Mortlake, found him, after a five minute desperate search, crouched on the wall at the end of the garden, and arrived at Paddington with three minutes to spare. Monty was an admirable conspirator. He remained perfectly still as she rushed him along the platform wrapped in a rug. Not a miaow. Not a growl. And nobody would ever have known that the night train had carried a cat, had Jeannie been able to curb her vociferous enthusiasm when she arrived at Penzance.

But she behaved as if the Crown Jewels were in her compartment. She was in such a high state of excitement when I met her that she did not notice the car attendant was directly behind me as she slid open the door to disclose her secret.

Monty's aplomb was superb. He stared at the man with regal indifference from the bunk. And as I recovered from my surprise and Jeannie muttered feeble excuses, all the car attendant found himself able to say was: 'Good heavens, what a beautiful cat!'

Five minutes later we were in the car on the road to Minack.

Monty was wary in the beginning at Minack. He did not relax on those initial short visits, seldom put his nose outside the cottage, making even a walk of a few yards in our company a notable occasion. He was seven years old and needed time for readjustment.

Minack is a cottage a few hundred yards from the cliff and cupped in a shallow valley with a wood behind it. The walls grow up from great rocks which some crofter a few centuries ago decided would make the ideal foundation. The stones of the walls are bound together with clay and, when we first came, the floor inside the cottage was of earth layered over by thin boards. There are two rooms; one, which is the length of the cottage is our living-room and kitchen, the other a tiny one, is our bedroom; and there is a third room which we added as an extension along with a bathroom that became known in his lifetime as Monty's room. On one side of the cottage the windows stare out undisturbed, except for the old barn buildings, across moorland to the sea and the distant coastline rimming Mount's Bay; on the other, two small windows on either side of the door face a pocket of a garden. The old crofter, the architect of Minack, wished to defend the cottage against the south westerlies; and so this little garden, and the cottage, were set in the hill that rose away to the west. Thus, if we walk up the hill fifty yards and look back, the eye is level with the massive granite chimney; the chimney which to fishermen sailing back to Mousehole and Newlyn in a stormy sea gives the comfortable feeling they are near home.

There is no house or eyesore in sight; and this freedom amid such untamed country provides a sense of immortality. As if here is a life that belongs to any century, that there is no harsh division in time, that the value of true happiness lies in the enduring qualities of nature. The wind blows as it did when the old crofter lived at Minack, so too the robin's song, and the flight of the curlew, and the woodpecker's knock on an elm. This sense of continuity may be unimportant in a world with the knowledge to reach the stars; but to us it provided the antidote to the life we had led. It was a positive reminder that generations had been able to find contentment without becoming slaves of the machine. Here around us were the ghosts of men and animals, long forgotten storms and hot summer days, gathered harvests and the hopes of spring. They were all one, and our future was part of them.

Our plan was to earn a living by growing flowers and, the speciality of the district, early potatoes in pocket meadows on the cliff. We were, however, more influenced by the beauty of the environment than by its practical value; hence we presented ourselves with difficulties which had to be borne as a sacrifice to our whim. There was, for instance, no lane to the cottage. A lane ran from the main road a half mile to a group of farm buildings at the top of the valley; but once past these buildings it became rougher and rougher until it stuttered to a stop amid brambles and gorse. In due course we cut a way through and made a road, but in the beginning the nearest we could take the car to Minack was the distance of two fields; and across these two fields we used to carry our luggage . . . and Monty.

Jeannie on the first visit put butter on his paws. There had been a sad, remarkable case in a newspaper of a cat that had been taken away from his home near Truro to another near Chester from which he had immediately disappeared. Several weeks later he arrived back to his old Truro home but so exhausted and close to starvation that he died a day or two later. I do not pretend to believe this story, documented in detail as it was, but Jeannie did, and she had a vision of Monty dashing from Minack and making for Mortlake. Thus she used the old wives' recipe for keeping a cat at home by buttering his paws; the theory being of course that the cat licks off the butter and says to himself that such a nice taste is worth staying for. A slender theory, I think, though comforting.

But it was soon made clear on that first visit and repeated on succeeding ones that Monty had no intention of running away. It was the opposite that provided us with problems. He never had the slightest wish to leave.

During this period, as I have said, he distrusted the outside around the cottage, made nervous perhaps by the unaccustomed silence and the unknown mysterious scents; and when we urged him to come out with us, he would usually turn tail as soon as we dropped him to the ground and rush back indoors. He was, in fact, sometimes so timid that he annoyed me, and I would pick him up again, deliberately deposit him a hundred yards from the cottage, then, impotently, crossly, watch him race back again.

Why, then, did he always disappear when we were due to start back for Mortlake? The bags would be packed, one load perhaps already lugged across the fields to the car, and there would be no sign of Monty. Obstinately remaining inside the cottage when we wanted him to be out, he was now out when we wanted him to be in. But where? The first disappearance resulted in a delay of two hours in our departure for we had no clue where to look. He had no haunts to which he might have sneaked, because he had never been long enough out of the cottage on his own to find one; no haunts, that is, that we knew of. Yet apparently on one of his brief excursions he had made a note of the barn, and how at the bottom of the barn door was a hole big enough for him to wriggle through; and that as the barn at the time was not ours and the door was kept locked, and the key kept by a farmer ten minutes away, it was a wonderful place to hide in. It became a ritual for him to hide there at the end of each visit. The key fetched, the key returned, and in between I would have had to climb to a beam near the ceiling where Monty glared balefully down at me. Or was he saying: 'I like it here. Hurry up and make it my home?'

It became his home one April evening when the moon was high. We had now cleared a way through the brush of the lane and though the surface was too rough for ordinary cars, it was suitable enough for a Land Rover. On this particular evening we bumped our way along it, the canvas hood bulging with our belongings. Monty alert on Jeannie's lap, both of us ecstatically happy that at last the time-wasting preliminaries had been completed. We drew up with a jerk and I switched off the engine. It was a beautiful moment. No sound but that of the surf in the distance. The moon shimmering the cottage as if it were a ghost cottage. Here was journey's end and adventure's beginning. All we had worked for had materialized.

'Good heavens, we're lucky,' I said, then added briskly as if to foreshadow the practical instead of the romantic side of our life to come, 'I'll get the luggage out ... you go ahead with Monty and light the candles.'

But it was Monty who went ahead. He jumped from Jeannie's lap, paused for a moment to see she was ready to follow, then sedately led the way up the path. A confident cat. A cat who knew he was home. A cat, in fact, who was happy.

Monty's transition into a country cat was a gradual affair. An urban gentleman does not become a country gentleman simply by changing his clothes. He must learn to adopt a new code of manners and a new approach to the outdoors; to be less suave and to show more bluster, to accept the countryside as a jungle which has to be mastered by skill and experience. Monty, as an urban cat, had therefore a lot to learn.

He first had to acclimatize himself to having us always around and he showed his delight in various ways. There was, for instance, the in-and-out window game, a game which was designed not only to display his affection but also to confirm his wonderment that we were now always present to obey his orders. Thus he would jump on a windowsill and ask to be let out, only, a few minutes later, to be outside another window asking to be let in. This performance would continue for an hour until one of us lost patience, saying crossly: 'For goodness' sake, Monty, make up your mind what you want to do.' He would then have the good sense to stop the game, replacing it probably by a short, though vigorous, wash.

There were the unsolicited purrs. A cat has to be in a very bad mood if a human cannot coax him to purr. There is little honour in this achievement, only the satisfaction that a minute or two is being soothed by such a pleasant sound. But the unsolicited purrs belong to quite another category. These are the jewels of the cat fraternity distributed sparingly like high honours in a kingdom. They are brought about by great general contentment. No special incident induces them. No memory of past or prospect of future banquets. Just a whole series of happy thoughts suddenly combine together and whoever is near is lucky enough to hear the result. Thus did Monty from time to time reward us.

My own preference was for the midnight unsolicited purr. For the first years, until we found a fox waiting for Monty to jump out, he had the freedom of the window at night. He used to go in and out and we were never disturbed if he chose to spend the night outside, perhaps in the barn. But when he did choose to remain indoors, and instead of settling on the sofa, preferred a corner of our bed, we felt flattered. It was then that I have relished when sometimes I lay awake, the rich, rolling tones of an unsolicited purr.

In those early days the unsolicited purr was bestowed on us frequently. Later, when country life became to him a continuously happy routine it became rarer; but in the beginning the new pattern of his life was so ebulliently wonderful that he could not restrain himself. There he would be on the carpet in the posture of a Trafalgar lion and suddenly the music would begin. For no reason that we could see. Just his personal ecstasy.

There were other times when his show of affection was awkward. It was then that he posed a question that as a cat hater I used to find easy to answer, but now as a cat lover I found most difficult. How do you summon up courage to dismiss a cat who is paying you the compliment of sitting on your lap?

If you have a train to catch, if your life is governed by rules not of your own making, the excuse for removal is ready made. But in my case time was my own, the work to be done was the product of my own self-discipline, I could not blame anyone else if I shoved off Monty who was comfortably enjoying a rest on my lap. I would gingerly start to lift him up, my hands softly encircling his middle, with the intention of placing him gently on the spot I was about to vacate; and he would hiss, growl and very likely bite my hand. True this was a momentary flash of temper with more noise than harm in it; but the prospect of its display, the certainty I was offending him, were enough time and again for me to postpone any action.

My subservience was made to look even more foolish when Jeannie, as she often did, served a meal on a tray. My seat was always the corner one of the sofa and so I used to endeavour to balance the plate-filled tray partly on the sofa arm, partly on Monty's back; trying, of course, to take great care not to put any weight on Monty. If, however, he showed signs of annoyance, if he woke up from his sleep and turned his head crossly round at me, I would edge the tray further over the arm so that it balanced like the plank of a see-saw. I enjoyed many meals this way in the greatest discomfort.

Rational people would not behave like that. I can imagine my own sneers if a few years before I had seen into the future and found I was going to behave in such a fashion. But there it was, I enjoyed it. I was glad to be of some service, and I used to be tinged with jealousy if he chose on occasions to honour Jeannie instead. Such occasions were rare because her lap was not up to his measurements. He overfilled it. He was like a large man on a small stool. She would sit, transfixed into immobility, and if at the time anything was being cooked in the oven it was sure to be burnt. Pleasure is relative to the desire of the individual. I do not know what pleasure Jeannie could have been offered in exchange for such moments with Monty.

These incidents may suggest that, now that the three of us were always together, Monty was spoilt. But is not a cat's nature, any cat, impervious to being spoilt? You can spoil a child and it can become a nuisance. You can spoil a dog and everyone except its owner is certain to suffer. A cat on the other hand, however luscious may be the bribes, remains cool and collected. Indulgence never goes to its head. It observes flattery instead of accepting it. Monty, for instance, did not consider himself an inferior member of the household; a pet, in fact. Thus he loathed it when condescension was shown to him; and many a misguided stranger trying to lure him with snapping fingers and 'pussy talk' has seen his haughty back. He was co-tenant of the cottage. He was not to be treated in that imbecile fashion so many people reserve for animals. The compliments he wished for were of the kind we gave him; we set out to implement any decision he made on his own by helping to make the result as successful as possible. We played the role of the ideal servants and we won our reward by watching his enjoyment. And there was another reward which Jeannie called 'paying his rent'.

His rent was making him do what he did not want to do. Hence this was the reward we forced him to give us when we felt in the mood to assert our authority. Jeannie might suddenly pick him up, hold him in her arms and hug him, when it was perfectly obvious that he wished to be left by himself. He would lie in her arms, a pained expression on his face, as she talked sweet nothings to him; and then, the rent paid, he would rush across the room to a windowsill and sit there, tail slashing like a scythe, demanding to be let out.

I always maintained that Jeannie demanded more rent than I did. I think she had good reason to do so because she was responsible for his catering; and she was always filling plates or picking up empty ones or asking him to make up his mind what he wanted. 'Oh really, Monty,' she would say in mock fierceness, with Monty looking up at her as she stood by the sink, 'I've just thrown one saucer of milk away, you can't want another!' Or it might be one more morsel of fish required, and out would come the pan and down would go the plate.

His menu, now that we lived near a fishing port, was splendidly varied, and twice a week Jeannie would collect from Newlyn a supply of fresh fish. None of that shop-soiled whiting he used to have but sea-fish whiting, boned megram sole or a little halibut or, what became his most favourite of all – John Dorey, the fish which fishermen themselves take home for their suppers. He would gobble John Dorey until he bulged, one of the few things which lured him to greed; and to satisfy this greed he would try to show his most endearing self to Jeannie. The spot where his saucers were placed was opposite the front door on the carpet at the foot of a bookcase which hid one corner of the sink. When he was hungry, a normal hunger not too demanding, he would sit on this spot, upright with front paws neatly together and the tip of his tail gently flicking them. His eyes would be half closed and he would sway imperceptibly to and fro. A meal was due but he was in no hurry.

Yet if John Dorey was on the menu and was simmering in a pan on the stove he could never restrain his impatience. He would walk excitedly up and down the room, roaring with anticipated pleasure, rubbing himself against Jeannie's legs, looking up at her as if he were saying: 'I love you, I love you.' Here was a cat who was no longer retaining his dignity. Nothing could hide the fact that at this particular moment Monty was thinking that Jeannie was the most wonderful cook in the world.

He would then have been ready to promise her, I am sure, all the rent she required.

Monty's hunting at Mortlake had been limited to indoor mice, or indoor mice which happened to be outside. He soon began to find at Minack a variety of potential victims the like of which he had never seen before; and in some cases he was at a loss to the technique of attack required. I found him once, for instance, staring at a patch of ground under which a mole was digging.

My own first experience of a mole digging was the morning after a night out. It upset me. I was walking across a field, my head down, when I was suddenly aware that a patch of soil the size of a hat was moving. I stopped, stared and pinched myself. The soil circled like a slow spinning top, rising upwards, the texture of a seed bed. Monty saw this for the first time and was as startled as I had been. He put out a paw as if he were thinking of touching a red-hot coal, then leapt backwards with a growl. 'It's only a mole, old chap,' I said knowledgeably, 'only a mole digging a mole hill.' He was reassured enough to advance again. He touched the soil with his paw, then, meeting with no reaction, in fact finding there was no danger or excitement for him at all, he walked away with nonchalant composure; as cats do when they suspect they have made fools of themselves.

Another puzzle for him was what to do when he found an adder. A lizard, a slow worm or an ordinary grass snake was an easy excuse for a few minutes' play, but an adder he sensed was a danger; and he was certainly right. We have too many of them about. We were always on guard during the summer wearing wellington boots whenever we walk through the undergrowth; although it is in a warm spring when they are at their most viperish. I have been happily picking Scilly Whites on the cliff when I have suddenly seen the poised head of one within a few inches of my hand, hissing like escaped steam. In the summer they will wriggle away as you advance towards them and will whip up their heads and strike only if you step on them or tease them. In the spring they will attack at the slightest provocation and, as they have been hibernating through the winter, the venom injected into the wounds made by the fangs is a dose built up over the months. I learnt my lesson after the Scilly Whites, but Monty never learnt his lesson not to tease.

I have seen him touching the tail of an adder with his paw as if he were playing a dare game. It might have been even a form of Russian roulette because an adder can kill a cat, though this is very rare. As an adder is thirty inches long, perhaps he was deceived into thinking that the head was too far away to catch him, or perhaps I was worrying unnecessarily. He certainly never was bitten by an adder, nor for that matter did he ever kill one. He flirted with the danger. It was a game . . . and yet, I wonder. There is a tradition in Cornwall that the capture and killing of an adder is the peak of a cat's hunting career; and when the rare victory is achieved the trophy is ceremoniously dragged whatever distance to the home and deposited on the floor of the kitchen for all to admire. Perhaps this was Monty's secret ambition. Perhaps above all he longed for the plaudits awarded to an adder killer. If so, the fates were against him.

I will not, fortunately, ever know the differences in flavour of mice – indoor mice, harvest mice, long-tailed mice, short-eared mice and so on. Shrews must be unpleasant because Monty, although he would catch them for fun, never ate them. But it seems obvious to me after watching the attitude of Monty that outdoor mice have a far better flavour than the ordinary household mice. At Mortlake, he became, without being flamboyantly successful, a sound indoor-mouse catcher. At Minack he spent so much time outside on the alert that often he lost the desire to fulfil his inside duties; and since the excitement of the chase should be the same both in and out, it occurred to me sometimes that the cause of his extraordinary behaviour may have been a bored palate.

I would be quite wrong to suggest that we were riddled with mice at Minack. For months we would be totally free of any sign of a mouse but at intervals one or two would arrive and cause us annoyance. They would make an unwelcome noise on the boards which provided our ceiling, and on occasions would descend to the sitting-room. Here Monty was often sleeping on the sofa. 'Monty!' I would say sharply. 'There's a mouse in the cupboard.' And Monty would go on sleeping.

The cupboard concerned was the shape of a large wardrobe, shelves climbing two sides while the back was the wall of the cottage. Apart from the china on the shelves with cups on hooks, there was a table in the cupboard on which stood a Calor gas refrigerator; and under the table was the gas cylinder, pots and pans, a bread bin and various other household paraphernalia. Thus the cupboard was crowded and a mouse had a wonderful place to hide unless we set about clearing a space by removing the chattels into the sitting-room. We would perform this tedious task, then wake up Monty, carry him to the cupboard, and deposit him there. He was alone, except for the gas cylinder which was too much trouble to move, with the mouse.

Here, then, was a situation that was often repeated. Monty one side of the gas cylinder and the mouse on the other, and Monty had only to race once round the cylinder to catch it. Yet he would not budge. He would sit looking at me as if he were trying to tell me the mouse was his dearest friend. 'Go on, Monty!' my voice rising to a crescendo. 'Go on, you ass. Catch it!' The mouse would move its position and I would push Monty towards it so that they met nose to nose. Still not a whisker of interest. Nor any sign of fear from the mouse. I would push and exhort and be angry and in the end give up in despair. Monty had a pact with the mouse and nothing I could do would make him break it.

But why? He was swift as a panther when outside. He would be across the land and into the hedge and back again 'with his capture inside a few seconds; and when necessary he had infinite patience. I always found it an endearing sight to look through the window and see him in the distance perched on a rock, staring intently at the grass a yard away; then begin to gather himself for the pounce; shifting the stance of his paws, swaying gently forwards and backwards, until he gauged the great moment had come. And when he missed, when by some miscalculation he ended up in the grass with his back legs spreadeagled and a waving tail denoting his failure, I sensed with him his disappointment. His successes, of course, were loudly trumpeted. He consumed his victims not at the place of execution but on a square yard of ground on the edge of the path leading up to the cottage. No matter how distant the capture he would return with it to this spot; and I would see him coming jauntily up the lane, a mouthful of grass as well as the mouse. A few minutes later when nothing was left he would let out the bellow of victory. 'Well done, Monty,' we would say, 'well done!'

He was a wonderful hunter of rabbits, and he had an earnest idea that these should always be brought into the cottage and left under my desk until I had seen them. This behaviour was prompted by my enthusiasm for the first rabbit he caught. It was a baby one and the incident took place within a month of his arrival at Minack; and because I was so anxious to see him settle down, my enthusiasm and that of Jeannie was far too vociferous.

I was writing a letter and never knew he had entered the room until I heard a soft jungle cry at my feet; and there was Monty, like a retriever, looking up at me with the rabbit beside him. He was inordinately proud of himself. He strode up and down the room as we praised him, with purrs loud enough for three cats, rubbing against us, then scampering back across the room to have another sniff. He never forgot the glory of this moment, and time and again we had to suffer a repeat performance. If we saw him coming we shut the door, and there was always plenty of time to do so. A rabbit was far too big for him to carry in his mouth, and he would pull it along on the ground. 'Poor rabbit,' Jeannie would say, dead though it was.

Monty never touched birds, except once when I saw him catch a wren which annoyed him. Wrens can be foolish and this one was foolish. They are so small that if they kept themselves to themselves no one need know their whereabouts; instead they proclaim their presence by the cross rattle of warning and, in spring, enjoy baiting any objects they dislike. There was Monty lying somnolent in the garden while a pair of wrens rattled around him until he lost his temper and snatched one. I dashed forward, caught him, and put a hand to his mouth; and as I did so, he let the wren go and it flew safely away to a bush where it began its rattle again. And Monty went back to doze.

Monty's docile attitude to birds met its response from them. They showed no fear of him. It was I, if anything, who felt fear. I was always waiting for the incident that never happened.

Flush

VIRGINIA WOOLF

Elizabeth Barrett, poet and invalid, found solace and companionship, before her subsequent marriage to Robert Browning, in the devoted love and loyalty of her golden cocker spaniel, Flush...

ALL RESEARCHES HAVE failed to fix with any certainty the exact year of Flush's birth, let alone the month or the day; but it is likely that he was born some time early in the year 1842. It is also probable that he was directly descended from Tray (*c.* 1816), whose points, preserved unfortunately only in the untrustworthy medium of poetry, prove him to have been a red cocker spaniel of merit. There is every reason to think that Flush was the son of that 'real old cocking spaniel' for whom Dr. Mitford refused twenty guineas 'on account of his excellence in the field'. It is to poetry, alas, that we have to trust for our most detailed description of Flush himself as a young dog. He was of that particular shade of dark brown which in sunshine flashes 'all over into gold'. His eyes were 'startled eyes of hazel bland'. His ears were 'tasselled'; his 'slender feet' were 'canopied in fringes' and his tail was broad. Making allowance for the exigencies of rhyme and the inaccuracies of poetic diction, there is nothing here but what would meet with the approval of the Spaniel Club. We cannot doubt that Flush was a pure-bred Cocker of the red variety marked by all the characteristic excellences of his kind.

The first months of his life were passed at Three Mile Cross, a working man's cottage near Reading. Since the Mitfords had fallen on evil days – Kerenhappock was the only servant – the chair-covers were made by Miss Mitford herself and of the cheapest material; the most important article of furniture seems to have been a large table; the most important room a large greenhouse – it is unlikely that Flush was surrounded by any of those luxuries, rain-proof kennels, cement walks, a maid or boy attached to her person, that would now be accorded a dog of his rank. But he throve; he enjoyed with all the vivacity of his temperament most of the pleasures and some of the licences natural to his youth and sex. Miss Mitford, it is true, was much confined to the cottage. She had to read aloud to her father hour after hour; then to play cribbage; then, when at last he slumbered, to write and write and write at the table in the greenhouse in the attempt to pay their bills and settle their debts. But at last the longed-for moment would come. She thrust her papers aside, clapped a hat on her head, took her umbrella and set off for a walk across the fields with her dogs. Spaniels are by nature sympathetic; Flush, as his story proves, had an even excessive appreciation of human emotions. The sight of his dear mistress snuffing the fresh air at last, letting it ruffle her white hair and redden the natural freshness of her face, while the lines on her huge brow smoothed themselves out, excited him to gambols whose wildness was half sympathy with her own delight. As she strode through the long grass so he leapt hither and thither, parting its green curtain. The cool globes of dew or rain broke in showers of iridescent spray about his nose; the earth, here hard, here soft, here hot, here cold, stung, teased and tickled the soft pads of his feet. Then what a variety of smells interwoven in subtlest combination thrilled his nostrils; strong smells of earth, sweet smells of flowers; nameless smells of leaf and bramble; sour smells as they crossed the road; pungent smells as they entered beanfields. But suddenly down the wind came tearing a smell sharper, stronger, more lacerating than any – a smell that ripped across his brain stirring a thousand instincts, releasing a million memories – the smell of hare, the smell of fox. Off he flashed like a fish drawn in a rush through water further and further. He forgot his mistress; he forgot all human kind. He heard dark men cry 'Span! Span!' He heard whips crack. He raced; he rushed. At last he stopped bewildered; the incantation faded; very slowly, wagging his tail sheepishly, he trotted back across the fields to where Miss Mitford stood shouting 'Flush! Flush! Flush!' and waving her umbrella. And once at least the call was even more imperious; the hunting horn roused deeper instincts, summoned wilder and stronger emotions that transcended memory and obliterated grass, trees, hare, rabbit, fox in one wild shout of ecstasy. Love blazed her torch in his eyes; he heard the hunting horn of Venus. Before he was well out of his puppyhood, Flush was a father.

Such conduct in a man even, in the year 1842, would have called for some excuse from a biographer; in a woman no excuse could have availed; her name must have been blotted in ignominy from the page. But the moral code of dogs, whether better or worse, is certainly different from ours, and there was nothing in Flush's conduct in this respect that requires a veil now, or unfitted him for the society of the purest and the chastest in the land then. There is evidence, that is to say, that the elder brother of Dr. Pusey was anxious to buy him. Deducing from the known character of Dr. Pusey the probable character of his brother, there must have been something serious, solid, promising well for future excellence whatever might be the levity of the present in Flush even as a puppy. But a much more significant testimony to the attractive nature of his gifts is that, even though Mr. Pusey wished to buy him, Miss Mitford refused to sell him. As she was at her wits' end for money, scarcely knew indeed what tragedy to spin, what annual to edit, and was reduced to the repulsive expedient of asking her friends for help, it must have gone hard with her to refuse the sum offered by the elder brother of Dr. Pusey. Twenty pounds had been offered for Flush's father. Miss Mitford might well have asked ten or fifteen for Flush. Ten or fifteen pounds was a princely sum, a magnificent sum to have at her disposal. With ten or fifteen pounds she might have re-covered her chairs, she might have re-stocked her greenhouse, she might have bought herself an entire wardrobe, and 'I have not bought a bonnet, a cloak, a gown, hardly a pair of gloves', she wrote in 1842, 'for four years'.

But to sell Flush was unthinkable. He was of the rare order of objects that cannot be associated with money. Was he not of the still rarer kind that, because they typify what is spiritual, what is beyond price, become a fitting token of the disinterestedness of friendship; may be offered in that spirit to a friend, if one is lucky enough to have one, who is more like a daughter than a friend; to a friend who lies secluded all through the summer months in a back bedroom in Wimpole Street, to a friend who is no other than England's foremost poetess, the brilliant, the doomed, the adored Elizabeth Barrett herself? Such were the thoughts that came more and more frequently to Miss Mitford as she watched Flush rolling and scampering in the sunshine; as she sat by the couch of Miss Barrett in her dark, ivy-shaded London bedroom. Yes; Flush was worthy of Miss Barrett; Miss Barrett was worthy of Flush. The sacrifice was a great one; but the sacrifice must be made. Thus, one day, probably in the early summer of the year 1842, a remarkable couple might have been seen taking their way down Wimpole Street – a very short, stout, shabby, elderly lady, with a bright red face and bright white hair, who led by the chain a very spirited, very inquisitive, very well-bred golden cocker spaniel puppy. They walked almost the whole length of the street until at last they paused at No. 50. Not without trepidation, Miss Mitford rang the bell.

Even now perhaps nobody rings the bell of a house in Wimpole Street without trepidation. It is the most august of London streets, the most impersonal. Indeed, when the world seems tumbling to ruin, and civilization rocks on its foundations, one has only to go to Wimpole Street; to pace that avenue; to survey those houses; to consider their uniformity; to marvel at the window curtains and their consistency; to admire the brass knockers and their regularity; to observe butchers tendering joints and cooks receiving them; to reckon the incomes of the inhabitants and infer their consequent submission to the laws of God and man – one has only to go to Wimpole Street and drink deep of the peace breathed by authority in order to heave a sigh of thankfulness that, while Corinth has fallen and Messina has tumbled, while crowns have blown down the wind and old Empires have gone up in flames, Wimpole Street has remained unmoved, and, turning from Wimpole Street into Oxford Street, a prayer rises in the heart and bursts from the lips that not a brick of Wimpole Street may be re-pointed, not a curtain washed, not a butcher fail to tender or a cook to receive the sirloin, the haunch, the breast, the ribs of mutton and beef for ever and ever, for as long as Wimpole Street remains, civilization is secure.

The butlers of Wimpole Street move ponderously even to-day; in the summer of 1842 they were more deliberate still. The laws of livery were then more stringent; the ritual of the green baize apron for cleaning silver; of the striped waistcoat and swallow-tail black coat for opening the hall door, was more closely observed. It is likely then that Miss Mitford and Flush were kept waiting at least three minutes and a half on the door-step. At last, however, the door of number fifty was flung wide; Miss Mitford and Flush were ushered in. Miss Mitford was a frequent visitor; there was nothing to surprise, though something to subdue her, in the sight of the Barrett family mansion. But the effect upon Flush must have been overwhelming in the extreme. Until this moment he had set foot in no house but the working man's cottage at Three Mile Cross. The boards there were bare; the mats were frayed; the chairs were cheap. Here there was nothing bare, nothing frayed, nothing cheap – that Flush could see at a glance. Mr. Barrett, the owner, was a rich merchant; he had a large family of grown-up sons and daughters, and a retinue, proportionately large, of servants. His house was furnished in the fashion of the late 'thirties, with some tincture, no doubt, of that Eastern fantasy which had led him when he built a house in Shropshire to adorn it with the domes and crescents of Moorish architecture. Here in Wimpole Street such extravagance would not be allowed; but we may suppose that the high dark rooms were full of ottomans and carved mahogany; tables were twisted; filigree ornaments stood upon them; daggers and swords hung upon wine-dark walls; curious objects brought from his East Indian property stood in recesses, and thick rich carpets clothed the floors.

But as Flush trotted up behind Miss Mitford, who was behind the butler, he was more astonished by what he smelt than by what he saw. Up the funnel of the staircase came warm whiffs of joints roasting, of fowls basting, of soups simmering – ravishing almost as food itself to nostrils used to the meagre savour of Kerenhappock's penurious fries and hashes. Mixing with the smell of food were further smells – smells of cedarwood and sandalwood and mahogany; scents of male bodies and female bodies; of men servants and maid servants; of coats and trousers; of crinolines and mantles; of curtains of tapestry, of curtains of plush; of coal dust and fog; of wine and cigars. Each room as he passed it – dining-room, drawing-room, library, bedroom – wafted out its own contribution to the general stew; while, as he set down first one paw and then another, each was caressed and retained by the sensuality of rich pile carpets closing amorously over it. At length they reached a closed door at the back of the house. A gentle tap was given; gently the door was opened.

Miss Barrett's bedroom – for such it was – must by all accounts have been dark. The light, normally obscured by a curtain of green damask, was in summer further dimmed by the ivy, the scarlet runners, the convolvuluses and the nasturtiums which grew in the window-box. At first Flush could distinguish nothing in the pale greenish gloom but five white globes glimmering mysteriously in mid-air. But again it was the smell of the room that overpowered him. Only a scholar who has descended step by step into a mausoleum and there finds himself in a crypt, crusted with fungus, slimy with mould, exuding sour smells of decay and antiquity, while half-obliterated marble busts gleam in mid-air and all is dimly seen by the light of the small swinging lamp which he holds, and dips and turns, glancing now here, now there – only the sensations of such an explorer into the buried vaults of a ruined city can compare with the riot of emotions that flooded Flush's nerves as he stood for the first time in an invalid's bedroom, in Wimpole Street, and smelt eau-de-Cologne.

Very slowly, very dimly, with much sniffing and pawing, Flush by degrees distinguished the outlines of several articles of furniture. That huge object by the window was perhaps a wardrobe. Next to it stood, conceivably, a chest of drawers. In the middle of the room swam up to the surface what seemed to be a table with a ring round it; and then the vague amorphous shapes of armchair and table emerged. But everything was disguised. On top of the wardrobe stood three white busts; the chest of drawers was surmounted by a bookcase; the bookcase was pasted over with crimson merino; the washing-table had a coronal of shelves upon it; on top of the shelves that were on top of the washing-table stood two more busts. Nothing in the room was itself; everything was something else. Even the window-blind was not a simple muslin blind; it was a painted fabric with a design of castles and gateways and groves of trees, and there were several peasants taking a walk. Looking-glasses further distorted these already distorted objects so that there seemed to be ten busts of ten poets instead of five; four tables instead of two. And suddenly there was a more terrifying confusion still. Suddenly Flush saw staring back at him from a hole in the wall another dog with bright eyes flashing, and tongue lolling! He paused amazed. He advanced in awe.

Thus advancing, thus withdrawing, Flush scarcely heard, save as the distant drone of wind among the treetops, the murmur and patter of voices talking. He pursued his investigations, cautiously, nervously, as an explorer in a forest softly advances his foot, uncertain whether that shadow is a lion, or that root a cobra. At last, however, he was aware of huge objects in commotion over him; and, unstrung as he was by the experiences of the past hour, he hid himself, trembling, behind a screen. The voices ceased. A door shut. For one instant he paused, bewildered, unstrung. Then with a pounce as of clawed tigers memory fell upon him. He felt himself alone – deserted. He rushed to the door. It was shut. He pawed, he listened. He heard footsteps descending. He knew them for the familiar footsteps of his mistress. They stopped. But no – on they went, down they went. Miss Mitford was slowly, was heavily, was reluctantly descending the stairs. And as she went, as he heard her footsteps fade, panic seized upon him. Door after door shut in his face as Miss Mitford went downstairs; they shut on freedom; on fields; on hares, on grass; on his adored, his venerated mistress – on the dear old woman who had washed him and beaten him and fed him from her own plate when she had none too much to eat herself – on all he had known of happiness and love and human goodness! There! The front door slammed. He was alone. She had deserted him.

Then such a wave of despair and anguish overwhelmed him, the irrevocableness and implacability of fate so smote him, that he lifted up his head and howled aloud. A voice said 'Flush'. He did not hear it. 'Flush', it repeated a second time. He started. He had thought himself alone. He turned. Was there something alive in the room with him? Was there something on the sofa? In the wild hope that this being, whatever it was, might open the door, that he might still rush after Miss Mitford and find her – that this was some game of hide-and-seek such as they used to play in the greenhouse at home – Flush darted to the sofa.

'Oh, Flush!' said Miss Barrett. For the first time she looked him in the face. For the first time Flush looked at the lady lying on the sofa.

Each was surprised. Heavy curls hung down on either side of Miss Barrett's face; large bright eyes shone out; a large mouth smiled. Heavy ears hung down on either side of Flush's face; his eyes, too, were large and bright: his mouth was wide. There was a likeness between them. As they gazed at each other each felt: Here am I – and then each felt: But how different! Hers was the pale worn face of an invalid, cut off from air, light, freedom. His was the warm ruddy face of a young animal; instinct with health and energy. Broken asunder, yet made in the same mould, could it be that each completed what was dormant in the other? She might have been – all that; and he – But no. Between them lay the widest gulf that can separate one being from another. She spoke. He was dumb. She was woman; he was dog. Thus closely united, thus immensely divided, they gazed at each other. Then with one bound Flush sprang on to the sofa and laid himself where he was to lie for ever after – on the rug at Miss Barrett's feet.

The summer of 1842 was, historians tell us, not much different from other summers, yet to Flush it was so different that he must have doubted if the world itself were the same. It was a summer spent in a bedroom a summer spent with Miss Barrett. It was a summer spent in London, spent in the heart of civilization. At first he saw nothing but the bedroom and its furniture, but that alone was surprising enough. To identify, distinguish and call by their right names all the different articles he saw there was confusing enough. And he had scarcely accustomed himself to the tables, to the busts, to the washing-stands – the smell of eau-de-Cologne still affected his nostrils disagreeably, when there came one of those rare days which are fine but not windy, warm but not baking, dry but not dusty, when an invalid can take the air. The day came when Miss Barrett could safely risk the huge adventure of going shopping with her sister.

The carriage was ordered; Miss Barrett rose from her sofa; veiled and muffled, she descended the stairs. Flush of course went with her. He leapt into the carriage by her side. Couched on her lap, the whole pomp of London at its most splendid burst on his astonished eyes. They drove along Oxford Street. He saw houses made almost entirely of glass. He saw windows laced across with glittering streamers; heaped with gleaming mounds of pink, purple, yellow, rose. The carriage stopped. He entered mysterious arcades filmed with clouds and webs of tinted gauze. A million airs from China, from Arabia, wafted their frail incense into the remotest fibres of his senses. Swiftly over the counters flashed yards of gleaming silk; more darkly, more slowly rolled the ponderous bombazine. Scissors snipped; coins sparkled. Paper was folded; string tied. What with nodding plumes, waving streamers, tossing horses, yellow liveries, passing faces, leaping, dancing up, down, Flush, satiated with the multiplicity of his sensations, slept, drowsed, dreamt and knew no more until he was lifted out of the carriage and the door of Wimpole Street shut on him again.

And next day, as the fine weather continued, Miss Barrett ventured upon an even more daring exploit – she had herself drawn up Wimpole Street in a bath-chair. Again Flush went with her. For the first time he heard his nails click upon the hard paving-stones of London. For the first time the whole battery of a London street on a hot summer's day assaulted his nostrils. He smelt the swooning smells that lie in the gutters; the bitter smells that corrode iron railings; the fuming, heady smells that rise from basements – smells more complex, corrupt, violently contrasted and compounded than any he had smelt in the fields near Reading; smells that lay far beyond the range of the human nose; so that while the chair went on, he stopped, amazed; defining, savouring, until a jerk at his collar dragged him on. And also, as he trotted up Wimpole Street behind Miss Barrett's chair he was dazed by the passage of human bodies. Petticoats swished at his head; trousers brushed his flanks; sometimes a wheel whizzed an inch from his nose; the wind of destruction roared in his ears and fanned the feathers of his paws as a van passed. Then he plunged in terror. Mercifully the chain tugged at his collar; Miss Barrett held him tight, or he would have rushed to destruction.

At last, with every nerve throbbing and every sense singing, he reached Regent's Park. And then when he saw once more, after years of absence it seemed, grass, flowers and trees, the old hunting cry of the fields hallooed in his ears and he dashed forward to run as he had run in the fields at home. But now a heavy weight jerked at his throat; he was thrown back on his haunches. Were there not trees and grass? he asked. Were these not the signals of freedom? Had he not always leapt forward directly Miss Mitford started on her walk? Why was he a prisoner here? He paused. Here, he observed, the flowers were massed far more thickly than at home; they stood, plant by plant, rigidly in narrow plots. The plots were intersected by hard black paths. Men in shiny top-hats marched ominously up and down the paths. At the sight of them he shuddered closer to the chair. He gladly accepted the protection of the chain. Thus before many of these walks were over a new conception had entered his brain. Setting one thing beside another, he had arrived at a conclusion. Where there are flower-beds there are asphalt paths; where there are flower-bed and asphalt paths, there are men in shiny top-hats; where there are flower-beds and asphalt paths and men with shiny top-hats, dogs must be led on chains. Without being able to decipher a word of the placard at the Gate, he had learnt his lesson – in Regent's Park dogs must be led on chains.

And to this nucleus of knowledge, born from the strange experiences of the summer of 1842, soon adhered another; dogs are not equal, but different. At Three Mile Cross Flush had mixed impartially with tap-room dogs and the Squire's greyhounds; he had known no difference between the tinker's dog and himself. Indeed it is probable that the mother of his child, though by courtesy called Spaniel, was nothing but a mongrel, eared in one way, tailed in another. But the dogs of London, Flush soon discovered, are strictly divided into different classes. Some are chained dogs; some run wild. Some take their airings in carriages and drink from purple jars; others are unkempt and uncollared and pick up a living in the gutter. Dogs therefore, Flush began to suspect, differ; some are high, others low; and his suspicions were confirmed by snatches of talk held in passing with the dogs of Wimpole Street. 'See that scallywag? A mere mongrel! . . . By gad, that's a fine Spaniel. One of the best blood in Britain! . . . Pity his ears aren't a shade more curly . . . There's a topknot for you!'

From such phrases, from the accent of praise or derision in which they were spoken, at the pillar-box or outside the public-house where footmen were exchanging racing tips, Flush knew before the summer had passed that there is no equality among dogs: some dogs are high dogs; some are low. Which, then, was he? No sooner had Flush got home than he examined himself carefully in the looking-glass. Heaven be praised, he was a dog of birth and breeding! His head was smooth; his eyes were prominent but not gozzled; his feet were feathered; he was the equal of the best-bred cocker in Wimpole Street. He noted with approval the purple jar from which he drank – such are the privileges of rank; he bent his head quietly to have the chain fixed to his collar – such are its penalties. When about this time Miss Barrett observed him staring in the glass, she was mistaken. He was a philosopher, she thought, meditating the difference between appearance and reality. On the contrary, he was an aristocrat considering his points.

But the fine summer days were soon over; the autumn winds began to blow; and Miss Barrett settled down to a life of complete seclusion in her bedroom. Flush's life was also changed. His outdoor education was supplemented by that of the bedroom, and this, to a dog of Flush's temperament, was the most drastic that could have been invented. His only airings, and these were brief and perfunctory, were taken in the company of Wilson, Miss Barrett's maid. For the rest of the day he kept his station on the sofa at Miss Barrett's feet. All his natural instincts were thwarted and contradicted. When the autumn winds had blown last year in Berkshire he had run in wild scampering across the stubble; now at the sound of the ivy tapping on the pane Miss Barrett asked Wilson to see to the fastenings of the window. When the leaves of the scarlet runners and nasturtiums in the window-box yellowed and fell she drew her Indian shawl more closely round her. When the October rain lashed the window Wilson lit the fire and heaped up the coals. Autumn deepened into winter and the first fogs jaundiced the the air. Wilson and Flush could scarcely grope their way to the pillar-box or to the chemist. When they came back, nothing could be seen in the room but the pale busts glimmering wanly on the tops of the wardrobes; the peasants and the castle had vanished on the blind; blank yellow filled the pane. Flush felt that he and Miss Barrett lived alone together in a cushioned and firelit cave. The traffic droned on perpetually outside with muffled reverberations; now and again a voice went calling hoarsely, 'Old chairs and baskets to mend', down the street: sometimes there was a jangle of organ music, coming nearer and louder; going further and fading away. But none of these sounds meant freedom, or action, or exercise. The wind and the rain, the wild days of autumn and the cold days of mid-winter, all alike meant nothing to Flush except warmth and stillness; the lighting of lamps, the drawing of curtains and the poking of the fire.

At first the strain was too great to be borne. He could not help dancing round the room on a windy autumn day when the partridges must be scattering over the stubble. He thought he heard guns on the breeze. He could not help running to the door with his hackles raised when a dog barked outside. And yet when Miss Barrett called him back, when she laid her hand on his collar, he could not deny that another feeling, urgent, contradictory, disagreeable – he did not know what to call it or why he obeyed it – restrained him. He lay still at her feet. To resign, to control, to suppress the most violent instincts of his nature – that was the prime lesson of the bedroom school, and it was one of such portentous difficulty that many scholars have learnt Greek with less – many battles have been won that cost their generals not half such pain. But then, Miss Barrett was the teacher. Between them, Flush felt more and more strongly, as the weeks wore on, was a bond, an uncomfortable yet thrilling tightness; so that if his pleasure was her pain, then his pleasure was pleasure no longer but three parts pain. The truth of this was proved every day. Somebody opened the door and whistled him to come. Why should he not go out? He longed for air and exercise; his limbs were cramped with lying on the sofa. He had never grown altogether used to the smell of eau-de-Cologne. But no – though the door stood open, he would not leave Miss Barrett. He hesitated half-way to the door and then went back to the sofa. 'Flushie', wrote Miss Barrett, 'is my friend – my companion – and loves me better than he loves the sunshine without.' She could not go out. She was chained to the sofa. 'A bird in a cage would have as good a story,' she wrote, as she had. And Flush, to whom the whole world was free, chose to forfeit all the smells of Wimpole Street in order to lie by her side.

And yet sometimes the tie would almost break; there were vast gaps in their understanding. Sometimes they would lie and stare at each other in blank bewilderment. Why, Miss Barrett wondered, did Flush tremble suddenly, and whimper and start and listen? She could hear nothing; she could see nothing; there was nobody in the room with them. She could not guess that Folly, her sister's little King Charles, had passed the door; or that Catiline the Cuba bloodhound had been given a mutton-bone by a footman in the basement. But Flush knew; he heard; he was ravaged by the alternate rages of lust and greed. Then with all her poet's imagination Miss Barreett could not divine what Wilson's wet umbrella meant to Flush; what memories it recalled, of forests and parrots and wild trumpeting elephants; nor did she know, when Mr. Kenyon stumbled over the bell-pull, that Flush heard dark men cursing in the mountains; the cry, 'Span! Span!' rang in his ears, and it was in some muffled, ancestral rage that he bit him.

Flush was equally at a loss to account for Miss Barrett's emotions. There she would lie hour after hour passing her hand over a white page with a black stick; and her eyes would suddenly fill with tears; but why? 'Ah, my dear Mr. Horne,' she was writing. 'And then came the failure in my health . . . and then the enforced exile to Torquay . . . which gave a nightmare to my life for ever, and robbed it of more than I can speak of here; do not speak of that anywhere. *Do not speak of that,* dear Mr. Horne.' But there was no sound in the room, no smell to make Miss Barrett cry. Then again Miss Barrett, still agitating her stick, burst out laughing. She had drawn 'a very neat and characteristic portrait of Flush, humorously made rather like myself', and she had written under it 'only fails of being an excellent substitute for mine through being more worthy than I can be counted'. What was there to laugh at in the black smudge that she held out for Flush to look at? He could smell nothing; he could hear nothing. There was nobody in the room with them. The fact was that they could not communicate with words, and it was a fact that led undoubtedly to much misunderstanding. Yet did it not lead also to a peculiar intimacy? 'Writing,' Miss Barrett once exclaimed after a morning's toil, 'writing, writing . . .' After all, she may have thought, do words say everything? Can words say anything? Do not words destroy the symbols that lie beyond the reach of words? Once at least Miss Barrett seems to have found it so. She was lying, thinking; she had forgotten Flush altogether, and her thoughts were so sad that the tears fell upon the pillow. Then suddenly a hairy head was pressed against her; large bright eyes shone in hers; and she started. Was it Flush, or was it Pan? Was she no longer an invalid in Wimpole Street, but a Greek nymph in some dim grove in Arcady? And did the bearded god himself press his lips to hers? For a moment she was transformed; she was a nymph and Flush was Pan. The sun burnt and love blazed. But suppose Flush had been able to speak – would he not have said something sensible about the potato disease in Ireland? So, too, Flush felt strange stirrings at work within him. When he saw Miss Barrett's thin hands delicately lifting some silver box or pearl ornament from the ringed table, his own furry paws seemed to contract and he longed that they should fine themselves to ten separate fingers. When he heard her low voice syllabling innumerable sounds, he longed for the day when his own rough roar would issue like hers in the little simple sounds that had such mysterious meaning. And when he watched the same finger for ever crossing a white page with a straight stick, he longed for the time when he too should blacken paper as she did.

And yet, had he been able to write as she did? – The question is superfluous happily, for truth compels us to say that in the year 1842–43 Miss Barrett was not a nymph but an invalid; Flush was not a poet but a red cocker spaniel; and Wimpole Street was not Arcady but Wimpole Street.

African Game
SIR H. RIDER HAGGARD

*In the days before universal recognition of the need to conserve
the world's wildlife, Haggard's famous hero, Allan Quatermain,
pits his wits against the animals of the African plains . . .*

ON THE FOLLOWING MORNING at daylight I started out shooting. As we
were short of meat I determined to kill a buffalo, of which there were
plenty about, before looking for traces of elephants. Not more than half
a mile from camp we came across a trail broad as a cart-road, evidently
made by a great herd of buffaloes which had passed up at dawn from
their feeding ground in the marshes, to spend the day in the cool air of
the uplands. This trail I followed boldly; for such wind as there was
blew straight down the mountain-side, that is, from the direction in
which the buffaloes had gone, to me. About a mile further on the forest
began to be dense, and the nature of the trail showed me that I must be
close to my game. Another two hundred yards and the bush was so thick
that, had it not been for the trail, we could scarcely have passed through
it. As it was, Gobo, who carried my eight-bore rifle (for I had the
.570-express in my hand), and the other two men whom I had taken
with me, showed the very strongest dislike to going any further, pointing
out that there was 'no room to run away.' I told them that they need not
come unless they liked, but that I was certainly going on; and then,
growing ashamed, they came.

Another fifty yards, and the trail opened into a little glade. I knelt
down and peeped and peered, but no buffalo could I see. Evidently the
herd had broken up here – I knew that from the spoor – and penetrated
the opposite bush in little troops. I crossed the glade, and choosing one

line of spoor, followed it for some sixty yards, when it became clear to me that I was surrounded by buffaloes; and yet so dense was the cover that I could not see any. A few yards to my left I could hear one rubbing its horns against a tree, while from my right came an occasional low and throaty grunt which told me that I was uncomfortably near an old bull. I crept on towards him with my heart in my mouth, as gently as though I were walking upon eggs for a bet, lifting every little bit of wood in my path, and placing it behind me lest it should crack and warn the game. After me in single file came my three retainers, and I don't know which of them looked the most frightened. Presently Gobo touched my leg; I glanced round, and saw him pointing slantwise towards the left. I lifted my head a little and peeped over a mass of creepers; beyond the creepers was a dense bush of sharp-pointed aloes, of that kind of which the leaves project laterally, and on the other side of the aloes, not fifteen paces from us, I made out the horns, neck, and the ridge of the back of a tremendous old bull. I took my eight-bore, and getting on to my knee prepared to shoot him through the neck, taking my chance of cutting his spine. I had already covered him as well as the aloe leaves would allow, when he gave a kind of sigh and lay down.

I looked round in dismay. What was to be done now? I could not see to shoot him lying down, even if my bullet would have pierced the intervening aloes – which was doubtful – and if I stood up he would either run away or charge me. I reflected, and came to the conclusion that the only thing to do was to lie down also; for I did not fancy wandering after other buffaloes in that dense bush. If a buffalo lies down, it is clear that he must get up again some time, so it was only a case of patience – 'fighting the fight of sit down,' as the Zulus say.

Accordingly I sat down and lighted a pipe, thinking that the smell of it might reach the buffalo and make him get up. But the wind was the wrong way, and it did not; so when it was done I lit another. Afterwards I had cause to regret that pipe.

Well, we squatted like this for between half and three quarters of an hour, till at length I began to grow heartily sick of the performance. It was about as dull a business as the last hour of a comic opera. I could hear buffaloes snorting and moving all round, and see the red-beaked tic birds flying up off their backs, making a kind of hiss as they did so, something like that of an English missel-thrush, but I could not see a single buffalo. As for my old bull, I think he must have slept the sleep of the just, for he never even stirred.

Just as I was making up my mind that something must be done to save the situation, my attention was attracted by a curious grinding noise. At first I thought that it must be a buffalo chewing the cud, but was obliged to abandon the idea because the noise was too loud. I shifted myself round and stared through the cracks in the bush, in the direction whence the sound seemed to come, and once I thought that I saw something gray moving about fifty yards off, but could not make certain. Although the grinding noise still continued I could see nothing more, so I gave up thinking about it, and once again turned my attention to the buffalo. Presently, however, something happened. Suddenly from about forty yards away there came a tremendous snorting sound, more like that made by an engine getting a heavy train under weigh than anything else in the world.

'By Jove,' I thought, turning round in the direction from which the grinding sound had come, 'that must be a rhinoceros, and he has got our wind.' For, as you fellows know, there is no mistaking the sound made by a rhinoceros when he gets wind of you.

Another second, and I heard a most tremendous crashing noise. Before I could think what to do, before I could even get up, the bush behind me seemed to burst asunder, and there appeared not eight yards from us, the great horn and wicked twinkling eye of a charging rhinoceros. He had winded us or my pipe, I do not know which, and, after the fashion of these brutes, had charged up the scent. I could not rise, I could not even get the gun up, I had no time. All that I was able to do was to roll over as far out of the monster's path as the bush would allow. Another second and he was over me, his great bulk towering above me like a mountain, and, upon my word, I could not get his smell out of my nostrils for a week. Circumstances impressed it on my memory, at least I suppose so. His hot breath blew upon my face, one of his front feet just missed my head, and his hind one actually trod upon the loose part of my trousers and pinched a little bit of my skin. I saw him pass over me lying as I was upon my back, and next second I saw something else. My men were a little behind me, and therefore straight in the path of the rhinoceros. One of them flung himself backwards into the bush, and thus avoided him. The second with a wild yell sprung to his feet, and bounded like an india-rubber ball right into the aloe bush, landing well among the spikes. But the third, it was my friend Gobo, could not by any means get away. He managed to gain his feet, and that was all. The rhinoceros was charging with his head low; his horn passed between Gobo's legs, and feeling something on his nose, he jerked it up. Away went Gobo, high into the air. He turned a complete somersault at the apex of the curve, and as he did so, I caught sight of his face. It was gray with terror, and his mouth was wide open. Down he came, right on to the great brute's back, and that broke his fall. Luckily for him the rhinoceros never turned, but crashed straight through the aloe bush, only missing the man who had jumped into it by about a yard.

Then followed a complication. The sleeping buffalo on the further side of the bush, hearing the noise, sprang to his feet, and for a second, not knowing what to do, stood still. At that instant the huge rhinoceros blundered right on to him, and getting his horn beneath his stomach gave him such a fearful dig that the buffalo was turned over on to his back,

311

while his assailant went a most amazing cropper over his carcase. In another moment, however, the rhinoceros was up, and wheeling round to the left, crashed through the bush down-hill and towards the open country.

Instantly the whole place became alive with alarming sounds. In every direction troops of snorting buffaloes charged through the forest, wild with fright, while the injured bull on the further side of the bush began to bellow like a mad thing. I lay quite still for a moment, devoutly praying that none of the flying buffaloes would come my way. Then when the danger lessened I got on to my feet, shook myself, and looked round. One of my boys, he who had thrown himself backward into the bush, was already half way up a tree – if heaven had been at the top of it he could not have climbed quicker. Gobo was lying close to me, groaning vigorously, but, as I suspected, quite unhurt; while from the aloe bush into which No. 3 had bounded like a tennis ball, issued a succession of the most piercing yells.

I looked, and saw that this unfortunate fellow was in a very tight place. A great spike of aloe had run through the back of his skin waist-belt, though without piercing his flesh, in such a fashion that it was impossible for him to move, while within six feet of him the injured buffalo bull, thinking, no doubt, that he was the aggressor, bellowed and ramped to get at him, tearing the thick aloes with his great horns. That no time was to be lost, if I wished to save the man's life, was very clear. So seizing my eight-bore, which was fortunately uninjured, I took a pace to the left, for the rhinoceros had enlarged the hole in the bush, and aimed at the point of the buffalo's shoulder, since on account of my position I could not get a fair side shot for the heart. As I did so I saw that the rhinoceros had given the bull a tremendous wound in the stomach, and that the shock of the encounter had put his left hind-leg out of joint at the hip. I fired, and the bullet striking the shoulder broke it, and knocked the buffalo down. I knew that he could not get up any more, because he was now injured fore and aft, so notwithstanding his terrific bellows I scrambled round to where he was. There he lay glaring furiously and tearing up the soil with his horns. Stepping up to within two yards of him I aimed at the vertebra of his neck and fired. The bullet struck true, and with a thud he dropped his head upon the ground, groaned, and died.

This little matter having been attended to with the assistance of Gobo, who had now found his feet, I went on to extricate our unfortunate companion from the aloe bush. This we found a thorny task, but at last he was dragged forth uninjured, though in a very pious and prayerful frame of mind. His 'spirit had certainly looked that way,' he said, or he would now have been dead. As I never like to interfere with true piety, I did not venture to suggest that his spirit had deigned to make use of my eight-bore in his interest.

Having despatched this boy back to the camp to tell the bearers to come and cut the buffalo up, I bethought me that I owed that rhinoceros a grudge which I should love to repay. So without saying a word of what was in my mind to Gobo, who was now more than ever convinced that Fate walked about loose in Wambe's country, I just followed on the brute's spoor. He had crashed through the bush till he reached the little glade. Then moderating his pace somewhat, he had followed the glade down its entire length, and once more turned to the right through the forest, shaping his course for the open land that lies between the edge of the bush and the river. Having followed him for a mile or so further, I found myself quite on the open. I took out my glasses and searched the plain. About a mile ahead was something brown – as I thought, the rhinoceros. I advanced another quarter of a mile, and looked once more – it was not the rhinoceros, but a big ant-heap. This was puzzling, but I did not like to give it up, because I knew from his spoor that he must be somewhere ahead. But as the wind was blowing straight from me towards the line that he had followed, and as a rhinoceros can smell you for about a mile, it would not, I felt, be safe to follow his trail any further; so I made a détour of a mile and more, till I was nearly opposite the ant-heap, and then once more searched the plain. It was no good, I could see nothing of him, and was about to give it up and start after some oryx I saw on the skyline, when suddenly at a distance of about three hundred yards from the ant-heap, and on its further side, I saw my rhino stand up in a patch of grass.

'Heavens!' I thought to myself, 'he's off again;' but no, after standing staring for a minute or two he once more lay down.

Now I found myself in a quandary. As you know, a rhinoceros is a very short-sighted brute, indeed his sight is as bad as his scent is good. Of this fact he is perfectly aware, but he always makes the most of his natural gifts. For instance, when he lies down he invariably does so with his head down wind. Thus, if any enemy crosses his wind he will still be able to escape, or attack him; and if, on the other hand, the danger approaches up wind he will at least have a chance of seeing it. Otherwise, by walking delicately, one might actually kick him up like a partridge, if only the advance was made up wind.

Well, the point was, how on earth should I get within shot of this rhinoceros? After much deliberation I determined to try a side approach, thinking that in this way I might get a shoulder shot. Accordingly we started in a crouching attitude, I first, Gobo holding on to my coat tails, and the other boy on to Gobo's moocha. I always adopt this plan when stalking big game, for if you follow any other system the bearers will get out of line. We arrived within three hundred yards safely enough, and then the real difficulties began. The grass had been so closely eaten off by game that there was scarcely any cover. Consequently it was necessary to go on to our hands and knees, which in my case involved laying down the eightbore at every step and then lifting it up again. However, I wriggled along somehow, and if it had not been for Gobo and his friend no doubt everything would have gone well. But as you have, I dare say, observed, a native out stalking is always of that mind which is supposed to actuate an ostrich – so long as his head is hidden he seems to think that nothing else can be seen. So it was in this instance, Gobo and the other boy crept along on their hands and toes with their heads well down, but, though unfortunately I did not notice it till too late, bearing the fundamental portions of their frames high in the air. Now all animals are quite as suspicious of this end of mankind as they are of his face, and of that fact I soon had a proof. Just when we had got within about two hundred yards, and I was congratulating myself that I had not had this long crawl with the sun beating on the back of my neck like a furnace for nothing, I heard the hissing note of the rhinoceros birds, and up flew four or five of them from the brute's back, where they had been comfortably employed in catching tics. Now this performance on the part of the birds is to a rhinoceros what the word 'cave' is to a schoolboy – it puts him on the *qui vive* at once. Before the birds were well in the air I saw the grass stir.

'Down you go,' I whispered to the boys, and as I did so the rhinoceros got up and glared suspiciously around. But he could see nothing, indeed if we had been standing up I doubt if he would have seen us at that distance; so he merely gave two or three sniffs and then lay down, his head still down wind, the birds once more settling on his back.

But it was clear to me that he was sleeping with one eye open, being generally in a suspicious and unchristian frame of mind, and that it was useless to proceed further on this stalk, so we quietly withdrew to consider the position and study the ground. The results were not satisfactory. There was absolutely no cover about except the ant-heap, which was some three hundred yards from the rhinocerous upon his up-wind side. I knew that if I tried to stalk him in front I should fail, and so I should if I attempted to do so from the further side – he or the birds would see me; so I came to a conclusion: I would go to the ant-heap, which would give him my wind, and instead of stalking him I would let him stalk me. It was a bold step, and one which I should never advise a hunter to take, but somehow I felt as though rhino and I must play the hand out.

I explained my intentions to the men, who both held up their arms in horror. Their fears for my safety were a little mitigated, however, when I told them that I did not expect them to come with me.

Gobo breathed a prayer that I might not meet Fate walking about, and the other one sincerely trusted that my spirit might look my way when the rhinoceros charged, and then they both departed to a place of safety.

Taking my eight-bore, and half-a-dozen spare cartridges in my pocket, I made a détour, and reaching the ant-heap in safety lay down. For a moment the wind had dropped, but presently a gentle puff of air passed over me, and blew on towards the rhinoceros. By the way, I wonder what it is that smells so strong about a man? Is it his body or his breath? I have never been able to make out, but I saw it stated the other day, that in the duck decoys the man who is working the ducks holds a little piece of burning turf before his mouth, and that if he does this they cannot smell him, which looks as though it were the breath. Well, whatever it was about me that attracted his attention, the rhinoceros soon smelt me, for within half a minute after the puff of wind had passed he was on his legs, and turning round to get his head up wind. There he stood for a few seconds and sniffed, and then he began to move, first of all at a trot, then, as the scent grew stronger, at a furious gallop. On he came, snorting like a runaway engine, with his tail stuck straight up in the air; if he had seen me lie down there he could not have made a better line. It was rather nervous work, I can tell you, lying there waiting for his onslaught, for he looked like a mountain of flesh. I determined, however, not to fire till I could plainly see his eye, for I think that rule always gives one the right distance for big game; so I rested my rifle on the ant-heap and waited for him, kneeling. At last, when he was about forty yards away, I saw that the time had come, and aiming straight for the middle of the chest I pulled.

Thud went the heavy bullet, and with a tremendous snort over rolled the rhinoceros beneath its shock, just like a shot rabbit. But if I had thought that he was done for I was mistaken, for in another second he was up again, and coming at me as hard as ever, only with his head held low. I waited till he was within ten yards, in the hope that he would expose his chest, but he would do nothing of the sort; so I just had to fire at his head with the left barrel, and take my chance. Well, as luck would have it, of course the animal put its horn in the way of the bullet, which cut clean through it about three inches above the root and then glanced off into space.

After that things got rather serious. My gun was empty and the rhinoceros was rapidly arriving, so rapidly indeed that I came to the conclusion that I had better make way for him. Accordingly I jumped to my feet and ran to the right as hard as I could go. As I did so he arrived full tilt, knocked my friendly ant-heap flat, and for the third time that day went a most magnificent cropper. This gave me a few seconds' start, and I ran down wind – my word, I did run! Unfortunately, however, my modest retreat was observed, and the rhinoceros, as soon as he found his legs again, set to work to run after me. Now no man on earth can run so fast as an irritated rhinoceros can gallop, and I knew that he must soon catch me up. But having some slight experience of this sort of thing, luckily for myself, I kept my head, and as I fled I managed to open my rifle, get the old cartridges out, and put in two fresh ones. To do this I was obliged to steady my pace a little, and by the time that I had snapped the rifle to I heard the beast snorting and thundering away within a few paces of my back. I stopped, and as I did so rapidly cocked the rifle and slued round upon my heel. By this time the brute was within six or seven yards of me, but luckily his head was up. I lifted the rifle and fired at him. It was a snap shot, but the bullet struck him in the chest within three inches of the first, and found its way into his lungs. It did not stop him, however, so all I could do was to bound to one side, which I did with suprising activity, and as he brushed past me to fire the other barrel into his side. That did for him. The ball passed in behind the shoulder and right through his heart. He fell over on to his side, gave one most awful squeal, – a dozen pigs could not have made such a noise, – and promptly died, keeping his wicked eyes wide open all the time.

As for me, I blew my nose, and going up to the rhinoceros sat on his head, and reflected that I had done a capital morning's shooting.

After this, as it was now midday, and I had killed enough meat, we marched back triumphantly to camp, where I proceeded to concoct a stew of buffalo beef and compressed vegetables. When this was ready we ate the stew, and then I took a nap. About four o'clock Gobo woke me up, and told me that the head man of one of Wambe's kraals had arrived to see me. I ordered him to be brought up, and presently he came, a little, wizened, talkative old man, with a waistcloth round his middle, and a greasy, frayed kaross made of the skins of rock rabbits over his shoulders.

I told him to sit down, and then abused him roundly. 'What did he mean,' I asked, 'by disturbing me in this rude way? How did he dare to cause a person of my quality and evident importance to be awakened in order to interview his entirely contemptible self?'

I spoke thus because I knew that it would produce an impression on him. Nobody, except a really great man, he would argue, would dare to speak to him in that fashion. Most savages are desperate bullies at heart, and look on insolence as a sign of power.

The old man instantly collapsed. He was utterly overcome, he said; his heart was split in two, and well realized the extent of his misbehaviour. But the occasion was very urgent. He heard that a mighty hunter was in the neighbourhood, a beautiful white man, how beautiful he could not have imagined had he not seen (this to me!), and he came to beg his assistance. The truth was, that three bull elephants such as no man ever saw had for years been the terror of their kraal, which was but a small place – a cattle kraal of the great chief Wambe's, where they lived to keep the cattle. And now of late these elephants had done them much damage; but last night they had destroyed a whole patch of mealie land, and he feared that if they came back they would all starve next season for want of food. Would the mighty white man then be pleased to come and kill the elephants? It would be easy for him to do – oh, most easy! It was only necessary that he should hide himself in a tree, for there was a full moon, and then when the elephants appeared he would speak to them with the gun, and they would fall down dead, and there would be an end of their troubling.

Of course I hummed and hawed, and made a great favour of consenting to this proposal, though really I was delighted to have such a chance. One of the conditions that I made was that a messenger should at once be despatched to Wambe, whose kraal was two days' journey from where I was, telling him that I proposed to come and pay my respects to him in a few days, and to ask his formal permission to shoot in his country. Also I intimated that I was prepared to present him with 'hongo,' that is, blackmail, and that I hoped to do a little trade with him in ivory, of which I heard he had a great quantity.

This message the old gentleman promised to despatch at once, though there was something about his manner which showed me that he was doubtful as to how it would be received. After that we struck our camp and moved on to the kraal, which we reached about an hour before sunset. This kraal was a collection of huts surrounded by a slight thorn-fence, perhaps there were ten of them in all. It was situated in a kloof of the mountain down which a rivulet flowed. The kloof was densely wooded, but for some distance above the kraal it was free from bush, and here on the rich deep ground brought down by the rivulet were the cultivated lands, in extent somewhere about twenty or twenty-five acres. On the kraal side of these lands stood a single hut, that served for a mealie store, which at the moment was used as a dwelling-place by an old woman, the first wife of our friend the head man.

It appears that this lady, having had some difference of opinion with her husband about the extent of authority allowed to a younger and more amiable wife, had refused to dwell in the kraal any more, and, by way of marking her displeasure, had taken up her abode among the mealies. As the issue will show, she was, it happened, cutting off her nose to spite her face.

Close by this hut grew a large baobab tree. A glance at the mealie grounds showed me that the old head man had not exaggerated the mischief done by the elephants to his crops, which were now getting ripe. Nearly half of the entire patch was destroyed. The great brutes had eaten all they could, and the rest they had trampled down. I went up to their spoor and started back in amazement – never had I seen such spoor before. It was simply enormous, more especially that of one old bull, that carried, so said the natives, but a single tusk. One might have used any of the footprints for a hip-bath.

Having taken stock of the position, my next step was to make arrangements for the fray. The three bulls, according to the natives, had been spoored into the dense patch of bush above the kloof. Now it seemed to me very probable that they would return to-night to feed on the remainder of the ripening mealies. If so, there was a bright moon, and it struck me

317

that by the exercise of a little ingenuity I might bag one or more of them without exposing myself to any risk, which, having the highest respect for the aggressive powers of bull elephants, was a great consideration to me.

This then was my plan. To the right of the huts as you look up the kloof, and commanding the mealie lands, stands the baobab tree that I have mentioned. Into that baobab tree I made up my mind to go. Then if the elephants appeared I should get a shot at them. I announced my intentions to the head man of the kraal, who was delighted. 'Now,' he said, 'his people might sleep in peace, for while the mighty white hunter sat aloft like a spirit watching over the welfare of his kraal what was there to fear?'

I told him that he was an ungrateful brute to think of sleeping in peace while, perched like a wounded vulture on a tree, I watched for his welfare in wakeful sorrow; and once more he collapsed, and owned that my words were 'sharp but just.'

However, as I have said, confidence was completely restored; and that evening everybody in the kraal, including the superannuated victim of jealousy in the little hut where the mealie cobs were stored, went to bed with a sense of sweet security from elephants and all other animals that prowl by night.

For my part, I pitched my camp below the kraal; and then, having procured a beam of wood from the head man – rather a rotten one, by the way – I set it across two boughs that ran out laterally from the baobab tree, at a height of about twenty-five feet from the ground, in such fashion that I and another man could sit upon it with our legs hanging down, and rest our backs against the bole of the tree. This done I went back to the camp and ate my supper. About nine o'clock, half-an-hour before the moon-rise, I summoned Gobo, who, thinking that he had seen about enough of the delights of big game hunting for that day, did not altogether relish the job; and, despite his remonstrances, gave him my eight-bore to carry, I having the .570–express. Then we set out for the tree. It was very dark, but we found it without difficulty, though climbing it was a more complicated matter. However, at last we got up and sat down, like two little boys on a form that is too high for them, and waited. I did not dare to smoke, because I remembered the rhinoceros, and feared that the elephants might wind the tobacco if they should come my way, and this made the business more wearisome, so I fell to thinking and wondering at the completeness of the silence.

At last the moon came up, and with it a moaning wind, at the breath of which the silence began to whisper mysteriously. Lonely enough in the newborn light looked the wide expanse of mountain, plain, and forest, more like some vision of a dream, some reflection from a fair world of peace beyond our ken, than the mere face of garish earth made soft with sleep. Indeed, had it not been for the fact that I was beginning to find the log on which I sat very hard, I should have grown quite sentimental over the beautiful sight; but I will defy anybody to become sentimental when seated in the damp, on a very rough beam of wood, and half-way up a tree. So I merely made a mental note that it was a particularly lovely night, and turned my attention to the prospect of elephants. But no elephants came, and after waiting for another hour or so, I think that what between weariness and disgust, I must have dropped into a gentle doze. Presently I awoke with a start. Gobo, who was perched close to me, but as far off as the beam would allow – for neither white man nor black like the aroma which each vows is the peculiar and disagreeable property of the other – was faintly, very faintly clicking his forefinger against his thumb. I knew by this signal, a very favourite one among native hunters and gun-bearers, that he must have seen or heard something. I looked at his face, and saw that he was staring excitedly towards the dim edge of the bush beyond the deep green line of mealies. I stared too, and listened. Presently I heard a soft large sound as though a giant were gently stretching out his hands and pressing back the ears of standing corn. Then came a pause, and then, out into the open majestically stalked the largest elephant I ever saw or ever shall see. Heavens! what a monster he was; and how the moonlight gleamed upon his one splendid tusk – for the other was missing – as he stood among the mealies gently moving his enormous ears to and fro, and testing the wind with his trunk. While I was still marvelling at his girth, and speculating upon the weight of that huge tusk, which I swore should be my tusk before very long, out stepped a second bull and stood beside him. He was not quite so tall, but he seemed to me to be almost thicker-set than the first; and even in that light I could see that both his tusks were perfect. Another pause, and the third emerged. He was shorter than either of the others, but higher in the shoulder than No. 2; and when I tell you, as I afterwards learnt from actual measurement, that the smallest of these three mighty bulls measured twelve feet one and a half inches at the shoulder, it will give you some idea of their size. The three formed into line and stood still for a minute, the one-tusked bull gently caressing the elephant on the left with his trunk.

Then they began to feed, walking forward and slightly to the right as they gathered great bunches of the sweet mealies and thrust them into their mouths. All this time they were more than a hundred and twenty yards away from me (this I knew, because I had paced the distances from the tree to various points), much too far to allow of my attempting a shot at them in that uncertain light. They fed in a semicircle, gradually drawing round towards the hut near my tree, in which the corn was stored and the old woman slept.

This went on for between an hour and an hour and a half, till, what between excitement and hope, that maketh the heart sick, I grew so weary that I was actually contemplating a descent from the tree and a

319

moonlight stalk. Such an act in ground so open would have been that of a stark staring lunatic, and that I should even have been contemplating it will show you the condition of my mind. But everything comes to him who knows how to wait, and sometimes too to him who doesn't, and so at last those elephants, or rather one of them, came to me.

After they had fed their fill, which was a very large one, the noble three stood once more in line some seventy yards to the left of the hut, and on the edge of the cultivated lands, or in all about eighty-five yards from where I was perched. Then at last the one with a single tusk made a peculiar rattling noise in his trunk, just as though he were blowing his nose, and without more ado began to walk deliberately toward the hut where the old woman slept. I made my rifle ready and glanced up at the moon, only to discover that a new complication was looming in the immediate future. I have said that a wind rose with the moon. Well, the wind brought rain-clouds along its track. Several light ones had already lessened the light for a little while, though without obscuring it, and now two more were coming up rapidly, both of them very black and dense. The first cloud was small and long, and the one behind big and broad. I remember noticing that the pair of them bore a most comical resemblance to a dray drawn by a very long raw-boned horse. As luck would have it, just as the elephant arrived within twenty-five yards or so of me, the head of the horse-cloud floated over the face of the moon, rendering it impossible for me to fire. In the faint twilight which remained, however, I could just make out the gray mass of the great brute still advancing towards the hut. Then the light went altogether and I had to trust to my ears. I heard him fumbling with his trunk, apparently at the roof of the hut; next came a sound as of straw being drawn out, and then for a little while there was complete silence.

The cloud began to pass; I could see the outline of the elephant; he was standing with his head quite over the top of the hut. But I could not see his trunk, and no wonder, for it was *inside the hut*. He had thrust it through the roof, and, attracted no doubt by the smell of the mealies, was groping about with it inside. It was growing light now, and I got my rifle ready, when suddenly there was a most awful yell, and I saw the trunk reappear, and in its mighty fold the old woman who had been sleeping in the hut. Out she came through the hole like a periwinkle on the point of a pin, still wrapped up in her blanket, and with her skinny legs and arms stretched to the four points of the compass, and as she did so, gave that most alarming screech. I really don't know who was most frightened, she, or I, or the elephant. At any rate the last was considerably startled; he had been fishing for mealies – the old woman was a mere accident, and one that greatly discomposed his nerves. He gave a sort of trumpet, and threw her away from him right into the crown of a low mimosa tree, where she stuck shrieking like a metropolitan engine. The old bull lifted his tail, and flapping his great ears prepared for flight. I put up my eight-bore, and aiming hastily at the point of his shoulder (for he was broadside on), I fired. The report rang out like thunder, making a thousand echoes in the quiet hills. I saw him go down all of a heap as though he were stone dead. Then, alas! whether it was the kick of a heavy rifle, or the excited bump of that idiot Gobo, or both together, or merely an unhappy coincidence, I do not know, but the rotton beam broke and I went down too, landing flat at the foot of the tree upon a certain humble portion of the human frame. The shock was so severe that I felt as though all my teeth were flying through the roof of my mouth, but although I sat slightly stunned for a few seconds, luckily for me I fell light, and was not in any way injured.

Meanwhile the elephant began to scream with fear and fury, and, attracted by his cries, the other two charged up. I felt for my rifle; it was not there. Then I remembered that I had rested it on a fork of the bough in order to fire, and doubtless there it remained. My position now was very unpleasant. I did not dare to try and climb the tree again, which, shaken as I was, would have been a task of some difficulty, because the elephants would certainly see me, and Gobo, who had clung to a bough, was still aloft with the other rifle. I could not run because there was no shelter near. Under these circumstances I did the only thing feasible, clambered round the trunk as softly as possible, and keeping one eye on the elephants, whispered to Gobo to bring down the rifle, and awaited the developement of the situation. I knew that if the elephants did not see me – which, luckily, they were too enraged to do – they would not smell me, for I was up-wind. Gobo, however, either did not, or, preferring the safety of the tree, would not hear me. He said the former, but I believed the latter, for I knew that he was not enough of a sportsman to really enjoy shooting elephants by moonlight in the open. So there I was behind my tree, dismayed, unarmed, but highly interested, for I was witnessing a remarkable performance.

When the two other bulls arrived the wounded elephant on the ground ceased to scream, but began to make a low moaning noise, and to gently touch the wound near his shoulder, from which the blood was literally spouting. The other two seemed to understand; at any rate, they did this. Kneeling down on either side, they placed their trunks and tusks underneath him, and, aided by his own efforts, with one great lift got him on to his feet. Then leaning against him on either side to support him, they marched off at a walk in the direction of the village. It was a pitiful sight, and even then it made me feel a brute.

Presently, from a walk, as the wounded elephant gathered himself together a little, they broke into a trot, and after that I could follow them no longer with my eyes, for the second black cloud came up over the moon and put her out, as an extinguisher puts out a dip. I say with my eyes, but my ears still gave me a very fair notion of what was going on. When the cloud came up the three terrified animals were heading directly for the kraal, probably because the way was open and the path easy. I fancy that they grew confused in the darkness, for when they came to the kraal fence they did not turn aside, but crashed straight through it. Then there were 'times,' as the Irish servant-girl says in the American book. Having taken the fence, they thought that they might as well take the kraal also, so they just ran over it. One hive-shaped hut was turned quite over on to its top, and when I arrived upon the scene the people who had been sleeping there were bumbling about inside like bees disturbed at night, while two more were crushed flat, and a third had all its side torn out. Oddly enough, however, nobody was hurt, though several people had a narrow escape of being trodden to death.

On arrival I found the old head man in a state painfully like that favoured by Greek art, dancing about in front of his ruined abodes as vigorously as though he had just been stung by a scorpion.

I asked him what ailed him, and he burst out into a flood of abuse. He called me a Wizard, a Sham, a Fraud, a Bringer of bad luck! I had promised to kill the elephants, and I had so arranged things that the elephants had nearly killed him, etc.

This, still smarting, or rather aching, as I was from that most terrific bump, was too much for my feelings, so I just made a rush at my friend, and getting him by the ear, I banged his head against the doorway of his own hut, which was all that was left of it.

'You wicked old scoundrel,' I said, 'you dare to complain about your own trifling inconveniences, when you gave me a rotten beam to sit on, and thereby delivered me to the fury of the elephant' (*bump! bump! bump!*), 'when your own wife' (*bump!*) 'has just been dragged out of her hut' (*bump!*) 'like a snail from its shell, and thrown by the Earth-shaker into a tree' (*bump! bump!*).

'Mercy, my father, mercy!' gasped the old fellow. 'Truly I have done amiss – my heart tells me so.'

'I should hope it did, you old villain' (*bump!*).

'Mercy, great white man! I thought the log was sound. But what says the unequalled chief – is the old woman, my wife, indeed dead? Ah, if she is dead all may yet prove to have been for the very best;' and he clasped his hands and looked up piously to heaven, in which the moon was once more shining brightly.

I let go his ear and burst out laughing, the whole scene and his devout aspirations for the decease of the partner of his joys, or rather woes, were so intensely ridiculous.

'No, you old iniquity,' I answered; 'I left her in the top of a thorn-tree, screaming like a thousand bluejays. The elephant put her there.'

'Alas! alas!' he said, 'surely the back of the ox is shaped to the burden, Doubtless, my father, she will come down when she is tired;' and without troubling himself further about the matter, he began to blow at the smouldering embers of the fire.

And, as a matter of fact, she did appear a few minutes later, considerably scratched and startled, but none the worse.

After that I made my way to my little camp, which, fortunately, the elephants had not walked over, and wrapping myself up in a blanket, was soon fast asleep.

And so ended my first round with those three elephants.

On the morrow I woke up full of painful recollections, and not without a certain feeling of gratitude to the Powers above that I was there to wake up. Yesterday had been a tempestuous day; indeed, what between buffalo, rhinoceros, and elephant, it had been very tempestuous. Having realized this fact, I next bethought me of those magnificent tusks, and instantly, early as it was, broke the tenth commandment. I coveted my neighbour's tusks, if an elephant could be said to be my neighbour *de jure*, as certainly, so recently as the previous night, he had been *de facto* – a much closer neighbour than I cared for, indeed. Now when you covet your neighbour's goods, the best thing, if not the most moral thing, to do is to enter his house as a strong man armed, and take them. I was not a strong man, but having recovered my eight-bore I was armed, and so was the other strong man – the elephant with the tusks. Consequently I prepared for a struggle to the death. In other words, I summoned my faithful retainers, and told them that I was now going to follow those elephants over the edge of the world, if necessary. They showed a certain bashfulness about the business, but they did not gainsay me, because they dared not. Ever since I had prepared with all due solemnity to execute the rebellious Gobo they had conceived a great respect for me.

So I went up to bid adieu to the old head man, whom I found alternately contemplating the ruins of his kraal and, with the able assistance of his last wife, thrashing the jealous lady who had slept in the mealie hut, because she was, as he declared, the fount of all his sorrows.

Leaving them to work a way through their domestic differences, I levied a supply of vegetable food from the kraal in consideration of services rendered, and left them with my blessing. I do not know how they settled matters, because I have not seen them since.

Then I started on the spoor of the three bulls. For a couple of miles or so below the kraal – as far, indeed, as the belt of swamp that borders the river – the ground is at this spot rather stony, and clothed with scattered bushes. Rain had fallen towards the daybreak, and this fact, together with the nature of the soil, made spooring a very difficult business. The wounded bull had indeed bled freely, but the rain had washed the blood off the leaves and grass, and the ground being so rough and hard did not take the footmarks so clearly as was convenient. However, we got along, though slowly, partly by the spoor, and partly by carefully lifting leaves and blades of grass, and finding blood underneath them, for the blood gushing from a wounded animal often falls

323

upon their inner surfaces, and then, of course, unless the rain is very heavy, it is not washed away. It took us something over an hour and a half to reach the edge of the marsh, but once there our task became much easier, for the soft soil showed plentiful evidences of the great brutes' passage. Threading our way through the swampy land, we came at last to a ford of the river, and here we could see where the poor wounded animal had lain down in the mud and water in the hope of easing himself of his pain, and could see also how his two faithful companions had assisted him to rise again. We crossed the ford, and took up the spoor on the further side, and followed it into the marsh-like land beyond. No rain had fallen on this side of the river, and the blood-marks were consequently much more frequent.

All that day we followed the three bulls, now across open plains, and now through patches of bush. They seemed to have travelled on almost without stopping, and I noticed that as they went the wounded bull recovered his strength a little. This I could see from his spoor, which had become firmer, and also from the fact that the other two had ceased to support him. At last evening closed in, and having travelled some eighteen miles, we camped, thoroughly tired out.

Before dawn on the following day we were up, and the first break of light found us once more on the spoor. About half-past five o'clock we reached the place where the elephants had fed and slept. The two unwounded bulls had taken their fill, as the condition of the neighbouring bushes showed, but the wounded one had eaten nothing. He had spent the night leaning against a good-sized tree, which his weight had pushed out of the perpendicular. They had not long left this place, and could not be very far ahead, especially as the wounded bull was now again so stiff after his night's rest that for the first few miles the other two had been obliged to support him. But elephants go very quick, even when they seem to be travelling slowly, for shrub and creepers that almost stop a man's progress are no hindrance to them. The three had now turned to the left, and were travelling back again in a semicircular line toward the mountains, probably with the idea of working round to their old feeding grounds on the further side of the river.

There was nothing for it but to follow their lead, and accordingly we followed with industry. Through all that long hot day did we tramp, passing quantities of every sort of game, and even coming across the spoor of other elephants. But, in spite of my men's entreaties, I would not turn aside after these. I would have those mighty tusks or none.

By evening we were quite close to our game, probably within a quarter of a mile, but the bush was dense, and we could see nothing of them, so once more we must camp, thoroughly disgusted with our luck. That night, just after the moon rose, while I was sitting smoking my pipe with my back against a tree, I heard an elephant trumpet, as though something had startled it, and not three hundred yards away. I was very tired, but my curiosity overcame my weariness, so, without saying a word to any of the men, all of whom were asleep, I took my eight-bore and a few spare cartridges, and steered toward the sound. The game path which we had been following all day ran straight on in the direction from which the elephant had trumpeted. It was narrow, but well trodden, and the light struck down upon it in a straight white line. I crept along it cautiously for some two hundred yards, when it opened suddenly into a most beautiful glade some hundred yards or more in width, wherein tall grass grew and flat-topped trees stood singly. With the caution born of long experience I watched for a few moments before I entered the glade, and then I saw why the elephant had trumped. There in the middle of the glade stood a large maned lion. He stood quite still, making a soft purring noise, and waving his tail to and fro. Presently the grass about forty yards on the hither side of him gave a wide ripple, and a lioness sprang out of it like a flash, and bounded noiselessly up to the lion. Reaching him, the great cat halted suddenly, and rubbed her head against his shoulder. Then they both began to purr loudly, so loudly that I believe that in the stillness one might have heard them two hundred yards or more away.

After a time, while I was still hesitating what to do, either they got a whiff of my wind, or they wearied of standing still, and determined to start in search of game. At any rate, as though moved by a common impulse, they bounded suddenly away, leap by leap, and vanished in the depths of the forest to the left. I waited for a little while longer to see if there were any more yellow skins about, and seeing none, came to the conclusion that the lions must have frightened the elephants away, and that I had taken my stroll for nothing. But just as I was turning back I thought that I heard a bough break upon the further side of the glade, and, rash as the act was, I followed the sound. I crossed the glade as silently as my own shadow. On its further side the path went on. Albeit with many fears, I went on too. The jungle growth was so thick here that it almost met overhead, leaving so small a passage for the light that I could scarcely see to grope my way along. Presently, however, it widened, and then opened into a second glade slightly smaller than the first, and there, on the further side of it, about eighty yards from me, stood the three enormous elephants.

They stood thus: – Immediately opposite and facing me was the wounded one-tusked bull. He was leaning his bulk against a dead thorn-tree, the only one in the place, and looked very sick indeed. Near him stood the second bull as though keeping a watch over him. The third elephant was a good deal nearer to me and broadside on. While I was still staring at them, this elephant suddenly walked off and vanished down a path in the bush to the right.

There were now two things to be done – either I could go back to the camp and advance upon the elephants at dawn, or I could attack them at once. The first was, of course, by far the wiser and safer course. To engage one elephant by moonlight and single-handed is a sufficiently rash proceeding; to tackle three was little short of lunacy. But, on the other hand, I knew that they would be on the marsh again before daylight, and there might come another day of weary trudging before I could catch them up, or they might escape me altogether.

'No,' I thought to myself, 'faint heart never won fair tusk. I'll risk it, and have a slap at them. But how?' I could not advance across the open, for they would see me; clearly the only thing to do was to creep round in the shadow of the bush and try to come upon them so. So I started. Seven or eight minutes of careful stalking brought me to the mouth of the path down which the third elephant had walked. The other two were now about fifty yards from me, and the nature of the wall of bush was such that I could not see how to get nearer to them without being discovered. I hesitated, and peeped down the path which the elephant had followed. About five yards in, it took a turn round a shrub. I thought that I would just have a look behind it, and advanced, expecting that I should be able to catch a sight of the elephant's tail. As it happened, however, I met his trunk coming round the corner. It is very disconcerting to see an elephant's trunk when you expect to see his tail, and for a moment I stood paralyzed almost under the vast brute's head, for he was not five yards from me. He too halted, having seen or winded me, probably the latter, and then threw up his trunk and trumpeted preparatory to a charge. I was in for it now, for I could not escape either to the right or left, on account of the bush, and I did not dare turn my back. So I did the only thing that I could do – raised the rifle and fired at the black mass of his chest. It was too dark for me to pick a shot; I could only brown him, as it were.

The shot rung out like thunder on the quiet air, and the elephant answered it with a scream, then dropped his trunk and stood for a second or two as still as though he had been cut in stone. I confess that I lost my head; I ought to have fired my second barrel, but I did not. Instead of doing so, I rapidly opened my rifle, pulled out the old cartridge from the right barrel and replaced it. But before I could snap the breech to, the bull was at me. I saw his great trunk fly up like a brown beam, and I waited no longer. Turning, I fled for dear life, and after me thundered the elephant. Right into the open glade I ran, and then, thank Heaven, just as he was coming up with me the bullet took effect on him, He had been shot right through the heart, or lungs, and down he fell with a crash, stone dead.

But in escaping from Scylla I had run into the jaws of Charybdis. I heard the elephant fall, and glanced round. Straight in front of me, and not fifteen paces away, were the other two bulls. They were staring about, and at that moment they caught sight of me. Then they came, the pair of them – came like thunderbolts, and from different angles. I had only time to snap my rifle to, lift it, and fire, almost at haphazard, at the head of the nearest, the unwounded bull.

Now, as you know, in the case of the African elephant, whose skull is convex, and not concave like that of the Indian, this is always a most risky and very frequently a perfectly useless shot. The bullet loses itself in the masses of bone, that is all. But there is one little vital place, and should the bullet happen to strike there, it will follow the channel of the nostrils – at least I suppose it is that of the nostrils – and reach the brain. And this was what happened in the present case – the ball struck the fatal spot in the region of the eye and travelled to the brain. Down came the great bull all of a heap, and rolled on to his side as dead as a stone. I swung round at that instant to face the third, the monster bull with one tusk that I had wounded two days before. He was already almost over me, and in the dim moonlight seemed to tower above me like a house. I lifted the rifle and pulled at his neck. It would not go off ! Then, in a flash, as it were, I remembered that it was on the half-cock. The lock of this barrel was a little weak, and a few days before, in firing at a cow eland, the left barrel had jarred off at the shock of the discharge of the right, knocking me backwards with the recoil; so after that I had kept it on the half-cock till I actually wanted to fire it.

I gave one desperate bound to the right, and, my lame leg notwith-standing, I believe that few men could have made a better jump. At any rate, it was none too soon, for as I jumped I felt the wind made by the tremendous downward stroke of the monster's trunk. Then I ran for it.

I ran like a buck, still keeping hold of my gun, however. My idea, so far as I could be said to have any fixed idea, was to bolt down the pathway up which I had come, like a rabbit down a burrow, trusting that he would lose sight of me in the uncertain light. I sped across the glade. Fortunately the bull, being wounded, could not go full speed; but wounded or no, he could go quite as fast as I could. I was unable to gain an inch, and away we went, with just about three feet between our separate extremities. We were at the other side now, and a glance served to show me that I had miscalculated and overshot the opening. To reach it now was hopeless; I should have blundered straight into the elephant. So I did the only thing I could do: I swerved like a course hare, and started off round the edge of the glade, seeking for some opening into which I could plunge. This gave me a moment's start, for the bull could not turn as quickly as I could, and I made the most of it. But no opening could I see; the bush was like a wall. We were speeding round the edge of the glade, and the elephant was coming up again. Now he was within about six feet, and now, as he trumpeted or rather screamed, I could feel the fierce hot blast of his breath strike upon my head. Heavens! how it frightened me!

We were three parts round the glade now, and about fifty yards ahead

327

was the single large dead thorn-tree against which the bull had been leaning. I spurted for it; it was my last chance of safety. But spurt as I would, it seemed hours before I got there. Putting out my right hand, I swung round the tree, thus bringing myself face to face with the elephant. I had not time to lift the rifle to fire, I had barely time to cock it, and run sideways and backward, when he was on to me. Crash! he came, striking the tree full with his forehead. It snapped like a carrot about forty inches from the ground. Fortunately I was clear of the trunk, but one of the dead branches struck me on the chest as it went down and swept me to the ground. I fell upon my back, and the elephant blundered past me as I lay. More by instinct than anything else I lifted the rifle with one hand and pulled the trigger. It exploded, and, as I discovered afterwards, the bullet struck him in the ribs. But the recoil of the heavy rifle held thus was very severe; it bent my arm up, and sent the butt with a thud against the top of my shoulder and the side of my neck, for the moment quite paralyzing me, and causing the weapon to jump from my grasp. Meanwhile the bull was rushing on. He travelled for some twenty paces, and then suddenly he stopped. Faintly I reflected that he was coming back to finish me, but even the prospect of imminent and dreadful death could not rouse me into action. I was utterly spent; I could not move.

Idly, almost indifferently, I watched his movements. For a moment he stood still, next he trumpeted till the welkin rang, and then very slowly, and with great dignity, he knelt down. At this point I swooned away.

When I came to myself again I saw from the moon that I must have been insensible for quite two hours. I was drenched with dew, and shivering all over. At first I could not think where I was, when, on lifting my head, I saw the outline of the one-tusked bull still kneeling some five-and-twenty paces from me. Then I remembered. Slowly I raised myself, and was instantly taken with a violent sickness, the result of over-exertion, after which I very nearly fainted a second time. Presently I grew better, and considered the position. Two of the elephants were, as I knew, dead; but how about No. 3? There he knelt in majesty in the lonely moonlight. The question was, was he resting, or dead? I rose on my hands and knees, loaded my rifle, and painfully crept a few paces nearer. I could see his eye now, for the moonlight fell full upon it – it was open, and rather prominent. I crouched and watched; the eyelid did not move, nor did the great brown body, or the trunk, or the ear, or the tail – nothing moved. Then I knew that he must be dead.

I crept up to him, still keeping the rifle well forward, and gave him a thump, reflecting as I did so how very near I had been to being thumped instead of thumping. He never stirred; certainly he was dead, though to this day I do not know if it was my random shot that killed him, or if he died from concussion of the brain consequent upon the tremendous shock of his contact with the tree. Anyhow, there he was. Cold and beautiful he lay, or rather knelt, as the poet neatly puts it. Indeed, I do not think that I have ever seen a sight more imposing in its way than that of the mighty beast crouched in majestic death, and shone upon by the lonely moon.

And Who, With Eden
JOHN COLLIER

'YOU MARRY THE MENTAL age of ten, and you end up being a bedroom steward on a blasted Noah's Ark.' Mr. Jensen muttered this bitter conclusion to a toucan, whose cage he was resentfully cleaning out. He even gave the well-beaked bird a push with his scraper, to move it to the far end of its perch, so that he could scrape.

Other cages, of all shapes and sizes, stood around what was incorrectly called the *patio*. These, the warm wind advised him, were also in need of cleaning. Otherwise – no beer!

Mr. Jensen, when he proposed marriage to a lady as young in mind as he described, had looked forward confidently to control of the exchequer. He had failed entirely to take notice of the attitude of small girls to their pennies. From this it may be inferred that theirs was no mismating, mentally, of May and December. It might better have been described as a March-April marriage in I.Q., though it was a ripe September union in terms of A.D.

What Mr. Jensen had referred to as a Noah's Ark had been called, by the real-estate man, a Spanish style bungalette. The term, though harsh, was not altogether unjust. It was one of a straggle of its kind, littered like a tide-mark between the listless levels of swamp and sea on an inexpensive-looking beach in mid-Florida. Their architecture, which would have harmonized with few landscapes, harmonized with this one. Both offered an illusion of attractiveness which evaporated suddenly and without trace, so there was no telling who or what had taken one in. Years ago, when this development was dreamed up, slapped together and sold off, the Jensens, pale and blinking from the north, gazing dazedly around at sunshine and sea-shine, had declared it to be quite a picture. Myra had not long signed upon the dotted line when Mr. Jensen, though he was not in the very least an artist, felt obscurely that he could have done better himself. It is probable that, given a certain facility, he would have done exactly the same thing. Everything was executed in those pastel colours which are at once obvious and unbelievable. There were long, vague, horizontal smears of blues and yellows and pinks, fretted here and there by the easily drawn palmetto, and enlivened by the all too simple pelican, a cute touch, but one which soon loses its appeal.

When these weak and leaky pleasure-boxes were first run up, three coconut palms and a bougainvillea had been planted in each skimpy lot. The purpose was, to provide glamour. This objective had not been achieved. After ten years, the beach colony looked cheaper than ever and, even more distressing, it was no longer cheap at all. The Jensens had been washed up there on the tepid wave of Myra's low fixed income; that pillowing billow had sunk beneath them, and now, like stranded jellyfish, they found it uncomfortable to remain and impossible to depart.

Mr. Jensen longed desperately to depart. He longed for Brooklyn. It may be observed of nostalgia that, the less agreeable its object, the more valid and the more excruciating its pang. Mr. Jensen frequently said he wanted a real saloon and a decent delicatessen, but the howling within and the physical pain in his chest were oftenest evoked by an idea of the grimy wind blowing off the Hudson and the expectorations frozen on the sidewalks.

Sometimes he experienced a species of olfactory mirage; he seemed to snuff up again the snug fume of the one-Swede apartment house, where he, as doorman, elevator man and janitor, had been the one Swede. Myra, new-widowed of her builder, cut off in more or less his youth, before he had had time to make the builder's post-war pile, had come there with her low fixed income, and there Mr. Jensen had wooed, and won and married her for it. Now, possibly for want of petting, that warm-hearted woman had taken intemperately to pets.

'First a lot of stinking animals! Then a lot of squawking birds! And, now, by Jiminy, if she isn't kissing a turtle!'

Mrs. Jensen, her extremely light housekeeping already postponed, was in truth lying in a long chair on the porch, clad in a play-suit rich in humour and suspense, and she was lavishing caresses on the outworks and bastions of the newly acquired reptile, which had coyly retreated its head into its shell. It was this ingeuous lady's misfortune, that her many pets, beginning with Mr. Jensen himself, had all found her endearments a little overwhelming, and had turned aside or drawn back their heads and ended up in the collection of jerry-built cages in the *patio*.

'Like an addict!' said Mr. Jensen. 'Like a dope fiend! Lower all the time! All I can say is, you can't say she isn't asking for it!'

The toucan could not say this. According to the limitations of its kind, it could say nothing at all. No doubt it had its thoughts, but no one ever knows what a toucan is thinking of, except perhaps during April and

May. It may be hazarded, however, that this one thought very little of Mr. Jensen, indeed, had it been as talkative as a parrot, and as wise as an owl, and as hawk-eyed as a hawk, and as burned-up, over the push with the scraper, as a phoenix, it might quite conceivably have expressed itself as follows:

'Can the moral indignation, Jensen! You are trying to work yourself up. You are trying to nerve yourself to a deed altogether beyond your capacity. My advice to you is – don't! Throw away that scrap of paper with the small ad upon it! Abandon your dangerous dream! Don't talk to me of freedom! Freedom, my friend is strictly for the birds. Take a look at these! They are wings. Where are yours! I thought so, and I need say no more.'

'What I will say, however, is that you are in no way equipped to carry out the abominable enterprise you have in mind. Your brain is sluggish, your nerves are shot, your judgment is poor, you are deplorably over-weight, and you cholesterol level is perilously high. Consider – still worse! – the darkness, the depth and the wide extent, like night over the Matto Grosso, of your ignorance. Look around you at the limitless panorama of the things you don't know. One or other of these may make all the difference between success and failure. You are ignorant of almost everything I can think of, even during April and May. You disagree on this last point? Let us appeal to Mrs. Jensen.

'Let us get down to concrete examples. You don't know your reptiles. You have just mistaken a common gopher tortoise for a turtle. Your values are all wrong; you implied that the reptile, *qua* reptile, is low. It is true that, like you, it has no feathers, but you forget that, like me, it can lay an egg. You may, of course, do something in the latter line if you persist in your foolhardy project, but that will be only in a figurative sense, and it will add nothing at all to your credit or your comfort. And, speaking of comfort, there are several things about the service around here—'

But we need follow no further this purely hypothetical discourse of the toucan, for it was not endowed with the necessary qualifications, and therefore it didn't say a single word. This was a great pity, for it is more than likely that a frank talk more or less along these lines would have had very considerable weight with Mr. Jensen.

Instead, unfortunately, the wind shifted a point or two towards the south-west, and Mr. Jensen was assailed by the hot breath of the Great Cypress Swamp, a district from which emanates a moral as well as a physical halitosis. A smell of ooze, a smell of serpents, a smell of darkness, a smell of decay! Mr. Jensen was not the first man, nor the beach colony the first Eden, to be exposed to this insidious influence.

He was at once afflicted by a vision, as piercing as a toothache, of sleet and skyscrapers. The unreal lineaments of a real saloon rose up about him. He lifted up his eyes to the heights of shadowy apartment houses where the janitor was authorized to insist that no pets of any sort were allowed.

Not even tropical fish?

Not even tropical fish!

Next moment the mirage had faded, and, after the fashion of fading mirages, it left its victim more lost, more desperate and thirstier than before. The Great Cypress Swamp got him on the rebound, which was exactly according to plan. The Great Cypress Swamp did not, through the agency of its pestilential messenger, fill his ear with a long sales-talk about how dignified how comfortable, how independent, how well supplied with the best of beer and of delicatessen a single Swede might be who was in a position to add, to the emoluments and perquisites of doorman, elevator operator and janitor, a low fixed income which was entirely his own. The Great Cypress Swamp leaves all that sort of thing to the individual, who never lets it down. The Great Cypress Swamp has one message, and one message only, for mankind. It says, as softly as a prompter, 'What the hell!'

'What the hell!' said Mr. Jensen, and straightening up, he left the scraper among the scrapings and padded over to where his wife lay in her chair. She was peering wistfully in at the tortoise, which wore an expression of reserve, and showed no inclination to come out and play.

'The pet shop said they're affectionate,' she complained. 'He seems kind of self-centred to me.'

'I told you don't get a lousy turtle,' rejoined her spouse. 'You fall for any line those fellows hand you. Let me tell you something, Myra. I've been thinking. You know what *you* ought to do, honey?' you ought to get yourself a snake.'

'Cold blooded again!' objected Mrs. Jensen. 'I guess when they're cold-blooded they don't ever get real fond of you. Look at him! He's gone right inside.'

'You don't want to judge everything by a turtle,' said Mr. Jensen. 'How can a snake go inside? Where could it go? And if it could, it wouldn't want to. A snake's affectionate. You get the right snake, you got a real pal.'

'People say they hate the sight of a snake,' said Mrs. Jensen, but in a tone not entirely preclusive of sympathy for the underdog.

'That's a lot of prejudice,' said Mr. Jensen. 'Besides, everyone don't think that way. People that know snakes in person don't think that way at all. Remember that act in Tampa you wouldn't go in to see? *Snake Dance Strip-Tease!* That dame had 'em twining all around her. There was a picture of it on the billboard.'

'What do they eat, Hermie?' asked his wife, setting the tortoise on the floor, where it remained as if waiting for a handle and a porter.

'They eat an egg,' said Mr. Jensen. 'All you do is whistle when it's dinner time, and they sit up and beg. Some sorts eat a rabbit, but they're the big ones. What you want is a nice *little* snake.'

'I could carry it around,' said Mrs. Jensen, tentatively.

'Sure you could,' affirmed her husband. 'Down the front of your dress; that's where they carry them. It could look out at people. Cute as hell!'

'But I don't think I'd like a snake,' said Mrs. Jensen, after a movement which suggested that she was, in imagination, trying one on.

'Okay!' said Mr. Jensen. 'Okay! Okay! Don't have one! No snake! Snake's out! Finished! *I'm* not trying to sell you any bill of goods on a snake, honey – don't get me wrong! You know what I always say: we got too much damned zoo around here already. Only seeing you were so disappointed in that no-good, do-nothing turtle— Well, forget it! The hell with the snake! Let 'em kill it, and skin it, and make a pair of shoes for a midget.'

'You mean you know of one?' asked Mrs. Jensen.

'Of course I do,' he assured her. 'A fellow was telling me. He's got a pet shop in Miami, and he's stuck with this snake, and he don't know what to do!'

'He's got to get rid of it?'

'Well, you know what the price of eggs has gone up to,' said Mr. Jensen.

'Maybe he'd give it away, to a real good home?'

'A snake-skin's worth money,' said Mr. Jensen. 'This guy's got to eat. All the same, he said he couldn't scarcely face up to killing it. It's so goddam loyal. He said it's got an eye like a dog.'

'Well, I don't know,' said Mrs. Jensen.

'It takes all day to die, a snake does,' continued her husband.

'Do they come very high,' asked Mrs. Jensen after a pause.

'He said twenty,' said her husband, 'but I got an idea I could get it for less. What d'you say, honey? Would you like me to get it for you, for a surprise?'

'Well, not *too much* of a surprise,' said she.

'No,' said he. 'But, *you* know – coming in a box. Gift wrapped, eh? It can be for our anniversary. Give me a twenty and I'll get going right after we eat. Maybe I'll get it for ten; maybe for five.'

'I'll come with you,' said Mrs. Jensen, but Mr. Jensen shook his head.

'That's where you went wrong with the turtle,' said he. 'He's got you tied up in his mind with the pet shop where he's been so miserable. Now look at him – all withdrawn! Like that dame in the movie, and all she needed was love and affection. Listen, if I was a snake I'd like to be put in a box and not know where I was going, and find myself being unwrapped by someone just like you, Myra, in a nice quiet room with the door shut. 'Then I'd know things were different.'

'I'll have an egg ready for him,' said Mrs. Jensen. 'I suppose he eats it raw?'

'He'll come with directions,' said her husband. 'Let's get the food on the table and I'll be off as soon as we've ate.'

A good husband is always eager to gratify his wife's little fancy, and Mr. Jensen was off almost before the end of their meal; he was still chewing as he drove out to the coastal highway. He did not, however, follow that broad and easy path into Miami, but soon took a narrower road inland, which still dwindled, like a stream nearing its source, as he penetrated deeper and deeper into the wide, vacant and misleading smile of the country north of the Everglades. He was looking for a village called Melodie.

This little number is so elusive, so fugitive, that Mr. Jensen passed it two or three times before he realized it was there. At last he noticed a cluster of mail boxes at the entrance of a stretch of dirt which might conceivably be called a road. The boxes, at their haphazard heights, had something of the appearance of the notes of a bar or two of music, and no doubt those notes, if sketchily whistled over by a talented wayfarer, would have expressed all the sweetness and allure, like that of a pretty girl, of the village they represented. Mr. Jensen was not musically gifted, but even to him the mail boxes expressed quite a good deal.

For example, they indicated that the village he was seeking must lie somewhere down the dirt road, because it could not possibly be anywhere else. If it could, it unquestionably would have been. They also had a rustic simplicity about them, which gave him new hope he might get his snake for five. He left his car on the side of the State highway, and ventured down the track, and was soon rewarded by the sight of some unpretentious roofs. These lay at a little distance, on the other side of a creek. This creek was crossed by what was quite definitely a bridge; in fact on one side of it there was a sort of hand-rail. One part of this hand-rail must have been much firmer than it looked, for a boy was leaning on it. He was a boy of thirteen, but rather small for his age, which was just as well.

On or over the bridge there were also a number of mosquitoes, of the black and day-faring type which are so interesting a feature of the locality. Mr. Jensen did not notice them at first, but they noticed him, and soon began to introduce themselves.

'Is this place called Melodie?' asked Mr. Jensen. 'Where'll I find this snakeologist that hangs out here?'

The small boy looked at Mr. Jensen through a pair of spectacles that seemed rounder and more uncompromising than the ordinary. 'Herpetologist,' he said.

'Listen, bud,' said Mr. Jensen, 'if ever I get the shingles again I won't be coming up *this* neck of the woods for treatment, believe you me! I'm looking for the fellow that runs this ad.' With that, he pulled out his scrap of newspaper, two mosquitoes taking full advantage of the moment that his hand was in his pocket. 'Jesus!' exclaimed Mr. Jensen, slapping his neck and his brow in rapid succession.

'Eidelpfeffer, herpetologist,' said the boy. 'That's me.'

'You?' said Mr. Jensen staring at him in the sort of surprise that is sometimes thought to be unflattering, and was, indeed, thought to be so in this case.

'*Naturalist, pet shops, museums and medical schools supplied,*' quoted the youngster, without deigning to glance at the familiar text. '*Live reptiles for scientific purposes. Rare collectors' items.* Want to buy one?'

'Maybe,' said Mr. Jensen. 'You see, son, I'm a sort of professor from up north. My experiments are going to save a lot of the human race. I've driven all the way down here to get a tip-top, high-powered, poisonous snake. A real stinger.'

'Professor, eh?' said the small boy, who, Mr. Jensen now noted, had an air of being, mentally if not physically, somewhat older than his years. This characteristic was vaguely distasteful to Mr. Jensen, just as was his wife's girlishness; perhaps he was hard to please where mental ages were concerned.

'Well, let's see,' continued the village Ditmars. 'Crotalus? Crotalus adamanteus? Horridus? Or what about Ancistrodon?'

'Nothing important,' said Mr. Jensen. 'I want a decent, straight-forward American snake like you'd find in your own back-yard.'

'Those are rattlers and copperheads, Professor,' said the boy, eyeing Mr. Jensen with a very offensive, scientific sort of expression. 'I was just giving you the Latin names of them, Professor.'

Fortunately, Mr. Jensen was inspired by a mosquito to slap his brow at that very moment. This not only relieved a certain frustration but it also cued him to the dramatic mimicry of a scientist who has absent-mindedly mislaid his Latin. The interpretation would have done credit to a student of *the Method*. 'Why sure! Sure! Of course!' said he. 'Don't know what the hell I'm thinking of, what with these goddam mosquitoes buzzing me all the time! But look, kid I'm not interested in a rattler. I want something with a bit of class to it; little and cute and yet plenty of zip.'

The boy ruminated for a little. 'Well Professor,' said he at last, 'I wonder what you'd say to Tyrannosaurus Rex?'

'I came here,' cried Mr. Jensen, 'for a yard of snake, not a yard of highbrow talk. If you've got something like what I said, let's do business. If not, say so, and don't keep me standing here getting bit.'

'I know what you want,' said the boy. 'You want a Coral snake.'

'How's that for size?'

'Twenty inches.'

'Packs a high grade of poison?'

'It certainly does.'

'Good-looking?'

'It's got bands around it; red, black and yellow. It looks like the King snake, and that's the best looking species there is. Here you are!' And the boy fished out a slim handbook from the hip pocket of his jeans and showed Mr. Jensen an attractive colour print of the reptile, banded as described. 'Read what it says,' said he. 'Deadliest type of poison in North or South America. Akin to that of the cobra.'

'That's my baby!' said Mr. Jensen.

'What do you want it for?' asked the boy.

Mosquitoes and questions are one of worse combinations in the world. 'They've got no right,' said Mr. Jensen, 'to let a kid advertise. Here's the country needing scientists, and my time being wasted driving all the way down here to talk to a runty, four-eyed, question-asking little bastard who don't know a snake from a tape worm! Keep your snake, punk, and I'll keep my top secret information, and my dough as well.' With that he turned away.

He had not gone very far, however, when, the picture of the snake being very clear in his mind's eye, and its colour and general equipment appealing to him very strongly, and reflecting that he had no idea where he might find such another, he swallowed his resentment and turned back to the bridge.

'Listen, pal,' said he, 'let's make a deal. How do you sell 'em? A little bitsy one like that can't come so very high, I guess? Three bucks? Four? You know, son, they don't give us scientists all the dough in the world to toss around, the way the Reds do. Gee, if I'd had four bucks all to myself when I was your age, I'd have been right on the top of the world!' And Mr. Jensen gave this boy, absolutely free of charge, and, it proved, with no strings attatched, a big, wide, warm, genial, man-to-man sort of smile. 'Four bucks, eh?' said he.

Alas, the ungrateful child was sharper than the teeth of the serpents in which he dealt. He turned round, unresponsive spectacles on Mr. Jensen, and these spectacles, in spite of their chilly detachment, seemed to peer into the recesses of that gentleman's heart, or, at the very least, of his pocket-book. And sure enough, when Pint-size at last condescended to acknowledge the offer, he uttered only one word, but that was right on the button. 'Twenty.'

It would be tedious to rehearse each of the dolorous steps by which Mr. Jensen slowly climbed from the low level of his original offer up the almost vertical face of this dreadful boy's cliff-like indifference. That cliff had to be climbed, however, because, as another mountaineer said of another Everest, it was there. Even so, had he not been goaded by the mosquitoes, Mr. Jensen might never have made it. In the end he clinched the bargain at eighteen-fifty; this to include a trustworthy box in which to carry the reptile home. The boy retired to a shed in the backyard of one of the shacks on the other side of the bridge, and soon returned with a neat green carton and a dollar fifty in change.

Mr. Jensen quitted the company of Master Eidelpfeffer and of the mosquitoes without any profuse thanks or farewells. He felt that both had put the bite on him. He looked back when he reached the turn in the dirt road, and the boy was looking after him with a peculiar expression. Nothing is more upsetting, when one is engaged in an operation of great delicacy, than to be looked at with a peculiar expression.

Mr. Jensen breathed hard as he drove home. There was a small bar at the junction of the inland road with Highway No. 1. Outside it presented the refreshing appearance of half a grapefruit; within, it was as cold, and nearly as dark, as the inside of a deep freeze. It had an atmosphere of the greatest refinement, distinction and exclusiveness; this was achieved by having the juke box turned extremely low. In this retreat Mr. Jensen killed half an hour, four bottles of ice-cold beer and his dollar fifty. It was his purpose to arrive home at exactly six o'clock, that being the hour at which Mrs. Jensen changed from her playsuit into whatever she decided to wear at the evening meal.

Passing through the patio, Mr. Jensen looked upon the toucan, and the toucan looked upon Mr. Jensen. Nothing was said.

Mr. Jensen went into the house, and into the marital chamber where as he expected, his wife, rosy from the bath, was dimmimg the highlights a little by the application of a very delicious talcum powder, strongly scented with violets. 'If this snake likes violets,' thought Mr. Jensen 'we're in business.'

'Here we are, honey!' said he to his wife. 'Here's your surprise.'

'Oh, thank you, Hermie!' said Mrs. Jensen happily. But then, her face falling a little, she said, 'I thought you were going to get it gift-wrapped.'

'The guy where I got this snake,' said Mr. Jensen sombrely, 'was all out of gift-wrapping paper.'

'Never mind,' said Myra. 'We'll put him back next week and wrap him properly for the anniversary.'

'Great!' said Mr. Jensen, and for a moment he could say no more. He felt, at this critical juncture in his affairs, a certain oppression in his chest, as if his ice-cold beer had frozen into a solid block when only half way down.

'Let's open him right away,' said Myra.

'Now just a minute!' said Mr. Jensen, putting back her hand. 'That's a trained snake, Myra. It's tame. It's affectionate. It does an act. You can tie it round your leg for a garter, or around your neck, or anywhere. You just stick its tail in its mouth like the two ends of a necklace. The guy said you got to love him up; you got to make a pet of him; you got to let him do his stuff, right from the start. He'll be just crazy about you.'

'All right,' said Myra. 'Now let's undo him.'

'Let me get out,' said Mr. Jensen. 'I don't want him seeing me first. He might take to me instead of you. I'll take a little walk, sweetie, and you get real friendly with him.'

He thereupon closed the door very firmly and went for a stroll on the beach. He saw, through the Bates's picture window, the Bates's sitting with their evening Collins. Had Mr. Jensen been a lover of the pictorial arts, he might have engaged in some interesting reflections as to the vastly different schools of the art offered us by a picture window, according to whether we are looking in or looking out. As it was, he thought only of whether he should pay a brief visit to these neighbours, for the purpose of mentioning that he had bought his wife a King snake for a present, so that afterwards he might maintain that Master Eidelpfeffer had wrapped him a Coral snake in error. He was detained from this by noticing that the brother-in-law was there. Brother-in-law should never be there. This brother-in-law was a game warden from Ocala, and might be too curious or know too much. Mr. Jensen at this point was against intellectual curiosity, knowledge, etc., on general principles, so he reverted to his original plan, which anyway was the better, of representing his deadly purchase as a mere passing snake which had just dropped in, so to speak, for a bite.

As he went back towards the house, Mr. Jensen stopped at the incinerator, and put in a little paper and some dry fragments of palm branches, for at that late moment it struck him that he had better destroy all traces of the green carton, on which the publicity-mad youngster had stencilled his noticeable name. He wondered if by any chance he had overlooked any other detail of such importance, and the thought caused his nerves to twang like fiddle strings and a perspiration to break out upon his brow. At this moment Mr. Jensen repented deeply and sincerely for his wicked act and he prayed that some guardian angel might have stayed Myra's hand in the opening of the box, or struck the snake with a toothache, or anything that would get him of the hook. He listened, but all was deathly quiet within the house. He picked up a heavy stick and opened the door and went in.

'Is that you, Hermie?' called his wife. 'Oh, come in here, Hermie! Hermie, I don't think he likes me!'

Mr. Jensen went into the bedroom, all his fears vanished, and feeling only that the snake or his wife, or both of them, had somehow let him down. Some people are never satisfied. 'Afraid to pick him up?' said he morosely.

'I picked him up,' said Myra tearfully, 'I wanted to give him a kiss. But he kept turning his head away. 'It's cold-blooded, that's what it is! They never get real fond of you when they're cold-blooded.'

'Oh, shucks! You don't know how to handle a snake,' said Mr. Jensen. 'Where is he now, anyway?

'I put him to bed,' said Myra. 'I'll feed him an egg later, and maybe he'll act different.'

'Maybe,' said Mr. Jensen, glancing at the green box. He suddenly felt that his day had been too much for him, and he lowered himself, with

a grunt on to the connubial couch. 'You and your goddam menagerie!'
said he a little crossly.

'I'll put him back in the box,' said Myra.

'You said you had!' cried Mr. Jensen, hastily lifting his feet from the
floor.

'Bed, dear,' said Myra. 'Not box. To bed, I said I put him. For his
blood to be warmer. Watch out! You'll squash the poor little thing!'

But Mr. Jensen had already done so, in putting back his hand to gain
purchase for a quick spring from the bed. 'Oh, my God!' said he. 'It's got
me! I'm bit!'

'Better let me put some mecurochrome on it dear,' exclaimed his careful
wife. 'You never know where their teeth have been.'

'They been in me,' said her husband. 'That's where they've been!' He
uttered these words quietly and sadly, with a weariness and detachment
which represented only the calm before the storm. 'I'm done for,' he
observed.

'It don't look very deep,' said Myra, taking his hand and looking at
the two tiny punctures. 'It's not like it was one of those poisonous snakes
that bit that poor dog those people had—'

At this point Mr. Jensen recovered his power of speech and a full
sense of urgency of the occasion.

'It is! It's worse! It's deadly!' cried he. 'I'm dying! Get someone quick!'

'Why, Hermie!' cried Myra with a fond woman's emphasis on the
sentimental rather than the practical side of things. 'You didn't ever bring
me home one of those poisonous snakes, did you? Hermie, *don't* say you
did a thing like that! Not for our anniversary, and all! Oh, Hermie say
you were joking!'

'Joking!' cried Mr. Jensen. 'I'm dying, I tell you! Run!'

Myra ran, but she ran like a hen, in all directions at once. It was
several minutes before she returned with Mr. Bates and his brother-in-
law, the game warden. Mr. Jensen was to be heard making some very
shocking sounds as they approached the house, but, as they entered, he
fell silent.

'I'm afraid he's gone, Mrs. Jensen,' said Mr. Bates, speaking from a
discreet position in the bedroom doorway. It was not necessary for him
to adventure into the bedroom itself, for he had retired only the previous
year from the operation of a small but enterprising funeral parlour, and
he could have recognized Mr. Jensen's unfortunate condition six blocks
away.

'Where's that snake?' said the brother-in-law, advancing into the room,
stick in hand.

'Oh, Hermie!' wailed Myra. 'How could you have done it to me? How
could you be so bad?'

'Look out!' shouted the game warden suddenly. 'Here it is! Got it!'

It takes very little to put a small snake out of action, and the next moment the two men were bending over this one. 'If this is the snake,' said the game warden to Myra, 'your husband never died of any bite. For a moment I thought it was a Coral, but this here's a King snake, Mrs. Jensen. It's perfectly harmless.'

'Of course, it's for a qualified medical practitioner to have the say so,' said Mr. Bates, 'but you can take it from me, Mrs. Jensen, because I've had nearly forty years' experience, your poor husband passed away from a heart attack.'

'Oh, Hermie,' cried Myra, on a gush of softer tears, 'I knew you was only joking!'

A Buffalo Hunt

WASHINGTON IRVING

With his two companions, the Captain and the Virtuoso, the narrator embarks on a hunt across the Great Prairie. Like most heedless but not insensitive sportsmen, when faced with the reality of the kill, the inexperienced hunter finds his feelings are of shame and pity for the great beast ...

AFTER PROCEEDING ABOUT two hours in a southerly direction, we emerged towards mid-day from the dreary belt of the Cross Timber, and to our infinite delight beheld 'the Great Prairie', stretching to the right and left before us. We could distinctly trace the meandering course of the Main Canadian, and various smaller streams, by the strips of green forests that bordered them. The landscape was vast and beautiful. There is always an expansion of feeling in looking upon these boundless and fertile wastes; but I was doubly conscious of it after emerging from our 'close dungeon of innumerous boughs.'

From a rising ground Beatte pointed out the place where he and his comrades had killed the buffaloes; and we beheld several black objects moving in the distance, which he said were part of the herd. The Captain determined to shape his course to a woody bottom about a mile distant, and to encamp there for a day or two, by way of having a regular buffalo-hunt, and getting a supply of provisions. As the troop defiled along the slope of the hill towards the camping ground, Beatte proposed to my messmates and myself, that we should put ourselves under his guidance, promising to take us where we should have plenty of sport. Leaving the line of march, therefore, we diverged towards the prairie; traversing a small valley, and ascending a gentle swell of land. As we reached the summit, we beheld a gang of wild horses about a mile off.

Beatte was immediately on the alert, and no longer thought of buffalo hunting. He was mounted on his powerful half wild horse, with a lariat coiled at the saddle-bow, and set off in pursuit; while we remained on a rising ground watching his manoeuvres with great solicitude. Taking advantage of a strip of woodland, he stole quietly along, so as to get close to them before he was perceived. The moment they caught sight of him a grand scamper took place. We watched him skirting along the horizon like a privateer in full chase of a merchantman; at length he passed over the brow of a ridge, and down a shallow valley; in a few moments he was on the opposite hill, and close upon one of the horses. He was soon head and head, and appeared to be trying to noose his prey; but they both disappeared again behind the hill, and we saw no more of them. It turned out afterwards that he had noosed a powerful horse, but could not hold him, and had lost his lariat in the attempt.

While we were waiting for his return, we perceived two buffalo descending a slope, towards a stream, which wound through a ravine fringed with trees. The young Count and myself endeavored to get near them under covert of the trees. They discovered us while we were yet three of four hundred yards off, and turning about, retreated up the rising ground. We urged our horses across the ravine, and gave chase. The immense weight of head and shoulders causes the buffalo to labour heavily up-hill; but it accelerates his descent. We had the advantage, therefore, and gained rapidly upon the fugitives, though it was difficult to get our horses to approach them, their very scent inspiring them with terror. The Count, who had a double-barrelled gun loaded with ball, fired, but it missed. The bulls now altered their course, and galloped down-hill with headlong rapidity. As they ran in different directions, we each singled one and separated. I was provided with a brace of veteran brass-barrelled pistols, which I had borrowed at Fort Gibson, and which had evidently seen some service. Pistols are very effective in buffalo hunting, as the hunter can ride up close to the animal, and fire it while at full speed; whereas the long heavy rifles used on the frontier, cannot be easily managed, nor discharged with accurate aim from horseback. My object, therefore, was to get within pistol-shot of the buffalo. This was no very easy matter. I was well mounted on a horse of excellent speed and bottom, that seemed eager for the chase, and soon overtook the game; but the moment he came nearly parallel, he would keep sheering off, with ears forked and pricked forward, and every symptom of aversion and alarm. It was no wonder. Of all animals, a buffalo, when close pressed by the hunter, has an aspect the most diabolical. His two short black horns curve out of a huge frontlet of shaggy hair; his eyes glow like coals; his mouth is open; his tongue parched and drawn up into a half crescent; his tail is erect, and tufted and whisking about in the air; he is a perfect picture of mingled rage and terror.

It was with difficulty I urged my horse sufficiently near, when, taking aim, to my chagrin both pistols missed fire. Unfortunately the locks of these veteran weapons were so much worn, that in the gallop the priming had been shaken out of the pans. At the snapping of the last pistol I was close upon the buffalo, when, in his despair, he turned round with a sudden snort, and rushed upon me. My horse wheeled about as if on a pivot, made a convulsive spring, and, as I had been leaning on one side with pistol extended, I came near being thrown at the feet of the buffalo.

Three or four bounds of the horse carried us out of the reach of the enemy, who, having merely turned in desperate self-defence, quickly resumed his flight. As soon as I could gather in my panic-stricken horse, and prime the pistols afresh, I again spurred in pursuit of the buffalo, who had slackened his speed to take breath. On my approach he again set off full tilt, heaving himself forward with a heavy rolling gallop, dashing with headlong precipitation through brakes and ravines, while several deer and wolves, startled from their coverts by his thundering career, ran helter-skelter to right and left across the waste.

A gallop across the prairies in pursuit of game is by no means so smooth a career as those may imagine who have only the idea of an open level plain. It is true, the prairies of the hunting ground are not so much entangled with flowering plants and long herbage as the lower prairies, and are principally covered with short buffalo-grass; but they are diversified by hill and dale, and where most level, are apt to be cut up by deep rifts and ravines, made by torrents after rains; and which, yawning from an even surface, are almost like pitfalls in the way of the hunter, checking him suddenly when in full career, or subjecting him to the risk of limb and life. The plains, too, are beset by burrowing-holes of small animals, in which the horse is apt to sink to the fetlock, and throw both himself and his rider. The late rain had covered some parts of the prairie, where the ground was hard, with a thin sheet of water, through which which the horse had to splash his way. In other parts there were innumerable shallow hollows, eight or ten feet in diameter, made by the buffaloes, who wallow in sand and mud like swine. These being filled with water, shone like mirrors, so that the horse was continually leaping over them or springing on one side. We had reached, too, a rough part of the prairie, very much broken and cut up; the buffalo, who was running for life, took no heed to his course, plunging down break-neck ravines, where it was necessary to skirt the borders in search of a safer descent. At length we came to where a winter stream had torn a deep chasm across the whole prairie, leaving open jagged rocks, and forming a long glen bordered by steep crumbling cliffs of mingled stone and clay. Down one of these the buffalo flung himself, half tumbling, half leaping, and then scuttled along the bottom; while I, seeing all further pursuit useless, pulled up, and gazed quietly after him from the border of the cliff, until he disappeared amidst the windings of the ravine.

Nothing now remained but to turn my steed and rejoin my companions.

Here at first was some little difficulty. The ardor of the chase had betrayed me into a long, heedless gallop. I now found myself in the midst of a lonely waste, in which the prospect was bounded by undulating swells of land, naked and uniform, where, from the deficiency of land-marks and distinct features, an inexperienced man may become bewild-ered, and lose his way as readily as in the wastes of the ocean. The day, too, was overcast, so that I could not guide myself by the sun; my only mode was to retrace the track my horse had made in coming, though this I would often lose sight of, where the ground was covered with parched herbage.

To one unaccustomed to it, there is something inexpressibly lonely in the solitude of a prairie. The loneliness of a forest seems nothing to it. There the view is shut in by trees, and the imagination is left free to picture some livelier scene beyond. But here we have an immense extent of landscape without a sign of human existence. We have the consciousness of being far, far beyond the bounds of human habitation; we feel as if moving in the midst of a desert world. As my horse lagged slowly back over the scenes of our late scamper, and the delirium of the chase had passed away, I was peculiarly sensible to these circumstances. The silence of the waste was now and then broken by the cry of a distant flock of pelicans, stalking like spectres about a shallow pool; sometimes by the sinister croaking of a raven in the air, while occasionally a scoundrel wolf would scour off from before me, and, having attained a safe distance, would sit down and howl and whine with tones that gave a dreariness to the surrounding solitude.

After pursuing my way for some time, I descried a horseman on the edge of a distant hill, and soon recognized him to be the Count. He had been equally unsuccessful with myself; we were shortly after rejoined by our worthy comrade, the Virtuoso, who, with spectacles on nose, had made two or three ineffectual shots from horseback.

We determined not to seek the camp until we had made one more effort. Casting our eyes about the surrounding waste, we descried a herd of buffalo about two miles distant, scattered apart, and quietly grazing near a small strip of trees and bushes. It required but little stretch of fancy to picture them so many cattle grazing on the edge of a common, and that the grove might shelter some lonely farm-house.

We now formed our plan to circumvent the herd, and by getting on the other side of them, to hunt them in the direction where we knew our camp to be situated: otherwise, the pursuit might take us to such a distance as to render it impossible to find our way back before nightfall. Taking a wide circuit, therefore, we moved slowly and cautiously, pausing occasionally when we saw any of the herd desist from grazing. The wind fortunately set from them, otherwise they might have scented us and have taken the alarm. In this way we succeeding in getting round the herd without disturbing it. It consisted of about forty head; bulls, cows, and calves. Separating to some distance from each other, we now approached slowly in a parallel line, hoping by degrees to steal near without exciting attention. They began, however, to move off quietly, stopping at every step or two to graze, when suddenly a bull, that, unobserved by us, had been taking his siesta under a clump of trees to our left, roused himself from his lair, and hastened to join his companions. We were still at a considerable distance, but the game had taken the alarm. We quickened our pace; they broke into a gallop, and now commenced a full chase.

As the ground was level, they shouldered along with great speed, following each other in a line; two or three bulls bringing up the rear, the last of whom, from his enormous size and venerable frontlet, and beard of sunburnt hair, looked like the patriarch of the herd, and as if he might long have reigned the monarch of the prairie.

There is a mixture of the awful and the comic in the look of these huge animals, as they bear their great bulk forwards, with an up and down motion of the unwieldy head and shoulders, their tails cocked up like the cue of a Pantaloon in a pantomime, the end whisking about in a fierce yet whimsical style, and their eyes glaring venomously with an expression of fright and fury.

For some time I kept parallel with the line, without being able to force my horse within pistol-shot, so much had he been alarmed by the assault of the buffalo in the preceding chase. At length I succeeded, but was again balked by my pistols missing fire. My companions, whose horses were less fleet and more wayworn, could not overtake the herd; at length Mr. L., who was in the rear of the line, and losing ground, levelled his double-barrelled gun, and fired a long raking shot. It struck a buffalo just above the loins, broke its back-bone, and brought it to the ground. He stopped and alighted to dispatch his prey, when, borrowing his gun, which had yet a charge remaining in it, I put my horse to his speed, again overtook the herd which was thundering along, pursued by the Count. With my present weapon there was no need of urging my horse to such close quarters; galloping along parallel, therefore, I singled out a buffalo, and by a fortunate shot brought it down on the spot. The ball had struck a vital part; it could not move from the place where it fell, but lay there struggling in mortal agony, while the rest of the herd kept on their headlong career across the prairie.

Dismounting, I now fettered my horse to prevent his straying, and advanced to contemplate my victim. I am nothing of a sportsman; I had been prompted to this unwonted exploit by the magnitude of the game and the excitement of an adventurous chase. Now that the excitement was over, I could not but look with commiseration upon the poor animal that lay struggling and bleeding at my feet. His very size and importance, which had before inspired me with eagerness, now increased my compunction. It seemed as if I had inflicted pain in proportion to the bulk of my victim, and as if there were a hundred-fold greater waste of life than there would have been in the destruction of an animal of inferior size.

To add to these after-qualms of conscience, the poor animal lingered in his agony. He had evidently received a mortal wound, but death might be long in coming. It would not do to leave him here to be torn piecemeal while yet alive, by the wolves that had already snuffed his blood, and were skulking and howling at a distance, and waiting for my departure; and by the ravens that were flapping about, croaking dismally in the air. It became now an act of mercy to give him his quietus, and put him out of his misery. I primed one of the pistols, therefore, and advanced close up to the buffalo. To inflict a wound thus in cold blood, I found a totally different thing from firing in the heat of the chase. Taking aim, however, just behind the fore-shoulder, my pistol for once proved true; the ball must have passed through the heart, for the animal gave one convulsive throe and expired.

While I stood meditating and moralizing over the wreck I had so wantonly produced, with my horse grazing near me, I was rejoined by my fellow-sportsman the Virtuoso, who, being a man of universal adroitness, and withal more experienced and hardened in the gentle art of 'venerie', soon managed to carve out the tongue of the buffalo, and delivered it to me to bear back to the camp as a trophy.

Troubles in the Fold

THOMAS HARDY

Bathsheba Everdene has dismissed her shepherd, Gabriel Oak, for criticising her flirtacious conduct towards Farmer Bold- wood. Himself in love with her, Gabriel vows never to return to Bathsheba's service . . .

GABRIEL OAK HAD CEASED to feed the Weatherbury flock for about four- and-twenty hours, when on Sunday afternoon the elderly gentlemen Joseph Poorgrass, Matthew Moon, Fray, and half-a-dozen others, came running up to the house of the mistress of the Upper Farm.

'Whatever *is* the matter, men?' she said, meeting them at the door just as she was coming out on her way to church, and ceasing in a moment from the close compression of her two red lips, with which she had accompanied the exertion of pulling on a tight glove.

'Sixty!' said Joseph Poorgrass.

'Seventy!' said Moon.

'Fifty-nine!' said Susan Tall's husband.

' – Sheep have broken fence,' said Fray.

' – And got into a field of young clover,' said Tall.

' – Young clover!' said Joseph Poorgrass.

'And they be getting blasted,' said Henery Fray.

'That they be,' said Joseph.

'And will all die as dead as nits, if they bain't got out and cured!' said Tall.

Joseph's countenance was drawn into lines and puckers by his concern. Fray's forehead was wrinkled both perpendicularly and crosswise, after the pattern of a portcullis, expressive of a double despair. Laban Tall's lips were thin, and his face was rigid. Matthew's jaws sank, and his eyes turned whichever way the strongest muscle happened to pull them.

'Yes,' said Joseph, 'and I was sitting at home looking for Ephesians, and says I to myself, " 'Tis nothing but Corinthians and Thessalonians in this danged Testament," when who should come in but Henery there: "Joseph," he said, "the sheep have blasted theirselves – " '

With Bathsheba it was a moment when thought was speech and speech exclamation. Moreover, she had hardly recovered her equanimity since the disturbance which she had suffered from Oak's remarks.

'That's enough – that's enough! – O you fools!' she cried, throwing the parasol and Prayer-book into the passage, and running out of doors in the direction signified. 'To come to me, and not go and get them out directly! O, the stupid numskulls!'

Her eyes were at their darkest and brightest now. Bathsheba's beauty belonging rather to the demonian than to the angelic school, she never looked so well as when she was angry – and particularly when the effect was heightened by a rather dashing velvet dress, carefully put on before a glass.

All the ancient men ran in a jumbled throng after her to the clover-field, Joseph sinking down in the midst when about half-way, like an individual withering in a world which was more and more insupportable. Having once received the stimulus that her presence always gave them they went round among the sheep with a will. The majority of the afflicted animals were lying down, and could not be stirred. These were bodily lifted out, and the others driven into the adjoining field. Here, after the lapse of a few minutes, several more fell down, and lay helpless and livid as the rest.

Bathsheba, with a sad, bursting heart, looked at these primest specimens of her prime flock as they rolled there –

Swoln with wind and the rank mist they drew.

Many of them foamed at the mouth, their breathing being quick and short, whilst the bodies of all were fearfully distended.

'O, what can I do, what can I do!' said Bathsheba, helplessly. 'Sheep are such unfortunate animals! – there's always something happening to them! I never knew a flock pass a year without getting into some scrape or other.'

'There's only one way of saving them,' said Tall.

'What way? Tell me quick!'

'They must be pierced in the side with a thing made on purpose.'

'Can you do it? Can I?'

'No, ma'am. We can't, nor you neither. It must be done in a particular spot. If ye go to the right or left but an inch you stab the ewe and kill her. Not even a shepherd can do it, as a rule.'

'Then they must die,' she said, in a resigned tone.

'Only one man in the neighbourhood knows the way,' said Joseph, now just come up. 'He could cure 'em all if he were here.'

'Who is he? Let's get him!'

'Shepherd Oak,' said Matthew. 'Ah, he's a clever man in talents!'

'Ah, that he is so!' said Joseph Poorgrass.

'True – he's the man,' said Laban Tall.

'How dare you name that man in my presence!' she said excitedly. 'I told you never to allude to him, nor shall you if you stay with me. Ah!' she added, brightening, 'Farmer Boldwood knows!'

'O no, ma'am,' said Matthew. 'Two of his store ewes got into some vetches t'other day, and were just like these. He sent a man on horseback here post-haste for Gable, and Gable went and saved 'em. Farmer Boldwood hev got the thing they do it with. 'Tis a holler pipe, with a sharp pricker inside. Isn't it, Joseph?'

'Ay – a holler pipe,' echoed Joseph. 'That's what 'tis.'

'Ay, sure – that's the machine,' chimed in Henery Fray reflectively, with an Oriental indifference to the flight of time.

'Well,' burst out Bathsheba, 'don't stand there with your "ayes" and your "sures", talking at me! Get somebody to cure the sheep instantly!'

All then stalked off in consternation, to get somebody as directed, without any idea of who it was to be. In a minute they had vanished through the gate, and she stood alone with the dying flock.

'Never will I send for him – never!' she said firmly.

One of the ewes here contracted its muscles horribly, extended itself, and jumped high into the air. The leap was an astonishing one. The ewe fell heavily, and lay still.

Bathsheba went up to it. The sheep was dead.

'O, what shall I do – what shall I do!' she again exclaimed, wringing her hands. 'I won't send for him. No, I won't!'

The most vigorous expression of a resolution does not always coincide with the greatest vigour of the resolution itself. It is often flung out as a sort of prop to support a decaying conviction which, whilst strong, required no enunciation to prove it so. The 'No, I won't' of Bathsheba meant virtually, 'I think I must.'

She followed her assistants through the gate, and lifted her hand to one of them. Laban answered her signal.

'Where is Oak staying?'

'Across the valley at Nest Cottage.'

'Jump on the bay mare, and ride across, and say he must return instantly – that I say so.'

Tall scrambled off to a field, and in two minutes was on Poll, the bay, bare-backed, and with only a halter by way of rein. He diminished down the hill.

Bathsheba watched. So did all the rest. Tall cantered along the bridle-path through Sixteen Acres, Sheeplands, Middle Field, The Flats, Cappel's Piece, shrank almost to a point, crossed the bridge, and ascended from the valley through Springmead and Whitepits on the other side. The cottage to which Gabriel had retired before taking his final departure from the locality was visible as a white spot on the opposite hill, backed by blue firs, Bathsheba walked up and down. The men entered the field and endeavoured to ease the anguish of the dumb creatures by rubbing them. Nothing availed.

Bathsheba continued walking. The horse was seen descending the hill, and the wearisome series had to be repeated in reverse order: Whitepits, Springmead, Cappel's Piece, The Flats, Middle Field, Sheeplands, Sixteen Acres. She hoped Tall had had presence of mind enough to give the mare up to Gabriel, and return himself on foot. The rider neared them. It was Tall.

'O what folly!' said Bathsheba.

Gabriel was not visible anywhere.

'Perhaps he is already gone!' she said.

Tall came into the inclosure, and leapt off, his face tragic as Morton's after the battle of Shrewsbury.

'Well?' said Bathsheba, unwilling to believe that her verbal *lettre-de-cachet* could possibly have miscarried.

'He says *beggars mustn't be choosers,*' replied Laban.

'What!' said the young farmer, opening her eyes and drawing in her breath for an outburst. Joseph Poorgrass retired a few steps behind a hurdle.

'He says he shall not come onless you request en to come civilly and in a proper manner, as becomes any 'ooman begging a favour.'

'Oh, oh, that's his answer! Where does he get his airs? Who am I, then, to be treated like that? Shall I beg to a man who has begged to me?'

Another of the flock sprang into the air, and fell dead.

The men looked grave, as if they suppressed opinion.

Bathsheba turned aside, her eyes full of tears. The strait she was in through pride and shrewishness could not be disguised longer: she burst out crying bitterly: they all saw it; and she attempted no further concealment.

'I wouldn't cry about it, miss,' said William Smallbury compassionately. 'Why not ask him softer like? I'm sure he'd come then. Gable is a true man in that way.'

Bathsheba checked her grief and wiped her eyes. 'O, it is a wicked cruelty to me – it is – it is!' she murmured. 'And he drives me to do what I wouldn't; yes, he does! – Tall, come indoors.'

After this collapse, not very dignified for the head of an establishment, she went into the house, Tall at her heels. Here she sat down and hastily scribbled a note between the small convulsive sobs of convalescence which follow a fit of crying as a ground-swell follows a storm. The note was none the less polite for being written in a hurry. She held it at a distance, was about to fold it, then added these words at the bottom: –

Do not desert me, Gabriel!

She looked a little redder in refolding it, and closed her lips, as if thereby to suspend till too late in the action of conscience in examining whether such stategy were justifiable. The note was despatched as the message had been, and Bathsheba waited indoors for the result.

It was an anxious quarter of an hour that intervened between the messenger's departure and the sound of the horse's tramp again outside. She could not watch this time, but, leaning over the old bureau at which she had written the letter, closed her eyes, as if to keep out both hope and fear.

The case, however, was a promising one, Gabriel was not angry: he was simply neutral, although her first command had been so haughty. Such imperiousness would have damned a little less beauty; and on the other hand, such beauty would have redeemed a little less imperiousness.

She went out when the horse was heard, and looked up. A mounted figure passed between her and the sky, and drew on towards the field of sheep, the rider turning his face in receding. Gabriel looked at her. It was a moment when a woman's eyes and tongue tell distinctly opposite tales. Bathsheba looked full of gratitude, and she said: –

'O, Gabriel, how could you serve me so unkindly!'

Such a tenderly-shaped reproach for his previous delay was the one speech in the language that he could pardon for not being commendation of his readiness now.

Gabriel murmered a confused reply, and hastened on. She knew from the look which sentence in her note had brought him. Bathsheba followed to the field.

Gabriel was already among the turgid, prostrate forms. He had flung off his coat, rolled up his shirt-sleeves, and taken from his pocket the instrument of salvation. It was a small tube or trochar, with a lance passing down the inside; and Gabriel began to use it with a dexterity that would have graced a hospital-surgeon. Passing his hand over the sheep's left flank, and selecting the proper point, he punctured the skin and rumen with the lance as it stood in the tube; then he suddenly withdrew the lance, retaining the tube in its place. A current of air rushed up the tube, forcible enough to have extinguished a candle held at the orifice.

It has been said that mere ease after torment is delightful for a time; and the countenances of these poor creatures expressed it now. Forty-nine operations were successfully performed. Owing to the great hurry necessitated by the far-gone state of some of the flock, Gabriel missed his aim in one case, and in one only – striking wide of the mark, and inflicting a mortal blow at once upon the suffering ewe. Four had died; three recovered without an operation. The total number of sheep which had thus strayed and injured themselves so dangerously was fifty-seven.

When the love-led man had ceased from his labours Bathsheba came and looked him in the face.

'Gabriel, will you stay on with me?' she said, smiling winningly, and not troubling to bring her lips quite together again at the end, because there was going to be another smile soon.

'I will,' said Gabriel.

And she smiled on him again.

We Think the World of You
J. R. ACKERLEY

*A pedigree Alsatian bitch, Evie, is left in the uncaring charge
of the Winders family when her feckless young owner, Johnny,
is sent to prison. After a social worker has advised that the dog
be put down, Johnny's friend, Frank, a middle-aged civil
servant, rescues her for a weekend of freedom . . .*

THE DAYLIGHT HOURS we spent mostly in the open air. Evie saw to that.
And it was borne in upon me that, without perceiving it, I had grown
old and dull, I had forgotten that life itself was an adventure. She
corrected this. She held the key to what I had lost, the secret of delight.
It was a word I often used, but what did I know of the quality itself, I
thought, as I watched her inextinguishable high spirits, her insatiable
appetite, not for food, in which she seemed scarcely interested, but for
fun, the way she welcomed life like a lover? So extreme was her excitement
when outings were proposed that it looked as though she could not bear
the very thing she wanted, but, as with her collar in the Winders' kitchen,
must do all she could to frustrate or postpone the fulfilment of her heart's
desire. This she did by removing from me my clothes as fast as I tried
to put them on, my socks, my shoes, my gloves, and bounding with them
all over the flat in a transport of joy. Hysterical with laughter I would
pursue her from room to room, only to find myself continually deprived
again of the thing-before-the-last I had managed to retrieve. Then, when
I had eventually assembled everything, she would fly into the kitchen
and hurl about the vegetables from the vegetable basket, strewing the
passage with carrots, onions, and potatoes as though they were flowers
upon a triumphal way. She was childish, she was charming, and to me

it seemed both strange and touching that anyone should find the world so wonderful.

Yet at the same time, and although it would seem unfair to criticize the character of a creature the surprising thing about whom was that she had managed to preserve any good character at all, I had to admit that she showed at once certain traits which it was difficult not to regret; she had a tendency to be both a bully and a nag. These features were constantly observable in her behaviour towards the human race. Either she was nervous of people, or she simply did not like them, it was hard to tell which; at any rate not merely would she not permit them to touch her, she would not permit them even to approach or address her; from which it naturally followed, since we were always together, that she would not permit them to approach or address me. She challenged, she interrupted, she threatened, and I soon gave up attempting to take her into pubs or shops, she made such deplorable scenes. Her notion of life was perfectly clear and perfectly simple; it was to be out with me all day on the towing-path or Barnes Common and to be always on the move. I gratified her wishes in everything; it was, after all, what I had brought her away to do; but it must be added that I derived from it all a sense of personal satisfaction also, for it was a long time, I thought sourly, since anyone had seemed to want my company so much.

Whatever else might happen, it was plain, Evie was not going to let me out of her sight again. I could not go from one room of my flat to another but she instantly followed, as though fearing that if I turned a corner and her eyes lost their grip on me I might vanish quite away. When dusk fell and the curtains were drawn she accepted this, without demur, as the end of the day's play, and sat peacefully with me in my study, curled up in my big arm-chair or reclined upon the divan bed, while I read or wrote. There was, however, one quiet little indoor game with which, on the second evening, she entertained me and, to speak the truth, momentarily disturbed my mind. Not that I could have retreated then, even had I wished to retreat, I say to myself looking back; I was already too deeply involved. In any case the whole thing could easily be laughed off ... It began simply enough. She was sitting on the divan facing me, staring at me, her long forelegs close together, the paw joints flexed over the edge of the bed. Sitting thus, she suddenly picked up her ball which, with various other objects to which she seemed to attach a value, she had collected about her, and set it on her legs. It rolled down them, as upon rails, fell to the floor and bounced across the room towards me. This was nothing. Pure accident. Merely amusing. The mechanics were easy; our relative positions directed the ball inevitably from her to me. Receiving it into my hand I returned it with a laugh. She caught it in her jaws. But then she it on her legs again; down them it rolled, bounced across the carpet and reached my hand. Now I looked at her with more particularity and put my book away. The ball was in my hand and she was gazing at me expectantly. For a second I hesitated, as though a cautionary hand had been laid upon me. Then I cast it back into her waiting jaws. She placed it upon her legs a third time. It did not move. Peering down at it, as if in perplexity, she gave it, with her long black nose, a shove, and it began once more its slow conversational journey from her to me. But now, just as it reached the verge – was it simply because she childishly felt she could not after all bear to part with it, or because the hitch that had occurred had vexed her? – she suddenly seized it back with a swift, almost scolding, thrust of the head and replaced it on her legs. It rolled. It fell. It bounced. It crossed the room and came into my hand. Yes, yes, of course. I know; it is absurd to read too much into animal behaviour, and afterwards, as I have said, I laughed it off; but at that moment I did take the uncanny impression that, in a deliberate and purposeful way, she had gathered up all her poor resources and, in order to reach me directly and upon my own ground, had managed to cross that uncrossable barrier that separates man and beast. The expression on her face contributed to this fleeting illusion. Some animals have a furrow above their eyes very like that furrow, etched by a lifetime of meditation, that we see upon the brow of sages. In the animal's case, of course, it is merely the loose skin wrinkling upon the line of the socket bone; but it often imparts to their faces a similar look of wisdom. Evie had this 'intellectual' line, and it lent to her expression now an appearance of the profoundest concentration. With her nose pointing down and her ears cocked forward she followed, with the utmost gravity, the progress of the ball as it travelled down her legs, fell over the edge, bounded across the carpet and reached my hand; then, without altering the bent position of her head, she raised her eyes beneath their furrowed brows to mine and directed at me the kind of look that two scientists might exchange after successfully bringing off some critical experiment in physics. Yet, when I returned the ball to her now, it was as though the effort she had been making – if effort it was – suddenly failed; she became a mere dog once more, kicking up her legs and rolling about with the toy in her mouth; and when I offered out of curiosity, to replay the game next evening, I could not get it going; she seemed worried and confused; the inspiration, having done its work, had apparently gone out of her for ever.

But if I could not refix her attention upon that, her eyes seldom left my face. Throughout the evenings as we sat I was conscious always of her presence; looking up I would find her gaze upon me, and each time I would be struck afresh by the astounding variety of her beauty. The device in the midst of her forehead had altered again; perhaps her ducking in the river had exposed detail which coal-dust had hitherto obscured; the black caste mark was diamond-shaped still, but deep shadows had now developed upon either side of it, stretching across her brow, so that in certain lights the diamond looked like the body of a bird with its wings spread, a bird in flight. These dark markings on her chalky face – the diamond with its wing-like stains, the oblique black-rimmed eyes with the small jet eyebrow tufts set like accents above them, the long sooty lips – symmetrically divided it up into zones of delicate pastel colours, like a stained-glass window. The skull, bisected by the thread, was two oval pools of the palest honey, the centre of her face was stone grey, her cheeks were silvery white and upon each a *patte de mouche* had been tastefully set. Framed in its soft white ruff, this strange face with its heavily leaded features and the occasional expression of sadness imparted to it by some slight movement of the brows, was the face of a clown, a clown by Rouault.

Then she would move and be something quite different. She might sit in the attitude of the Sphinx, with her thick fur collar flounced upon her shoulders; or she might lower her head to rest it on her outstretched paws, so that, lying there, long and flat, the ears invisibly laid back against the dark upcurving neck, it resembled the head of some legendary serpent; or she might recline on her flank with one silver arm extended, the other doubled up upon its knuckles, in the posture of those heraldic lions that have one paw resting on an orb; or she might make herself so small and compact, withdrawing all her legs beneath her and coiling her long tail close around her, that, with the shaft of her neck rising out of the pool of her body, she looked more like a doe than a dog. I would glance up and meet her gaze which I felt to be upon me, and instantly the tall ears would crumple back and an expression of such sweetness come over her face that it was impossible not to go and caress her, this charming Krishna beast with her caste mark and her long almond eyes. I would have to go to her; she would not come to me. All the fawning sentiment that had characterized her puppy days had gone. Her love was now aloof. I would call her but she would not come. Motionless as a carven image she would sit, her head drawn back, her glowing eyes fixed tenderly and stead-fastly upon me, and I would put my book away and go to her, moved by her love and her beauty. Shoot her indeed!

At night she slept as she pleased, in an arm-chair in my bedroom, or on my bed. If she began on the chair she usually ended up on the bed. It was a double bed, and sometimes she would curl up at my feet, but mostly against the pillow, laying down her head beside my own. She was quite odourless; the faint sweet smell, perhaps, of fur or feather. And when the room was darkened she fell asleep at once. In the morning she would wake me by dabbing a paw on my face; sometimes I would be roused to find her lying with all her length upon me, her forearms on my shoulders, looking gaily down into my eyes. Another day had begun . . .

Saturday, Sunday, Monday . . . the week-end slipped away. Tomorrow I would have to take her back. I could keep her no longer. 'I must make a plan,' I said to myself as I turned out the light on the last day. 'I'll think it over before I go to sleep.' But I did not think it over; my mind seemed unable to grasp the fact and I fell asleep without considering it at all. 'I must make a plan,' I said to myself the following morning as I drank my tea. 'I suppose I'd better ring up Liverpool Street and find out about trains.' But I did not. The morning was bright and beautiful; I stared through the window instead at the boats passing up and down on the river below. Separated from me now not merely by distance but by the memory of that nightmare journey – for that was the obstacle my thoughts gripped on – Stratford seemed as remote as the Hebrides, and to get Evie back to it required, in my imagination, a resolution so dauntless, an effort so stupendous, that I could not even begin to think how it could be accomplished. Conversely, now that she had entered into my life, that other inconceivable proposition, as I had once envisaged it, of keeping her there, appeared, although it had not yet been put to any test, less impracticable. My mind, indeed, if it could be said to be busy at all, was busy with that. To leave her behind in my flat was out of the question. I had deserted her twice on Saturday to do a little shopping, and the change in her expression from jubilation as she bounded with me to the door, to the most poignant dismay and despair when I shut it in her face, had upset me so much that, tired though I was, I had rushed like a madman from shop to shop, muttering audibly at the slowness of other customers, even in one shop earning a rebuke for trying to push in front of them. On neither errand was I gone more than fifteen minutes, yet to my fond and guilty mind they had both seemed interminable. When I returned she was still standing where I had left her, her forehead against the door. ... But why make plans? My office, after all, was on the way to Liverpool Street. ... I had a room of my own ... no harm in trying. ... I could always take her on if it didn't work. And I could cover myself against all eventualities by phoning a wire to Millie. This, at least, so far as planning went, was no sooner thought of than done: I said we might be delayed and she was not to worry if we did not turn up today. Perhaps she should have a letter of explanation too, just in case. ... She would get it in the afternoon if I posted it now. I sat down to it at once, and my pen positively flew along as though the letter had been written for a long time in my head and was only waiting to come out. I described everything that had happened since I left her, the frightful journey, the walk across the parks ('If you could have seen her delighting in her youth and strength you would have understood more clearly what I mean about the wretched life she's been leading and how frustrating it is'); I told her what Miss Sweeting had said and that I was now asking Johnny through Megan to let me put Evie in a kennel until he was free ('I'm sure he'll agree. Since he's a prisoner himself and knows what loss of freedom means he would not be so cruel as to condemn his dog to a similar fate'); and I ended by saying that Evie was still so intensely nervous that I doubted whether I should be able to induce her to enter another train just yet ('If I can't I must try to work her into my life for a bit longer, though I don't at the moment see how. But she's in good health, so don't worry, and I'll be writing to you again soon'). Besides being too quickly written, this letter was far too long; I realized that when I took it to the post. Millie was no great reader and used to find, I remembered, as much difficulty with my normal calligraphy as she found with my normal speech; but I had been too carried away to think of using the special childish round-hand I generally employed when writing to her.

As soon as I had done all this I felt extraordinarily light-hearted, almost light-headed. Nothing was resolved, but some tension had been released and it was in the blithest spirits that I set out with Evie, like Dick Whittington and his cat, to walk to London. In my despatch-case I carried a few biscuits to sustain her while I worked and a tin receptacle for water. But I had not gone far before I was annoyed and perturbed to find that the joints of my legs were painfully stiff. I had, after all, covered during the week-end as great a distance as I normally walked in months. When we reached Hammersmith Bridge I looked hopefully about for a taxi to carry us at least as far as Palace Gate; but to walk I had set out and to walk I was obliged. My objective was Gladstone House, a large block of government offices in the neighbourhood of Regent's Park; my own room was on the topmost floor, the sixth. Limping into the vestibule two-and-a-half hours later I gazed longingly, though doubtfully, at the lift . . . Surely Evie, who had been using the one in my block of flats, could be said to be lift-minded by now? But, alas, as I feared, there was to her all the difference in the world between a self-operating lift that carried no one but ourselves and went non-stop to our destination, and one that not only contained a suspicious stranger in the person of the lift-man, but took on other suspicious strangers at every floor. When we reached the third, with half a dozen nervous people aboard, and I saw another half-dozen waiting to get in, I realized that it was time to get out, that no one would attempt to detain us if we did, and that the lift-man would not feel offended if Evie never used his lift again.

The working day, which had begun so fatiguingly, ended no better. I had entertained a hope that the six-mile walk which had almost worn me out would tire Evie a little too, and that she would be disposed to lie down and doze while I attended to my correspondence. This proved the fondest of illusions. She prowled restlessly about, whining and complaining, or stood staring at me as though she could scarcely believe the evidence of her senses; she uttered loud sighs or even louder cavernous yawns, subsiding from time to time into a heap on the floor, with a startling thud, as much as to say 'Oh hell!', only to get up again immediately; she tried, by all her usual tricks of stealing and pretending to destroy my gloves, to draw attention to herself and her wishes; when this did not work she instituted noisy cat-and-mouse games with her biscuits (none of which did she actually eat), hurling them all over the carpet until it was littered with their fragments; and she barked violently with her excruciating bitch's bark, not only at everyone who entered the room but at every footstep in the busy passage outside. When I cuffed her in exasperation she put her fore-paws on my desk, upsetting the ink on my papers, in order to lick my face forgivingly. She was nevertheless much admired by my colleagues and had, for a time, a novelty value even beyond the department, so that a number of curious sightseers arrived throughout the morning. But she received them all so ungraciously that they did not call again.

Although I had considered the question of *her* lunch (needlessly, as I have said) I had given no thought to my own; when the time for it arrived the prospect of obtaining any was not bright. I could not take her into the canteen, nor could I leave her shut up for half an hour while I visited it myself. Her feelings, and mine, apart, my room had no key, and anyone might look in on me in my absence. . . . My only chance, it seemed to me, and it involved further physical strain, was to find some small, unfrequented pub which would provide me with a sandwich and a pint of beer. Evie's intense, petrified anxiety when she saw me preparing to leave, the almost mad stare with which her starting eyes pierced and searched my own for the answer to the only question in the world: 'Me too?', unwelcome though it was, touched me as it always did. It also affected me with a sensation of hysteria similar perhaps to her own, a feeling that if I did not take care I should begin to laugh, or to cry, or possibly to bark, and never be able to stop, for I knew that as soon as I settled the matter by clipping on her lead I should be practically raped and then sucked down the spiral staircase like a leaf in the wind. These prospects afforded me so little pleasure in my present state of fatigue that I considered letting her follow me down uncontrolled, but I was afraid she might spiral impetuously out into the dangerous road and be run over. A number of staid officials plodding up from the floors below shrank against the wall as we sped past.

The expedition was more rewarding than I had dared hope. An almost deserted pub on the far side of Regent's Park supplied me with what I most needed, a couple of pints of refreshing beer, also with a plate of meat-and-two-veg. which I shared with Evie. On our return I decided to let her mount the stairs by herself, for she could not very well spiral out of the roof; and the experiment was interesting in that the twisting staircase seemed to make her as giddy when she was off the lead as it made me when she was on it. She started off with such speed that I wondered whether she might not acquire a permanent curve in her backbone; but the curve she did acquire was in her mind, for when she reached the landings she constantly lost her sense of direction and, circling still, came flying down again without stopping, so that I was forever meeting and parting from her, gaining her, as it were, only to repel and lose her once more.

The success of the break ended there. The afternoon passed much as the morning had done, excepting that I was left more severely alone. My outgoing mail, such little as I managed to write, was not collected unless I placed it on the mat outside my door where the incoming mail was now deposited, for the post-girls were too scared to come in. Even so, Evie heard their timid steps and never failed to issue her warning. I left early and, having once more negotiated Baker Street, Hyde Park, and Kensington Gardens, had the good fortune to find a taxi at Palace Gate to convey us to Hammersmith Bridge. Evie, when we reached home, was as fresh as a daisy; I was not; but strenuous though the day had been I derived retrospective satisfaction from it nevertheless; at any rate I had brought her through it; she had been initiated into my working life, and meeting her strange gaze as she reclined on the bed, I told her that I hoped she had learnt a rope or two and would do better on the morrow.

When she woke me I heard a pattering on the roof. The weather was another thing I had omitted from my calculations. What on earth should I do now? Perhaps the rain would stop by the time I was up and dressed. On the contrary it was coming down harder than ever. I knew from experience that one phoned for taxis in vain. I phoned, in vain. Buses were out of the question. How could I walk her to London in this downpour? I stared at her alert, expectant face in dismay. At the base of her ears, in the openings, I noticed, the system of head hair began in a kind of spray. It was as though she had a light grey flower, a puff-ball, struck in front of each.

'You little bitch!' I said crossly.

Then I remembered the Metropolitan Railway in Hammersmith, which I seldom used, though what I regarded as its cynical humour always entertained me when I did. Fair promise, foul reward! After luring one on with the offer of a choice of stations romantically rural in their names – Royal Oak, Goldhawk Road, Shepherd's Bush, Ladbroke Grove, Westbourne Park – it then ushered one through some of the ugliest and grimiest districts of Central London. But it presented me with a practical solution now; Hammersmith was a terminus; there were no complications of any kind; a train was always waiting, level with the platform, and it would take us direct to Baker Street. When the rain had abated a little we set out.

Evie behaved abominably. I removed her from the train at Royal Oak, I could no longer endure her, piercing and violent challenge to everyone else who got in, nor the cold looks and indignant mutterings cast at me from the other end of the compartment where the rest of the passengers huddled. Why, oh why, I asked myself as I took the intolerable creature out and walked her on through the rain, did she have to go on like that?

The same thought recurred to me in my office throughout the day. So obviously brimming with intelligence, so fond of me, why, why, in spite of everything I said to her, did she seem unable to understand that my director and other members of the staff, with whom she saw me constantly in conversation, were therefore friends and could be permitted, they at least, to enter my room without being repeatedly threatened? Before the day's work was half done she had reduced the whole department to a palpable state of nerves. In the afternoon, in extremity. I fell upon her with an exclamation of rage and gave her the soundest biffing with my hands that she had so far received from me. For a moment she concealed herself beneath my desk; then she emerged and stood looking at me with an expression of such sorrow and, at the same time, such dignity, that, falling forward upon my letters, I sank my head on my arms. 'Evie, Evie,' I said miserably as her nose pushed in against my cheek, 'what are we to do?' But I knew the answer already. I could not go on. I could not bear another day. I had had enough. The strain and the worry were too great. Her meat was finished and mine too, for I had given her my week's ration: how could I shop for more? She would have to go back to the Winders in the morning.

The Stolen White Elephant

MARK TWAIN

This story, which was first published in the United States of America in 1882, reveals the extraordinary lengths to which some owners will go to rescue their weird and wonderful pets from the hands of unscrupulous villains. . .

THE FOLLOWING CURIOUS history was related to me by a chance railway acquaintance. He was a gentleman more than seventy years of age, and his thoroughly good and gentle face and earnest and sincere manner imprinted the unmistakable stamp of truth upon every statement which fell from his lips. He said:—

You know in what reverence the royal white elephant of Siam is held by the people of that country. You know it is sacred to kings, only kings may possess it, and that it is indeed in a measure even superior to kings, since it receives not merely honor but worship. Very well; five years ago, when the troubles concerning the frontier line arose between Great Britain and Siam, it was presently manifest that Siam had been in the wrong. Therefore every reparation was quickly made, and the British representative stated that he was satisfied and the past should be forgotten. This greatly relieved the King of Siam, and partly as a token of gratitude, but partly also, perhaps, to wipe out any little remaining vestige of unpleasantness which England might feel toward him, he wished to send the Queen a present, – the sole sure way of propitiating an enemy, according to Oriental ideas. This present ought not only to be a royal one, but transcendently royal. Wherefore, what offering could be so meet as that of a white elephant? My position in the Indian civil service was such that I was deemed peculiarly worthy of the honor of conveying the present to Her Majesty. A ship was fitted out for me and my servants and the officers and attendants of the elephant, and in due time I arrived in New York harbor and placed my royal charge in admirable quarters in Jersey City. It was necessary to remain awhile in order to recruit the animal's health before resuming the voyage.

All went well during a fortnight, – then my calamities began. The white elephant was stolen! I was called up at dead of night and informed of this fearful misfortune. For some moments I was beside myself with terror and anxiety; I was helpless. Then I grew calmer and collected my faculties. I soon saw my course, – for indeed there was but the one course for an intelligent man to pursue. Late as it was, I flew to New York and got a policeman to conduct me to the headquarters of the detective force. Fortunately I arrived in time, though the chief of the force, the celebrated Inspector Blunt, was just on the point of leaving for his home. He was a man of middle size and compact frame, and when he was thinking deeply he had a way of knitting his brows and tapping his forehead reflectively with his finger, which impressed you at once with the conviction that you stood in the presence of a person of no common order. The very sight of him gave me confidence and made me hopeful. I stated my errand. It did not flurry him in the least; it had no more visible effect upon his iron self-possession than if I had told him somebody had stolen my dog. He motioned me to a seat, and said calmly, –

'Allow me to think a moment, please.'

So saying, he sat down at his office table and leaned his head upon his hand. Several clerks were at work at the other end of the room; the scratching of their pens was all the sound I heard during the next six or seven minutes. Meantime the inspector sat there, buried in thought. Finally he raised his head, and there was that in the firm lines of his face which showed me that his brain had done its work and his plan was made. Said he, – and his voice was low and impressive, –

'This is no ordinary case. Every step must be warily taken; each step must be made sure before the next is ventured. And secrecy must be observed, – secrecy profound and absolute. Speak to no one about the matter, not even the reporters. I will take care of *them*; I will see that they get only what it may suit my ends to let them know.' He touched a bell; a youth appeared. 'Alaric, tell the reporters to remain for the present.' The boy retired. 'Now let us proceed to business, – and systematically. Nothing can be accomplished in this trade of mine without strict and minute method.'

He took a pen and some paper. 'Now – name of the elephant?'

'Hassan Ben Ali Ben Selim Abdallah Mohammed Moisé Alhammal Jamsetjejeebhoy Dhuleep Sultan Ebu Bhudpoor.'

'Very well. Given name?'

'Jumbo.'

'Very well. Place of birth?'

'The capital city of Siam.'

'Parents living?'

'No, – dead.'

'Had they any other issue besides this one?'

'None. He was an only child.'

'Very well. These matters are sufficient under that head. Now please describe the elephant, and leave out no particular, however insignificant, – that is, insignificant from *your* point of view. To men in my profession there *are* no insignificant particulars; they do not exist.'

I described, – he wrote. When I was done, he said, –

'Now listen. If I have made any mistakes, correct me.'

He read as follows:–

'Height, 19 feet; length from apex of forehead to insertion of tail, 26 feet; length of trunk, 16 feet; length of tail, 6 feet; total length, including trunk and tail, 48 feet; length of tusks, 9½ feet; ears in keeping with these dimensions; footprint resembles the mark left when one up-ends a barrel in the snow; color of the elephant, a dull white; has a hole the size of a plate in each ear for the insertion of jewelry, and possesses the habit in a remarkable degree of squirting water upon spectators and of maltreating with his trunk not only such persons as he is acquainted with, but even entire strangers; limps slightly with his right hind leg, and has a small scar in his left armpit caused by a former boil; had on, when stolen, a castle containing seats for fifteen persons, and a gold-cloth saddle-blanket the size of an ordinary carpet.'

There were no mistakes. The inspector touched the bell, handed the description to Alaric, and said, –

'Have fifty thousand copies of this printed at once and mailed to every detective office and pawnbroker's shop on the continent.' Alaric retired. 'There, – so far, so good. Next, I must have a photograph of the property.'

I gave him one. He examined it critically, and said, –

'It must do, since we can do no better; but he has his trunk curled up and tucked into his mouth. That is unfortunate, and is calculated to mislead, for of course he does not usually have it in that position.' He touched his bell.

'Alaric, have fifty thousand copies of this photograph made, the first thing in the morning, and mail them with the descriptive circulars.'

Alaric retired to execute his orders. The inspector said, –

'It will be necessary to offer a reward, of course. Now as to the amount?'

'What sum would you suggest?'

'To *begin* with, I should say, – well, twenty-five thousand dollars. It is an intricate and difficult business; there are a thousand avenues of escape and opportunities of concealment. These thieves have friends and pals everywhere—'

'Bless me, do you know who they are?'

The wary face, practised in concealing the thoughts and feelings within, gave me no token, nor yet the replying words, so quietly uttered:–

'Never mind about that. I may, and I may not. We generally gather a pretty shrewd inkling of who our man is by the manner of his work and the size of the game he goes after. We are not dealing with a pickpocket or a hall thief, now, make up your mind to that. This property was not "lifted" by a novice. But, as I was saying, considering the amount of travel which will have to be done, and the diligence with which the thieves will cover up their traces as they move along, twenty-five thousand may be too small a sum to offer, yet I think it worth while to start with that.'

So we determined upon that figure, as a beginning. Then this man, whom nothing escaped which could by any possibility be made to serve as a clew, said:–

'There are cases in detective history to show that criminals have been detected through peculiarities in their appetites. Now, what does this elephant eat, and how much?'

'Well, as to *what* he eats, he will eat *anything*. He will eat a man, he will eat a Bible, – he will eat anything *between* a man and a Bible.'

'Good, – very good indeed, but too general. Details are necessary, – details are the only valuable things in our trade. Very well, – as to men. At one meal, – or, if you prefer, during one day, – how many men will he eat, if fresh?'

'He would not care whether they were fresh or not; at a single meal he would eat five ordinary men.'

'Very good; five men; we will put that down. What nationalities would he prefer?'

'He is indifferent about nationalities. He prefers acquaintances, but is not prejudiced against strangers.'

'Very good. Now, as to Bibles. How many Bibles would he eat at a meal?'

'He would eat an entire edition.'

'It is hardly succinct enough. Do you mean the ordinary octavo, or the family illustrated?'

'I think he would be indifferent to illustrations; that is, I think he would not value illustrations above simple letterpress.'

'No, you do not get my idea. I refer to bulk. The ordinary octavo Bible weighs about two pounds and a half, while the great quarto with the illustrations weighs ten or twelve. How many Doré Bibles would he eat at a meal?'

'If you knew this elephant, you could not ask. He would take what they had.'

'Well, put it in dollars and cents, then. We must get at it somehow. The Doré costs a hundred dollars a copy, Russia leather, bevelled.'

'He would require about fifty thousand dollars' worth, – say an edition of five hundred copies.'

'Now that is more exact. I will put that down. Very well; he likes men and Bibles; so far, so good. What else will he eat? I want particulars.'

'He will leave Bibles to eat bricks, he will leave bricks to eat bottles, he will leave bottles to eat clothing, he will leave clothing to eat cats, he will leave cats to eat oysters, he will leave oysters to eat ham, he will leave ham to eat sugar, he will leave sugar to eat pie, he will leave pie to eat potatoes, he will leave potatoes to eat bran, he will leave bran to eat hay, he will leave hay to eat oats, he will leave oats to eat rice, for he was mainly raised on it. There is nothing whatever that he will not eat but European butter, and he would eat that if he could taste it.'

'Very good. General quantity at a meal, – say about—'

'Well, anywhere from a quarter to half a ton.'

'And he drinks—'

'Everything that is fluid. Milk, water, whiskey, molasses, castor oil, camphene, carbolic acid, – it is no use to go into particulars; whatever fluid occurs to you set it down. He will drink anything that is fluid, except European coffee.'

'Very good. As to quantity?'

'Put it down five to fifteen barrels, – his thirst varies; his other appetites do not.'

'These things are unusual. They ought to furnish quite good clews toward tracing him.'

He touched the bell.

'Alaric, summon Captain Burns.'

Burns appeared. Inspector Blunt unfolded the whole matter to him, detail by detail. Then he said in the clear, decisive tones of a man whose plans are clearly defined in his head, and who is accustomed to command, –

'Captain Burns, detail Detectives Jones, Davis, Halsey, Bates, and Hackett to shadow the elephant.'

'Yes, sir.'

'Detail Detectives Moses, Dakin, Murphy, Rogers, Tupper, Higgins, and Bartholomew to shadow the thieves.'

'Yes, sir.'

'Place a strong guard – a guard of thirty picked men, with a relief of thirty – over the place from whence the elephant was stolen, to keep strict watch there night and day, and allow none to approach – except reporters – without written authority from me.'

'Yes, sir.'

'Place detectives in plain clothes in the railway, steamship, and ferry depots, and upon all roadways leading out of Jersey City, with orders to search all suspicious persons.'

'Yes, sir.'

'Furnish all these men with photograph and accompanying description of the elephant, and instruct them to search all trains and outgoing ferry-boats and other vessels.'

'Yes, sir.'

'If the elephant should be found, let him be seized, and the information forwarded to me by telegraph.'

'Yes, sir.'

'Let me be informed at once if any clews should be found, – footprints of the animal, or anything of that kind.'

'Yes, sir.'

'Get an order commanding the harbor police to patrol the frontages vigilantly.'

'Yes, sir.'

'Despatch detectives in plain clothes over all the railways, north as far as Canada, west as far as Ohio, south as far as Washington.'

'Yes, sir.'

'Place experts in all the telegraph offices to listen to all messages; and let them require that all cipher despatches be interpreted to them.'

'Yes, sir.'

'Let all these things be done with the utmost secrecy, – mind, the most impenetrable secrecy.'

'Yes, sir.'

'Report to me promptly at the usual hour.'

'Yes, sir.'

'Go!'

'Yes, sir.'

He was gone.

Inspector Blunt was silent and thoughtful a moment, while the fire in his eye cooled down and faded out. Then he turned to me and said in a placid voice, –

'I am not given to boasting, it is not my habit; but – we shall find the elephant.'

I shook him warmly by the hand and thanked him; and I *felt* my thanks, too. The more I had seen of the man the more I liked him, and the more I admired him and marvelled over the mysterious wonders of his profession. Then we parted for the night, and I went home with a far happier heart than I had carried with me to his office.

Next morning it was all in the newspapers, in the minutest detail. It even had additions, – consisting of Detective This, Detective That, and Detective The Other's 'Theory' as to how the robbery was done, who the robbers were, and whither they had flown with their booty. There were eleven of these theories, and they covered all the possibilities; and this single fact shows what independent thinkers detectives are. No two theories were alike, or even much resembled each other, save in one striking particular, and in that one all the eleven theories were absolutely agreed. That was, that although the rear of my building was torn out and the only door remained locked, the elephant had not been removed through the rent, but by some other (undiscovered) outlet. All agreed that the robbers had made that rent only to mislead the detectives. That never would have occurred to me or to any other layman, perhaps, but it had not deceived the detectives for a moment. Thus, what I had supposed was the only thing that had no mystery about it was in fact the very thing I had gone furthest astray in. The eleven theories all named the supposed robbers, but no two named the same robbers; the total number of suspected persons was thirty-seven. The various newspaper accounts all closed with the most important opinion of all, – that of Chief Inspector Blunt. A portion of this statement read as follows:–

'The chief knows who the principals are, namely, "Brick" Duffy and "Red" McFadden. Ten days before the robbery was achieved he was already aware that it was to be attempted, and had quietly proceeded to shadow these two noted villains; but unfortunately on the night in question their track was lost, and before it could be found again the bird was flown, – that is, the elephant.

'Duffy and McFadden are the boldest scoundrels in the profession; the chief has reasons for believing that they are the men who stole the stove out of the detective headquarters on a bitter night last winter, – in consequence of which the chief and every detective present were in the hands of the physicians before morning, some with frozen feet, others with frozen fingers, ears, and other members.'

When I read the first half of that I was more astonished than ever at the wonderful sagacity of this strange man. He not only saw everything in the present with a clear eye, but even the future could not be hidden from him. I was soon at his office, and said I could not help wishing he had had those men arrested, and so prevented the trouble and loss; but his reply was simple and unanswerable:–

'It is not our province to prevent crime, but to punish it. We cannot punish it until it is committed.'

I remarked that the secrecy with which we had begun had been marred by the newspapers; not only all our facts but all our plans and purposes had been revealed; even all the suspected persons had been named; these would doubtless disguise themselves now, or go into hiding.

'Let them. They will find that when I am ready for them my hand will descend upon them, in their secret places, as unerringly as the hand of fate. As to the newspapers, we *must* keep in with them. Fame, reputation, constant public mention, – these are the detective's bread and butter. He must publish his facts, else he will be supposed to have none; he must publish his theory, for nothing is so strange or striking as a detective's theory, or brings him so much wondering respect; we must publish our plans, for these the journals insist upon having, and we could not deny them without offending. We must constantly show the public what we are doing, or they will believe we are doing nothing. It is much pleasanter to have a newspaper say, "Inspector Blunt's ingenious and extraordinary theory is as follows," than to have it say some harsh thing, or, worse still, some sarcastic one.'

'I see the force of what you say. But I noticed that in one part of your remarks in the papers this morning you refused to reveal your opinion upon a certain minor point.'

'Yes, we always do that; it has a good effect. Besides, I had not formed any opinion on that point, any way.'

I deposited a considerable sum of money with the inspector, to meet current expenses, and sat down to wait for news. We were expecting the telegrams to begin to arrive at any moment now. Meantime I reread the newspapers and also our descriptive circular, and observed that our $25,000 reward seemed to be offered only to detectives. I said I thought it ought to be offered to anybody who would catch the elephant. The inspector said:-

'It is the detectives who will find the elephant, hence the reward will go to the right place. If other people found the animal, it would only be by watching the detectives and taking advantage of clews and indications stolen from them, and that would entitle the detectives to the reward, after all. The proper office of a reward is to stimulate the men who deliver up their time and their trained sagacities to this sort of work, and not to confer benefits upon chance citizens who stumble upon a capture without having earned the benefits by their own merits and labors.'

This was reasonable enough, certainly. Now the telegraphic machine in the corner began to click, and the following despatch was the result:-

> FLOWER STATION, N.Y., 7.30 A.M.
>
> Have got a clew. Found a succession of deep tracks across a farm near here. Followed them two miles east without result; think elephant went west. Shall now shadow him in that direction.
>
> DARLEY, *Detective.*

'Darley's one of the best men on the force,' said the inspector. 'We shall hear from him again before long.'

Telegram No. 2 came:-

> BARKER'S, N.J., 7.40 A.M.
>
> Just arrived. Glass factory broken open here during night, and eight hundred bottles taken. Only water in large quantity near here is five miles distant. Shall strike for there. Elephant will be thirsty. Bottles were empty.
>
> BAKER, *Detective.*

'That promises well, too,' said the inspector. 'I told you the creature's appetites would not be bad clews.'

Telegram No. 3:-

> TAYLORVILLE, L.I., 8.15 A.M.
>
> A haystack near here disappeared during night. Probably eaten. Have got a clew, and am off.
>
> HUBBARD, *Detective.*

'How he does move around!' said the inspector. 'I knew we had a difficult job on hand, but we shall catch him yet.'

> FLOWER STATION, N.Y., 9 A.M.
>
> Shadowed the tracks three miles westward. Large, deep and ragged. Have just met a farmer who says they are not elephant tracks. Says they are holes where he dug up saplings for shade-trees when ground was frozen last winter. Give me orders how to proceed.
>
> DARLEY, *Detective.*

'Aha! a confederate of the thieves! The thing grows warm,' said the inspector.

He dictated the following telegram to Darley:–

Arrest the man and force him to name his pals. Continue to follow the tracks, – to the Pacific, if necessary.

Chief BLUNT.

Next telegram:–

CONEY POINT, PA, 8.45 A.M.

Gas office broken open here during night and three months' unpaid gas bills taken. Have got a clew and am away.

MURPHY, *Detective.*

'Heavens!' said the inspector; 'would he eat gas bills?'

'Through ignorance, – yes; but they cannot support life. At least, unassisted.'

Now came this exciting telegram:–

IRONVILLE, N.Y., 9.30 A.M.

Just arrived. This village in consternation. Elephant passed through here at five this morning. Some say he went east, some say west, some north, some south, – but all say they did not wait to notice particularly. He killed a horse; have secured a piece of it for a clew. Killed it with his trunk; from style of blow, think he struck it left-handed. From position in which horse lies, think elephant travelled northward along line of Berkley railway. Has four and a half hours' start, but I move on his track at once.

HAWES, *Detective.*

I uttered exclamations of joy. The inspector was as self-contained as a graven image. He calmly touched his bell.

'Alaric, send Captain Burns here.'

Burns appeared.

'How many men are ready for instant orders?'

'Ninety-six, sir.'

'Send them north at once. Let them concentrate along the line of the Berkley road north of Ironville.'

'Yes, sir.'

'Let them conduct their movements with the utmost secrecy. As fast as others are at liberty, hold them for orders.'

'Yes, sir.'

'Go!'

'Yes, sir.'

Presently came another telegram:–

SAGE CORNERS, N.Y., 10.30.

Just arrived. Elephant passed through here at 8.15. All escaped from the town but a policeman. Apparently elephant did not strike at policeman, but at the lamp-post. Got both. I have secured a portion of the policeman as clew.

STUMM, *Detective.*

'So the elephant has turned westward,' said the inspector. 'However, he will not escape, for my men are scattered all over that region.'

The next telegram said:–

GROVER'S, 11.15.

Just arrived. Village deserted, except sick and aged. Elephant passed through three quarters of an hour ago. The anti-temperance mass meeting was in session; he put his trunk in at a window and washed it out with water from cistern. Some swallowed it – since dead; several drowned. Detectives Cross and O'Shaughnessy were passing through town, but going south, – so missed elephant. Whole region for many miles around in terror, – people flying from their homes. Wherever they turn they meet elephant, and many are killed.

BRANT, Detective.

I could have shed tears, this havoc so distressed me. But the inspector only said, –

'You see, – we are closing in on him. He feels our presence; he has turned eastward again.'

Yet further troublous news was in store for us. The telegraph brought this:–

HOGANPORT, 12.19.

Just arrived. Elephant passed through half an hour ago, creating wildest fright and excitement. Elephant raged around streets; two plumbers going by, killed one – other escaped. Regret general.

O'FLAHERTY, Detective.

'Now he is right in the midst of my men,' said the inspector. 'Nothing can save him.'

A succession of telegrams came from detectives who were scattered through New Jersey and Pennsylvania, and who were following clews consisting of ravaged barns, factories, and Sunday school libraries, with high hopes, – hopes amounting to certainties, indeed. The inspector said, –

'I wish I could communicate with them and order them north, but that is impossible. A detective only visits a telegraph office to send his report; then he is off again, and you don't know where to put your hand on him.'

Now came this despatch:–

BRIDGEPORT, CT., 12.15.

Barnum offers rate of $4,000 a year for exclusive privilege of using elephant as travelling advertising medium from now till detectives find him. Wants to paste circus-posters on him. Desires immediate answer.

BOGGS, Detective.

'That is perfectly absurd!' I exclaimed.

'Of course it is,' said the inspector. 'Evidently Mr. Barnum, who thinks he is so sharp, does not know me, – but I know him.'

Then he dictated this answer to the despatch:–

Mr. Barnum's offer declined. Make it $7,000 or nothing.

Chief BLUNT.

'There. We shall not have to wait long for an answer. Mr. Barnum is not at home; he is in the telegraph office, – it is his way when he has business on hand. Inside of three—'

DONE – P.T. BARNUM.

So interrupted the clicking telegraphic instrument. Before I could make a comment upon this extraordinary episode, the following despatch carried my thoughts into another and very distressing channel:–

BOLIVIA, N.Y., 12.50.

Elephant arrived here from the south and passed through toward the forest at 11.50, dispersing a funeral on the way, and diminishing the mourners by two. Citizens fired some small cannon-balls into him, and then fled. Detective Burke and I arrived ten minutes later, from the north, but mistook some excavations for footprints, and so lost a good deal of time; but at last we struck the right trail and followed it to the woods. We then got down on our hands and knees and continued to keep a sharp eye on the track, and so shadowed it into the brush. Burke was in advance. Unfortunately the animal had stopped to rest; therefore, Burke having his head down, intent upon the track, butted up against the elephant's hind legs before he was aware of his vicinity. Burke instantly rose to his feet, seized the tail, and exclaimed joyfully, 'I claim the re—' but got no further, for a single blow of the huge trunk laid the brave fellow's fragments low in death. I fled rearward, and the elephant turned and shadowed me to the edge of the wood, making tremendous speed, and I should inevitably have been lost, but that the remains of the funeral providentially intervened again and diverted his attention. I have just learned that nothing of that funeral is now left; but this is no loss, for there is an abundance of material for another. Meantime, the elephant has disappeared again.

MULROONEY, Detective.

We heard no news except from the diligent and confident detectives scattered about New Jersey, Pennsylvania, Delaware, and Virginia, – who were all following fresh and encouraging clews, – until shortly after 2 P.M., when this telegram came:–

BAXTER CENTRE, 2.15.

Elephant been here, plastered over with circus-bills, and broke up a revival, striking down and damaging many who were on the point of entering upon a better life. Citizens penned him up, and established a guard. When Detective Brown and I arrived, some time after, we entered enclosure and proceeded to identify elephant by photograph and description. All marks tallied exactly except one, which we could not see, – the boil-scar under armpit. To make sure, Brown crept under to look, and was immediately brained, – that is, head crushed and destroyed, though nothing issued from debris. All fled; so did elephant, striking right and left with much effect. Has escaped, but left bold blood-track from cannon-wounds. Rediscovery certain. He broke southward, through a dense forest.

BRENT, Detective.

That was the last telegram. At nightfall a fog shut down which was so dense that objects but three feet away could not be discerned. This lasted all night. The ferry-boats and even the omnibuses had to stop running.

Next morning the papers were as full of detective theories as before; they had all our tragic facts in detail also, and a great many more which

373

they had received from their telegraphic correspondents. Column after column was occupied, a third of its way down, with glaring head-lines, which it made my heart sick to read. Their general tone was like this:–

The White Elephant at Large! He moves upon his Fatal March! Whole Villages deserted by their Fright-Stricken Occupants! Pale Terror goes before Him. Death and Devastation follow after! After these. The Detectives. Barns destroyed, Factories gutted, Harvests devoured, Public Assemblages dispersed, accompanied by Scenes of Carnage impossible to describe! Theories of thirty-four of the most distinguished Detectives on the Force! Theory of Chief Blunt!'

'There!' said Inspector Blunt, almost betrayed into excitement, 'this is magnificent! This is the greatest windfall that any detective organization ever had. The fame of it will travel to the ends of the earth, and endure to the end of time, and my name with it.'

But there was no joy for me. I felt as if I had committed all those red crimes, and that the elephant was only my irresponsible agent. And how the list had grown! In one place he had 'interfered with an election and killed five repeaters.' He had followed this act with the destruction of two poor fellows, named O'Donahue and McFlannigan, who had 'found a refuge in the home of the oppressed of all lands only the day before, and were in the act of exercising for the first time the noble right of American citizens at the polls, when stricken down by the relentless hand of the Scourge of Siam.' In another, he had 'found a crazy sensation-preacher preparing his next season's heroic attacks on the dance, the theatre, and other things which can't strike back, and had stepped on him.' And in still another place he had 'killed a lightning-rod agent.' And so the list went on, growing redder and redder, and more and more heartbreaking. Sixty persons had been killed, and two hundred and forty wounded. All the accounts bore just testimony to the activity and devotion of the detectives, and all closed with the remark that 'three hundred thousand citizens and four detectives saw the dread creature, and two of the latter he destroyed.'

I dreaded to hear the telegraphic instrument begin to click again. By and by the messages began to pour in, but I was happily disappointed in their nature. It was soon apparent that all trace of the elephant was lost. The fog had enabled him to search out a good hiding-place unobserved. Telegrams from the most absurdly distant points reported that a dim vast mass had been glimpsed there through the fog at such and such an hour, and was 'undoubtedly the elephant.' This dim vast mass had been glimpsed in New Haven, in New Jersey, in Pennsylvania, in interior New York, in Brooklyn, and even in the city of New York itself! But in all cases the dim vast mass had vanished quickly and left no trace. Every detective of the large force scattered over this huge extent of country sent his hourly report, and each and every one of them had a clew, and was shadowing something, and was hot upon the heels of it.

But the day passed without other result.

The next day the same.

The next just the same.

The newspaper reports began to grow monotonous with facts that amounted to nothing, clews which led to nothing, and theories which had nearly exhausted the elements which surprise and delight and dazzle.

By advice of the inspector I doubled the reward.

Four more dull days followed. Then came a bitter blow to the poor, hard-working detectives, – the journalist declined to print their theories, and coldly said, 'Give us a rest.'

Two weeks after the elephant's disappearance I raised the reward to $75,000 by the inspector's advice. It was a great sum, but I felt that I would rather sacrifice my whole private fortune than lose my credit with my government. Now that the detectives were in adversity, the newspapers turned upon them, and began to fling the most stinging sarcasms at them. This gave the minstrels an idea, and they dressed themselves as detectives and hunted the elephant on the stage in the most extravagant way. The caricaturists made pictures of detectives scanning the country with spy-glasses, while the elephant, at their backs, stole apples out of their pockets. And they made all sorts of ridiculous pictures of the detective badge, – you have seen that badge printed in gold on the back of detective novels, no doubt, – it is a wide-staring eye, with the legend, 'We Never Sleep.' When detectives called for a drink, the would-be facetious bar-keeper resurrected an obsolete form of expression and said, 'Will you have an eye-opener?' All the air was thick with sarcasms.

But there was one man who moved calm, untouched, unaffected, through it all. It was that heart of oak, the Chief Inspector. His brave eye never drooped, his serene confidence never wavered. He always said, –

'Let them rail on; he laughs best who laughs last.'

My admiration for the man grew into a species of worship. I was at his side always. His office had become an unpleasant place to me, and now became daily more and more so. Yet if he could endure it I meant to do so also; at least, as long as I could. So I came regularly, and stayed, – the only outsider who seemed to be capable of it. Everybody wondered how I could; and often it seemed to me that I must desert, but at such times I looked into that calm and apparently unconscious face, and held my ground.

About three weeks after the elephant's disappearance I was about to say, one morning, that I should *have* to strike my colors and retire, when the great detective arrested the thought by proposing one more superb and masterly move.

This was to compromise with the robbers. The fertility of this man's invention exceeded anything I have ever seen, and I have had a wide intercourse with the world's finest minds. He said he was confident he could compromise for $100,000 and recover the elephant. I said I believed I could scrape the amount together, but what would become of the poor detectives who had worked so faithfully? He said, –

'In compromises they always get half.'

This removed my only objection. So the inspector wrote two notes, in this form:–

DEAR MADAM. – Your husband can make a large sum of money (and be entirely protected from the law) by making an immediate appointment with me.

Chief BLUNT.

He sent one of these by his confidential messenger to the 'reputed wife' of Brick Duffy, and the other to the reputed wife of Red McFadden.

Within the hour these offensive answers came:–

YE OWLD FOOL: brick McDuffys bin ded 2 yere.

BRIDGET MAHONEY.

CHIEF BAT, – Red McFadden is hung and in heving 18 month. Any Ass but a detective knose that.

MARY O'HOOLIGAN.

'I had long suspected these facts,' said the inspector; 'this testimony proves the unerring accuracy of my instinct.'

The moment one resource failed him he was ready with another. He immediately wrote an advertisement for the morning papers, and I kept a copy of it:–

A. – xwblv.242N. Tjnd – fz328wmlg. Ozpo, –; 2m!ogw. Mum.

He said that if the thief was alive this would bring him to the usual rendezvous. He further explained that the usual rendezvous was a place where all business affairs between detectives and criminals were conducted. This meeting would take place at twelve the next night.

We could do nothing till then, and I lost no time in getting out of the office, and was grateful indeed for the privilege.

At 11 the next night I brought $100,000 in bank-notes and put them into the chief's hands, and shortly afterward he took his leave, with the brave old undimmed confidence in his eye. An almost intolerable hour dragged to a close; then I heard his welcome tread, and rose gasping and tottered to meet him. How his fine eyes flamed with triumph! He said, –

'We've compromised! The jokers will sing a different tune to-morrow! Follow me!'

He took a lighted candle and strode down into the vast vaulted basement where sixty detectives always slept, and where a score were now playing cards to while the time. I followed close after him. He walked swiftly down to the dim remote end of the place, and just as I succumbed to the pangs of suffocation and was swooning away he stumbled and fell over the outlying members of a mighty object, and I heard him exclaim as he went down, –

'Our noble profession is vindicated. Here is your elephant!'

I was carried to the office above and restored with carbolic acid. The whole detective force swarmed in, and such another season of triumphant rejoicing ensued as I had never witnessed before. The reporters were called, baskets of champagne were opened, toasts were drunk, the handshakings and congratulations were continuous and enthusiastic. Naturally the chief was the hero of the hour, and his happiness was so complete and had been so patiently and worthily and bravely won that it made me happy to see it, though I stood there a homeless beggar, my priceless charge dead, and my position in my country's service lost to me through what would always seem my fatally careless execution of a great trust. Many an eloquent eye testified its deep admiration for the chief, and many a detective's voice murmured, 'Look at him, – just the king of the profession, – only give him a clew, it's all he wants, and there ain't anything hid that he can't find.' The dividing of the $50,000 made great pleasure; when it was finished the chief made a little speech while he put his share in his pocket, in which he said, 'Enjoy it, boys, for you've earned it; and more than that you've earned for the detective profession undying fame.'

A telegram arrived, which read:–

MONROE, MICH., 10 P.M.

First time I've struck a telegraph office in over three weeks. Have followed those footprints, horseback, through the woods, a thousand miles to here, and they get stronger and bigger and fresher every day. Don't worry – inside of another week I'll have the elephant. This is dead sure.

DARLEY, *Detective.*

The chief ordered three cheers for 'Darley, one of the finest minds on the force,' and then commanded that he be telegraphed to come home and receive his share of the reward.

So ended that marvelous episode of the stolen elephant. The newspapers were pleasant with praises once more, the next day, with one contemptible exception. This sheet said, 'Great is the detective! He may be a little slow in finding a little thing like a mislaid elephant, – he may hunt him all day and sleep with his rotting carcass all night for three weeks, but he will find him at last – if he can get the man who mislaid him to show him the place!'

Poor Hassan was lost to me forever. The cannon-shots had wounded him fatally, he had crept to that unfriendly place in the fog, and there, surrounded by his enemies and in constant danger of detection, he has wasted away with hunger and suffering till death gave him peace.

The compromise cost me $100,000; my detective expenses were $42,000 more; I never applied for a place again under my government; I am a ruined man and a wanderer in the earth, – but my admiration for that man, whom I believe to be the greatest detective the world has ever produced, remains undimmed to this day, and will so remain unto the end.

Acknowledgments

The Publishers gratefully acknowledge permission granted by the following to reprint the copyright material included in this volume:

Bel Ria by Sheila Burnford. From the novel of the same name, published by Michael Joseph Ltd. Reprinted by permission of the Publishers.

Life With Mij by Gavin Maxwell. From Gavin Maxwell: 'Ring of Bright Water' (Penguin Books, 1974) pp. 114-139; copyright © Gavin Maxwell Enterprises Ltd., 1960. Reprinted by permission of Penguin Books Ltd. and Campbell Thomson & McLaughlin Ltd.

Gilded Cage by Alan Coren. From 'The Rhinestone As Big As the Ritz'; copyright © Alan Coren, 1979. Reprinted by permission of the Author.

The Rat Who Wasn't Having Any by William Garnett. From 'Morals of the Beastly World'; copyright © William Garnett 1958. Reprinted by permission of the Author.

Animals at Alconleigh by Nancy Mitford. From 'The Pursuit of Love'. Reprinted by permission of A. D. Peters & Co. Ltd.

Trinket's Colt by E. Somerville and M. Ross. From 'Some Experiences of an Irish R.M.', published by J. M. Dent & Sons Ltd. Reprinted by permission of John Farquharson Ltd.

A Sea of Headwaiters by Gerald Durrell. From 'The Whispering Land', published by Granada Publishing Ltd. Reprinted by permission of the Publishers and Curtis Brown Ltd.

Stumberleap by Henry Williamson. From 'Collected Nature Stories', published by Macdonald Futura Publishers Ltd. Reprinted by permission of the Publishers.

The Dog That Bit People by James Thurber. From 'My Life and Hard Times', published in Great Britain by Hamish Hamilton Ltd., © the Collection copyright 1963; published in the United States by Harper & Row Inc., copr. © 1933, 1961 James Thurber. Reprinted by permission of the Publishers and Mrs James Thurber.

The Bull That Thought by Rudyard Kipling. From 'Debits and Credits', published in Great Britain by Macmillan London Ltd.; published in the United States by Doubleday & Company, Inc., copyright © 1924 by Rudyard Kipling. Reprinted by permission of the National Trust and the Publishers.

Tobermory by Saki. From 'The Complete Short Stories of Saki (H. H. Munro)'; copyright © 1958 by The Viking Press, Inc. Reprinted by permission of Viking Penguin Inc.

Pig-Hoo-o-o-o-ey! by P. G. Wodehouse. From 'Blandings Castle', published by Hutchinson Publishing Group Ltd. Reprinted by permission of the Publishers, the Estate of the late P. G. Wodehouse and their Agents, Scott Meredith Literary Agency, Inc., 845 Third Avenue, New York, New York 10022 and A. P. Watt Ltd.

It Shouldn't Happen to a Vet by James Herriot. From the book of the same name, published in Great Britain by Michael Joseph Ltd.; published in the United States by St Martin's Press Inc. Macmillan & Co., Ltd. Reprinted by permission of the Publishers and David Higham Associates.

Lady Into Fox by David Garnett. From the novel of the same name, published by Chatto & Windus Ltd. Reprinted by permission of the Author's Literary Estate, the Publishers and A. P. Watt Ltd.

A Cat in the Window by Derek Tangye. From the book of the same name, published by Michael Joseph Ltd. Reprinted by permission of the Publishers.

Flush by Virginia Woolf. From the book of the same name, published in Great Britain by The Hogarth Press Ltd., and in the United States by Harcourt Brace Jovanovich, Inc.; copyright 1933 by Harcourt Brace Jovanovich, Inc.; renewed 1961 by Leonard Woolf. Reprinted by permission of the Author's Literary Estate and the Publishers.

And Who, With Eden . . . by John Collier. Reprinted by permission of A. D. Peters & Co. Ltd.

We Think the World of You by J. R. Ackerley. Reprinted with permission of The Bodley Head from the novel of the same name.